WHEN THE TIDE RISES

DAVID DRAKE

WHEN THE TIDE RISES

Copyright © 2008 by David Drake

A Baen Books Original

Baen Publishing Enterprises
P.O. Box 1403
Riverdale, NY 10471
www.baen.com

ISBN 10: 1-4165-9156-7
ISBN 13: 978-1-4165-9156-6

Cover art by Stephen Hickman

First Baen paperback printing, April 2009

Library of Congress Control Number: 2007051118

Distributed by Simon & Schuster
1230 Avenue of the Americas
New York, NY 10020

Pages by Joy Freeman (www.pagesbyjoy.com)
Printed in the United States of America

Daniel ran through the garden. The hedge was dense and the sculptured boxwood branches raked him like so many fingernails, but he'd hunted in brush before. He forced his way between trunks, holding the impeller vertical before him. He sprinted around the penthouse to reach the back, just as an open aircar roared out of the garage housed in the rear half of the suite.

Hogg fired a burst. Where the sub-machine gun's light projectiles hit, they stressed the car's black thermoplastic skin to gray-white.

The driver hauled his vehicle into a tight spiral as he gained altitude. The car banked, fifty yards out from the garage and ten or a dozen feet above the level of Daniel's head.

Daniel fired twice. The impeller's heavy recoil woke nostalgic memories of his childhood. The aircar was just a bigger bird, and the buttplate's punch against his shoulder was much the same as that of a shotgun using full charges.

Daniel saw a tiny spark in the car's rear fan housing. For a moment the vehicle continued to spiral upward, its fans howling.

Hogg stepped out of the garage, pointing his sub-machine gun. "Don't shoot!" Daniel shouted.

"Shoot, you pup!" Hogg shouted. "You bloody missed it, you did."

The car howled. There was a *Blang!* and the rear fan blasted shreds of itself out of the housing.

"Sorry, master," Hogg muttered in embarrassment. "Shoulda knowed you wouldn't miss a clout shot like that."

"I put holes in a couple blades instead of shooting out the motor," Daniel explained quietly. "I want them to have a chance to set down. Remember, I'm trying to capture the Governor alive."

To John Lambshead, my guide to many of the places I've used in this and other recent books; And the man who changed the way I look at nematodes.

ACKNOWLEDGMENTS

Dan Breen continues as my first reader, catching instances where the subject and verb don't agree, infelicities of phrasing, and not infrequently size issues. He's enough bigger than me (and than most people) that he'll do till a real giant comes around.

Dorothy Day and Karen Zimmerman archived my texts, a safety measure that takes a considerable weight off my mind. In fact, none of the computers I blew up this time were my primary work computer . . . but they could've been. Unless simultaneous asteroids hit Seattle and Indianapolis, I'd still have been able to proceed without losing a beat. (I'm not daring anybody when I say that. Really, I'm not.)

Dorothy also provided continuity help on dates and character names. This is invaluable.

Whereas Evan Ladouceur handled naval continuity, which is also invaluable. I have a team of remarkable experts.

Which of course includes Karen, my webmaster and the person who researches things for me in an eyeblink. She was not the model for Adele Mundy, but she's a real human example of how truly remarkable a trained research librarian is.

I mentioned blowing up computers, pretty much as usual. My son Jonathan twice rebuilt my desktop unit and kept me operational. I honestly don't know what it is about me and computers; I'm really a very gentle person who wants only the best for his machines.

One oddity that occurred with this book is that I

was asked to use the names of various people in the text. (The technical term is Tuckerizing, named for the fan and author Wilson Tucker who popularized the practice in the 1930s.) Having a long list of real names is handy for a writer, especially for a writer like me who likes to name characters rather than referring to them by epithets alone (the tall cop; the doctor; etc.).

I should emphasize that I used *only* the names, not the characters of the persons themselves. In many cases, that's a Good Thing.

My wife Jo bore up nobly, fed me amazingly well, and tramped around warships, castles, tanks (quite a number of tanks), and various other places while I researched the novel.

I owe a great deal to all of the above people and to many more as well. There are times I find life pretty difficult. Without my network of friends and family, it'd be—for me—literally impossible. Thank you all.

AUTHOR'S NOTE

The genesis of my RCN novels was Patrick O'Brian's wonderful Aubrey/Maturin series, set during and after the Napoleonic Wars. It therefore won't surprise many of you to find a number of plot points common to O'Brian's last novels and *When the Tide Rises*. This is a case of convergent evolution, however, rather than direct borrowing on my part: we're both working from Lord Cochrane's memoirs of service under the revolutionary governments of Chili (sic) and Brazil.

Jack Aubrey and Daniel Leary are supporting independence movements as agents of their governments. In reality, the British government threatened Cochrane with prosecution if he accepted the Chilean offer, and the British warships which Cochrane encountered during his operations against the Spanish empire baulked him at every possible opportunity.

Mr. O'Brian isn't around to ask, but I suspect we diverge from Cochrane's reality for the same reason. If you're writing a series, you create an enormous problem for yourself if your hero is seen as a traitor by his government. Cochrane himself returned to favor, but it took more than thirty years for that to happen.

Lord Cochrane was skilled, intelligent, and personally brave. Having said that, his memoirs often make uncomfortable reading. It's not that he was too stupid to see the political ramifications of his actions; rather, he looked on such considerations as unworthy of a superior being like himself. The political disasters which follow military victories throughout Cochrane's career, with the Royal Navy and then with foreign governments, seem to the reader as inevitable as night following day.

Cochrane frequently says about the people with whom he dealt, "He swore to do something, but he didn't carry through on his promises." After a while, I became exasperated with this nonsense. Cochrane was an extremely intelligent and experienced man who *must* have expected the bad result. As with a woman who's married three abusive drunks in a row, there's more involved than bad luck or even bad judgment.

But what that means is that Cochrane was unwilling to work within the system when his undoubted brilliance made it possible for him to have done so. It is equally true that the systems he was involved with were deeply flawed—the Royal Navy in the early nineteenth century, and the South American revolutionary governments.

What comes through powerfully in every English memoir I've read involving Latin America at that time is that almost none of the players (Bolivar may have been an exception) had a concept of a nation that was greater than the individual's own clan/family/tribe ruling as many of its neighbors as possible. Consistently when a region revolted from the colonial power (Spain or Portugal), the districts revolted from the capital and then the wealthy magnates revolted from the district government (which was generally run by one of the several powerful families in that district). The magnates than spent their time in burning out rival magnates.

If you've been following Latin American politics for

the past fifty years or so (I suspect the problems go much farther back, but I personally don't), you might reasonably come to the conclusion that nothing much has changed. For even more vivid modern examples of clan-based politics, consider Iraq and Afghanistan.

The business of *When the Tide Rises* is taken largely from real events in Chile, Peru, and Brazil. The major naval action, however, is based on the 1811 Battle of Lissa. (The 1866 Battle of Lissa is fascinating, but in fiction you couldn't make one side as incompetent as the historical losing side was. As one example, the gun crews of the defeated flagship forgot to load shells and therefore fought the battle firing blank charges.)

I write to entertain readers, not to advance a personal or political philosophy (I don't have a political philosophy); nonetheless, my fiction is almost always based on historical models. When you read *When the Tide Rises*, you might occasionally think about today's news and remember that it'll be tomorrow's history.

Heaven knows, I thought about the news while I was writing.

— Dave Drake
david-drake.com

When the sands are all dry, he is gay as a lark,
   And will talk in contemptuous tones of the Shark:
But, when the tide rises and sharks are around,
   His voice has a timid and tremulous sound.

—*Alice's Recitation*
   (from *Alice in Wonderland*)
   Lewis Carroll

CHAPTER 1

Xenos on Cinnabar

Commander Daniel Leary sipped whiskey from a glass with the Quenzer monogram as he surveyed his fellow guests; he held his lips in a neutral smile. He didn't know any of those present except for Miranda Dorst, his "plus one," but Sarah Sterret, the brunette wearing a diamond tiara, looked vaguely familiar.

Vaguely familiar. Mistress Sterret wasn't bad-looking, but she hadn't seen thirty in a while. Her husband, Nathan Sterret, a senior captain who was part of the complement of Navy House, needn't fear that the dashing Commander Leary would stray into *his* pastures.

Besides, Daniel was with Miranda now.

"Thank you, my good man," Miranda said as she took the faintly fizzy drink she'd ordered from an offered tray. She smiled, every inch the gracious lady.

Daniel swelled with pride. She fitted perfectly into this gathering; fitted better than a country boy like him, truth to tell, for all that the Dorsts, mother and

1

daughter, had made the simple black dress she was wearing. They and Miranda's late brother Timothy had lived in straitened circumstances ever since the early death of Captain Dorst, but class will tell.

The hostess gave a tiny nod; the footman in the doorway tapped the silver bell in his left hand.

"Please join me in the dining room," said Dame Cathleen Quenzer, a tall woman of sixty-odd who made her bulk look imposing rather than soft. "You'll find cards at your places."

Her politeness went no deeper than the words. Daniel had heard warrant-officer trainers at the Academy shout "Hop it, you miserable worms!" and sound less certain that they'd be obeyed.

"We're all here, then?" said the extremely handsome young man. He seemed to be with Senator Forbes, the chair of the Finance Committee. She was a small woman but birdlike only if you were thinking of hawks. Daniel doubted the relationship was grandmother and grandson, though the age difference made that possible. "It doesn't seem very many. Eight?"

Andrew Cummins glanced back over his shoulder as he entered the dining room. "Cathleen follows the old maxim that guests at a dinner party should number more than the Graces and fewer than the Muses, dear boy," he said.

Smirking he added, "That's three and nine, if you were wondering. I don't suppose you have much experience of the Muses, though your grace is beyond question."

Cummins too was a senator, though not nearly as powerful as Forbes. His fame came from being the most successful criminal advocate in Xenos—and thereby on the hundred and more worlds owing allegiance to the Republic of Cinnabar.

Cinnabar citizens didn't like to think of themselves as ruling an empire, but Daniel had studied enough history at the Naval Academy to know that was the reality. The fact didn't concern him, of course. He was an officer of the Republic of Cinnabar Navy, and he'd carry out any orders his superiors in the RCN gave him. If he'd been interested in philosophy, he'd be in another line of work.

Besides, being ruled by the Cinnabar Senate was better by any standard than being being a citizen of the so-called Alliance of Free Stars and living under the thumb of Guarantor Porra. The Alliance wouldn't stop expanding of its own will, but it could *be* stopped. The RCN had been doing a very good job of that, and the medals on both breasts of Daniel's Dress Whites proved to anyone who saw him that he'd taken an active part of that process.

"Commander?" said a footman obsequiously. "I'll guide you to your seat, if you will."

"Yes, of course," Daniel said. Another servant was murmuring to Miranda; even Cummins, obviously a regular at these dinners, was being escorted.

Daniel found it interesting that the servants wore not the cream-and-russet livery of the late Senator Quenzer but the orange-and-azure of Dame Cathleen's own family, the D'Almeidas. He wasn't interested in Society in the sense that Dame Cathleen was, but he was the son of Corder Leary, once Speaker of the Senate and even now one of the most powerful members of that body. Families and family alliances had been matters of life and death when Speaker

Leary crushed the Three Circles Conspiracy seventeen years ago.

The rectangular table wouldn't have seated more than eight diners comfortably, nor would a larger table have fit the room. There was an assembly hall on the second floor—Daniel had attended a rout at Quenzer House two years before when he was an up-and-coming lieutenant—but at the time he couldn't have imagined he'd be invited to one of the intimate dinners for which Dame Cathleen was famous.

Let alone that he'd be seated to the right of his hostess, with Senator Forbes to his own right. Captain Sterret was at the end of the row. Miranda was across the table from him, sitting beside Cummins.

From the way the attorney leered as he spoke to Miranda in a low voice, he fancied himself a ladies' man. He must be corseted to fit into his coat and dazzling vest, and that made his red face bulge the more. Miranda laughed lightly and avoided eye contact, sipping from the glass she'd brought to the table while looking toward Captain Sterret.

Sarah Sterret—*why* did she look familiar?—was opposite Daniel. He couldn't read her expression as she watched him, but it was something more than polite curiosity. Mind, he was used to drawing women's attention when he glittered in full dress, but he wasn't at all sure Sterret's look was positive.

The steward at the sideboard beside the doorway began ladling the soup course into bowls. Senator Forbes had brought servants for herself and her pretty boy, but the remaining guests would be served by the household staff.

Hogg had accompanied Daniel and Miranda to the

dinner, but he was in the kitchen now . . . or possibly in the butler's pantry, looking over the bottled goods with an eye for kick rather than for delicate bouquet. Daniel wouldn't trade Hogg for a hundred ordinary footmen, but bringing him into this dining room would demolish all his hopes of gaining allies in what he was being forced to view as his battle with Navy House.

"You're recently back on Cinnabar, are you not, Commander?" Dame Cathleen said. "From some sort of hush-hush derring-do, I'm sure?"

Daniel set down his whiskey—well, the last sip of his whiskey—and said, "Oh, nothing whatever romantic, Dame Cathleen. It was an advisory mission to the back of beyond, deep into Ganpat's Reach, if that means anything to you. No reason it should, of course."

"No doubt you gathered some more pretty medals, though, haven't you, Commander?" said Sarah Sterret archly. She glanced around her fellow guests with an icy smile. "Commander Leary seems to have a new medal every time you see him."

She leaned forward slightly to look down the table at Miranda. "Medals and other sorts of trophies, that is."

Oh my God, I have met her! Daniel realized. Though he hadn't paid much attention to her at the time, which was at least part of the problem. Was she married then?

That'd been several years ago when he was just back from a triumph on Kostroma that'd made him a nine-days wonder. It'd been at a ball, not here at Quenzer House but in a similar venue. He was with a cute blonde named Bobbi, Bobbi . . . well, it didn't matter. He and Bobbi hadn't really been on a last-name basis.

Daniel'd known at the time that Mistress Sterret wasn't best pleased by the way he'd ignored her increasingly blatant suggestions, but good heavens! Had she really thought that he'd be interested in a woman *her* age?

Apparently she had, and here she was across the small table from him. And—he glanced sidelong at Dame Cathleen, who wore an impish smile—his hostess had probably been aware of the fact when she made up the dinner invitations. People often became whimsical when they had considerable power and no proper outlet for it.

Corder Leary had never been whimsical.

"Why no, mistress, I don't believe there'll be any medals," Daniel said easily. The best way he could see to handle the situation was to be polite and a trifle distant; the last thing he needed was to raise the emotional temperature. "Nor is there any call for them. It was just an ordinary advisory mission, the sort of duty that goes to officers who're between ships."

He smiled wider and included the whole table in it.

"As I still am, I'm afraid," he went on. "Though I'm hopeful Navy House will find a way for me to serve the Republic again soon."

Daniel hadn't exactly been a protégé of Admiral Anston, the former Chief of the Navy Board, but Anston had seemed to see in Daniel the sort of cleverness that'd brought him to wealth and the leadership of the RCN.

But Anston had retired abruptly after a heart attack. The new Chief, Admiral Vocaine, viewed as an enemy anyone whom he saw as having been close to his predecessor.

Daniel grinned despite himself. Unfortunately, he wasn't powerful enough to really count as Vocaine's enemy.

The servants set bowls of oxtail soup before the guests with the precision of a drill team. Dame Cathleen was likely as stern as any Land Forces drillmaster. If she didn't herself correct errors with a baton, that was simply because she had senior servants to whip the footmen for her.

"Hmmph!" snorted Captain Sterret, staring fixedly at his soup as he thrust his spoon into it. "A lot of young officers think the Personnel Bureau should make assignments for their convenience, not the RCN's. Why—"

He raised his eyes and swept the table. His jaw twitched as his gaze passed over Daniel, but he didn't linger to glare.

"—you wouldn't believe the demands some of them make. Demands!"

"Ah, but Commander Leary isn't simply another young officer, is he, Captain?" said Cummins. "Why—"

He was speaking to the whole table, but he shifted his eyes from Sterret to Daniel, who'd been looking toward the ormolu-and-crystal light fixture on the opposite wall. It was a remarkably ornate thing which nonetheless seemed to work as well as a simpler unit at providing diffuse illumination.

There was nothing wrong with looking pretty, of course, so long as it didn't affect function. He'd had the name of his yacht, the *Princess Cecile*, inlaid in gold on her bow. Anybody who thought the *Sissie* couldn't see off an opponent of anything close to her tonnage hadn't read the log of her service under Daniel Leary.

"—even as we speak there's a documentary showing at all the best playhouses in Xenos: *The Conquest of Dunbar's World*. That, Commander, that isn't the sort of thing that happens after an ordinary advisory mission."

The spoon in Daniel's hand jumped. *Hogg'd burn him a new one if he slopped soup on his Dress Whites.*

"What?" he said. "You're joking!"

"Oh, come, Commander!" said Sarah Sterret. "Do you expect us to believe that you weren't aware of the play? It's been quite the sensation all over Cinnabar. All over the dependent worlds, I shouldn't wonder."

Daniel set down his spoon. "I hope you'll believe me, madame," he said. "Because it's the truth."

He paused. "On my honor as a Leary of Bantry."

"I think it's just terrible the way the playwrights make things up," said Miranda brightly. "And they put real people's names on what's all lies. Andrew, couldn't there be a law to keep them from doing that?"

She turned to the man beside her and simpered, an expression which Daniel wouldn't have believed she was capable of before he saw it. "Couldn't you propose something? I'm sure the Senate would pass it if *you* proposed it."

Daniel spooned up more oxtail soup; Dame Cathleen's chef was as skilled as one would expect.

Miranda had just defused what could very easily have led to a duel, for all that by RCN regulation both Daniel and Captain Sterret would have to resign their commissions in order to fight one. Uniquely among the girls with whom Daniel'd kept company, she was very clever.

"I scarcely think I have such influence in the Senate,

my dear," Cummins said dryly. "I'm sure Senator Forbes would agree with me there. Besides, there doesn't seem to be any harm done. Even if the play's a complete lie, it's a positive lie, isn't it?"

The soup had been whisked away; the steward leaned in to offer Dame Cathleen the fish. She accepted a slice and he moved down to Daniel.

It was in a cream sauce with chopped greens. The firm yellow flesh was probably that of a saffron hake, a flatfish which sometimes grew to the size of a man. No matter how good the chef was, this wouldn't be able to match the hake sprats Daniel and Hogg had gigged near shore at Bantry and grilled only minutes later . . .

"Well, I for one don't mind the citizens getting a little good news," said Senator Forbes as the steward served her. "And I don't care if it's true. Though from what I've heard, Leary—"

She looked at him. Her eyes reminded him even more of a hawk's.

"—that business on Dunbar's World wasn't a simple thing at all. According to the Summaries—"

She must mean the Intelligence Summaries, which she'd see as the chair of a Senatorial committee.

"—your very nice piece of work saved the Republic from a future headache." Grimacing, she added, "Now, if somebody'd just do the same in the Jewel System."

"I assure you, Senator," Captain Sterret said stiffly, "that the RCN is doing everything possible with the limited resources available. Admiral James is a first-rate fighting spacer. If anybody can break the siege of Diamondia, it's him."

Daniel nodded, though cautiously. A senior officer

in a bad mood could interpret enthusiastic agreement as an attempt by a junior to sit in judgment on him. Sterret's mood hadn't been good even before Forbes brought up Diamondia.

Daniel could've been honestly enthusiastic, though. James of Kithran, Admiral James, was of aristocratic birth. This hadn't hurt his chances of promotion, but if the RCN'd been a democracy—which thank the Gods it was not!—James might well've won a vote of serving officers to command the defense of the Jewel System.

He and his squadron were nonetheless being asked to make bricks without straw, and it'd take a lot of bricks to save Diamondia from the Alliance forces besieging it. Perhaps an impossible number of bricks.

"One wonders whether Admiral James is getting the support he needs and deserves, though, doesn't one?" said Dame Cathleen in a tone of false concern. She looked at Senator Forbes and raised an eyebrow. "It just seems that a trade nexus as important as Diamondia should have enough ships to defend itself. Still, no doubt the Senate has been following events carefully, haven't you, Beverly?"

"We are, yes," said Forbes. The words were neutral, but the glance she directed toward Captain Sterret at her side was not. "Though of course we can't interfere in the operational control of the navy. That's the responsibility of Navy House, whom we're told are the professionals."

Captain Sterret had only a horseshoe of hair running from ear to ear around the back of his head. When he flushed, his bald pate turned scarlet.

"Look, Senator . . ." he said. He was a tall man and

could probably be imposing in the right setting, but his features and personality both appeared to've had the edges rounded off. "It's all well and good to say James should have more ships, but where are they to come from? And if we had the ships, where would the crews come from? Why, we've stripped the merchant fleet bare to man the ships in commission now!"

"And yet the Alliance doesn't seem to have problems manning its warships," Cummins said. "More warships than the Republic has in service, as I understand?"

The fish plates vanished in their turn. The dish had indeed been hake, and the memories of foggy mornings at Bantry gave Daniel a twinge. Life had been simpler then, and it hadn't been so long ago. He was only twenty-five now, very young for a full commander.

"Guarantor Porra fills his crews with drafts from the relief rolls, Patron," Daniel said to Cummins. "You're better placed than I to say whether that'd be politically acceptable in the Republic—"

Speaker Leary's son didn't need Cummins to tell him that it'd lead to riots sufficient to level Xenos.

"—but speaking as an RCN officer, I'd very much regret seeing us go that route. The crews are likely to be disaffected and are sure to be inefficient. The Fleet—the naval arm of the Alliance—tries to get around the problem by assigning three crewmen where we'd use two, but that leads to overcrowding even though Fleet vessels are larger for their class. And in many circumstances, most in fact, more unskilled hands mean more confusion."

Servants to right and left offered Daniel tiny cutlets on a bed of rice, or squab with a bright purple root vegetable. Because his hobby was natural history, he was able to identify the "feathers" covering the bird as petals from the hearts of Hussite cardoons. With Hus deep within the Alliance, Dame Cathleen must've paid a fancy price for a product that hadn't been naturalized off its home world.

He took a squab. It'd been expertly boned and was remarkably tender. Force-meat stuffing preserved its shape.

Daniel'd seen Sterret relax noticeably as he spoke. The captain'd been getting even redder as he struggled to find words that wouldn't cost him a reprimand when they got back to the Navy Board. However Admiral Vocaine might feel about the Senate, it was from that body that the RCN's appropriations came. Even Senators who disliked Cummins personally would close ranks if one of their own were insulted by a mere servant from the permanent establishment.

"The Republic will not be drafting spacers, Commander," Senator Forbes said dryly. "There's enough unrest already in Dockside and the Lowlands."

Those were the old working-class districts of Xenos. Daniel suspected that the worst problems would come from the newer tenements ringing the city, however. These housed recent immigrants from the worlds dependent on Cinnabar.

"Oh, the proles are always making trouble, Betty," Forbes's companion said petulantly. Daniel hadn't caught the boy's name, but he doubted that the information would be of future use to him. "Really, I wish somebody would *do* something about them."

"No doubt someone will if it becomes necessary, dear boy," said Cummins with an unctuous chuckle.

"But I'm sure we all hope that it won't be necessary, don't we?"

"What *I* hope is that the Alliance navy will prove as negligible as the Commander implies," Forbes said. "With respect, Leary—"

She turned and nodded.

"—I must say that neither history nor the present Diamondia situation gives me much reason to agree with you."

"Do diamonds come from Diamondia?" asked the handsome youth. He made a moue. "I'd hate for the Alliance to take all our diamonds."

He toyed with the three-inch rope of little stones hanging from the lobe of his right ear. Senator Forbes hunched as though she'd been struck, but she continued stolidly chewing on a mouthful of cutlet.

"The Jewel System lies near a junction point within the Matrix," said Captain Sterret. "Were we to lose Diamondia, routes from Cinnabar to several of our allied worlds would be lengthened by as much as thirty days."

After the recent exchange, another man might've crowed at Forbes's embarrassment. Sterret—wisely—sounded rather relieved to change the subject to something that didn't bear directly on Navy House.

"Conversely," he went on, "if the Alliance held the system, they'd cut a comparable length of time off voyages from Pleasaunce to the Bagarian Cluster. A rebellion against Guarantor Porra broke out there a few months ago."

He looked up, at Forbes rather than her companion. "The Alliance won't succeed in capturing Diamondia," he said earnestly. "Admiral James won't permit that to happen."

"It's hard to imagine how Admiral James can prevent it, as badly as his fleet is outnumbered," said Dame Cathleen. "Unless you send him reinforcements, Captain?"

"You should send Commander Leary, Sterret," said Cummins. It was obvious to Daniel that he and their hostess entertained themselves with a routine of baiting guests to fight one another. "He only needed thirty men to capture a base held by thousands of troops on Dunbar's World. I'll bet he could do just as well in the Jewel System."

"That . . ." said the captain in a tone between shout and a snarl. He was looking at Daniel as he spoke between clenched teeth. "Is bollocks!"

"Yes," said Daniel, pleased to notice that he sounded calm. "That's bollocks. There *was* an initial assault by thirty spacers to disable the anti-starship defenses on the base, but I wasn't within a hundred miles at the time. It was led by one of my officers, and under other circumstances—"

At the time there'd been good reason to fear that the RCN would repudiate the whole business as an act of piracy. It'd seemed best to Daniel not to force Navy House to look closely at what'd happened.

"—medals would certainly have been appropriate. Not for me but for the leader of the assault force. That is, for—"

He paused, wondering what Adele would want him to say.

Adele isn't here. I'll tell the truth and to bloody Hell with what she'd want!

"—my signals officer, Adele Mundy."

"Ah, that would be Mundy of Chatsworth, would

it not?" Dame Cathleen said. "We should have her at one of these little gatherings, don't you think, Andrew?"

"Lady Mundy, yes," Daniel said thickly. Now that he'd spoken he regretted it. Besides her RCN duties, Adele worked for Mistress Bernis Sand, the Republic's spymaster. Publicity could make that portion of her activities more dangerous.

"You called her your 'signals officer,' Commander?" said Sarah Sterret. "Goodness, I'd never heard that euphemism before. To be honest, I'd expected to see her here tonight, but I see—"

She leaned over the table again to glare at Miranda. Her eyes had a reptilian glitter.

"—that you've already replaced her with this very *healthy* young person."

Nobody spoke for a moment. Miranda set her fork neatly on the plate so that a servant could clear it for the rib roast which the steward was carving on the sideboard.

"Why my goodness, Sarah," Miranda said sweetly. "Surely you didn't imagine there was anything romantic between Lady Mundy and Daniel? You must not know Daniel very well. Why dear, Lady Mundy is almost as old as *you* are."

She gave a silvery laugh. Daniel forced his lips tight on the rim of his glass. When everyone else at the table except the two Sterrets began to guffaw, he joined in as well.

A *very* clever young woman . . .

Adele Mundy glared at the mirror, checking the hang of the new gray suit. She didn't care very much about her appearance, but she'd look ridiculous if she'd fitted the closures askew. She *did* care about not becoming a laughingstock.

There was a tap on the door. Tovera looked at the security monitor. It was fed by optical fibers from microcameras in every room and passage of Chatsworth Minor.

That degree of paranoid concern seemed wildly excessive to Adele. This was not only her home when she was on Cinnabar, it'd been the family's townhouse during the sixteen years before she'd left to finish her education in the Academic Collections on Bryce.

"Mistress, it's Annette," squeaked one of the maids. Adele frequently got the impression that the servants were afraid of her, though they were also enormously proud to be in the service of Mundy of Chatsworth. "There's a young gentleman below asking to see you. His name's Cazelet."

"It's Annette and she's alone," Tovera said. She was keying the security monitor, no doubt trying to find significance in the name Cazelet. Tovera was a competent information technician, but Adele could've done much better if she'd chosen to.

She restrained herself with an effort of will, then sighed. Sometimes even the most extreme paranoia wouldn't be enough, of course. "I'm coming down, Annette," she said. "I'll see him, but I'm going out in a few minutes."

Tovera preceded Adele through the door, holding her attaché case in front of her. Annette was already skipping downstairs. The servants might be afraid of Lady Mundy, but they were—rightly—terrified by Lady Mundy's secretary.

Adele's decision to go to Bryce, the cultural heart of the Alliance, instead of taking further instruction in the Library of Celsus here in Xenos hadn't been whimsical. Even then, nothing the serious elder Mundy girl did was whimsical. She'd made her choice, however, purely on the ground of what facility would at this stage best advance her plan of becoming a skilled archivist.

It hadn't crossed Adele's mind that she'd save her life by going off-planet, but she did. Reports of a coup plot on Cinnabar and its bloody suppression by Corder Leary, the Speaker of the Senate, reached Bryce a few days after she did. Save for Adele's own, the head of every member of the Mundy family was displayed on the Speaker's Rock in the center of Xenos.

Adele's ten-year-old sister Agatha was killed a few days after their parents. Former family friends had turned the little girl away, so she'd wandered in the street until a pair of sergeants in the Land Forces of the Republic had recognized her. They'd cut her head off with their knives.

In the entryway at the base of the stairs, a boy of twenty-four or five waited with the doorman. His black hair was cut short in an unfamiliar style, but his thin features were vaguely familiar.

He nodded acknowledgment as Adele followed Tovera down. His hands had been clasped behind his back; now he brought them into sight and let his arms hang by his sides.

"I'm Adele Mundy," she said without preamble. The boy was wearing a conservative business suit similar to Adele's own, though the base color of his was beige. "I'm going out in two and a half minutes, so please state your business without wasting both our time."

Adele didn't like visitors. They were intrusive, and she much preferred getting information electronically. Her personal data unit rode in a thigh pocket. There were similar pockets in every pair of trousers she owned, even—in defiance of regulation—those of her RCN dress uniforms.

When Adele wielded the unit's control wands, she had an answer to almost any factual question that she could ask. What information the personal unit didn't itself have was available from some other database. Thanks to her skills and the tools which Mistress Sand had provided, there were few electronic repositories from which she was barred.

"Thank you," said Cazelet. He nodded twice as though he were resetting his memory, then continued, "A month ago my father and mother were arrested on Pleasaunce by agents of the Fifth Bureau. They were charged with conduct prejudicial to the good order of the State, which is treason under the War Emergency Powers proclaimed by Guarantor Porra. Their trial was of course secret, but it seems a foregone conclusion that they were executed."

He paused. Adele nodded. "Yes, it does," she said in a neutral tone.

She touched her data unit but she didn't take it out. The Fifth Bureau was the security directorate which reported to Porra personally. Its agents were known to be skilled and ruthless beyond the norm of most secret police organizations.

"I wasn't arrested at the time," Cazelet continued, "because I was with my grandmother. I was studying information storage and retrieval techniques to help me in my duties for Phoenix Starfreight, the shipping line which my father owned. We had twelve vessels, though—again, of course—they'll have been confiscated by the State under the treason regulations. My grandmother has provided full documentation of my personal and family background."

He held out a data chip. Tovera reached past Adele and said, "I'll see to it."

"Why have you come to me?" Adele said quietly.

She knew that Tovera was holding a gun on the boy, but she herself was sure he meant no harm. The disquieting aspect of the business was that from his preamble, he was aware that she was involved with the Republic's intelligence apparatus. Adele's connection with Mistress Sand shouldn't have been so generally known that a refugee from the Alliance would seek her out as his first choice for that purpose.

"My grandmother said that you'd help me," Cazelet said. He twisted off the ring on his left little finger and offered it to her. It was a small ruby signet. Meeting Adele's eyes, he said, "My grandmother is Mistress Boileau."

Tovera reached for the signet. "No," said Adele. She didn't raise her voice, but the syllable was as hard as a shard of glass.

Tovera's face was without expression, but she withdrew her hand. Adele took the ring and turned it to catch the light. The intaglio of the Boileau crest, an armed lion, was too small to really make out, but Adele's wasn't in doubt that it was really Mistress Boileau's signet.

"The Fifth Bureau could've provided him with your friend's eyes as easily as they could her ring," Tovera said. She was a colorless woman with a colorless voice, and she had no conscience at all. That had made her a great asset to the Fifth Bureau when she was part of it. "It proves nothing."

"I recognize his features," Adele said, returning the ring. "He's a Boileau."

She frowned, then added, "We may even have met. Did we?"

Cazelet bobbed his head twice again, but he said, "My mother brought me to Bryce twice to visit Granna, when I was twelve and again when I was fourteen. I saw you both times, but we weren't introduced."

He cleared his throat and added, "Mistress? Granna says you're an artist. She says that no one ever could accomplish what you do with information systems, and that nobody'll ever equal you in the future either."

Adele sniffed. "I was well trained," she said.

The doorman had turned away to watch the street through the door's sidelight. Tovera eyed the youth in cold fury.

"Tovera," Adele said crisply, "there's been a change of plans. Master Cazelet will accompany me to the playhouse. I want you to deliver the data he's brought to those who'll want to see it. When they've digested it, I'll discuss the situation with them."

Mistress Sand would be as angry as Tovera. While she wasn't likely to shoot anyone herself, she had the whole resources of the Republic to command if she wished to.

"Mistress, it doesn't mean anything even if he *is* her grandson!" Tovera said.

Adele stepped between her servant and Rene Cazelet. Tovera couldn't use the sub-machine gun in her attaché case without shooting her mistress first.

"On the contrary, Tovera," Adele said. "Family obligations mean a great deal to a Mundy of Chatsworth. Now, if you're in my service—carry out your orders! And if you're not, get out of my house and my sight, because I'll shoot you like a snake if I ever see you again."

Tovera closed her case and bowed slightly. Her complexion was ordinarily so pale that only one who knew her well would realize that she'd gone even whiter.

"I'll deliver the chip as you direct, mistress," she said quietly. "Shall I await your return here at Chatsworth Minor?"

"Yes, unless there's a reason for you to do otherwise," Adele said. "I'll leave that to your judgment."

Tovera smiled faintly in acknowledgment of the conciliatory words. "Mistress," she repeated. She went out the door like a wisp of cold air.

Adele shrugged to loosen her muscles. Her left hand had been in the pocket of her tunic, gripping a little pistol. She hadn't expected to shoot it out with her servant, but in times of tension her subconscious took her hands to one machine or the other: the personal data unit or the pistol. She was rarely without both.

"A playhouse, mistress?" Rene Cazelet said. He stood unusually straight; she wondered how much he'd understood of what'd just happened.

"Yes, Master Cazelet," Adele said, crooking a finger toward the doorman. He opened the panel which'd been carved out of wood from the Mundy country estate of Chatsworth Major. "We're going to a play. It's called *The Conquest of Dunbar's World*, and I'd very much like to see how it describes that business."

CHAPTER 2

Xenos on Cinnabar

Though the staff at Chatsworth Minor wore Mundy livery, they were actually employed by the Shippers' and Merchants' Treasury. The bank rented the townhouse for clients and clandestine meetings during the long periods in which the owner and her other tenant, Commander Leary, were off Cinnabar. Daniel hadn't been told of the connection, because the bank's major partner was his estranged father, Corder Leary.

Adele *did* know. Given her family's history with Speaker Leary, the situation made her uncomfortable and therefore distant toward the servants; though she was unlikely to've become close to them anyway. In the present instance she'd told the majordomo to get her two tickets at the nearest playhouse showing *The Conquest of Dunbar's World.*

The Palace Theatre was located on the Penta-crest, in the center of Xenos. It was fashionable and therefore ornate, but since it was close to Chatsworth Minor—Adele would've walked instead of taking a tram if time hadn't been short—the choice hadn't surprised her.

She'd been surprised to learn that the Palace had a Speaker's Box, however, and even more surprised that she and her guest had the use of it tonight. Her first reaction had been that this was probably costing a week's income for an RCN signals officer. Her second, noticing how obsequious the manager was as he led them to the box in the center of the third tier, was that more than money had to be involved. *What in heaven's name did the majordomo say?*

As the manager latched the door to the box behind them, Adele settled into one of the plush chairs. The lights went down and martial music began to rumble. She frowned. She'd intended to time their arrival to miss the opening nonsense attached to the features, but Cazelet's arrival should have made her late.

Cazelet reached into his pocket and squeezed his watch. It was a hunter; instead of displaying numerals, chimes bonged softly; they were followed by a snatch of an air which gave the minutes in increments of five.

"They held the show for us, mistress," he said. Adele had taken a center seat; he took one beside her. He was smiling faintly.

"I had nothing to do with that!" Adele said, angry at Cazelet's assumption and even more angry to realize that he might be correct. Had Daniel's sister Deirdre, the managing partner of the Treasury, given the servants at Chatsworth instructions that'd been kept secret from Adele?

As the music throbbed, holographic lightning spelled the names of players above the virtual stage. Adele knew displays: they were the means by which she absorbed most of the information that was her life. The Palace's projection apparatus was aligned to provide ninety-seven percent comprehension throughout the 180-degree arc of spectators, but the optimum viewing location was the center of the Speaker's Box.

A voice—normally documentaries were narrated by newsreaders, but here Adele recognized the tones of Michael Beasley, a leading player—said, "Though we who play the roles in this drama are civilians, the incidents which we portray are entirely true and are based on imagery collected by the heroic men and women of the Cinnabar navy. It is with profound humility and respect that we offer to the citizens of this great Republic a lifelike account of—"

The music and Beasley's voice swelled together.

"—the conquest of Dunbar's World!"

Adele set her data unit on her knees. She didn't need it at present, but she'd found that gripping the control wands settled her mind. Cazelet divided his attention between her and the documentary.

"Port Dunbar!" boomed Beasley. "A city being crushed by the relentless brutality of Guarantor Porra's goons."

The image panned across a ruined urban landscape. It was early dusk, though the sky was bright enough to show buildings already shattered by explosives. The tracking flares of bombardment rockets gleamed all the way to the orange blasts at the end of their quick arcs.

"Now, how did they . . . ?" Adele whispered; her wands flickered, calling up data.

"Is that wrong, mistress?" Cazelet said, giving her a start. She'd forgotten that she wasn't alone.

"On the contrary," she said, adjusting her data unit so that he could view its holographic display also. "It's right. They're using real images, images *my* helmet gathered when we flew into Port Dunbar."

"In orbit above the planet," Beasley's voice continued, "hangs a powerful Alliance squadron manned by picked crews, the finest spacers to be found among those willing to serve the megalomaniac tyrant Porra!"

Images of warships cascaded across the display: a cruiser/minelayer and another light cruiser, two heavy cruisers, and a modern battleship. The mix was seasoned with at least a dozen destroyers. Adele couldn't identify the vessels because she didn't have the background to sort one ship from another by the length of the antennas or the shape of the outrigger pontoons.

Daniel would've recognized them, however, and Adele remembered the names which her data unit supplied: the *Bremse*, the *Caio Duilio*, the *Bluecher*, the *Scheer*, and the battleship *Der Grosser Karl*. Oh, yes, she remembered them.

"And the only hope for the cowering residents of Dunbar's World . . ." continued the voice, this time rolling with oily smoothness over an image of Beasley himself, ". . . is the corvette *Princess Cecile* and her captain, Daniel Leary—as bold a spacer as ever wore the uniform of the Cinnabar navy!"

The image of Beasley was wearing a heavily embellished version of an RCN first-class uniform. As factual errors went in this presentation, that was a fairly mild one. In any case, it was what the producers had gotten right that concerned Adele, not their mistakes.

"Is that really Commander Leary, mistress?" Cazelet asked quietly.

"Good heavens, no!" Adele blurted. "Daniel, the commander, that is, is six inches shorter than that player and younger by fifteen years. Why, he's—"

She turned to Cazelet, shocked to realize what she was about to say. "Commander Leary is your age, sir. I tend to forget that sometimes. He has a youthful enthusiasm for all manner of things—"

Certainly including young pretty bubbleheads. He'd been seeing the sister of the late Midshipman Dorst on this return to Xenos, however, and *that* young lady appeared to have not only her own share of intelligence but also the share which her brother Timothy, brave and steadfast though he was, had undoubtedly lacked.

"—but his presence in a crisis has an impressive maturity."

Beasley/Daniel was addressing what were apparently his officers on the bridge of what might've been a battleship. Certainly it was too spacious for a 1,300-ton corvette like the *Princess Cecile*.

"Fellow citizens of the great Republic of Cinnabar!" he said. "You've joined me to lift the iron heel of tyranny from the necks of the innocent people of Dunbar's World. I swear to you that we will succeed, even if it means our deaths. As you know, a Cinnabar spacer never backs down!"

"Is the speech from the records also, mistress?" Cazelet asked. He was keeping his voice carefully neutral, but the doubt behind the question was obvious.

Well, it would've been obvious to a pet monkey!

"It is not," Adele said dryly. "To begin with, Cinnabar citizens are a minority in most RCN crews. They were a *small* minority on the vessels which we operated in Ganpat's Reach. More important—"

She paused, watching as a delegation from the government of Dunbar's World begged Commander Leary for his support in their struggle against tyranny. Makeup and artfully torn garments emphasized their wretchedness, and the holographic imagery had apparently been manipulated to reduce the height of the civilian players in comparison with the stalwart spacers of the RCN.

Adele snorted. "Good *heavens*!" she muttered. "They're in uniform."

"The uniforms are wrong, you mean?" Cazelet asked.

"What?" said Adele. She'd forgotten him again. "No—well, yes, that too. But it's the fact the spacers are wearing *any* uniform. They'd be in slops of some color that wouldn't show grease too badly. Unless they were going on liberty, of course, and then they'd be covered in so many ribbons and bangles that you'd be hard put to tell what the fabric was underneath."

"I wondered about that," Cazelet said. "Crews in the Fleet dressed the same as those who signed with us in Phoenix Starfreight. I thought it might be different in the RCN, though."

Adele looked at the boy—he *wasn't* a boy—sharply. Simply by listening to her, Cazelet had picked up on something that civilians almost never got: it wasn't "our navy" or even "the Cinnabar navy," it was the RCN to those who lifted on the Republic's paybill. And that brought her to another point.

"The other and better reason that Daniel wouldn't call his crew 'citizens' . . ." Adele said. She didn't ordinarily refer to her friend as Daniel rather than Commander Leary in public or among strangers. She was doing so consistently tonight, and she decided to stop fighting the tendency. ". . . is that they'd take it as an insult. Citizens are civilians. RCN crews are *spacers* and proud of it."

Signals Officer Mundy couldn't properly claim to be a spacer, despite what by now was very considerable experience aboard RCN vessels on active service. When she was on the hull of a ship under way, she was always clipped to a safety line. Nevertheless everyone in sight watched her nervously.

Despite Adele's awkwardness, she'd been adopted by the crew of the *Princess Cecile* and by every crew since which the *Sissie*'s veterans leavened. She'd been a studious child and never really one of the politically focused Mundys, but she was truly part of the RCN family.

Mistress Mundy had various skills which even the toughest spacer could appreciate. She'd demonstrated them again on Dunbar's World. . . .

On the stage, the *Princess Cecile*—a computer image too sparklingly perfect for even an admiral's yacht—battled a cruiser/minelayer with plasma cannon. The guns were primarily defensive armament intended to divert incoming missiles, but they could damage rigging or even worse if the range was really short.

The *Sissie*'s 4-inch weapons weren't sufficient to harm a cruiser's hull, of course. When her opponent exploded in a fireball swelling to fill the stage, Cazelet snorted in derision.

"I realize it's fiction," he said, "but couldn't they try to make it at least vaguely believable?"

"That's real imagery," Adele said. "Oh, it didn't happen off Dunbar's World, and of course it wasn't the *Sissie's* guns that were responsible. The *Bremse* detonated one of her own mines."

"By the Gods," Cazelet said softly. He turned to meet her eyes. "There are safety devices, are there not?"

The false Commander Leary was making another speech. In fact Daniel was a very effective orator, but Adele was sure that hadn't affected the "documentary" in the least.

"The lockouts were disconnected," Adele said. *I disconnected them, thereby killing several hundred Alliance spacers. Though I'm not sure it counts unless you watch them over your gunsight as they die.*

Riggers danced up and down the *Sissie's* antennas in light air suits, probably because the rigging suits they really wore were too stiff and depersonalizing for properly dramatic effects. Commander Leary— who wore Dress Whites under his translucent air suit—leaped into the void to save two spacers who'd slipped from the yard.

The computer-generated *Princess Cecile* was back in action, this time against a heavy cruiser. The enemy vessel crumbled under the lash of incoming missiles.

"That's true too?" Cazelet said. "I'll admit it looks like real imagery, but I don't see how it could be."

Adele smiled faintly. "It can be real if you realize that there's an allied battleship launching from out of the image area," she said. "That was two years ago and nowhere near Dunbar's World. But it was real."

The battles—and the heroic speeches, none of which mentioned loot or sexual partners like the speeches Daniel was in the habit of making to his crews—continued. Adele clipped scenes and made notes, feeling a grim fascination.

Almost no part of the documentary was "right" except for the historical images, but they could only have come from the RCN archives. There was nothing unusual about Navy House surreptitiously releasing documents and imagery to enhance the RCN's reputation or to do a favor to a powerful politician. There was vanishingly little chance of Admiral Vocaine providing information to make Daniel Leary a national hero, however.

On stage *Der Grosser Karl* limped into the Matrix, badly injured by the *Sissie*'s missiles. That was true too, in part. Adele had been present, but she couldn't say that she really remembered the battleship's 8-inch cannon raking them at point-blank range. At the time her duties had kept her too busy to worry about whether or not she was about to be killed. Besides, the chance of death wasn't something that'd have greatly exercised her even if she weren't occupied.

Assuming that the play had climaxed when the *Princess Cecile* chased away a battleship, Adele straightened. She looked forward to returning to Chatsworth Minor, where she'd have privacy to explore the questions which the performance raised.

Rene Cazelet had lapsed into silence. He was watching the stage intently, though occasionally he glanced sidelong at Adele. Her control wands flickered, gathering images and comparing them with stored data.

"There was still one hurdle for Commander Leary and his heroic crew," boomed Michael Beasley in a voice-over.

On stage the *Princess Cecile* swept low across the single continent of Dunbar's World, then braked hard. *They won't show that,* surely *they won't!*

"They had to capture the Alliance base and disable the missile battery there!"

They were going to show it.

The corvette landed on a muddy island, crushing barracks and military equipment beneath its outriggers. The main hatch crashed down immediately—Adele wondered whether that was dramatic license or if the producers simply didn't understand how slowly a multi-ton section of hull plating had to move if it weren't to be battered to scrap metal. The supposed crew of the *Sissie* rushed down the ramp without waiting for the ground baked by the plasma jets to cool. Commander Daniel Leary was in the lead.

Please. Please. Please.

Adele didn't know who she was speaking to. Praying to, she supposed, though she didn't believe in gods or Gods or anything at all except the working of blind chance.

Commander Leary held a sub-machine gun in one hand and a stocked impeller in the other. He raced toward the berm protecting the pit where ship-killing missiles were emplaced, using both weapons as he ran. For some reason the Alliance troops jumped out of their bunkers before they shot at him; they spun artistically and fell.

The gate into the emplacement was of razor ribbon stretched on a frame. *Just like the real gate.*

Commander Leary sawed through the obstruction with a burst from his sub-machine gun. *Alliance projectiles hitting wires, hitting tubing; howling, ricocheting in neon colors. Occasionally a wire parting with a sickening jangle.*

"Follow me, my heroes!" Commander Leary shouted

as he ran through the gap in the gate. The corvette's whole crew was with him. *Bunched like that, a single automatic impeller would slaughter the lot of them. They'd be dead!*

"Mistress, are you all right?" Cazelet said. His left arm was around her back; his hands were gripping her shoulders firmly. "Would you like to leave?"

There were bunkers inside the emplacement. Troops in Alliance uniforms—which was wrong, they'd been Pellegrinians, all but the communications detachment—threw down their weapons and stood, waving white flags.

"Victory!" boomed the voice-over. "And permanent safety for Dunbar's World under the protection of the Republic of Cinnabar!"

"I'm sorry," Adele whispered. "I'm all right."

Light flickering from the firing slits of the bunkers, the traces of driving bands ionized by the charges that accelerate them up the gun barrels. Her holographic sights twitching as she fires two rounds and moves to the next target. The faces of the Pellegrinian soldiers are shadowed, but she sees every one of them clearly as they bulge under the impact of her projectiles.

The martial music resumed as the house lights came up. Adele closed her personal data unit and slid it back into its pocket. Cazelet had taken his hands away from her but he continued to watch with a concerned expression.

"We'll return to Chatsworth Minor," Adele said as she stood. She didn't meet his eyes. "You'll have a room in the servants' quarters while I look into matters."

"Mistress, I have a room already," Cazelet said.

"It's best that you stay at Chatsworth," she said sharply. "That'll prevent accidents. Some of them, at least."

"Yes, ma'am," Cazelet said. Did he realize that she was worried about Mistress Sand, or rather what someone in Mistress Sand's organization might do to prevent the compromise of an asset as valuable as Adele Mundy?

He touched the door latch, but he paused and looked at Adele until she met his eyes. "Mistress," he said, "that last scene? Did Commander Leary really assault a strong point that way?"

"No," said Adele, stepping past the boy to open the door herself. "I did."

It occurred to Daniel, walking back to find a seat with the numbered chit in his hand, that the waiting room of the Navy Office was very like a cathedral. He grinned, a familiar expression on his broad features. There were probably more prayers—and certainly more sincere ones—offered here than in any religious edifice on Cinnabar.

Even the hall's front five benches weren't crowded, and the twenty or so beyond held only a scattering of suppliants. Most of those waiting were lieutenants, but there were some passed midshipmen hoping for their first assignment. On the other end of the continuum, several superannuated captains sat in stiff dignity with all the decorations they could claim, hoping the Republic's need would bring them out of forced retirement.

All were well dressed. This morning Daniel had donned his best second-class uniform, his Grays, but a good number of senior officers and those with private incomes were in Dress Whites.

As Daniel prepared to sit some ten rows back, he noticed a familiar face across the aisle. "Why, hello, Christopher," he said in a low voice, stepping toward the thin lieutenant seated there. "Haven't seen you since the Academy."

Christopher Cha continued to sit stiffly, gripping his chit between the thumbs and forefingers of both hands. Instead of looking up when Daniel spoke his name, he turned his face the other way as if he were searching for something farther down the empty row.

I didn't go home with his girlfriend after a party, did I? Daniel wondered. He certainly didn't remember doing so, but there were some nights during graduation week that were at best hazy.

"Leary!" said a lieutenant commander in the fourth row. He was making an effort to mute his voice, but the resulting husky whisper could be heard for a dozen paces in every direction. "Come tell me about the hero's life, bold fellow!"

Daniel went back and slid past the slanted knees of four strangers, all lieutenants, to get to Scott Morgan. They'd been classmates at the Academy. Morgan had run with a faster crowd than Daniel, estranged from his father, could afford to follow, but they'd gotten on well enough during such contact as they'd had.

"Pretty, eh?" said Morgan, tapping the pip-in-a-circle on the epaulette of his Dress Whites. As Daniel slid onto the backless bench beside him, Morgan touched the solid rectangle of a full commander on the collar tab of his Grays and went on, "Of course, they're not nearly as pretty as these, Danny-my-boy.

Congratulations, and further congratulations for still being alive. I'd say the rank is pretty much a given if you do the sorts of things you've done and manage to survive."

"I think you're overstating things, Scott," Daniel said, "but I appreciate your congratulations."

Without being really conscious of what he was doing, he glanced back at Lieutenant Cha. Morgan caught his expression and laughed. "Little Chrissie is afraid that if the Chief learns that he knows you, it'll hurt his chances of an appointment. As if Admiral Vocaine cares two pins about him! If we'd given a class award to the Least Likely to Be Promoted, it'd've been engraved CHRISTOPHER CHA!"

"You think that's it, Morgan?" Daniel said. He smiled, but it was a little lopsided. He'd always gotten on well with others, and it disturbed him to think that people he'd known for the best part of a decade would shun him because of his difficulties with the Chief of the Navy Board.

"Of course that's it!" Morgan said. "But I have to correct you on one point, laddy: I'm not Morgan, I'm Fanshawe—as in the son and heir of Senator Fanshawe. My uncle, that's the one with the money in the family, adopted me last month."

He grinned widely and added, "I'd still sit with you, Danny; you're good company and no bloody admiral is going to tell me who my friends are. But under the circumstances, I don't care whether the Republic chooses to keep me on half pay."

"Ah!" said Daniel. "Then hearty congratulations to you too, Fanshawe!"

He'd always believed that Morgan's birth parents

had quite enough money as it was, but no doubt there were as many gradations at the higher levels of these things as there were with poverty. Corder Leary would probably understand better than his son did.

A green light blinked on the desk of the functionary who guarded the gate between the benches and the clerks beyond the railing. He glared at the screen before him, then called, "Number twenty-two!" in a stentorian voice.

A lieutenant of forty rose so abruptly that she almost overbalanced and fell backward over the bench. Her second-class uniform was clean but nearly threadbare. She bustled to the gate, her face in a rictus of mingled hope and terror.

It would've been possible—and a great deal more practical—to've left the whole process to technology. Officers between assignments could've been paged electronically to report to a given office at a given time. For that matter, their orders could've been delivered without human involvement. Not only would the process be more efficient, it would avoid awkwardness and embarrassment for those waiting day after day in the echoing hall.

Daniel doubted there was an officer in the RCN who would've preferred that cold, impersonal world. Certainly he wouldn't have.

He looked again at his chit: the numerals 414 were inlaid in black on the ivroid. Or was it . . . ?

"Why, look at this, Morgan!" Daniel said, too excited to remember his friend's current name. "This is one of the originals, I'm sure of it! It's not a synthetic at all, it's cut from a moonfish eye."

"Sorry, I don't follow you, laddy," Fanshawe said. "Is

it valuable, do you mean? There's a plum assignment waiting for you if you draw this chip?"

"Well, not that," Daniel said. It'd be easy to mistake Morgan, now Fanshawe, for a buffoon. He'd never been that: his scores at the Academy ranged from good to remarkably good, and he'd come as close as anyone in their class to matching Daniel Leary in astrogation. "Though it's a prize in its own right. Only the original run of chits were cut from the natural substance. They date from when Navy House was opened a century and a half ago! And the moonfish has been extinct for, well, for very nearly that long."

He pursed his lips. "I wonder how many of the originals remain in use?"

"For now, my lad," said Fanshawe, "I suggest you forget about natural history and hand the thing back to Cerberus at the bar, there. He's just called your number."

"Thanks, Fanshawe," Daniel said as he rose and slid past the lieutenants again. "Thank you indeed."

The thanks were for much more than telling Daniel that he'd been paged. Wealthy connections had doubtless created an interest furthering Fanshawe's promotion, but the RCN would be fortunate if all its lieutenant commanders were his equal.

The attendant at the gate examined Daniel's chit with sour thoroughness, as if he thought it might be a counterfeit. The clerical staff of Navy House were not members of the RCN and tended to view themselves as superior to the serving officers who came to them as suppliants. Daniel understood the mechanism—his study of lower animals as a hobby had given him more than a few insights into human society as well—but it didn't make him like it any better.

The attendant replaced the chit in the hopper from which it would be dispensed to future generations of waiting officers, perhaps over another hundred and fifty years. "Office 12B," he said, swinging the gate open with his right hand.

"Pardon?" said Daniel. He'd been expecting to be sent to the desk of one of the clerks on the other side of the bar, but "office" meant—

"Through the door and ask the guard for directions," said the attendant peevishly. For the first time in the process, he looked up at Daniel's face. "Or have him guide you, if you don't think you can find your way to the second floor!"

"Ah," said Daniel. He reached into his pocket—an advantage of Grays over Dress Whites was that they *had* pockets—and dropped a florin on the attendant's desk. The coin rang clearly. "Thank you, my good man."

The attendant was still spluttering in amazed fury when Daniel reached the door at the back of the hall. He heard snorts of laughter from officers in the waiting area, and he himself was smiling.

There were two guards, RCN warrant officers whose lack of collar insignia meant they were from the provost marshal's division. They could probably handle themselves if push came to shove, but neither they nor anybody else expected trouble. When they retired in a few years, the white enamel on their sheathed batons would still be unmarked.

"I've been directed to 12B, Sauter," Daniel said, taking the name from the tag over the taller guard's breast pocket. He gestured toward the steps at the end of the corridor. The runner of blue carpeting was worn to the weft in the center of each tread, but the brass rods holding it in place were brightly polished. "Upstairs, I believe?"

"And to the right, Commander," Sauter agreed, "about midway down. That'll be the Liaison Office with Captain Britten."

Daniel pursed his lips as he dredged out a memory. "Britten," he repeated. "Was he perhaps in the Ten Star Cluster a few years ago?"

Sauter frowned. "The very man," said Leckie, his partner. "But promoted since then, I believe."

Daniel climbed the stairs two at a time. He wasn't in a particular hurry, but he was used to going up that way. Taking the treads normally would feel as awkward as mincing down the hallway instead of taking full strides.

The doors along the right-hand corridor were closed, though a clerk—an RCN rating, not a civilian—carried a file folder out of one as Daniel reached 12B. She seemed to look through him as she strode past in the direction he'd come from.

He knocked on the frame beside the panel of frosted glass. "Come in, dammit!" boomed a voice. Daniel swallowed his smile as he obeyed. Yes, this was the same officer whom he'd met on Todos Santos, all right.

Daniel closed the door behind him. The room was long and narrow. There were cabinets for paper files along one sidewall, and a desk—unoccupied at present—beside the door for a clerk. At the far end was another desk, so wide that it only fit the long way.

Captain Britten, built like a fireplug with cropped gray hair, sat at the big desk and typed on a virtual keyboard. He slammed the holographic keys as though he thought he could hammer out the answers he wanted. Daniel smiled; Adele had accused him of doing the same thing.

"Sit down, Leary," Britten said as he glared at his display. "I gather you've been making trouble again."

"Ah . . ." said Daniel. "Well, only for the enemies of the Republic, I believe, sir."

He ought to salute and report formally, but he was quite certain that Britten'd tear a strip off him if he did. Given that Daniel's salutes rarely rose to a level of minimal competence, he decided just to sit down as he'd been ordered to.

Britten snorted, then collapsed his display into a quiver of electrons and met Daniel's eyes. "Well, you stick to your story, Leary," he said. "Maybe one day you'll find somebody to believe it. For now, though—"

He stretched his arms sideways, then lifted them over his head. Britten's scowl of frustration was probably his normal expression, but he looked tired and a decade older than he had two years before on Todos Santos.

"—the problem is the Bagarian Cluster. My problem, and about to become your problem. What do you know about the place, eh?"

"Well, very little, sir," Daniel said, "though I can rectify that quickly, if you like."

The *Sailing Directions* which Navy House provided for all regions of the galaxy, both in and out of the Cinnabar Confederation, would give him everything an RCN officer was likely to need. Adele and her sources could provide much greater detail if for some reason that were necessary.

"The cluster's been part of the Alliance for over three hundred years," Daniel said. "Some heavy metals, a fair amount of agricultural produce; nothing of real importance. Frankly, the Bagarian Cluster's what you'd point to if you wanted to give an example of the boondocks. Ah, and there's a revolt going on there at the moment, I've been told."

"Right, I've been told that too, Leary," said Britten. "In fact the Independent Republic of Bagaria has requested the help of the RCN to organize its navy and put it in a state to defeat Alliance attempts to retake the cluster. It's my job, so now it's your job, to provide that help."

"Ah," said Daniel. "Ah, sir. . . . If I may ask, sir, is this a decision that's been made in Navy House, or has it been imposed by, ah, political elements?"

"Like the business in Ganpat's Reach that you just got back from, you mean?" Britten said. "No, this was our idea. My idea, Leary, not to put too fine a point on it. You know what's happening in the Jewel System?"

"Well sir," Daniel said, very carefully. "I know Admiral James only by reputation, but a very good reputation it is, sir."

"A *bloody* good reputation, couldn't agree more," said Britten. He brought up, then collapsed his holographic display again; a nervous tic that made him frown like a thundercloud when he realized what he was doing. "But he's got two battleships and the *Lao-tze* is eighty years old. *Eighty*, Leary, and don't tell me that she's still well found. For an eighty-year-old ship she *is* well found, but eighty bloody years take a toll. The Alliance squadron has two modern battleships and a pair of battle cruisers that can outsail anything in the RCN. *Plus* supporting forces in proportion."

Daniel tried not to frown, but given the direction his thoughts were headed, that was a losing proposition. "Ah, sir," he said. "Are you hoping that the Bagarian Republic will be able to reinforce Admiral James?"

Britten stared at him in disbelief. "May the Gods bugger me with a flagpole!" he said. "Have you lost your mind, Leary?"

"Ah, sorry sir," Daniel said in relief. He thought for a moment, then decided that with Britten he'd be better off to voice the rest of his thought. "No sir, I haven't; and I'm glad to see that you haven't either."

Britten laughed. He opened a drawer of his desk and brought out a quart of rye whiskey. The brand was a good one—Breen's Reserve—but not so exceptional that people would remark to see it on their host's sideboard.

An upended water glass covered the open bottle. "I've got another . . ." Britten muttered. He rummaged further, then chortled as he plunked a second glass onto the desktop.

"There's water down the hall," Britten said doubtfully as he slid a generous two fingers of liquor toward Daniel. "No? Well, I can't say I think it needs it either."

He set down his glass and resumed, "All I want you to do, Leary, is to give Fleet Command on Pleasaunce something to worry about besides reinforcing Admiral Guphill in the Jewel System. I want—we want, the

Republic wants—somebody to make enough scary headlines about the Bagarian Cluster that Guarantor Porra scrapes up all the ships he can spare and sends them to recapture Pelosi, that's where the government is. Instead of worrying mines out of the Diamondia defenses even quicker."

Daniel sipped, focused for the moment on the situation in the Jewel System. Diamondia was defended by a planetary defense array, a constellation of nuclear mines. Each when triggered used magnetic lenses to focus ions through the target; a single mine could destroy even a battleship.

The array could be swept by projectiles launched from beyond the range of the ion jets, but individual mines had a degree of mobility which made the process time-consuming as well as dangerous. Further, warships from the defended world could attack the sweepers while remaining within the minefield themselves. Knowing Admiral James, the defense of Diamondia was an active one.

"What sort of time scale are you considering, if I may ask, sir?" Daniel said. The factor controlling how quickly a planetary defense array could be cleared was the number of assets the enemy put to the task.

"At the present rate . . ." said Britten. He raised his glass, noticed it was empty, and banged it back on the desk. His eyes flicked to the bottle, but he didn't pour himself another.

"At the present rate, three months more or less," he went on. "We're slipping additional mines through the blockade on light craft, two or three at a time. That doesn't replace wastage, but it slows the rate somewhat. The Alliance could reduce the time to thirty days with the forces they *could* muster, according to my guesstimate."

He chuckled grimly. "And if you're wondering what's going to happen in that extra sixty days, Leary," he said, "I don't have a bloody clue. Maybe Porra'll keel over dead. Or maybe I will, which'll at least solve *my* problem."

Britten picked up the whiskey after all. "You?" he said, tilting the bottle toward Daniel.

Daniel swirled the last ounce of his present drink. He could hold his liquor—that was taken as a given for an RCN officer, much like courage—but there was no percentage in tripping in front of somebody who'd run to Admiral Vocaine with a story about Leary being drunk and incapable here in Navy House.

"Thank you, no, sir," Daniel said. "What assets can you give me for this mission, please?"

Britten chuckled again and splashed no more than an ounce in his glass. "'Bugger all,' you expect me to say, don't you?" he said. "Well, you're bloody near right. But you can have your corvette. She's free to contract to Navy House, isn't she?"

"Yes, sir!" Daniel said. Learning that he'd be commanding the *Princess Cecile* again cheered him to an unreasonable degree.

"And you can have the crew you came back with," Britten continued. "The ones who're pretending to be Kostroman laborers working in your father's dockyard. Admiral Vocaine may not want to pick a fight with Speaker Leary, but he's not such a bloody fool that he doesn't know what's going on, Commander."

Daniel cleared his throat. "Ah, yes, sir," he said.

Because there weren't enough spacers to supply both

the merchant service and the RCN on a war footing, Admiral Vocaine had begun sequestering—imprisoning, for all intents and purposes—the crews of vessels arriving on Cinnabar until they could be transferred aboard another RCN warship. Daniel had asked his sister to save his crew from that if she could.

Deirdre being Deirdre—and Corder Leary being Speaker Leary—there'd been a way. Daniel didn't trade on his family connections—he'd broken with his father forever when he joined the RCN—but he was a Leary of Bantry. He'd take care of his retainers—which the Sissies were, in his mind—even if that meant bending his principles.

Britten stared at his empty whiskey glass. "Bloody thing," he muttered. He clinked it upside down over the mouth of the bottle.

"Do you wonder where Admiral Vocaine stands on this, Leary?" he demanded. "Of *course* you bloody well do. Well, he's approved it. I wouldn't be giving you the assignment if I hadn't gotten the go-ahead from him."

"I'll try to justify the admiral's confidence, sir," Daniel said cautiously. He didn't see any benefit in discussing the Chief of the Navy Board, particularly in Navy House. "And yours."

"Oh, I don't mean Vocaine'll shed tears if you get yourself blown to ions, boy," Britten said. "He bloody well won't. But it's a job that's going to take flair to carry out, and your worst enemy—which Vocaine may very well be, Leary—will grant you flair."

He opened the drawer and slid the bottle away. "The clerk at Desk Five will have your orders," he said. "But I wanted to tell you the part that won't be written down."

"Thank you, sir," Daniel said, rising to his feet. He set the glass, now empty, on Britten's desk. "The *Sissie*, that's my corvette, will have a full missile magazine?"

"There'll be missiles," Britten grunted. "Regular naval units'll have priority . . . but I shouldn't wonder if you found a way around that."

I shouldn't wonder either, Captain, Daniel thought behind his smile. A few florins to a leading ordnanceman and new-manufacture dual-converter missiles could wind up marked as the sort of off-planet odds and ends that'd ordinarily be issued to a private yacht bought into service as an auxiliary.

"One thing, Leary, just to be clear," Britten said. "And maybe so that you understand Admiral Vocaine a little better. This is an open-ended appointment. You're to remain in the Bagarian Cluster until you're recalled, and that *won't* be before the end of the war."

"I understand, sir," said Daniel.

"But that's not all bad," Britten continued. "There's going to be a lot of things up in the air in the Bagarian Cluster. Money, for one, but more than that. A clever young fellow could just find himself life ruler of a rich planet. That's not a bad alternative to being an RCN officer, is it?"

"There are many who'd agree with you, sir," said Daniel. He did salute this time, then took himself quickly through the door.

I might consider that option myself, at some time after Hell freezes over.

CHAPTER 3

Bergen and Associates Yard, Cinnabar

The office of Bergen and Associates was built over the shops, so Daniel was forty feet in the air, looking down onto the *Princess Cecile*, which floated in the pool as the crew completed her outfitting. Behind him, his sister and the representatives of the Navy Office negotiated the terms of the corvette's lease.

"Now turn to Schedule 3, Depreciation," said Deirdre Leary, sitting at what'd once been Uncle Stacey's desk and now was Lieutenant Mon's. "You'll note that we've raised the figure by a half of a percent. That's based on actual wastage of spars and rigging during the previous RCN commission, as listed in the appendix. Now you'll note that we've—"

She was six years older than Daniel and their father's daughter in all respects except for physique. Where Corder was tall and craggy, Deirdre was shortish, soft if not exactly fat, and attractive if you liked full-figured brunettes. Attractiveness didn't matter: what Deirdre needed from a man

47

had nothing to do with romance, so she preferred to use professionals.

"One moment, mistress," said Ward Spears, the civilian clerk from the Navy Office, who was seated across from her. "I notice that you've increased depreciation on the hull as well, and that you're using the high figure for hull valuation . . ."

Daniel cleared his throat. "Ah, Deirdre?" he said. "The missiles have arrived and I believe I'd best oversee their stowage. You'll call me when you're ready for my signature?"

She flicked a hand toward him in dismissal. "Yes, of course we're applying the additional half percent to the hull, Master Spears," she said sharply. "While it's easier to measure the additional strain on the running gear, you surely don't claim that it doesn't involve the hull as well?"

The lieutenant commander who'd accompanied the clerk to represent the uniformed establishment watched longingly as Daniel started down the outside stairs. He must be as bored as Daniel was and, unlike the vessel's owner, didn't have the option of leaving the business to people who *liked* this sort of pettifoggery.

Which Deirdre really must. Her bank was leasing agent on the *Princess Cecile*, but that didn't mean she personally needed to handle these negotiations. She was haggling over a few hundred florins when she frequently dealt in tens of millions.

Better her than me, thought Daniel as he reached the concrete quay where Miranda stood beside Mon. A crew under Woetjans was swinging the fourth of twenty missiles cautiously from a lowboy and through the C Deck port serving the stern magazine. Even empty the missile weighed several tons. Filled with reaction mass—normally water—and accelerated to terminal velocity by its antimatter motors, it could deal a crippling blow to even a battleship.

If it hit, of course, and a corvette's small missile magazines made a hit over normal combat distances unlikely. Still, the *Sissie* had done some good in the past and might easily do so again. The present mission ought to provide a sufficiency of targets, at any rate.

"Oh, there's Daniel!" called Miranda happily. She was wearing green pastel slacks and a tunic with a floral pattern, cheerful without being garish. She was pretty rather than a classic beauty, but her personality made her the center of men's attention in almost any group. "Daniel, did you realize that these missiles are dual-converter RCN units? The manifest says they're a mix of single-converter foreign missiles."

Mon coughed and turned away in mild embarrassment. He'd been a good but unlucky officer during fourteen years of service with the RCN. When Daniel learned he owned the shipyard upon his Uncle Stacey's death two years before, he'd hired Mon to run it.

Mon now had a contented expression and an additional twenty pounds of comfortable fat. Daniel had a completely trustworthy manager who saw to it that Uncle Stacey's longtime employees were well treated. And the shipyard was making money hand over fist.

Of course, renewed hostilities with the Alliance had something to do with profitability. Navy House was getting first-rate workmanship on jobs that it hired done in the Bergen yard, though, so Daniel felt no embarrassment about being paid better as a civilian contractor than he was as a commander in the RCN.

."Well, Miranda," Daniel said, turning so that she could give him a friendly kiss on the cheek. "There may be some problems with paperwork, and it's even possible that I encouraged some problems with paperwork. But as I see it, missiles I ship aboard the *Princess Cecile* are very likely to be launched against enemies of the Republic. It's to everybody's advantage that they be modern units that accelerate quickly, don't you think?"

"Oh," said Miranda, looking stricken. "Oh, you must think I'm a *fool!*"

"Mistress, *nobody* thinks you're a fool!" said Mon fervently. He looked from her to the corvette, cleared his throat, and went on, "Well, what do you think of her, Commander? I don't mind saying that *I* think we did a good job."

The corvette's access ports were open while she was on the ground. Vesey—Lieutenant Vesey, Daniel's first officer—looked out from the bridge and waved.

"She's checking the astrogational updates," Mon said quietly. "Will Lady Mundy be able to help with the crewing situation, sir? Seeings as this really will be a combat mission."

Daniel grimaced. "We decided against pressing our luck," he said. Adele's ability to enter RCN databases at will and change assignments had been very useful in the past and might be again. Repeating the trick that'd gotten the *Princess Cecile* a crew when last she lifted from Cinnabar raised the risk of being caught to an unacceptable level. "And we've got eighty, that's enough to work and fight a corvette. They're all veterans, and they've sailed with me before."

"That's including the Pellegrinians, isn't it?" Mon said.

Daniel shrugged. "They're good men," he said. "And perfectly trustworthy."

A number of enemy spacers captured on Dunbar's World had preferred to join the RCN rather than return home and explain to Chancellor Arruns how they'd survived a disaster which'd claimed the life of his son and heir. In practice all members of the crew of a starship did their best in combat, regardless of their nationality or politics. That was their only chance of survival.

"Oh, they'll do, I know," said Mon. He laughed and added, "They'll have Captain Leary commanding them, after all. But a hundred and twenty would be better than eighty, even if it makes the berths a little tight."

Daniel tried to look at the *Princess Cecile* critically; to his surprise, he couldn't. Oh, he could rattle off the statistics: a three-hundred-foot cylinder with rounded ends; six rings of four antennas each, telescoped and folded along the hull while she was on the planetary surface. The plasma thrusters which drove her in an atmosphere were on the lower hull, clear of the water. High Drive motors annihilated antimatter to provide thrust more efficiently in a vacuum; they were recessed into the outriggers which steadied the ship after she'd landed.

The *Sissie* mounted paired 4-inch plasma cannon in turrets on the dorsal bow and ventral stern; the latter was inboard at the moment because it'd be under water if it were extended. For choice a starship always landed in water, which damped the flaring plasma exhaust and cushioned the process of settling many tons (1300 in the corvette's case, and she was small) onto a surface. Thrust reflected from rocky soil could flip a vessel if her captain were careless or unlucky.

"I think she's beautiful," Miranda said softly. "Generally I think Kostroma-built ships look stumpy, but the *Sissie*'s lines are perfect."

"I'm glad you think so, dear," Daniel said, choosing his words carefully.

To him the corvette was simply right: not pretty, not functional, just the way the universe had made her. He felt about the *Sissie* the same way he did about his nose. He knew there were many women and not a few men who obsessed about the details of their physical appearance, but not Daniel Leary; and the corvette was part of him.

He chuckled. Miranda looked at him and cocked an eyebrow in question. "I was thinking about the *Sissie* the way I do about my nose," Daniel said, wondering if that made any sense to the others. "Actually, she's more like my right hand, isn't she?"

The first lowboy was crawling down the quay to find room to reverse; a second, loaded with a further quartet of missiles, pulled up in its place. A stake-bed produce truck drove with a crashing of gears past the three more waiting lowboys and stopped beside Daniel and his companions.

Hogg got out of the cab. "All right, Bantries," he bellowed. "Hop down and wait till the master tells you where he wants you!"

He turned to Daniel, looking pleased, and said, "Good morning, young master. Woetjans thought you could use a heftier crew, so I went back to the estate and brought you twenty tenants that I was willing to vouch for. They'll need training before you can call'em spacers, but it seems to me some of what you need in this business is folks who'll jump when the master says jump. Aye, and knock heads when they're told, that too. This lot qualifies."

The men—and a few women—climbing from the back of the truck dipped their faces and touched forelocks to Daniel before shuffling into line. Most were young and one freckle-faced boy didn't look to be more than fourteen years old. If Hogg'd picked him, though, there was a reason.

Hogg was Daniel's servant. Hogg's ancestors had served Learys of Bantry for as far back as records ran. He looked dirty, unsophisticated, and *almost* bright enough to count to ten on his fingers.

In fact Hogg *was* dirty. He was also a skilled poacher, as clever—and ruthless—as a ferret, and utterly loyal to the young master.

Hogg had been the man in Daniel's life while he was growing up. Loyalty and devotion didn't mean that Hogg wouldn't whale the living daylights out of a boy he thought needed it. They'd both known that if Daniel had complained to his gentle mother, Hogg would be turned off the estate in disgrace.

Hogg had continued to raise the boy according to his standards of conduct, because it was his duty to do so. That willingness to put duty first had been the guiding light of Daniel's life ever since. It'd served him well in the RCN.

Daniel looked critically at the new recruits. It'd been nearly a decade since he'd been back to Bantry, so he didn't recognize many of the faces. Michael Polucha, though, had the streak of white in his hair where he'd fallen into the fish processor back when he and Daniel were both eleven.

"You, Stripey!" Daniel called. "Why did you decide to join the RCN?"

"Well, it's what Hogg told us, Master Daniel . . ." Polucha said, his eyes turned down toward his bare toes. "More money than anybody on Bantry ever seed—in the cottages I mean, saving your presence. And everybody bowing and scraping to us, 'cause we b'long t' Captain Leary."

Daniel scowled, wondering how to handle this. These folk were his responsibility, and the Learys didn't lie to their retainers. On the other hand, he had responsibilities to the *Princess Cecile* and the RCN also, and another twenty recruits could be *very* helpful . . .

"Just hold on before you say the wrong thing, young master," Hogg said. He turned to the *Sissie*'s main hatch, where Richard Campeny, the armorer, was chatting with the two power room ratings on guard with sub-machine guns.

"Campeny!" he called. "You heard what Polucha says I told him. Is it the truth?"

"Hell, yes, Hogg," said Campeny, straightening when he realized everybody—including Miranda—was watching him. "Though I won't pretend much of the money stuck to *my* fingers; I guess there's more could say that too. It's a bloody good time whenever we're on the ground, though, and they learn we're Sissies. A *bloody* good time!"

Hogg bobbed his head, then faced Daniel again. "Now, young master," he said forcefully. "Now what do you say?"

"All right, Campeny," Daniel said. "Since you seem to have time on your hands, take charge of this draft until Woetjans gets through stowing the missiles. Tell Lieutenant Vesey to set up the watches and make bunk assignments."

"You heard the master!" Hogg said. "Hop it, Bantries! You're going to make us proud or you'll rue the day you were born!"

The new draft clumped and clattered aboard the *Sissie*. Sun led and Hogg brought up the rear. They each carried a blanket roll; first order of business would be to get them proper footlockers. That'd mean Master Daniel—as opposed to Commander Leary—would need to advance modest amounts of money. . . .

"When will Lady Mundy be joining you, Daniel?" Miranda said. "Or is she already aboard?"

"Is she on board, Mon?" Daniel asked; Mon shook his head.

"To be honest," Daniel said to Miranda, "I don't know when she'll arrive. She said she had some business to take care of."

He pursed his lips. "And she said she'd be bringing an assistant, if I approved," he added. "Which of course I did."

"That'd be Tovera, you mean, sir?" Mon asked. He kept his tone very neutral, the way people did when they had to talk about Tovera.

"No, from the way she spoke, she's talking about a real assistant," Daniel said. "In addition to her servant Tovera. I, ah, I'm confident that Officer Mundy knows what she's doing."

Mon nodded. Pasternak, the Chief Engineer, leaned out of a stern hatch. "Mon!" he bellowed. "There's a bloody valve frozen on the feed to Number Eight thruster!"

"There bloody well isn't unless your own people have been monkeying with it!" Mon bellowed back. He glanced at Daniel. "With your leave?"

"Of course, Mon," Daniel said, but his manager was already striding up the *Sissie*'s entrance ramp. His boots hammered the non-skid surface.

"Is the assistant someone that Lady Mundy's other friends assigned to her, Daniel?" Miranda said in a very quiet voice.

"To be honest, my dear," Daniel said, "I don't know and I don't want to know. I'm happiest—"

He smiled warmly at the girl beside him, taking some of the sting out of what was nonetheless a rebuke.

"—when I don't know anything at all about Adele's other friends!"

Xenos on Cinnabar

The private car in which Adele shuttled along the tram lines of Xenos was marked with the crest of the Petrie family, three red mullets on a puce ground. It was common for wealthy families to keep personal cars at their townhouses; servants lifted them on and off the monorail as required.

Adele slipped her personal data unit back into its pocket so that she could grip a handhold as she faced the woman who'd summoned her into the vehicle. "Well," said Mistress Sand. "What did you learn?"

Adele shrugged. "That the Petries are a west-coast

family," she said. "Though they appear to be wealthy enough, they're not interested in the expense and ferment of Xenos. They don't have a townhouse here."

"I would have told you that," said Bernis Sand. "I suppose you wouldn't have trusted me, would you?"

"I ordinarily get information electronically," Adele said calmly. "When the question occurred to me, I answered it in my normal fashion."

She'd never seen the spymaster angry before. Sand's voice remained calm, but her stubby fingers fidgeted with a carved ivory snuff box, slipping it into and out of her waistcoat repeatedly.

"We looked at the information on the chip you sent us," Sand said, turning to face the opera window on the right side of the vehicle. The clear acrylic panel had been treated with a film that unrecognizably distorted objects seen through it. "To the extent we can cross-check, everything is confirmed."

She met Adele's eyes again and managed a slight smile. "It's in very good order," she added. "I was reminded of your own reports, Mundy."

Adele smiled faintly. "Thank you," she said. "Mistress Boileau trained me well."

"Bartram Cazelet was executed in Wellbank Prison on Pleasaunce," Sand continued. "It's possible but unlikely that Glenda Boileau Cazelet is still alive. You know about the Guarantor's prisons, so you realize that this possibility isn't good news."

Adele dipped her head in acknowledgment. "Yes, I realize that," she said.

"What we *don't* know, Mundy," Sand said in a harsher tone, "is who informed on the elder Cazelets. At this point there's a significant chance, a *significant* chance, that it was their own son. Your Rene Cazelet may well be not just an informer but an agent of the Fifth Bureau!"

A second tram with the Petrie crest, rather more battered than the first, followed theirs. That too was normal when members of the nobility wanted to retain their privacy but keep servants readily accessible. Today the second vehicle carried Tovera and Rene Cazelet, accompanied by four very solid men wearing Petrie livery.

"I don't believe that's the case, mistress," Adele said. "You may think the Fifth Bureau could delude Mistress Boileau in that fashion, but I do not. Regardless, I have a personal—a family—obligation to young Cazelet. He came to me for shelter, as I went to his grandmother."

"Mundy, you *can't* take him off planet with you," Sand said, "not given the nature of Commander Leary's mission. The risk to the Republic is unacceptable, completely unacceptable."

"I certainly can't leave him alone on Xenos while I'm gone for an indefinite period," Adele said quietly. "I'll keep an eye on him, mistress; and Tovera will, if you don't trust me. But he's going along."

"Are you saying that you won't accompany Commander Leary if this Cazelet doesn't go with you?" Sand said, raising her voice. She was a stocky woman given to tweed suits in earth tones. There was nothing distinctive about her appearance, but her personality dominated whatever room she was in.

Adele smiled faintly. Mistress Sand dominated the interior of this tramcar as surely as the sea covers a rock on the bottom; but in this case, as with the sea, the rock wasn't changed by the circumstances.

"The question doesn't arise, mistress," Adele said. "I *can* take Cazelet with me."

The emphasis was very mild, a barely noticeable stress on the syllable.

"Commander Leary would find room for him if the two of them had to share a bunk," she continued. "And he'll certainly find room for me, even if he had to smuggle me aboard in a section of spar."

Adele felt mild distress at the fact of this interview; Mistress Sand should know her better by now. Though the circumstances were unusual, of course.

The tram jolted across a set of points, rocking both of them. Mistress Sand grabbed a railing, then barked a laugh. "What I find interesting in talking to you, Mundy," she said, abruptly more relaxed, "is that you're not afraid of me. Most people *would* be under these circumstances."

Adele sniffed. "We're professional colleagues," she said. "We have a difference of opinion, but you've accepted my judgment in other difficult circumstances when I'm sure you had doubts. I'm *quite* sure that you don't wish me to come to harm."

Sand looked at her squarely. "No, I don't want you to come to harm, Mundy," she said softly. "I'd rather lose my right hand than lose you, for the Republic's sake."

With a flash of renewed anger she went on, "I read the after-action report on the assault on Mandelfarne Island. What in the name of the *gods* were you thinking? Do you know how important you are to Cinnabar?"

"I know I'm a Mundy of Chatsworth, mistress," Adele said. She smiled; her lips felt as it they'd been carved from ice. "And I know that if I ever put personal safety ahead of my duty, it won't be long before I lose the debate with the person in my head. The person who doesn't think there's any reason for my continued existence."

Sand sighed and inserted a key card into the tram's control panel. "It'll take you to the Bergen yard," she said. She hadn't bothered to punch a new destination. "That's what you want, isn't it?"

"That's correct," Adele said primly.

She hadn't been wholly truthful in implying that she wasn't afraid. There was a possibility that someone would decide to remove Rene Cazelet without—or even against—Sand's orders. Tovera was the best assurance of Cazelet's survival. The fact that Tovera herself wanted the boy dead wouldn't prevent her from killing anyone who tried to accomplish that result.

Sand looked at her again and shook her head. "Mundy," she said, "if you don't start showing a little common sense, you're going to be killed sooner rather than later. And I will regret that very much."

I *won't regret it*, Adele thought; but her lips merely gave a thin smile.

CHAPTER 4

Bergen and Associates Yard, Cinnabar

"Fellow officers," Adele said, awkwardly formal because of the awkward situation, "this is my assistant, Master Cazelet. He'll lodge in the midshipmen's quarters."

She'd called Vesey and the two midshipmen, Cory and Blantyre, to the Battle Direction Center in the corvette's stern. The senior warrant officers—Pasternak and Woetjans, Chief of Ship and Chief of Rig respectively—wouldn't have much direct contact with Cazelet, so she hadn't summoned them.

The BDC wasn't laid out for meetings: there was a star of three consoles in the center of the chamber which could control the *Sissie* if the bridge in the far bow were destroyed. The aisle between the consoles and the jumpseats against the bulkheads was narrow, but there was enough room for five people to meet face-to-face.

Also the BDC was out of the way of the jumble of testing and stowage before liftoff. Adele hadn't locked the armored hatch, but Tovera stood in the corridor outside; they wouldn't be disturbed.

The watch-standing officers eyed Cazelet. Vesey, a slim woman with plain features and mouse-brown hair, showed obvious distaste. Cory, a largish, soft-looking youth of modest intellect, appeared to be uninterested. Blantyre was a stocky, forceful girl; her guarded expression reminded Adele that Mistress Boileau's grandson was rather a good-looking young man.

Cazelet for his part stood straight with his legs spread slightly and his hands clasped over his belt buckle. He looked from one officer to another, smiling with the mild hopefulness of a puppy.

Vesey looked from Cazelet to Adele. "Is he to take instruction with the midshipmen also, then, mistress?" she said harshly. Vesey had been a skilled officer, particularly in astrogation, but she'd lacked confidence. When her fiancé died in battle, Vesey'd lost all zest for life.

Adele smiled faintly. On the credit side, Vesey no longer dithered because she was second-guessing herself. She had instead a fatalistic willingness to accept whatever happened. Because she *was* so highly skilled, the results of her crisply executed plans were consistently good.

For Vesey's sake, it was a pity that she wasn't happier. Happiness wasn't something that Adele herself had much experience of, however, and she certainly wasn't going to counsel someone else about how to achieve it.

"That won't be necessary—" Adele began.

"Instruction in astrogation, do you mean, Lieutenant?" Cazelet said unexpectedly.

Vesey's eyes narrowed slightly. "Primarily astrogation, yes," she said. "Shiphandling as well, but there's not very much chance to practice that while we're under way."

"I have some training in astrogation," Cazelet said. "And in shiphandling and Power Room operations; some, that is. I'd like to join Midshipmen Blantyre and Cory, if it's agreeable to you."

He looked at Adele. "And with you of course, mistress," he added.

"How did you happen to study those things?" Vesey said with a chilly lack of inflection.

"My family is in the shipping business," Cazelet said. "Was in business. My father wanted me to learn it from the ground up."

He cleared his throat. "I don't compare the smatterings I've picked up with your RCN training, of course," he added.

Cory looked at Cazelet, then nodded to Adele. "Lady Mundy doesn't have RCN training," he said, in a tone of challenge that surprised Adele to hear from him. "There's never been a signals officer like her before *ever*."

"That's what my grandmother says too, Cory," Cazelet said. He offered a friendly smile.

"Master Cazelet's grandmother trained me, you see, Cory," Adele said. "I'd be pleased if the three of you would make him feel at home aboard the *Sissie*, as Mistress Boileau did for me in the Academic Collections."

"She did?" Cory said in amazement. "Oh. *Oh*."

"Fine, I'll include him in the classes," Vesey said; still emotionless, but perhaps a degree less hostile. "Mistress, if I may—I have duties which I'd like to attend to?"

"Yes, of course," said Adele. "Thank you all for your time. I simply thought that since we'd be in close quarters for an indefinite period, it'd be best to have a formal introduction."

"Come along, Cazelet," Blantyre said brightly. "I'll show you to our berth."

Cazelet looked back at Adele; when she nodded, he followed Blantyre through the hatch that Vesey had just pushed open. Cory trailed out in the wake of the others.

That'd gone well enough, Adele thought. *The boy should fit in.*

Daniel luxuriated in the familiar contact between his back and the *Sissie's* command console. He grinned: this was home. The corvette had been his first command, and he knew that she'd always be first in his heart.

Along the bulkhead to his right were Sun at the gunnery console and Adele on signals. In theory the captain could slave the functions of every other station to himself at the command console; in practice, nobody else could enter Signals while Adele was aboard the *Princess Cecile*. The chores could be handled from either the command console or the Battle Direction Center, but it was impossible to gain access to the files stored in Adele's territory.

Cory sat at the navigator's console to Daniel's immediate left, though heaven help the *Sissie* if he had to pilot them home.

Daniel pursed his lips in disapproval of the thought. That wasn't fair: under his tutelage and Vesey's, Cory was becoming a decent astrogator. Oh, he didn't have a flair for the task, but he'd pass his boards for promotion to Lieutenant when he had a chance to sit for them. And Cory did, of all things, have real skill at communications—though that was properly the duty of a junior warrant, not a commissioned officer.

The remaining bridge console was the Chief Missileer's, filled at present by a former Pellegrinian named Borries. Daniel had run Borries through a lengthy series of tests and found him to be surprisingly good—better than most who came out of the RCN specialty school at Harbor Three near Xenos. Despite that, Daniel didn't intend for the fellow to actually control the corvette's primary armament in action.

Daniel had a touch which turned attacks into an art form—and besides, he *liked* launching missiles. Borries was on hand in case Daniel was incapacitated or too madly busy elsewhere to handle the task.

Vesey was in the BDC with Blantyre and three ratings, ready to take over if there was any reason that they should. Daniel rechecked the gauges on his holographic display. All hatches were sealed and the pumps were purring to circulate reaction mass. He hadn't ordered Pasternak to light the plasma thrusters yet, however.

"Center," Daniel said. His display immediately threw up the images of six personnel in the BDC. The last face puzzled him for an instant; then he realized it was Adele's new assistant, using the display on his commo helmet because there wasn't a console open for him. "Vesey, will you and your team be ready to take her up in five minutes, over?"

"*Aye aye, sir*," Vesey said. Her voice was neutral, but a touch of pleasure lifted the corners of her mouth.

That was as close to a smile as Daniel had seen her give since Miranda's brother died.

"You have the conn, Vesey," he said. "Out."

Daniel paused for a moment, gathering his thoughts. How many times had he addressed his crew before liftoff? Many, certainly, but every time was different; like a battle, like maneuvering closer to another woman. . . .

"Ship," he said. When he switched the intercom to the general communications channel, a multi-pointed star pulsed in the upper right of the display. If he moved the cursor onto it with his virtual keyboard, the real-time images of everybody aboard the *Sissie* would flash into life just as those in the BDC had done a moment earlier. In so doing, they'd mask the entire display. Daniel preferred to have the Power Room readouts as background to his thoughts.

"We're about to lift again, Sissies," he said, smiling easily. The crew, all those who weren't involved in the liftoff itself, were watching him even though he didn't see them. "Again, I say, because most of you've been with me for years by now. Those of you who're new to the *Sissie*—congratulations! You've signed aboard the finest ship in the RCN, which means the finest ship in the whole human universe."

The corvette shuddered heavily; Vesey had directed Pasternak to light two of the eight thrusters. They were on minimum output for the moment, the petals of each nozzle flared wide. Steam from the pool bloomed around the hull, mixing with iridescent exhaust ions which hadn't yet been damped by the atmosphere.

"I've been under orders not to tell you where we're lifting for," Daniel continued, "so I haven't; but most of you've been around long enough to have learned what our lords and masters in Navy House have not: you can't keep a secret in the RCN."

He heard the laughter and mild cheers he'd been playing for. A speech to people you're leading into battle is always a political speech, and nothing political is to be done without care. Corder Leary's son knew that, and—though Daniel didn't let the thought stiffen his face into a stern mask as it started to—the late Lucius Mundy's daughter probably knew it even better.

"For the record now . . ." Daniel continued. A second pair of thrusters lighted. "We're going to Pelosi in the Bagarian Cluster to help the rebels there organize against the Alliance."

He paused for effect, letting two more thrusters rumble into life. Even with them all on low output, the *Sissie* was rocking on her outriggers.

"That's for the record," Daniel said. "What *I* say to you, fellow spacers, is that we're being sent to stiffen some wog pricks. And no better crew in the RCN to do it. Is that right?"

"Right-t-t-t!" echoed through the corvette's passageways, punctuated by a few examples of "Yee-*ha*!" and less identifiable cheers.

"On the way there, we're going to touch down on Diamondia for reaction mass," he said. Adele would pick up the latest available information about Bagaria there, though he didn't say that. Diamondia received a constant trickle of Bagarian blockade runners. "We'll also have a chance to stretch our legs—and other things than legs, I shouldn't wonder—in a civilized place."

The final pair of thrusters lighted. They were running smoothly, all within the ninety-eighth percentile.

Mon's workmen had done the sort of job he expected of them. Daniel was pleased to co-own Bergen and Associates, even though that associate was his father Corder Leary.

"Now, I can't tell you how long the cruise is going to last," Daniel said. This was the nub of the speech; for his own conscience he had to tell his crew the truth, but he didn't plan to let them dwell on it. "It may be a long one. What I *do* know is that the Bagarian Cluster is bloody rich. With a war on, which there is, some of those riches are going to find their way into the pockets of likely spacers who know shiphandling and know how to fight. Now, do you know any spacers who fit that bill, Sissies?"

We do/Bloody well yes/Cinnabar forever! bounced and echoed through the corvette.

"I thought you might!" boomed Daniel. A green light glowed behind the Ship Readiness icon. "Lieutenant Vesey, you may lift ship."

And as the thruster apertures tightened to provide full power, Daniel shouted over the intercom, "RCN forever!"

CHAPTER 5

En route *to Diamondia*

Daniel went over his astrogational data one more time, comparing them with Vesey's solution, the computer's own solution, and—just for good measure—with the solutions offered by the two midshipmen. All were in close agreement, putting the *Princess Cecile* between forty-five and eighty light-minutes out from Diamondia.

Cory's solution was extremely similar to that of the computer. Well, there were worse things than trusting a machine when you realized that you'd blown your own computation.

"Signals," he said, glancing toward Adele as he spoke. "Is the message to Diamondia Control ready to go as soon as we drop into normal space, over?"

Adele didn't look up from her display, but he realized with a start—this was Adele, after all—that she was viewing his image coldly. *"Yes, Captain Leary,"* she said, *"it's ready to go. And I also put clothes on before I left my cabin this morning."*

Daniel grinned ruefully. She'd forgotten to say,

"Out," but communications protocol had never been her strength. "Thank you, Signals," he said. "Break. Ship, prepare to extract from the Matrix in thirty, that is three-oh, seconds from *mark*."

He pressed the virtual EXECUTE button with three fingers together. The charge on the starship's hull began to shift; Daniel's skin quivered in sympathy. The hairs on the back of both his forearms stood up, then flattened again. For a moment he felt a rushing sound.

Practical interstellar travel was possible because of varying physical constants among the bubble universes within the overarching Matrix of the cosmos. By slipping from the sidereal universe to others with different realities of space and time, a ship could adjust its position so that when it extracted again from the Matrix it was tens of thousands of light-years from the place where it entered.

The process had costs. Insertion and extraction strained a ship's fabric and often strained the minds of those aboard. Other universes weren't meant for man or even for life. All spacers had stories of things they'd seen or felt during a transit. Many scientists dismissed the stories, but not the ones who'd themselves spent time in the Matrix.

There were costs to everything, however. Most spacers had chosen this life, though that didn't mean they preferred service on an RCN warship to the higher wages and reduced danger of a merchant vessel. Even those who'd been pressed, however, would grant there'd be no safety for the merchant fleet unless the RCN was there to protect it.

As for Daniel Oliver Leary—he'd joined the RCN

in a fury, to spite his father. But regardless of the reason for what he'd done, it was the best decision he'd ever made in his life.

The *Princess Cecile* extracted from the Matrix. Nothing actually moved, but objects looked sharper and more textured. When a ship left sidereal space, Daniel *felt* that it became a manifold of possibilities which didn't register perfectly as they overlay one another.

His console brightened into a chart of the four light-hours volume surrounding the corvette. Carets indicated the sun Jewel and its inner planets including Diamondia.

The console bleeped softly. A legend in green light announced MESSAGE SENT.

"*Daniel,*" said Adele. She was using a two-way link and apparently not in her own mind discussing RCN business, so she ignored formality. "*The message will take sixty-two minutes to reach Diamondia; their response will take at least as long to reach us. May I go out on the hull?*"

"Ah . . ." said Daniel. "Why yes, of course, if you want to. Ah, would you like a companion?"

He couldn't go out himself at the moment, but perhaps Vesey? Adele wouldn't *certainly* drift off if she went out without a keeper, but there was a bloody good chance of that happening. What in heaven was she thinking of?

"*I'll take an escort, yes,*" she said. In a slightly different timbre—she'd switched to the command channel common to all officers—she continued, "*Mister Cory, I'd appreciate it if you'd suit up and accompany me onto the hull. Ah, out.*"

Cory started at his console and turned with a startled expression. He looked first at Adele, then met Daniel's eyes.

Daniel nodded minusculely. "Mister Cory," he said, "you're at the signal officer's disposal until I tell you otherwise. Six out."

Adele and the midshipman stepped to the rotunda outside the bridge hatch to don suits before exiting through the airlock onto the dorsal hull. Daniel rotated his console toward the bow so that his face wouldn't be visible; he knew that a variety of emotions were playing across it.

The only reason for anybody but a rigger or an astrogator to go onto the hull was to discuss something in a privacy that the strait hull of a corvette didn't permit. *What does Adele have to discuss with Cory?*

RCN midshipmen were expected to scramble up and down the antennas and to traverse the yards with the same swift certainty as enlisted riggers. Because they were young enough to think about adventure instead of danger, they generally took to the business.

Cory certainly had. He was quickly into his hard suit, then helped Adele don her much lighter, simpler air suit. Daniel and Woetjans had once pieced together a hard suit which fitted Adele as well as could be done. They'd thought that the rigid panels and reinforced joints would be safer for her than the flimsier suits which hull-side crewmen wore when they had to go out in vacuum.

It hadn't worked. Adele had bruised and scraped herself on the inside of the suit, and its stiffness made her even more awkward than she usually was. Because it was probably more dangerous and certainly less comfortable than an air suit, she'd refused to wear it again. She wasn't afraid to die, but she found nothing romantic in aches and pains.

Cory locked down her faceplate, then placed a hand on her shoulder to guide her into the airlock. While hydraulic rams drew the hatch closed, he clipped a safety line to the staple on her chest stiffener; the other end was already attached to his equipment belt.

It embarrassed Adele to be treated like a child, particularly by Cory, who wasn't notably competent by RCN standards. On the other hand, she *was* as helpless as a child; Cory was certainly more competent than she.

The pumps in the floor whirred, voiding the lock. The light flattened with the reduced number of air molecules to scatter it. In an emergency the outer hatch could be opened as soon as the inner hatch locked shut, but air was at a premium on a spaceship. The crew could always electrolyze reaction mass to free oxygen, but nitrogen migrated through the hull itself and was much harder to replace.

The telltale on the outer hatch went green. Cory looked at Adele, waiting for direction. She gave a curt nod; they could talk here in the lock, but there was enough traffic to and from the hull that they'd be in the way.

The hatch cycled open with a spill of tiny crystals frozen from remaining wisps of air; starlight caught them as they danced away. Adele led onto the outer hull, shuffling her magnetized boots in a fashion that marked her instantly as a landsman. Well, better that than to drift into vacuum and have Cory tug her back like a puppy on a leash.

Once they were out of the way, there was no need to go far. The dorsal antenna nearest the bow was only a few steps—well, shuffles—away. Adele set her back to it and waited while Cory transferred her safety line to the turnbuckle of a shroud.

The scene was of no particular interest to her. Stars were bright points on a background that was a negation of existence rather than a color. Adele wondered whether Jewel was visible from this angle—a light-hour shrank a normal-sized star into the galactic background—but then regretted the question. She'd reflexively reached for her data unit—which of course was unavailable beneath the air suit.

Adele smiled ruefully. She suddenly felt completely alone, cut off from the information that was her life . . . but she was on the hull by her own choice.

Cory leaned his helmet into contact with hers. "Mistress?" he said. "You wanted something?"

"Yes, Midshipman," Adele said, looking out toward stars glinting like the points of colored needles. "Why did you sell imagery from the *Princess Cecile*'s files to the producer of *The Conquest of Dunbar's World*? A Master Evrian Stanlas, though you may have worked through intermediaries."

Cory jerked upright, snatching his helmet away from hers. He wasn't deliberately breaking contact; he was simply stiffening in shock.

While a vessel was in the Matrix, the electrical potential of its sails controlled its course. The balances were so precise that any extraneous charge, no matter how minute, would throw the vessel unpredictably into the void.

A starship's rigging was set and lowered by hydraulic

rather than electrical motors. Riggers communicated by hand signals and took orders from the bridge through hydromechanical semaphores; a radio signal, even from a half-watt intercom, might send a ship into uncharted nothingness forever.

The only reason to avoid radios in sidereal space was that you might then use one by accident in the Matrix. That was reason enough: spacers faced enough risks without adding an avoidable one. RCN suits were only fitted with radios by the agreement of both the captain and the signal officer.

An unintended good result of this was that conversations on the hull required direct contact between the helmets of the two people speaking. They couldn't possibly be overheard.

Cory bent to touch her again. "How did you learn that?" he said. Even vibrating through his helmet and hers, she could hear the fear and anger.

The answer was that Adele had examined the bank records of everyone connected with the production until she found sums of money—about thirty-seven thousand florins; she had no idea how the figure'd been arrived at—being transferred to a familiar name. Cory wasn't who she'd expected to find, but she'd never been a person to let preconceptions overrule facts.

"Answer the question, Midshipman!" she said harshly.

The software that permitted Adele to enter bank records—and to transfer money, if she'd chosen to do so; which of course she did not—was part of the package with which Mistress Sand had equipped her. She didn't care whether an observer would agree that she was using the tools properly: she was Mundy of Chatsworth, and if others' perceptions conflicted with her own sense of right, so much the worse for the others.

"Yes, mistress," whispered Cory. Adele had to know what the words must be to recognize them. "Mistress, I thought you and Captain Leary should get credit for what you did. I knew that with the new Chief of the Navy Board, well, nothing good would come from that direction. So I found a producer who made that sort of documentary and then I went into the logs."

His helmet shifted away from hers, then clicked back. Adele smiled faintly; Cory must've turned to face her, forgetting that they could either see one another or speak—unless they wanted to be nose-to-nose. *She* certainly didn't want that.

"It wasn't hard, really," he said. "They wanted to bring something out right away while the story was still hot in the news, and this let them show the real thing. Well, it could've done. It did, sort of."

That's one way to describe the "documentary," Adele thought, but she supposed that judging by the standards of the entertainment industry, it was unusually accurate.

Which led to the next question. "So, you gave Stanlas the material free to help me and Captain Leary?" she said mildly.

"Oh, goodness, mistress, no!" Cory said unexpectedly. "They paid for it and paid well—I charged them ten florins a minute for what I transferred!"

Adele heard a rasp as the boy cleared his throat. "Look, mistress, I know you think . . . well, people think and maybe they're right, that I'm not very sharp. But my father's the biggest paving contractor on Florentine and I know how to negotiate a contract."

Before Adele could follow up on that, Cory went on, "Hoskins and Bladel were killed on Mandelfarne Island, you remember? And Dorsey lost a foot and can't walk anymore. They gave her a mechanical one but it doesn't work. So I split the money between Dorsey and the two families. That seemed right."

Yes, it certainly does, Adele thought. Aloud she said, "There were others injured in the attack. I believe you were yourself, Cory?"

"Well, sort of but that doesn't matter," he said earnestly. "I mean, mistress, that's just the job, isn't it? We're RCN, nobody minds about a few scrapes. But dead—and that happens too, sure, but since I had the money . . . And Dorsey was different, she's on crutches now, I guess till she dies. It wouldn't help having a wheelchair and her living up on the fourth floor where it's cheap."

Neither of them spoke for a moment. Cory cleared his throat again and said, "Ah, mistress? I didn't ask Six because, you know, he might not agree. Or you, because, well, I was afraid to. I never thought you'd learn, mistress. I should've asked."

But you didn't, because I'm Mistress Mundy, who's killed more people than you can count, Adele thought. *And you weren't sure how angry I might get if you told me what you planned.*

"All right, Cory," she said. "I don't suppose there's any reason for Captain Leary to learn what happened. But you must never do that again, do you understand?"

"Yes, mistress!" Cory said in relief. "Mistress, I swear I won't!"

The dorsal semaphore had six arms. They all suddenly stuck out from the post at equal intervals. Cory gasped and pointed, then touched helmets again.

"Mistress!" he said. "That's an emergency recall. What do you think Six wants us for?"

"I think we'll go in and learn," said Adele. She shuffled toward the airlock, but Cory held her by the shoulder for a moment to unclip her safety line from the antenna.

Like a baby, she thought. *But that's all right. I have a family to take care of me.*

CHAPTER 6

Above Diamondia

"Help me out of this thing!" Adele said even before the inner hatch was fully open. She didn't mind wearing the air suit at her console—it'd be uncomfortable, but personal comfort had never concerned her. That the suit kept her from getting at her data unit—and *why* hadn't she left it behind when she went onto the hull?—was another matter.

She needn't have spoken: Tovera, Cazelet, and Cory—who'd stripped off his gauntlets in the airlock—were already at work on her catches.

"Mistress, I'm going to lift you," Cory said—and did so, tilting her back as though she were sitting at her console. When Adele's feet came off the floor, Tovera tugged down the lower half of the suit; Cory shifted and Rene pulled the remainder from her torso.

They worked well as a team. The midshipman was well experienced with suits and Tovera could be expected to accomplish any physical task efficiently, but Adele had just learned something important about Cazelet.

She smiled as she settled onto her console. How nice that what she'd learned was positive. It wasn't always that way.

Daniel was absorbed in computations, and Sun in the console adjacent to hers was rotating the turrets to make sure the guns were ready. Rather than ask either of them what was going on, Adele echoed the command display onto her own. In truth, even when the person talking to her was a friend whom she trusted implicitly, she felt more comfortable with electronic data than she did spoken words.

The astrogation display was gibberish, but Daniel had inset the Plot-Position Indicator; that showed illuminated beads maneuvering at the edge of the minefield protecting Diamondia. The three red beads were careted with the names of RCN vessels, the *Aldgate*, *Ludgate*, and *Moorgate*. The names meant nothing to Adele and there wasn't time just now to call up full particulars.

The four blue pips weren't careted, which meant they'd turned off their IFF. Adele sniffed as her wands moved. As usual she'd slaved her console to her personal data unit, but that was just for comfort: she was adequately quick with any input device. A dumb machine might not be able to identify an uncooperative target at a light-hour's distance, but she was Adele Mundy.

If the ships had been closer, she'd have pinged the message drones that all but the very smallest vessels carried. A careful officer could disable that automatic facility, but with the exception of Adele herself she'd never seen anyone bother. Most captains didn't seem to know it existed.

That wasn't an answer for the present, since the signal and reply would take two hours. She'd make do with passive intelligence, the electronic signatures of the vessels themselves.

Adele grimaced as her wands sorted and compared. If she hadn't been in such a hurry to question Cory out of others' hearing, she'd have done a full-spectrum search as soon as the *Sissie* extracted into sidereal space. What'd taken Daniel fifteen minutes to notice would've been obvious to her immediately.

Still, she'd spent the fifteen minutes usefully. If Cory'd given the wrong answers, she or Tovera would've had to deal with the problem. A corvette on a mission of this sort couldn't afford an officer whose tongue could be bought. Grounding Cory on Diamondia might've been an adequate solution, but that risked leaving the problem for someone less prepared for it. Adele was glad not to have gone down that road.

A starship is a living community with the need to maintain its environment besides all the requirements of a ground-based military post. Each type of electric motor—and there were hundreds on even a small ship—has a unique frequency. To an analyst with a collection of templates and the skill to isolate one source at a time from an electronic hash, the cumulative symphony was as sure an identifier as close-range visuals.

Adele's fingers twitched and twitched again, cross-checking data before transmitting them to the command console. The *Cora*, the *Inca*, the *Cazique*—

And finally the large vessel, the *Stein*. Its volume of signatures slowed identification, though in the long run it was absolutely certain.

Daniel didn't turn or reply, but his image grinned in satisfaction when the data flashed onto his display. He brought up an attack board and selected one of the four plans already prepared, then announced, *"Ship, there's an engagement going on above Diamondia, three Alliance sloops backed by a light cruiser going after some mine-tenders from Admiral James' squadron. That doesn't seem like fair odds to me, so we're going to take a hand. Prepare to insert in thirty, that's three-zero, seconds."*

His fingers slammed down on the EXECUTE button. *"Break,"* he continued, now looking at Adele's icon on his display. *"Mundy, I want you to signal the friendlies as soon as we extract, telling them who we are and requesting passage. I'm not worried about them popping at us with whatever they've got for guns, but our course'll take us into the planetary defense array very quickly. Can you handle that while I'm busy with the attack board? Over."*

"Yes, Daniel," Adele said, preparing her gear. That wasn't proper protocol, but she'd apologize when she had time.

Normally she'd rely on laser communicators, one emitter to each of the RCN vessels, but under the circumstances she'd better double the message with tight-beam microwave. It didn't sound as though there was any margin for error, and any ship could have part of its communications suite fail.

Adele smiled coldly. It wouldn't bother her to die—indeed, if they triggered a nuclear mine, she probably wouldn't even be aware of it. But in the unlikely event that there *was* an afterlife, she'd be in certain Hell to realize that she'd been sloppy in performing her last task.

She was still smiling when a voice shouted, "*Up RCN!*" The *Princess Cecile* returned to the Matrix as the first stage in its attack run.

As the *Sissie* flickered out of the sidereal universe, Daniel took an instant to eye Borries's attack solutions. They were actually quite good, but they postulated that the *Sissie* might extract from the Matrix well in-planet from where Daniel proposed.

That wasn't going to happen—or at any rate if it did, they wouldn't be launching any missiles. The Pellegrinian was allowing for Diamondia's atmosphere: it'd destroy a vessel trying to extract within it. He'd forgotten the planetary defense array that extended much farther up from the surface, however. It was hostile unless and until somebody directed its controller to let them through.

Daniel felt the charge on the hull build as the corvette brought itself into equivalence with the sidereal universe. "*Extracting in three-zero seconds!*" Vesey announced from the BDC, but everybody in the veteran crew could feel it happening. It was an extremely short insertion, but the distance would've taken weeks to traverse in normal space.

The *Sissie* seemed to shake herself. Daniel turned his eyes to the attack board, frozen into an approximation of the situation they'd find when they reappeared. The computer had extrapolated it from the course, rate, and position of the vessels at the moment the corvette entered the Matrix and lost contact with the sidereal universe.

The display showed their point of extraction and initial course as being what Daniel'd predicted they'd be. At less than sixty light-minutes decent astrogators—and Daniel was much better than that—could come very close to their intention, but it'd be fantasy to expect that missiles programmed before inserting into the Matrix would hit their target. He'd need to refine his solution after they extracted.

The attack board flashed live; the approximation remained as a ghost image until Daniel switched it off. The PPI in a corner of the display sharpened from pearly radiance to a real three-dimensional chart; icons bloomed across the top of the screen as Adele connected with the RCN support vessels. She didn't copy her transmission to him since she knew he was busy.

The High Drive slammed on, nearly trebling Daniel's weight. Vesey was decelerating at maximum output or very nearly so, delaying the corvette's entry into the minefield as much as possible. Though they'd made this last insertion on a minimal rig, four of the twenty-four mainsails and nothing above them, they were still going to lose yards if not antennas very shortly. The antennas might've been able to take it if he'd doubled the standing rigging, but there hadn't been time.

First things first.

The Alliance attack on the mine-tenders had required either skill or luck. If the cruiser and her escorts had maneuvered close to Diamondia in normal fashion, the RCN support vessels would've dropped back onto the surface before they were in danger. The attackers must've launched themselves from their base on

Zmargadine Three in a single transit to Diamondia. An overshot would've put them in the minefield.

It wouldn't be a coincidence that the sloops were twenty years old and the cruiser was older than that. The Alliance admiral clearly regarded them as expendable if necessary in the cause of harassing the RCN squadron.

The cruiser's 15-cm guns would batter the minetenders to junk if they stayed in vacuum, and if they locked themselves into braking orbits to land they'd be sitting ducks for Alliance missiles.

The process of returning to sidereal space normally took between forty-five seconds and a minute. An enemy keeping a close lookout for anomalies in the electromagnetic spectrum could initiate an attack before the extracting vessel was able to respond.

The Alliance ships had no reason to expect they'd be attacked from the Matrix, nor was their training good enough that they were prepared for something they didn't expect. The cruiser's four 15-cm guns continued to track the *Moorgate*, firing whenever the tubes cooled enough to be reloaded, even after Daniel called, "Ship, launching two!"

The *Sissie* rang from paired hammer-blows five seconds apart. Water, flash-heated to steam, ejected the missiles from the corvette's two launching tubes. Their High Drive motors lighted when they were safely clear of the vessel, sputtering back a blue haze of antimatter particles which hadn't been destroyed in the reaction chambers.

Two more missiles rumbled down rollerways from the magazine to the tubes. "Borries, take over," Daniel shouted. "BDC, I have the conn, out!"

He wanted to do it all. He couldn't and he didn't have to, he had first-rate officers, but there hadn't been time to explain exactly what he had in mind. In truth, all Daniel had in mind was to react to the situation as it appeared when they extracted from the Matrix—launch missiles, swing the corvette into a landing pattern, and evade the Alliance response.

There *still* wasn't an Alliance response. *My, we've really caught them with their pants down.*

The three Alliance sloops were in polar orbits around Diamondia, well outside the range of the mines. They weren't shooting because at this range their 10-cm plasma cannon wouldn't be effective even against 200-ton mine-tenders.

The *Stein* was shadowing the *Moorgate*, slashing with 15-cm bolts. The mine-tender couldn't accelerate without rising into a higher orbit, nor could she decelerate without the atmosphere limiting her ability to maneuver. Plasma bolts would rupture the hull, probably sooner rather than later; whereupon the cruiser would transfer her attentions to the next of her victims.

Destroying three auxiliaries wouldn't have much practical effect on the siege, but it'd raise the spirits of Alliance crews stuck in a dangerous hardship posting. Even better from the Alliance viewpoint, it'd depress Admiral James' personnel. It'd be suicide for the ships of the RCN squadron to try to reinforce the mine-tenders. Even a battleship lifting through the atmosphere would be unable to defend itself against missiles launched from orbit.

Daniel reduced thrust to 1.5 g and set the antennas to retract so that the *Sissie* could land, assuming things worked out. If everything went as it should, the process—sails furling, yards rotating parallel with the antennas, and all folding down against the hull—would be automatic.

Even on a good day something jammed, though, and after Vesey's hard braking they'd be lucky if all four deployed antennas hadn't bent too badly to telescope. Woetjans was on the hull with her top people; they'd be able to clear problems even though the present deceleration was still significant.

Whatever happened now, the *Princess Cecile* wouldn't be able to reenter the Matrix.

"Princess Cecile, *you're cleared through!*" said an unfamiliar voice on Daniel's commo helmet. As usual, Adele was controlling access to him. She'd let this one pass, though, instead of handling it herself. *"This is Delacroix Control, you're cleared through the array, out!"*

Borries clanged out two more missiles. Daniel had calculated the corvette's extraction so that they'd enter normal space on the opposite side of the planet from the *Stein* and in a reciprocal orbit. The ships would pass within three thousand miles of one another, well within the range that the cruiser's plasma cannon could be punishing. It was a necessary risk but a calculated one: if the *Stein* turned her guns on the corvette, the corvette's missiles would almost certainly destroy her.

The cruiser's captain knew that as well as Daniel did. The 15-cm guns shifted from the *Moorgate* to the incoming missiles.

The *Stein*'s High Drive and plasma thrusters lit together at full output. Under normal circumstances that'd be a waste of reaction mass—the thrusters weren't nearly as efficient as matter-antimatter annihilation. The Alliance captain clearly realized that if the cruiser didn't get out of the kill zone as quickly as possible, that reaction mass would merely add to the size of the ball of wreckage expanding away from missile impacts.

The 15-cm guns were firing at high rate, spewing plasma bolts before the barrels had properly cooled from the previous rounds. This was certain to erode the tubes and might well lead to an explosion that damaged the turret, but need outweighed the risk.

The corvette's first missile burst before burnout; the second had just begun to separate into three pieces, widening the attack's footprint, when the guns caught them. Solid fragments caromed away, driven by the thrust of their vaporized mass.

The *Sissie* sliced past the minefield in a descending spiral; the mine-tenders were already diving for the surface. Borries launched a third pair of missiles.

"Cease fire!" Daniel ordered, his hands busy adjusting the High Drive, swinging the corvette's bow down slightly so that they'd enter the atmosphere on an even keel. "Borries, this is Six, cease fire!"

The *Stein* staggered as a mast snapped and carried away other rigging with it. The thrusters shut down, leaving a broad track of shimmering ions behind the glint of the High Drive exhaust.

Daniel hadn't been sure how the sloops would react— he hadn't attacked or even threatened them—but he was gratified to see they were accelerating away from the planet also. That wasn't cowardice: an Alliance corvette never would've attacked four RCN vessels. The sloops' captains assumed that the *Sissie* was the leading vessel of a powerful force.

The *Sissie*'s third pair of missiles were going to miss because the cruiser'd reduced acceleration abruptly, but the guns hammered them anyway. The sloops were already losing definition, fading into the Matrix; they weren't going anywhere, just *away* so that they wouldn't be caught when a large RCN squadron extracted. A moment later the *Stein* followed, sure that further missiles couldn't reach it before insertion was complete.

Contact between vessels, let alone combat, was possible only in sidereal space. A ship that escaped into the Matrix—it was extremely vulnerable during the minute or so of insertion—could lurk there until its air ran out. The Alliance ships might struggle toward Z3 using dead reckoning from their last recorded star sights or simply hide for a day or so before slipping briefly into the human universe to make proper astrogational computations. Either way, they were out of action.

The outer airlock clanged; Woetjans was bringing in her crew, so the rig'd been stowed for landing. Daniel'd have had to adjust the *Sissie*'s angle of descent shortly if they hadn't come in, and he hadn't been thinking about it.

He felt himself relax. He hadn't been thinking about landing formalities either, and it was past time that he do so. "Signals—" he began.

"*Princess Cecile, this is Port Delacroix Control,*" said an unfamiliar female voice. "*You are cleared for Berth 17 in the Outer Harbor, not 12 in Main as you were told before. We're bringing the* Moorgate *in there because she can't maneuver to her regular berth, over.*"

"Delacroix Control, this is *Princess Cecile*," said Daniel. He should've known he didn't have to worry about communications chores when he had a battle to fight. "Acknowledged that we're clear for Berth 17, Outer Harbor. Over."

There was a pause. The corvette slid deeper into the atmosphere, which began to buffet her seriously. A starship wasn't streamlined even when closed down for landing, so the rig had to be built to take a battering. The crew got used to it perforce.

Instead of "Acknowledged, out," as Daniel expected, the ground controller said, "*The Admiral says, 'Well done, Princess Cecile,' and will Captain Leary please attend him in the Residence at his earliest convenience. A car will be waiting, over.*"

"Acknowledged," Daniel said, feeling a smile spread across his face. "*Princess Cecile* out."

Hogg, who'd been sitting on the jumpseat attached to the back of the command console, got up and started toward the hatch. The *Sissie* was pitching like a skiff in a storm, but he kept walking. Hogg had ridden many skiffs in many storms.

"Guess I'll lay out your Whites, master," he called over back the wind roar.

Daniel smiled even more broadly.

CHAPTER 7

Port Delacroix on Diamondia

The terraces of the Governor's Residence overlooked the Inner Harbor of Port Delacroix. Just as Admiral James was now occupying the Residence, the RCN squadron had displaced civilian shipping. The *Zeno* and the ancient *Lao-tze* were moored bow-in on opposite sides of the pool. Between the two battleships floated the heavy cruiser *Alcubiere*, the light cruiser *Antigone*, and five destroyers; two more destroyers were in orbit.

"Doesn't seem like much to oppose what the Alliance's got on Z3, does it, Leary?" said Admiral James. He touched the decanter between them. "More whiskey?"

"Thank you, sir," Daniel said, sliding his glass over. "A splash, if you would."

That gave him time to consider how to respond . . . which didn't change the facts, unfortunately. Daniel smiled wryly: he generally fell back on the truth when he wasn't sure what to say. At least that way he didn't have to remember what story he'd told whom.

"And no, it isn't very much," he said, "but I don't imagine that a base on the moon of a gas giant is safe, let alone comfortable. So long as we hold out, there's the chance of luck turning our way. There've been cases where ships fell into a crevasse on an ice moon before, I recall."

James snorted as he lowered the decanter with a clack. The tabletop was made from scraps of fire opal, crushed and reconstituted in a bed of clear resin. Daniel had never thought of himself as an art fancier, but it struck him he'd seen whores on the strip outside Harbor Three dressed in better taste than this table.

His face must've shown how he felt, because James chuckled and said, "Governor Niven left his furnishings behind when he offered me the Residence and moved to his hunting lodge in the mountains. I may be doing him an injustice to remark that the lodge isn't as likely to be bombarded if things go wrong. On the other hand—"

He rang a fingertip on the decanter.

"—he didn't take time to pack his liquor cabinet."

The admiral gave Daniel a wan smile. He was a distinguished-looking man who wore his silvery hair longer than RCN regulations would've permitted in anyone of lesser rank. He lifted his glass against the clear sky to view the tawny liquor, then said, "I'm afraid I've been punishing it pretty badly, though, trying to figure out how to deal with Admiral Guphill's four capital ships. I'd say that two of them were only battle cruisers, but—"

The smile took on hard edges.

"—they're new, and either of them carries more missiles than the *Lao-tze* as well as being able to sail rings around her. And Leary? Thank you for the hope, but I'd already checked on the likelihood of the Alliance base sinking to the core of Z3. The only cases of that happening involve much larger primaries or satellites closer to the surface. I'm afraid we'll have to figure out a way to beat them ourselves."

In the harbor, sirens, whistles, and—from the *Laotze*—what must've been a brass gong sounded, not quite simultaneously. Daniel lifted an eyebrow.

"Local noon," James said with a chuckle. "The mayor, the Kaid they call him here, told me it was the custom from ships in the harbor to call noon. I saw no reason to object. The populace is being very supportive; more than the governor's staff, to be honest."

Then, sharply: "Are you religious, Leary? Do you pray?"

Daniel cleared his throat. "Ah," he said. "I'm not a freethinker, sir. But, well, with an officer's duties, I don't go to the temple as often as I might."

There were admirals who had the reputation of being priests in uniform, but Daniel hadn't heard that about James. May the gods help the Republic if the leader of Diamondia's defense had suddenly put his faith in heaven instead of the RCN!

"Good man," said James unexpectedly. "I never trust a young officer who doesn't spend more time with a bottle than he does with a prayer book. More whiskey?"

Daniel looked at his glass. A steward in black and white—Daniel didn't know if he was RCN or part of the governor's legacy like the liquor cabinet—stood silently beside the sliding doors back into the Residence. He hadn't moved since bringing out the decanter.

"Thank you, sir," Daniel said, sliding his glass over again. "Ah, Admiral? We expended six missiles on the way in, as you know?"

"I do know," said James, filling his own glass also. The decanter was getting low. "I do indeed. A brilliant little action, Leary; in the best traditions of the RCN."

"Thank you, sir," Daniel repeated. "To whom do I apply to replenish our magazines? Since we're not, the *Sissie*'s not I mean, part of the Diamondia Squadron?"

"You can save your breath, I'm afraid," the admiral said. He leaned back in his chair and sipped his drink. James was wearing Whites without medals or ribbons; from a distance he might've passed for a well-born gentleman in summer linens. "Leary, the only replenishment we've had since the squadron arrived on Diamondia has been blockade runners carrying mines, and few enough of those; seventeen small ships with forty-one mines aboard. The Alliance has already swept more than a hundred."

He set his glass down, empty again. His eyes were turned toward the harbor, but whatever he was seeing in his mind was much farther away than that.

"Leary," he said. "I'm not going to attach your ship to my squadron, though it'd be useful and you'd be bloody useful from what I saw this morning."

"Sir!" said Daniel, more sharply than he'd intended. "I'm afraid my mission from the Navy Office has precedence—"

"Do you think I care about Navy House here, Leary?" the admiral said. "Should I be afraid that Admiral Vocaine is going to slap my wrist? I've got four Alliance capital ships to do that!"

He lurched halfway to his feet, then fell back onto his chair. Its seat of reconstituted opal was set in a wrought-iron frame like the tabletop; the feet scraped on the patio tile.

"I shouldn't have drunk so much," James said mildly, musing on his empty glass. "Or I should drink more, of course. Well, I can't change the past, can I?"

He lifted the decanter, then paused. "More for you, Leary?" he asked.

"Go ahead and finish it, sir," Daniel said. "I've got a busy day ahead if we're to lift at dawn. Ah, as I intend."

"There's more where this comes from," James muttered vaguely, but when he set down the empty decanter he didn't call for a replacement. He sipped morosely, then looked across the table at Daniel.

"The reason I'm not holding you on Diamondia, Leary," he said, "isn't that I'm afraid of what it'd do to my career. I've never concerned myself much with that. I'm James of Kithran no matter what Navy House says."

Which is why you have *a career that's the envy of most other officers of your rank, sir*, Daniel thought; but this wasn't the time for him to speak, even in praise.

"In a few months," James continued, "the Alliance will clear a path through the defense array. Admiral Guphill will launch an attack on the planet, and I'll lead my squadron out to engage him. They'll know they've been in a fight!"

"Yes sir," Daniel murmured, meeting the admiral's fierce gaze.

"But there's not the slightest chance that we'll be able to stop them," James said. "I know that as well as Guphill does; and you know it too, Leary."

Daniel didn't speak. *Of course I know it. Guphill*

is competent, and he's got twice the strength of ships crewed with the best personnel in the Fleet.

James set his glass down; he hadn't emptied it. "You did my squadron a favor when you came in," he said. "And you're a good officer, the sort the RCN needs. I'm not going to tangle you to no purpose in this mare's nest. You go off on your special mission and keep well clear. All I ask you is this, if you've got the backbone."

He pointed his right index finger at Daniel's chest. "When you next see Eldridge Vocaine, say that I asked you to tell him that if he'd been doing his job, he'd have sent another battleship instead of a corvette; and that if he had, the battle off Diamondia would've had a different ending. Do you understand?"

Daniel rose to his feet. "Sir, I understand," he said. "And I have the backbone, yes. But I hope it won't be necessary to deliver that message."

"Go back to your duties, Leary," Admiral James said. He suddenly laughed. "I was young once too. But you go back and make the RCN proud of you."

The admiral tossed off the rest of his whiskey. As Daniel turned he thought James had started to smile.

"I'm sorry, Officer Mundy," said a secretary who sounded more hostile than regretful. Thick whitewashed walls made the room much more comfortable than the sun-blasted street; the only illumination bounced in from high windows onto a light shaft, though the small lamp on the desk could be lit if needed. "Master Torregrossa is out today and I don't expect him back. You might try his estate on Exos."

A two-stroke engine fired up, then drove down the

dirt street more slowly than the high-pitched jingle from its cooling fins suggested that it should. Rather than a scooter, it must power a jitney like the one that'd brought Adele here with Tovera and Cazelet.

Cazelet stepped past Adele and took the stylus which the secretary was holding upright on the desk. "What do you think you're—" the fellow protested, but he subsided to watch Cazelet bend over the notepad and began writing. He cupped his free hand to conceal the note from his companions.

Adele didn't comment, but when she realized that she'd started to dip into the pocket of her tunic she smiled coldly. Whatever was going on here, it wasn't grounds for shooting Cazelet instantly.

Cazelet held the pad up to the secretary's eyes, then ripped the note off and crumpled it into his pocket. The stylus and the pad, facedown, flopped onto the desktop.

"We'll see Torregrossa *now*, Ameneni," he said. He didn't raise his voice, but the syllables snapped like sparks. "If he's not in the building, you'll have him here in an hour or it'll be the worse for you."

Tovera grinned like a snake.

"I'm *very* sorry, Patron," the secretary said. "He's here, yes, in his office on the third floor."

He pointed to an unmarked door in the sidewall. "I'll ring ahead, or would you rather . . . ?"

Cazelet glanced at Adele and raised an eyebrow. "Yes, announce us," she said. "This is a friendly call."

That'd been her intention, anyway. It still was, but friendliness wasn't quite so high a priority as it'd been before the shipping agent directed his secretary to lie to them.

"The boy next," Tovera said. She opened the door and started up the staircase. Her attaché case was open, and her hand was inside it.

"Yes, all right," Adele said. She didn't approve of Tovera's paranoia, but there was no reason that Cazelet *shouldn't* be in the middle. She smiled wryly. Among other things, that put Adele in a better position to deal with anyone coming up the stairs behind them.

"There're Diamondian factors all over the Galactic West," Cazelet said, turning his head back toward her slightly. "Two of Torregrossa's cousins have done business of various sorts with Phoenix Starfreight."

"And you remembered that?" Adele said as her soft-soled boots scraped and whisked on the stair treads.

"No, mistress," said Cazelet. "But I brought the Phoenix database with me from Blythe and checked it against shippers on Diamondia when you told me what you were going to do."

Joseph Torregrossa, a dark-skinned little man in a cream business suit, leaned over the railing at the top of the stairs. The upturned points of his mustache were as sharp as styluses.

"Master Cazelet!" he said. "This is so unexpected—as you must see. I regret if my secretary Bhanu misunderstood your colleague's question!"

"That's all right, Torregrossa," said Cazelet as he reached the top of the stairs. His voice was as harsh as if he rather than Tovera were pointing a sub-machine gun. "So long as you don't misunderstand me. Let's go into your office."

"Yes, of course, of course," said the little man. He swept a bead curtain clatteringly back with his left arm.

When Cazelet curtly gestured, however, Torregrossa obediently stepped inside ahead of his guests.

Adele paused a moment before following the others, then entered with a faint smile. Though the curtain seemed only a visual barrier, it marked the edge of an active sound-cancellation system. No one outside could hear what was said in the office.

Torregrossa seated himself on the low dais against the wall to the left of the door; a fountain played in a waist-high alcove directly opposite. The remaining vertical surfaces were covered in traceries in high relief, molded rather than carved but astonishingly intricate nonetheless.

Cushions lay on the dais and around the walls, but there was no furniture; a virtual keyboard shimmered in the air before Torregrossa, however. The office was atmospheric but by no means low-tech.

"I was pained to hear the news of your father, Patron," Torregrossa said with unctuous care. "Please allow me to offer my condolences."

Cazelet grunted as he settled cross-legged onto a cushion covered with gleaming brocade. "Don't believe everything you hear, Torregrossa," he said. "Give me a quick rundown on this Independent Republic of Bagaria or whatever they're calling it."

"Ah!" said Torregrossa, spreading his hands wide. "Then you mean . . . ?"

"I mean that I want your analysis of the Bagarian situation," Cazelet said roughly. "And I need you to turn over your full electronic files to my colleague Mundy, here."

He nodded toward her. Adele sat primly erect, her data unit in her lap. Her wands twitched as she began by emulating the device waiting for Torregrossa's input.

"But that can wait. For now, what's your view of the Bagarian Republic?"

Adele was comfortable enough. She'd have preferred to sit directly on the floor instead of on this slick-finished cushion, but it would do. This had become Cazelet's show and she didn't intend to draw attention to herself.

Torregrossa laughed and interleaved his fingers repeatedly in the visual equivalent of tutting. "Well, there's a great deal of money to be made in the short term," he said. "I scarcely need to tell a Cazelet that, do I? They're a gang of criminals, worse than Platt, the Cluster Governor. There was only one of him, you see. The ministers of this new republic think they should be as rich as the governor was . . . and very shortly, they all are."

"What's the state of the Bagarian navy?" Adele asked, as much to see how Torregrossa responded as for the answer itself.

Torregrossa looked at her, then toward Cazelet with a raised eyebrow.

Cazelet made a quick wiping motion with his left hand. "Treat any question my colleague asks as a question from me," he said irritably. "Treat it as a question from my father!"

"As you wish, Patron," the factor said, dipping his head in a hint of a bow. "Whatever you and your noble father wish."

He turned slightly. "Mistress Mundy," he said, "there are ships and they are armed. Whether they have crews, that I do not know. The new ministry isn't good about letting pay trickle down to those on the bottom where the common spacers lie. There is desertion, there will be more desertions. But—"

He raised an index finger for attention. His nails were almond-shaped and had been tinted the soft pink of early dawn.

"—so long as all they have against them's a Cluster Command, they're enough. The Alliance's got some ships on Churchyard. The governor hides on Conyers with antiship missiles around him. Generalissima DeMarce and her little rebel friends'll play in the rest of the cluster. When the Alliance takes care of its business with Cinnabar or the other way around, it matters little. . . ."

Torregrossa spread his hands and contemplated the perfect nails. "It'll go hard, then, on the Generalissima and her ministers, whichever ones have survived their fellows' greed, that is. But there's money to be made by a firm big enough to take advantage of the situation. Not Torregrossa Brothers alone, no. But perhaps . . ."

He raised an eyebrow toward Cazelet.

"Perhaps . . ." he continued, "Phoenix Starfreight in cooperation with Torregrossa Brothers? We have good contacts in the cluster, you know that, Patron."

"I told you already that you'll need to provide all the information you've got to my colleague," Cazelet said. "Indeed, perhaps you could provide her with access right now while we're all here."

"That won't be necessary," said Adele as she slipped the wands into the case of her data unit. She stood. "I have the data. Master Cazelet, I believe the best use of our time now will be to begin analyzing it back aboard the *Princess Cecile*."

Cazelet rose by straightening his legs without touching a hand to the floor. Tovera had remained standing at the side of the doorway, her off-white suit blending with the delicate moldings.

"I assure you that your colleague does *not* have the information, Patron," Torregrossa said sharply. "While I have the greatest respect for you and your father, Torregrossa Brothers must respectfully refuse to unlock our files until there's been an agreement on, let us say, the division of the spoils between our companies."

"Thank you for your time, Torregrossa," Cazelet said, turning to follow Adele through the door.

"My files are protected!" Torregrossa said. "You *can*not enter them!"

"If Lady Mundy says she's copied your files, worm," Tovera said, "then it's as true as if I tell you I'll shoot your eyes out if you raise your voice to her again."

She lifted the sub-machine gun from her case, then giggled.

"I *will* shoot your eyes out if you raise your voice to her again," Tovera said. "In fact, maybe I'll shoot them out anyway."

"Put that away, Tovera," Adele snapped as she started back down the stairs. "We have work to do."

"Yes, mistress," Tovera said in a chastened tone. She concealed the gun again but didn't latch the case closed. Over her shoulder she called cheerfully, "But perhaps I'll be seeing you again soon, worm. I'll look forward to that!"

CHAPTER 8

Port Delacroix, Diamondia

Daniel kept a real-time exterior panorama running at the top of his display as he readied the *Princess Cecile* for liftoff. It didn't seem to him that the sky was brighter than it'd been a few minutes before, but now the water of the harbor shimmered in pale reflection.

"*Six, this is Three,*" announced Pasternak on the command channel. "*We're ready to light thrusters, over.*"

Daniel glanced at his holographic display. The Power Room readouts and the PPI shared the body of the tank, with an astrogational screen scrunched up below. He'd expand that last as soon as they made orbit and it had immediate bearing on his actions.

He keyed a two-way link, beyond the ability of anybody else on the *Sissie* to hear, and said, "Adele, when can we lift?"

"*In two minutes, fifty . . . three seconds, Daniel,*" Adele said calmly. "*After that we have a window of ninety-two minutes if you wish to wait.*"

"Roger," Daniel said, realizing that she wasn't going to close her transmission. "Thank you, Adele. Break, Pasternak? You can start lighting them in thirty seconds, over."

"*Roger, Three out*," muttered Pasternak as he broke the connection.

On the PPI the destroyers *Echo* and *Encounter* patrolled at the edge of the planetary defense array. They couldn't stop a major attack, but they kept the Alliance minesweepers at a distance from the array. The sweepers had the laborious task of slinging metallic junk toward the nuclear mines using electromagnetic charges; generally the projectors'd been modified from automatic impellers. Eventually a pellet would hit and neutralize the target; then the clearance vessel moved on to the next.

It was a dangerous job, too. Mines could be set at greater than the usual sensitivity so that they'd go off when a target was as much as a hundred thousand miles away. Though focused, the jet of X-rays wouldn't be dangerous even to a corvette at that range, but a mine-clearance vessel, basically a lifeboat, would crumple into lifeless, drifting slag.

Thrusters One and Eight lighted, licking glittering plumes of steam from the harbor. The Governor's Residence wasn't directly visible from the *Sissie*'s berth, but Daniel wondered whether Admiral James was watching remote imagery of the liftoff. No reason he should, of course. . . .

Daniel didn't know how Adele'd determined when the *Princess Cecile* should lift, but he assumed she'd based the determination on enemy commo traffic. The Alliance patrolled in the vicinity of Diamondia on a regular basis. Usually that involved a squadron of four cruisers and accompanying destroyers passing close to the minefield to chase any RCN ships in orbit back to harbor.

Two and Seven lighted. Though their nozzles were flared, the iridescent blooms beating the harbor set the corvette to rocking.

Occasionally Alliance capital ships would join the sweep in hopes that Admiral James would sally expecting cruisers and face battleships instead. Guphill's forces played it too safe to fool anybody, though. The battleships and battle cruisers doubled the usual hundred-and-fifty-thousand-kilometer safety cordon out from the minefield that their lighter vessels maintained.

Admiral James wasn't likely to come up to fight anyway, however much he and his spacers wished to. The attrition of frequent skirmishes between the screening forces would leave James without the missiles necessary to fight the fleet action that'd certainly come.

Thrusters Three and Four lighted. The Power Room display told Daniel what was happening, but he thought he could tell by the vibration alone. Each of the pumps feeding reaction mass to the thrusters had a slightly different rhythm. The *Princess Cecile* was as much part of Daniel Leary as his liver was.

Daniel expanded the astrogation display briefly. It was only seven days by Navy House charts from Diamondia to Pelosi, the capital of the Independent Republic of Bagaria; he thought that with him conning the *Sissie* they could shave a day off that.

It was only seven days from Diamondia to Pleasaunce as well. The Jewel System was at a node between bubble universes. Voyages staging through it were considerably shorter than other routes between many common destinations—most of which were in Alliance territory. The presence of Diamondia, a world providing a first-class harbor and amenities to travelers, in Cinnabar hands was a both a practical obstacle and a gross insult to Guarantor Porra and his government.

Its main importance to Cinnabar was as a point from which to attack the Alliance. From the RCN's viewpoint that was extremely important, but not *so* critical that additional resources could be diverted from sectors where the Republic's survival was threatened.

"*Six, this is Three,*" Pasternak reported. "*All thrusters are lighted and operating within parameters. Operating at high efficiency if I may say so, out.*"

"Roger, Three," Daniel said. "Break, Signals, are we cleared for liftoff, over?"

"*Princess Cecile, this is Delacroix Control,*" said the same female voice which'd cleared them in. Had Adele held the transmission or was the timing just fortunate? "*You are cleared for liftoff, over.*"

"Roger, Delacroix Control," said Daniel. "*Sissie* out. Break, Ship, prepare to lift in thirty, say again three-zero seconds. Six out."

He ran up the throttles, feeding reaction mass to the thrusters. For the moment he didn't sphincter down the nozzle petals for maximum efficiency.

He grinned and continued on the general push, "Ship, this is Six. I don't know what we're going to find in the Bagarian Cluster, but I do know anybody with ideas we don't go along with is going to find a lot more than they expected! Up Cinnabar!"

Responding cheers rang a descant to the roar of the *Sissie* lifting from the surface of another planet.

Above Diamondia

The plasma thrusters shut off and Adele's body lifted against the restraints. The console's upholstery expanded now that acceleration didn't ram her body into it. A moment later the High Drive coughed into life, returning the Sissies to the equivalent of normal gravity.

"Commander Leary always allows a slight gap when he switches propulsion modes, Cazelet," Adele said on the link she'd set up with the man at the jumpseat on the rear of her console. "That way a late surge from the one he's shutting down doesn't double the strain on the ship needlessly."

She winced as she heard herself. Adele knew she had a tendency to be pedantic, but this was *absurd*. And why was she bragging about her knowledge of shipboard life to this boy?

He wasn't really a boy. At twenty-four, Cazelet was older than Daniel had been when they met on Kostroma.

"I'd wondered," Cazelet said, *"because Captain Leary is clearly skillful enough to match the commands more closely than he chose to do. I hadn't thought about the possibility of mechanical failure."*

He cleared his throat. Adele had a miniature of Cazelet's face on the bottom of her display; his brow furrowed as his mind worked with a question.

"Ah, Lady Mundy, I don't mean to be forward . . ." he said. *"But I'd be much more comfortable if you called me Rene. It wouldn't be a breach of naval discipline because I'm not a member of the RCN.*

Ah. . . . But of course whatever you prefer is fine with me. Over."

Adele started to speak, then closed her mouth. She didn't know how she felt about the request.

She snorted. She'd noticed that lawyers, when asked questions which didn't have clear answers, always said, "No." That gave her a course of action in her own similar circumstances.

"All right, Rene," she said. "Now that the thrusters aren't spreading static across the whole RF spectrum, I'll show you how to identify the ships in the Alliance squadron."

She pursed her lips. "And you'd best call me Mundy," she added. "I'm not Lady Mundy in my own mind—or many other people's, I'm confident. Ah, or Adele, I suppose. Though generally only Daniel calls me that. In private."

"*Thank you,*" Cazelet said. "*Ah, since we're on a private channel—thank you, Adele.*"

"Yes," said Adele, working to keep her mind as neutral as the syllable. "I'm giving you control of the display, now."

She didn't, of course; she'd merely enabled the Training facility to allow Rene temporary access until she made an input herself. The jumpseat positions were intended to train ordinary spacers striking for a specialist rating and, secondarily, as backup in case something happened to the assigned officer. Ordinarily the rear controls were locked whenever the console proper was occupied.

To Adele's surprise, the first thing Rene did was call up the existing Order of Battle for the Alliance squadron, the data gathered by Naval Intelligence officers on Admiral James' staff. Face blank, she said, "I suspect that this was gathered mostly through visual identifications. We'll cross-check it using signals intelligence. I believe signals provide more accurate data than optical recognition, but I recognize that there can be a difference of opinion on the matter."

Adele cleared her throat. They couldn't look at one another directly through the shimmering holographic display, but she'd set a real-time image of Rene's face on her screen—and he'd done the same with hers. She'd expected the boy to interrupt with questions—nervous or pushy, unwelcome in either instance. He said nothing, merely waiting expectantly.

Ordinarily Tovera'd be in the jumpseat, just as Daniel's servant Hogg sat on his. Today she sat behind Cory at the navigation console, looking across the compartment at Adele. Her face had no more expression than the muzzle of a gun has.

"First," said Adele, "lock onto the nearest Alliance communications transponder."

The distance between Diamondia and the Alliance base was nearly 800 million miles, and Z3 would sometimes be on the other side of Zmargadine from ships that needed to communicate with their headquarters. Admiral Guphill had deployed a constellation of communications transceivers so that his forces could communicate in the event the RCN force tried to cut off a separated element.

Adele expected Rene to ask where to start, but he immediately went to work on his own. Instead of going to a sector which he'd memorized against need and setting the corvette's laser communicator to seek—which is what Adele herself would've done—he went into the database, found the listing of orbits, and entered the nearest manually.

It was more of a textbook solution than Adele's was, but it was adequately quick. It could've been duplicated by anybody aboard the *Sissie*—if someone had told them what to do.

Rene locked one of the laser heads on the satellite; it'd remain connected despite the motion of both corvette and satellite. If the head's own line of sight to the target were blocked, it'd hand off to another head. *"Ready, Adele,"* he said.

"All right, Cazelet," Adele said. "Enter the satellite by emulating an Alliance ship asking for an automated communications check."

"Yes, mistress," he said. She was subconsciously aware of the buzz of the High Drive and the chatter on intra-ship communications channels—all of which passed through her station. The corvette was building velocity in sidereal space before inserting into the Matrix. *"I'll be entering as the* Stein."

"Go ahead," said Adele. Cazelet hadn't asked permission, but he'd given her the opportunity to overrule him if she chose. Nor had he asked her for the cruiser's coded handshake: he'd apparently captured it himself from the BDC when the *Stein* signaled that she was under attack by an RCN corvette. Mistress Boileau must be very proud of her grandson.

"Here are the protocols we'll use when we get in," Adele said, opening one of her own files for Cazelet and then exiting from the console again. "We'll be looking for a ship that didn't sign out properly so that we can use its identity to enter the restricted files."

They had a wait of seven minutes for query and

response. The satellite was one of a tiara of five in orbit between Diamondia and the third planet, Samphire, an airless lump of blue-gray rock which didn't have a metallic core. It many respects it would've made a better base than Z3, but reaction mass would've had to come from Zmargadine regardless. Guphill had chosen to consolidate on Z3, a cold, shifting Hell that made the Jewel System a hardship posting for the Alliance personnel.

The handshake came back. The connection with the satellite was open but the *Princess Cecile* in her own guise couldn't go any farther with the operation.

"*The* Stein *herself didn't sign out, mistress!*" Cazelet said. "*I'm entering the satellite's data banks. Why, we could enter the headquarters system from here! This is amazing!*"

"If we had enough time, I'd do just that," Adele said with a wry smile. "We'll be inserting in a few minutes, though. Signals to and from Z3 would take several hours."

Cazelet was navigating the satellite's internal memory, using the codes Adele had supplied. The second part of the communications handshake required randomly variable code sets which synched perfectly. Without capturing a vessel equipped with the code generator, it was impossible to duplicate them.

When a ship opened a connection and didn't close it properly, however, that connection remained open. The *Stein* had inserted into the Matrix without signing out. That'd happened in the heat of battle, but six other connections were open, including that of Guphill's flagship, the *Pleasaunce*.

Most people were sloppy. Adele supposed she

should feel good about that, given that in the present case the people involved were enemies whom it was the RCN's job to destroy. She found that evidence of human failure made her a little more sour than she already was, though. Oh, well.

The Alliance protocols Cazelet was using to open directories in the satellite's data bank were part of the kit which Adele had received from Mistress Sand. She'd initially wondered why they weren't more generally available to the RCN, but a little experience had taught her that most officers wouldn't have been able to use them even if they'd been trained by an expert like Adele herself.

Whereas Rene Cazelet—given access but without training—was sorting and copying Alliance files with bright enthusiasm. "*Oh, mistress, this is amazing!*" he said. "*They're all here, and look! The second battle cruiser isn't the* Mackensen *as our files say, it's the* Stosch!*"

"That's correct," Adele said, "but we're not going to inform Diamondia of that."

"*We're not?*" Cazelet said, raising his eyes in puzzlement. He was trying to see through the display instead of looking at her image *on* the display. "*Why, mistress? Shouldn't they correct their files?*"

"Yes," said Adele, "in theory; but the information doesn't have tactical significance because the two ships are of equivalent force. Whereas if we transmit it back to Diamondia Control, the enemy may intercept the message and realize that we've entered their communications system. That *could* have tactical significance."

"*Oh,*" said Cazelet. "*Yes, of course. I'm sorry, I should've seen that.*"

"You may reasonably think that the Alliance forces in the Jewel System are barely competent to speak to one another, let alone intercept our communications," Adele went on with a hard smile. "But because we know our business, we won't take a chance that they don't have anybody who does."

"But this is just wonderful!" Cazelet said, bubbling again. *"Mistress, you're a genius, just as Granna says!"*

"You did the work, Rene," Adele said.

She might've said something further, but Daniel's voice announced, *"Ship, this is Six. We will insert into the Matrix in thirty, that's three-zero, seconds. Next stop, Pelosi, shipmates!"*

It was probably as well that Adele had been interrupted. Cazelet's enthusiasm was an entirely good thing, and he deserved to be pleased after such an impressive first essay into signals intelligence.

But even though Adele wasn't a commissioned officer, she'd spent enough time in the RCN to understand what the list they'd just called up meant: two battleships, two battle cruisers, four heavy cruisers, four light cruisers, six destroyers, and six sloops.

It meant certain doom for Admiral James and his squadron unless they got a considerable helping hand.

CHAPTER 9

Above Pelosi

Adele was vaguely aware of the bustle as the *Princess Cecile* prepared to extract from the Matrix, but she continued to pore over information she'd winnowed from the files of Torregrossa Brothers. The less she thought about the details of star travel, the happier— the less unhappy—she was.

"*Extraction!*" the intercom said enthusiastically. Adele felt her body turn inside out as the light around her changed. The communications screen that she'd embedded in the upper left quadrant of her display changed from a pearly blur to a web of color-coded traffic; she expanded it to the upper two-thirds of the total volume, shrinking everything else to a pair of bars across the bottom.

"*Ship, this is Five,*" said Lieutenant Vesey from the Battle Direction Center. "*I'd like you all to know that Captain Leary conned us by dead reckoning from Diamondia to within 153,000 miles of the surface of Pelosi, without a single extraction to check his*

114

calculations. When you next go on liberty around Harbor Three, you tell people that. And tell them you're Sissies! Five out!"

There were cheers.

Vesey's learning people skills, Adele thought. *She's always been a good astrogator, but now she's learning to lead. Learning from the best, of course.*

Adele concentrated on the message traffic and the ships on and around Pelosi.

Her wands flickered. There was so much. . . . Making an instant decision, she said, "Midshipman Cory, take over the commo duties, I'm busy."

That probably wasn't the right way to delegate, but she was *very* busy.

"Roger, Signals," Cory said. His voice threatened to crack but settled down. *"Navigation out."*

The Bagarian navy—the Naval Force of the Independent Republic of Bagaria—was in Morning Harbor on Pelosi, with the cruiser *Sacred Independence* orbiting the planet as a guard ship. At any rate the *Independence* was supposed to be on guard. Nobody aboard her appeared to be in the least concerned that a warship had just extracted in her immediate vicinity.

Calling the *Independence,* a 5,000-ton freighter from the Cinnabar-Kostroma run, a warship was stretching a point as well. When the rebellion broke out, the rebel government bought and converted her by the addition of plasma cannon—six 4-inch guns and a pair of the 10-cm Alliance equivalents—and adapting two cargo holds to carry missiles. Her full capacity was ninety-six missiles, but there were only twenty-one in her magazines.

That is, twenty-one missiles according to the manifest. Even without Master Torregrossa's warning, Adele had been on enough fringe planets to suspect the manifest might've been falsified to put money into a minister's pocket.

"Signals, what's the status of the guard ship?" Daniel demanded, his voice taut. *"I haven't received a challenge, over."*

"There's no challenge," Adele said as her fingers began to sort data from the ships in harbor below. "They're not on alert. A rating on the bridge noticed us appear, but the officer of the watch—who was sleeping—threatened to flog the fellow if he bothered him again."

The largest ship in the excellent natural harbor— Morning City was built on a lake of 700,000 acres with a crenellated shoreline—was 6,000 tons, another long-haul freighter. It'd been bought on Elgato, where it was due to be scrapped, and had become the *Generalissima DeMarce*. Besides a claimed eleven missiles, it was armed with four 4-inch guns and a pair of 15-cm weapons.

Adele sneered. These last would shake the *DeMarce*'s rusty plates apart if they were ever fired. Adele had personal experience of what the recoil of heavy plasma cannon did to a freighter's frames, and in that case the ship had been strengthened to take the weapons.

A number of small craft ranging from a hundred and fifty tons to nearly a thousand had been assigned to the Bagarian navy. None of them carried plasma cannon or missiles, though they probably mounted baskets of free-flight 8-inch rockets for protection against pirates . . . or for that matter, for piracy. At short range the rockets' high-explosive heads could dismast a ship and shred its sails, leaving it helpless and easily boarded.

Adele gathered particulars on the light craft, but optical examination was the only way to be sure of their armament and equipment. For that task her skills paled into insignificance beside Daniel's. Regardless of detail, the ships were a poor lot.

There was one more vessel of interest in Morning Harbor, and it was the most interesting of all. Adele frowned when her second attempt to enter its main computer failed because the configuration wasn't what she'd expected. The third time was the charm, but—

"Signals, there's an RCN light cruiser in harbor below," Daniel said in the same terse, metallic voice as when he'd queried her about the guard ship. *"I need complete information on it, over."*

Because she was irritated at Daniel prodding her, Adele dumped to the command console the entire contents of the cruiser's log. It would be as useless to Daniel as thirty tons of coal to someone who wanted a diamond.

Then, because even irritation couldn't prevent her from doing her duty, she said, "The ship's the Alliance cruiser *Victoria Luise*, assigned to the Bagarian Cluster Command. Captain Seward took the Bagarian, ah, navy to Schumer's World, and the planet revolted from the Alliance. The rebels captured the *Victoria Luise* on the ground and Seward brought it away with him when he returned here."

"That's a Financier-class light cruiser from the RCN, Adele," said Daniel in a tone of delighted wonder.

"I'd have thought that the last one of those'd been scrapped before you or I were born. The Alliance must've captured her, and of course the Protectorate Service—well, that's our term, the Cluster Commands as the Alliance calls them—that's where you'd find old foreign-built ships. We're looking at history, by the Gods we are."

Adele thought for a moment that Daniel had failed to close his transmission properly. Then he went on, *"All right, hail the guard ship and ask for landing permission. I'm afraid that they're suddenly going to wake up to the fact that we're here and attack in a panic. Six out."*

Adele nodded understanding as she engaged both the microwave and the 20-meter transmitters. *"Sacred Independence,"* she said, echoing her transmission on the *Sissie's* command channel, *"this is RCS Princess Cecile under Commander Leary, requesting clearance to land in Morning Harbor. Over."*

There was a flurry of activity on the bridge of the *Independence*. Adele monitored it through the Bagarians' intercom. She'd entered the system through the navigation sensors which updated the vessel's location by constant star sightings.

"Commander Leary?" the *Independence* replied by microwave. *"Commander Daniel Leary? This is Captain Andreas Hoppler, and I'm very glad to make your acquaintance, over."*

"Daniel, do you want to take over?" Adele said on a two-way link.

"Roger," he said. *"Break. Captain Hoppler, this is Captain Daniel Leary of the Princess Cecile. Are we cleared to land? To be honest, I was expecting you*

to challenge us when we extracted. What are the procedures here, over?"

The Bagarian captain had a rolling laugh which he exercised before answering, "*The procedures are that you call Morning Control and land, Captain,*" he said. "*This is Pelosi, not a civilized place; I myself am from Newbern, you must know. We're in orbit in case the Alliance tries to attack, but they are cowards; a small ship like yours is no security threat, over.*"

"*Roger, Captain Hoppler,*" Daniel said. Even on the compressed transmission, Adele could hear the edge in his voice. "Princess Cecile *out, break. Signals, connect me with Morning Control, over.*"

Then, in a tone of marvel he added, "*Adele, they may be right that a corvette with the sort of sweepings that Cluster Commands get for crews isn't a threat, but they'd better hope that the Alliance doesn't send real Fleet elements here. And they'd really better hope that they never get on the wrong side of me in the Sissie!*"

Morning City on Pelosi

"Don't look so glum, Woetjans," said Daniel as the crowd in holiday clothing cheered the procession. "We certainly can't complain that they're not friendly, can we?"

Daniel, Blantyre, and Cory waved from the front of a red-draped flatbed trailer pulled by an eight-wheeled farm tractor from which bunting fluttered. Twenty armed spacers under the bosun stood around the edges of the trailer. They were in liberty suits, utilities decorated with multicolored ribbons and patches, but it was hard to retain a festive expression when a mob kept pushing itself at you.

The male citizens lining the parade route were in business suits. Most wore black stovepipe hats with feathers stuck in the band. The women's dresses were in primary colors; frequently several children clung to the full skirts of mothers who threw handfuls of filmy, metallic-looking strips. When breezes flicked them over the procession, Daniel saw that they were leaves; their silvery veins stood out on a shimmering bronze background.

Adele and Tovera stood to the rear of the commissioned officers. Adele wore a set of Grays, while her servant was in a plain suit—beige rather than the off-white she usually affected.

Adele watched Daniel with a faint smile. He supposed she was amused that he was looking at the local vegetation while everybody in Morning City was cheering Daniel Leary like the arrival of a god.

Daniel grinned, then resumed waving to the crowd. Odd about Tovera being so drab; poisonous insects usually wore bright colors.

"They're friendly," Woetjans muttered in frustration. "Too bloody friendly. The next time one a these women tries to climb past me to kiss the great hero—begging your pardon, sir—I'm going to pop her in the mouth instead've pushing 'er back to 'er husband. Even if she's got a little sprat in her arms like the last one."

"I have every confidence you'll continue to be a disciplined spacer whom I can trust as my bosun, Woetjans," Daniel said in carefully molded reproof. "In any case, we've reached the House of Assembly and won't have to worry about the crowd any more."

When Pelosi was part of the Alliance, it'd had a local Assembly to advise the Legate, who in turn reported to the Cluster Governor. The legates generally ignored the Assemblymen, but the hall provided a suitable venue for the new Congress of the Republic.

Though the square in front of the building was packed, lines of men wearing scraps of uniform held open a corridor down which the tractor and trailer drove toward the temporary stand in front of the main entrance. Many of the soldiers were barefoot and carried short pikes instead of guns, but almost all of them wore a beret with a black, red, or white plume.

Dignitaries in gorgeous uniforms stood on the platform. Spectators of intermediate rank, perhaps the Members of Congress, looked down from the second- and third-story windows of the building.

Daniel glanced back at Adele. Her right hand touched her data unit, but it was still in its sheath; bringing it out would be an insult to the waiting officials and more generally to the new republic. Adele wasn't one to bow to authority—and certainly not to the authority of jumped-up farmers from the fringe worlds—but the RCN was on Pelosi to support the rebellion. Offending the locals would interfere with that goal, and Adele would rather die than fail in her duty.

Daniel grinned; so would he, of course. In fact he guessed that was by and large true of the *Princess Cecile*'s crew. In reality, though, his Sissies would rather die than have a bunch of wogs *watch* them fail, a truth that made their attitude rather less noble.

The tractor pulled hard left at the base of the platform and stopped. From this close Daniel could see that under the black, red, and white bunting, the stand had been knocked together from rough timber. It swayed noticeably when the dignitaries on it moved.

"Excellency Lord Leary, will you come with me, please?" said an officer of twenty or so. He wore scarlet trousers and a sky-blue tailcoat picked out with more medals than Daniel himself could claim. "And your officers, they may come also, if you will."

He bowed and swept an arm toward the flight of steps at one end. They didn't look any sturdier than the rest of the structure. Daniel half smiled, half grimaced, and said, "All right, Blantyre and Cory, follow me. You knew when you joined the RCN that the job was dangerous."

The midshipmen wore first-class uniforms, a tailored one in the case of Cory. Daniel was bringing them along simply to add to the display.

He exchanged glances with Adele as he started up the steps. The trailer was too close to the platform to be seen by those on top of it, and the spacers of their escort formed a wall, shoulder-to-shoulder, against the eyes of the crowd. Adele sank gratefully onto the bed of the trailer, opening the data unit on her crossed legs.

Though the platform was eight feet high, the heads of the seven people standing on it didn't quite rise to the course of stone separating the brick facades of the building's first and second stories. Six were men, making the squat, gray-haired woman in the center the head of state, Generalissima DeMarce. Bagarian uniforms emphasized padded shoulders and trousers bloused into riding boots, but DeMarce wore in addition a pelisse of lustrous golden fur.

Until he reached the top of the platform, Daniel hadn't appreciated that DeMarce and all her ministers would be in uniform. There was no help for it, then. He halted, clicked his heels to attention, and threw the Generalissima as sharp a salute as he could manage. It wouldn't have earned him a place on a drill team, but it was better than most of his attempts.

The Bagarians returned the salute in confusion. Daniel at least had four years of Drill and Ceremony at the Academy. It was staggeringly obvious that none of the ministers had had any military training until the revolution put them in power.

Despite Daniel's horror, the crowd cheered wildly at the spectacle. Maybe they thought an exchange of military courtesies was supposed to involve everybody's right arm going in a different direction.

"Commander Lord Leary!" said DeMarce, her voice booming through the loudspeakers concealed behind the bunting; the platform shook in rhythm with her words. "As the representative of the sacred Bagarian people, I welcome you and the unconquerable Republic of Cinnabar which you represent."

She turned from Daniel to the square below and swept up her arms in command. Obediently the crowd cheered.

DeMarce dropped her hands. Her amplified voice resumed over the trailing remnants of applause, "Commander, with you and the Gods supporting the cause of independence, we are invincible! And now, since the Bagarian people join all the rest of the galaxy in recognizing your unique merits, my colleague Douglas

Lampert will make a further presentation in his capacity as Minister of the Navy!"

Her arms shot up again; the crowd resumed its applause. It looked like a stage show, but in fact the enthusiasm seemed real—if choreographed.

Lampert stepped forward, holding a red, black, and white sash with gold fringes along both edges. He was a plump fellow who, judging from the way his uniform bulged, tried to control his midriff with a girdle instead of exercise. Daniel, who'd been laced into his Whites, had only sympathy for him.

"Lord Leary!" he said. The loudspeakers amplified his voice but didn't make it any less squeaky.

The form of address was incorrect, at least by Cinnabar usage. Daniel wasn't the Leary of Leary. He wouldn't be in the future, either, unless Deirdre predeceased him leaving no offspring. Given that she was a banker and he had a reputation for being the most daring officer in the RCN, that was a very low-probability outcome. Hogg, standing on the trailer below, was probably muttering, "What d'ye expect from wogs?"

Daniel grinned at himself. Because he was uncomfortable because he didn't know what was going on, the same uncharitable thought had drifted through his own mind.

"I bear in my hands the insignia of the Admiral in Chief of the Independent Republic of Bagaria," Lampert chirped, holding forward the sash. "As Minister of the Navy and with the full agreement of the head of state and of my colleagues, I present this to you, Lord Daniel Leary. Wear it in honor and with it sweep the enemy from our worlds and the space around them!"

By all the Gods! Whatever Daniel'd been thinking, that wasn't it.

Daniel bent slightly to let Lampert drape the sash over him. The saucer hat gave a little trouble, but Daniel straightened it with a hand when the minister stepped back. Something was written on the sash in gold embroidery, but that wasn't anything to worry about now.

He had a momentary concern that he'd forfeit his RCN rank if he accepted a foreign appointment, but that was silly: it was common for nations to grant naval honors to RCN officers. When Daniel thought about it, he remembered that his own investiture as a Royal Companion of Novy Sverdlovsk made him a Colonel of the Regiment of Guards.

What was different about Bagaria was that they appeared to mean it. It wasn't an honorary rank: they wanted him to lead their navy. That was in keeping with the purposes of the Navy Board in sending Daniel Leary to the cluster, and it was also very much to Daniel's taste.

"Your Excellency," Daniel said. "Honored representatives of the Bagarian Republic."

He made slight bows to Lampert and to the Generalissima, then nodded toward the remaining ministers.

"I accept your offer with humble gratitude," he said, pleased to see the loudspeakers were picking up his words. "With the united will of the Bagarian people behind us, we cannot fail to sweep the minions of the tyrant from your cluster!"

He smiled. Only the son of a great politician would've been able to tell so many lies, with such sincerity, in so few words.

Generalissima DeMarce stepped forward again. "In acknowledgment of this great occasion," she said, "I have decided after consultation with my ministers—"

She glanced over her shoulder.

"—to rename the ship just captured from the enemy. Henceforth the *Victoria Luise* shall be known as the *Admiral Leary*. May you and she go forward in triumph together against our enemies!"

DeMarce raised her arms again. Daniel's mind spun for a moment, then over the applause he thundered, "Your Excellency!"

The Generalissima eyed him narrowly but didn't speak. The cheers abated.

"Your Excellency, humbled though I am by this honor . . ." Daniel said. There probably wasn't a regulation against it, but he couldn't imagine anything that would wreck his RCN career more thoroughly than what even his friends would consider an act of incredible arrogance.

"I would ask instead that we use this occasion to proclaim the indissoluble bonds between our two great republics. Grant me that the *Victoria Luise* may revert to her former name in Cinnabar service, becoming henceforth the Independent Bagarian Ship *Ladouceur*!"

Taking a chance, Daniel raised his hands. The crowd responded with the wild cheering that he'd hoped for—

And even more important, the Generalissima and her ministers did also.

Daniel beamed happily. His first act as commander of the rebel navy had gone well. If he could just be half so lucky with the considerable remainder of the things he had to do . . .

CHAPTER 10

Morning City on Pelosi

Adele reached the entrance to the fenced area where the marquee for tonight's fete was set up. The event was a barbeque: whole animals were being roasted over beds of coals in the central park of Morning City. Lanterns of colored paper hung from the branches of trees, while guards in the livery of the Great Houses—as Pelosi defined them—patrolled the fence that kept out the riffraff. The onlookers outside were ragged, but they seemed glad just to watch.

There'd been a party each of the three nights since the *Princess Cecile* docked in Morning Lake. Adele had gone to the first as Lady Mundy, but she'd had no intention of attending another any time soon. Tonight, however, she needed to speak with Daniel as quickly as possible. He was young enough to drink and dance all night and still get his work done in the morning.

Adele smiled coldly. So was she, she supposed. At any rate, partying had never prevented her from meeting her own standards the next day. She didn't have a taste for it, however, while Daniel certainly did.

"Who're you?" said the functionary at the entrance. He stepped in front of her and put his knuckles on his hips. There were shiny patches on the elbows of his velvet coat. Adele didn't know whether the garment was livery or simply ordinary bad taste.

Rather than say any of the first things that came into her mind, Adele reached for the invitation in her breast pocket. Her face was stony, but she wasn't here to discipline somebody else's servants.

"Hey, wog, that's Mistress Mundy!" said Barnes, a husky rigger who'd been with Daniel—and therefore Adele—since Kostroma. Lest his words possibly not be insulting enough, he slapped the local man across the back of the head. "You watch your tongue, will you?"

"Sorry, mistress!" said Dasi, walking up behind Barnes. "It'd gotten pretty quiet and we thought we could catch ourselves a drink."

In silhouette the riggers were almost impossible to tell apart, for all that Dasi was as dark as Barnes was fair. They weren't the smartest members of the *Sissie*'s crew, but they were imperturbable and up for anything.

The local in velvet hunched at the slap and began to yowl. He fell silent when Barnes looked at him critically and said, "Mistress, would you like us to kick him a bit? I'm real sorry that happened."

"No, that's all right," Adele said. She was wearing her Grays, which didn't look like a dress uniform to a Bagarian. Having representatives from both communities on entrance duty should've avoided this problem, but she'd arrived late. "It's my own fault, I suppose."

Spacers weren't disciplined like soldiers or servants. Riggers in particular worked completely alone. They were no good to their ships if they didn't think and act for themselves, and they couldn't be threatened with any punishment that was worse than the risks they accepted every time they went out on the hull.

The Bagarian mewled; he'd raised his hands to cover his head against another slap—or worse. Dasi grinned and patted the fellow's buttocks. That brought another yelp.

"Cheer up, buddy," the spacer said. "If Tovera'd been here, you'd have a hole right between your eyes instead of a headache."

He and Barnes laughed. Adele smiled but didn't say anything further as she walked into the enclosure.

"I'd probably have asked the fellow to apologize," Tovera said through the bud in Adele's left ear. *"On his knees."*

She giggled. *"Probably."*

Tovera was on the roof of the Assembly Hall, observing the gathering electronically. The ear bud let her guide Adele to Daniel expeditiously through the rout, but Adele couldn't reply. Tovera had a parabolic microphone, however, which served much the same purpose as a two-way link.

Not even Tovera could really claim that Adele needed a bodyguard to walk into an upper-class party, but she was probably uncomfortable not to be within sub-machine gun range of any threat to her mistress. That was all right. Adele was often uncomfortable knowing that her servant might kill somebody beside her at any moment.

Tovera had her uses, though; and while she was in

Adele's charge, she was less likely to do something that civilized people would consider horrible. Perhaps that counterbalanced some of the things which Adele herself had done and which she considered horrible.

"*I see him, mistress,*" Tovera said. "*He's at the northeast corner of the refreshment tent, the one nearest you. Wait, he went back under it.*"

"Yes, I see it," Adele said, turning toward the marquee. A small orchestra on the bandstand played a galliard; well, played at a galliard. There was probably a dancing floor of boards at that end of the mall.

The gathering she'd attended the first night had been a ball at the Theatre Generale. The men had all wanted to dance with her, and the women had watched her with envious determination to learn the latest steps from Cinnabar.

Rene Cazelet had attended also. He could've had his choice of partners: for a dance, for the night, or for as long as he stayed on Pelosi. Although Adele didn't have personal knowledge of, well, mating rituals, she'd observed them as she'd observed many other things.

Instead Rene'd spent most of the evening at their table, drinking sparkling water and watching Adele with almost the determination that Tovera showed. *They both worry too much*, Adele thought.

Rene'd danced twice with her, though. He didn't wear riding boots like the men on Pelosi, and he didn't plant his feet on top of her toes—also in contrast to the men on Pelosi.

Adele hadn't permitted him to accompany her tonight. She could slip in and out while wearing her second-class uniform, but if Rene came he'd draw attention even if he dressed like a servant. She didn't usually think in those terms, but he was obviously an attractive man.

"He's coming out from under the marquee," Tovera said. *"He's with a local man. I'll have his name in a moment."*

"Why, Adele!" said Daniel, resplendent in his Whites with full medals. "I didn't know you were coming tonight, and I'm delighted to see you. May I present Master David Power? He's supplying us with munitions."

Power was tall but even so heavy for his height. His tailcoat was either black or a dark red that turned black under the fairy lights; its hems and lapels were gold, and his trousers were gold as well. Like Daniel, he held a ten-ounce glass from which he'd drunk half the clear liquor.

Power looked at Adele, frowned, and said in a slurred voice, "Who's this, then? She's important?"

"She's Lady Adele Mundy, my good man," Daniel said mildly. "Mundy of Chatsworth, don't you know? Well, I suppose we can't expect Bagarians to be up on Cinnabar society, can we, Lady Mundy?"

He clapped the big man on the shoulder with apparent bonhomie. Daniel had certainly been drinking, but Adele could tell he was putting on the appearance of tipsiness to make forgivable what would otherwise have been a cutting insult.

The drink had really affected him, however. Daniel wouldn't have let the implied slight to Adele cause him to retaliate that way against an ally if he'd been fully himself.

"I'm incognito, Master Power," Adele said as brightly

as she could manage. She wasn't angry with the fellow, but she was tired and she needed to speak to Daniel alone. "Admiral Leary should be more discreet. I trust we can count on you?"

"What?" said the local man, swaying. He was trying to stare at Adele, but his eyes didn't focus. "Count on me. Yes, count on me!"

"Might we get a drink, Admiral?" Adele said, gesturing with the fingers of her right hand. "Something's come up at the ship."

"Count on me!" Power said, wandering off. Instead of offending the fellow by ordering him away, Adele had said just enough to puzzle and bore him so that he left of his own accord. "Count!"

"He's gotten the contract to build missiles with plasma thrusters instead of High Drives," Daniel said, speaking in a low voice as they watched Power wobble into the crowd. "They'd be useless against warships, of course, but we can launch them from orbit into an atmosphere without antimatter destroying the nozzle in the first half mile. I think they'll let us force the Alliance forces to come up and fight—or smash them on the ground if they won't. Either way is fine."

"This was your idea, Daniel?" Adele said.

"Not mine, no," said Daniel with a satisfied smile. "But I brought the notion with me. Captain Burke used them on Grimmald and very kindly let me copy the plans before we lifted from Cinnabar. They're really quite simple, steel pipes full of water with a pump, a plasma thruster, and a very basic guidance system. Well within the manufacturing capability of Pelosi—or for that matter, any planet that can build water heaters!"

He grinned a little broader. "Well, that's a bit of an exaggeration," he said, "but they certainly can build them here on Pelosi."

The orchestra had begun playing an estampe which Adele'd heard on Cinnabar—not during her most recent landfall but when she was in Xenos two years before; now they shifted awkwardly into a tarantella. Was it a deliberate medley or had the players gotten their music scrambled?

Adele reached for her data unit while the back of her mind plotted routes to the solution of the puzzle. She caught herself.

"I'm sorry," she said, giving Daniel a smile that would've withered leaves. "I'm tired and I'm not concentrating well."

He didn't know what she was talking about. On the other hand, he did know *her*. He nodded in calm acceptance, waiting for her to get to the point.

"Yes," Adele said, clearing her mind with the syllable. She resumed, "Rene and I have been going over the records of trading companies in Morning City. Coupled with information we brought from Diamondia, a pattern has become clear."

"The locals are cooperating with you?" Daniel said. "If so, I need coaching, because *I'm* certainly not getting cooperation."

"They're not cooperating, no," Adele said with another cold smile. "But their security isn't very good. And—"

She felt her face muscles relax minutely.

"—Rene has provided context from his knowledge of Phoenix Starfreight. That's proved very helpful."

She cleared her throat and continued, "Although

contact between the cluster and the Alliance has been embargoed on both sides, Bagarian ships meet Alliance vessels on Dodd's Throne and trade normally. Generalissima DeMarce may not be involved, but all six of her ministers are."

Adele looked around her. Pastel light on the bright clothing gave the crowd a sinister look, but that probably came out of her mind rather than reality. "I dare say two-thirds of the guests here at least are members of companies which are currently trading with the Alliance."

"Dodd's Throne . . ." Daniel repeated, his mind sorting files. Adele started to bring out her data unit, but for this sort of question Daniel's way was faster. He would, of course, have committed to memory places that might be used as bases by either side. "Right, lies outside the cluster proper. Red sun, normal gravity, adequate atmosphere; no water to speak of, though. Some cobalt and nickel mining, but food has to be imported and it's a miserable place."

He smiled brightly. "Well, that's very interesting," he said. "How large-scale is it?"

Adele felt herself frowning. "At present there're eight ships here in Morning Harbor which arrived from Dodd's Throne with Alliance cargoes," she said. "That's about average over the past three months. Where we can check the manifests, the cargoes arrived on ships of larger capacity; therefore presumably fewer of them."

She cleared her throat, wondering if drink had fuddled Daniel more than it usually did. More than it ever had before . . . which would be a much worse problem than this business alone.

"Daniel, this means that the government we're here

to support doesn't want to rock a profitable boat," she said carefully. "They won't support—whatever they may say—actions that would prevent the Alliance from reinforcing its fleet in the Jewel System."

"Yes, I see that," Daniel said, still smiling. He swirled the remaining liquor in his glass but didn't taste it for the moment. "But I prefer to think of that as a problem for the past. Thanks to you and Master Cazelet—"

He dipped his head in a half-bow.

"—I can start working on a solution. And since that's Minister Lampert there by the roast ox, I believe I'll do that right now. Thank you, Adele!"

Daniel strode off toward the barbeque pits. He began whistling. As the first few notes drifted back to her, Adele recalled the song: *"Roll me over, in the clover . . ."*

Morning Harbor on Pelosi

If Daniel had been able to stand outside himself, he'd be the first to say that the *Ladouceur* would be a joke in a squadron of modern warships. At 3,800 tons she was smaller than any light cruiser built for a generation and more; she had a mixed armament of two 6-inch guns in a dorsal turret amidships and four 4-inch guns in lateral turrets offset to bow and stern; and her antennas, instead of telescoping within themselves, folded parallel like the yards.

The arrangements of armament and rigging had proved unsatisfactory in service. Rather than rebuild the

ships involved, the Financier class had been relegated
to colonial service, showing the flag on planets where
a kerosene lamp was high technology. At some point
in its history the *Ladouceur* had passed into Alliance
ownership; beyond a notation by a clerk in Navy House,
the RCN wouldn't have noticed her passing.

But the old cruiser was now Daniel's flagship, and
it was with pride that he gestured toward her with
his left hand and said, "Generalissima and gentlemen,
with the *Ladouceur* rerigged to my satisfaction and
the crews of the whole squadron worked up properly,
we'll have a force to keep the Alliance well away from
Bagaria. Guarantor Porra has enough problems that
he won't care to spend his resources in cracking as
hard a nut as he'll find us to be!"

Captain Seward of the *Generalissima DeMarce*
snorted; Captain Hoppler, who'd brought the *Independence* down from orbit this morning, shot his right
cuff and ostentatiously studied his shapely fingernails.
DeMarce exchanged a grimace with Minister Lampert, though both smoothed their expressions back
to neutrality when Daniel glanced over his shoulder
at them.

Because of Adele's warning, Daniel had couched
his praise more defensively than his personal taste
might've formed it in other circumstances. In truth,
the chance of Bagaria mounting offensive operations
with the means at hand would've been pretty slim,
were it not for the equally low caliber of the opposing Cluster Command. And though the government
might not want to disrupt trade, the undoubted greed
of his present audience offered another means of
manipulating them.

"And the amount of loot that'll come to the Republic when we take Churchyard and then Conyers . . ." Daniel said with bland enthusiasm. "Why, even the poor of Morning City will be wearing crowns!"

My *goodness* but that was a lie! But it wouldn't lie heavily on Daniel's conscience. From the feral looks on the faces of his companions, they had no intention of letting the imaginary loot trickle that far down the social scale.

"That's all very well to say, Admiral," said Seward, a girlishly slight Kostroman whose mustache turned up in spikes at the end. "But the crews are a problem. We seem to recruit only the dregs, I'm afraid, and not many of them. True patriotism is absent from the lower orders."

The Bagarian navy paid a common spacer eight ostrads per day; commercial vessels in the cluster paid eighteen. All the petty officers and most of the leading spacers were foreigners whom the new republic had recruited with promises of premium pay. Unfortunately that pay hadn't materialized, so desertions among skilled spacers were even more frequent than by the Bagarian natives.

"Well, I hope that self-interest will supply the place of patriotism once we get matters in hand," said Daniel in a tone of determined cheerfulness. "When they see the loot their fellows return with, I mean. But for now, we need to be sure that the major elements of our squadron can work together. That's the *Ladouceur* and your ships, gentlemen—"

He bowed to Seward and Hoppler.

"—the *DeMarce* and *Independence*."

"If by work together you mean maneuver in concert

in the Matrix, we *can't*," said Seward in a tone of scorn. He'd expected to retain command of the light cruiser he'd brought back from Schumer's World; his pique at the Cinnabar officer who'd been placed over him was understandable. "We're practical captains, Leary. We're not trained in this silly folderol that you Cinnabar *gentlemen* set such score by."

Daniel nodded pleasantly. "I understand that coming from a merchant background you wouldn't have experience in the concerted action that's necessary for successful naval operations, Captain," he said. "It's certainly no reflection on your skills."

That was no more than the truth; the only justification for taking it as an insult was that it replied to the Kostroman's own hostility. Mind, Daniel *did* intend it as an insult. Even if failure could be justified, it was nothing to brag about.

"I've allowed for that problem," Daniel went on smoothly while the reddening Seward spluttered toward finding words. "I'll put officers I've brought with me aboard the *Independence* and *DeMarce* as astrogators. It's not that they're more skilled than you gentlemen, of course—"

He nodded again toward the two captains. Vesey certainly *was* a better astrogator than either of them, and Blantyre might well be. Of course that left Cory as First Lieutenant of the *Ladouceur*, but at worst the midshipman knew how to use the astrogation computer.

"—but they've worked with me, and my little foibles won't throw them off. I propose to lift from Morning Harbor at 0600 tomorrow."

He turned to Generalissima DeMarce. "Your Excellency?" he said. "I expect to be back in between three days and a week. Can you have a thousand soldiers ready then? Because as soon as I have the ships worked up, I propose to move against Churchyard and take care of the Cluster Command once and for all."

The Generalissima flicked a hand to her head as though patting down an errant curl. "If you think that's wise . . ." she said without meeting Daniel's eyes. "Yes, all right, when you return."

"We don't have full crews!" Hoppler protested. "We don't even have minimal crews. Leary, you're a bold fellow I'm sure, but we can't go off!"

"Captain Hoppler, I've looked at the crew lists," Daniel said, letting the least touch of steel creep into his tone. "I'll be leaving the *Sissie* in Morning Harbor and splitting her crew among the three vessels of my new command, so we won't be short of skilled personnel. Some of the existing spacers may not be fully experienced yet, but that's what training's for. And as I told you, I believe that once we have a degree of success, the next stages will come easier."

"We won't have a success!" Seward said. "We'll have a mare's nest, that's all!"

"Captain Seward," Daniel said. "The government of Bagaria has seen fit to give me command of her naval forces."

He nodded toward DeMarce and Lampert. They were watching the discussion carefully, but neither tried to intervene.

"The government may remove me at any time, of course," Daniel went on, "but until then I intend to command to the best of my ability. The major elements of the fleet *will* lift for orbit at 0600 tomorrow. I very much hope you both will continue in the Bagarian service, but if you choose to resign your commissions instead—so be it. Do you understand me?"

The men scowled, but neither spoke.

"Gentlemen," Daniel said, "I must insist on a reply. Do you choose to continue in command of your present charges?"

"Yes," said Hoppler. "Yes, fine, but you'll see."

Seward didn't speak for a moment. Then he snarled, "You're a cocky bastard, Leary! Yes, all right, I command the *DeMarce*. That'll give me a good view of you falling on your high-and-mighty *face*."

"We're all agreed, then," Daniel said cheerfully, sweeping his four companions with another sunny smile. This seemed to be his morning for telling whopping lies. "Then Your Excellency, gentlemen—I'll be off. I have a great deal to do before liftoff tomorrow."

The main thing he had to do was to take Vesey and Blantyre into his confidence. He wasn't going to tell all the Sissies what was going to happen for fear one of them would blurt something to the locals on the way.

He wanted the Bagarian officers to be completely surprised when the squadron extracted from the Matrix above Dodd's Throne.

CHAPTER 11

Above Dodd's Throne

The process of extraction, so unpleasant if Adele had time to think about it, passed her unaware or at least unconcerned when she was busy. The *Ladouceur*'s extraction above Dodd's Throne made Adele *very* busy.

The planet, sunlit from the *Sissie*'s present position, was an unattractive yellow-orange lump. The *Sacred Independence* was already in normal space, 147,000 miles from the *Princess Cecile* and rather closer than that to the planet. Another ship hung in a free-fall orbit some 57,000 miles above the planetary surface. Ordinarily ships held 1 g to simulate gravity, but Rene'd warned Adele that Dodd's Throne might be an exception because it wouldn't be possible to replenish reaction mass upon landing.

Rene was a clever young man, and he learned quickly.

The orbiting ship was . . . "Daniel, the unfamiliar vessel is the freighter *Moore County* out of Rodham,"

Adele said. She'd keyed the command channel manually, which meant she should've called him Captain;
or perhaps Admiral? Well, they all knew that she'd
meant no disrespect; and she was in a hurry. "It's
just lifted with a cargo of holographic entertainment
centers from Mine Compound 73, which appears to
be the trading rendezvous on Dodd's Throne. It's
not a guardship, and there doesn't appear to be a
guardship. Over!"

"*Acknowledged, Signals,*" Daniel's voice said coolly.
"*Over.*"

She'd put too much emphasis on "over" because
she was embarrassed at calling Daniel by his name
in public. *Will I never get it right?*

Another ship appeared, the *Generalissima DeMarce.*
Blantyre was nearly a minute behind schedule, but
she'd brought her charge even closer than the 21,000
miles above the planet where Daniel had extracted
the *Ladouceur.*

Adele's wands assembled and analyzed data from
Dodd's Throne, then collated the results and transmitted them as a text block to Daniel's display. "Captain,"
she said, "there are six Bagarian ships on the ground
at MC 73, which I've highlighted. They're exchanging
cargo with two Pleasaunce-registered ships, the *Vieux
Carree* and *Babanguida.* The Alliance ships each have
two single 10-cm guns, but they don't appear to be
manned at present, over."

"*Roger, Signals,*" said Daniel. He didn't sound
excited, but Adele heard a quiver of hopeful enthusiasm in those few syllables. Perhaps she imagined it.
"*Connect me with our squadron mates, over.*"

"You're connected, Captain," Adele said, trying to

keep her voice free of the irritation she felt at being asked to do something she'd set up within seconds of extraction. And within seconds of the *DeMarce*'s extraction, of course, but that delay wasn't *her* fault.

She'd chosen the 20-meter short-wave frequency rather than laser or microwave links. SW transmissions were easy to intercept, but Adele didn't trust the personnel or equipment of the converted merchantmen to pick up the tight-beam communications she preferred.

"*Squadron, this is Squadron Six,*" Daniel said. "*The pair of 5,000-ton freighters on the planet below—*"

He transmitted a map file marked with the location of MC 73. He hadn't bothered to ask Adele to create it for him as some captains might've done.

"*—are Alliance-owned and therefore legitimate prizes. I want both of you to take your ships down, secure the enemy vessels, and put prize crews aboard. There shouldn't be any need for violence since we've caught them without hope of escape. Remember, this is about making us all rich, not about killing people. Do you understand, over?*"

While she gave Daniel her partial attention, Adele monitored communications among the merchant vessels. None of them—including the *Moore County*—seemed to have the slightest awareness, let alone concern, regarding the warships' arrival.

"*I bloody well* won't *be doing that, Leary!*" Seward snapped back immediately. "*There's no proper harbor down there, just bare rock that's bound to be irregular. It's not safe for a ship the size of the* DeMarce. *And just what do you propose to do while we're on the ground, can you tell me that, over?*"

"*The* Ladouceur *will be in orbit making sure no one surprises us on the ground the way we're about to surprise the* Vieux Carree *and* Babanguida," Daniel said. He sounded calm, almost bored. "*Break. Captain Hoppler, do you see your way clear to obeying orders, over?*"

The blue glint of the *Independence*'s High Drive brightened, dragging a hiss across the short-wave spectrum. "*Why yes, of course, Admiral,*" Andreas Hoppler said with studied nonchalance. "*Newbern is a real planet, not a spherical soup bowl like Kostroma where my colleague comes from. I'm used to landing on solid ground. I'm setting down now. Guard us well, Admiral. Hoppler out.*"

"*Squadron Six, this is DeMarce Five,*" announced Midshipman Blantyre, who'd presumably awarded herself the first lieutenant's call sign according to RCN protocol. "*I'm ready and willing to bring her in, sir. As you know, I've got hard-surface experience, over.*"

Is that true? Adele thought. She started to bring Blantyre's record up as a sidebar on her display, then realized that written documentation wouldn't go into that level of detail. Besides, Blantyre'd said that Daniel knew she had experience. If that'd been true in any meaningful sense, Adele would've known it too.

Blantyre was therefore not telling the truth. She was, in fact, lying in order to deceive Captain Seward, who'd otherwise obstruct Daniel's wishes. Adele supposed she ought to feel good about what Blantyre was doing, since it was bringing about a good result; the dishonesty still made her lip curl.

A smile softened what'd been a sneer of disgust. *Her* way of dealing with Seward would've been to offer to shoot him dead at his console if he didn't carry out Daniel's orders. Most people—Tovera was an exception—would agree that Blantyre's technique was preferable, and Adele decided that she would join the majority.

"*Yes, all right, DeMarce Five,*" Daniel said blandly. "*Captain Seward, Lieutenant Blantyre will land the vessel in the interests of safety if you like. Command will revert to you when you're on the ground, over.*"

"*I'll land the bloody ship, Leary!*" Seward said. His High Drive already glared with braking thrust. "*I don't need a brat who's still got her milk teeth to pilot my ship for me. But I want you to know that it's dangerous—though not for you up in orbit, of course! DeMarce out!*"

Adele kept real-time inserts of the *Ladouceur*'s companions on the upper register of her display. The *Independence* was already deep in the atmosphere. Even without expanding the image of Hoppler's ship, she could see it was wrapped in a shroud of rainbow ions as its plasma thrusters took over from its High Drive.

"*Adele, can you connect me with the ships on the ground?*" Daniel asked quietly over a two-way link. "*I want to warn them not to resist, over.*"

"Yes, of course," Adele said, adjusting her wands almost without thinking about it. "I can't guarantee that anybody will be manning the signals suite, of course, but if we use the 17-meter emergency frequency it should trip the ships' intercom circuits also. That should rouse somebody."

She tried to expand Daniel's real-time image on her display. Her attempt failed, though she wasn't sure if it was a problem with the command—she was using her

personal data unit as an input device, as usual—or if
the console she was using had a malfunction. Instead,
she looked at Daniel directly.

Though the *Ladouceur* wasn't large even for its class,
a cruiser's bridge was still far more spacious than that
of the *Princess Cecile*. The command console sat in the
middle of the circular compartment; by rotating on its
axis, the captain could face any quarter. Eight junior
positions surrounded it with the primary operator's
back to the bulkhead. Because Adele's display was
live, she leaned to the side to look past. It took her
a little aback to see that Daniel was staring directly
at her already.

"Daniel," she said, still using the link. The buzz
of the High Drive and the *whir/skree/clank* of the
various systems operating within the cruiser's steel
hull made it impractical to talk unaided, even when
both parties were in the same compartment. "Would
it really be safe for Blantyre to land on rock? That
is a dangerous business, isn't it?"

Daniel shrugged. "*It could have its moments,*" he
said. "*Thrust reflected between a solid surface and the
hull can set up a standing wave if you're not careful.
But there's eight ships on the ground now, Adele, and
I don't believe that the Bagarian Cluster is that thick
with master pilots.*"

He cleared his throat and grinned. "*I'm just as
pleased that Seward decided to take over the job
himself, though. All Blantyre's experience has been
on simulators, and those were emulating the* Sissie. *A
5,000-ton freighter is quite different—and I'm afraid
much more different than Blantyre would realize until
she started down.*"

Adele nodded in understanding. It hadn't been a bluff, exactly—Blantyre really would've tried to bring the *DeMarce* in. It might've been suicidally dangerous, but that was regularly a part of being an RCN officer.

"We'll be coming out of the shadow of the planet in ninety seconds," she said. "You'll be able speak to the ships on the ground, then. Dodd's Throne doesn't have a system of communications satellites, and though I could've used the *Moore County* as a transponder—"

She smiled slightly. She was making what was for her a joke.

"—I didn't think that was necessary."

"*Quite right*," agreed Daniel; dryly, she thought. "*Break. This is the IBS* Ladouceur. *Merchant vessels at Mine Compound 73, do not attempt to lift. Warships and troops of the Independent Republic of Bagaria have taken control of the planet. Bagarian registry ships will be examined and released, but the* Babanguida *and* Vieux Carree *will be taken to Pelosi for condemnation by a prize court.*"

Daniel took a deep breath; his first since he began speaking, Adele thought. In a firm, coolly distant voice he added, "*Vieux Carree, shut down your plasma thrusters. If you lift off the ground, you will be infallibly destroyed either by the ships landing at Compound 73 or by the vessels waiting in orbit. Spacers, I'm Commander Daniel Leary of the RCN, and I assure you that you will not escape me! Over.*"

Adele didn't recall hearing Daniel boast except when he did it for effect. That included the effect his heroism had on foolish young women, of course, but she supposed that was pardonable. A rational survival plan for the human species would certainly involve spreading the genes of warriors like Daniel Leary as widely as possible.

She grinned, then made a series of quick commands that burped further information to the Alliance vessels. It wasn't anything she'd planned to do, but she had the clips in her data unit and it seemed a suitable time to disseminate them.

"Captain," Adele said. "I transmitted excerpts from *The Conquest of Dunbar's World* to the ships on the surface. I thought it might add point to your threat."

"*Bloody Hell, Signals,*" Daniel said, but he chuckled. "*They'll think I'm a posturing idiot, over.*"

"*Yes sir,*" said Cory unexpectedly from the Battle Direction Center. Adele had keyed the command channel rather than a two-way link. "*But a very handsome one, sir. Five out.*"

He has a sense of humor, Adele thought. Of course Cory might always've had a sense of humor, but when he first met Lieutenant Leary aboard the tender *Hermes* he wouldn't've had the calm courage to joke in the midst of a tense situation. Daniel might not've been able to make Cory an astrogator, but he *had* made the boy a man.

Daniel cleared his throat. "*Ship, this is Six,*" he said. Borries looked at him, but Sun, the only other junior officer on the bridge besides Adele, continued to stare at his display. The gunner seemed to be willing a target to approach so that he could blast it.

"*The situation on the ground appears to have settled out peaceably, as it should've done,*" Daniel continued. "*The two Alliance prizes've shut down their thrusters and're waiting to be boarded. Our companion vessels have landed and will take charge of them momentarily.*

When they've all lifted to orbit, we'll set a course back to Pelosi. You're heroes, fellow spacers, and don't think the folks in Morning Harbor won't know it! Six out."

"Squadron Six, this is Independence Five," said Vesey. *"Emergency, emergency. The crews—the non-RCN spacers—are out of control and are looting ships. Repeat, they're looting the ships, the country craft as well as the prizes. Over!"*

She was speaking through a laser communicator. The high pitch of her voice might've been an artifact of transmission, but the words rattled out faster than Vesey ordinarily spoke.

Adele was filtering the cruiser's internal chatter away from Daniel. She'd set outside calls to appear as a text crawl on his display. She highlighted this one in red, then copied Daniel as she replied, *"Independence Five, this is Squadron. Hold for the Captain."*

"Vesey, this is Six," said Daniel. *"How many men can you dispose, over?"*

"Only the twenty-five I brought with me, sir," Vesey replied, audibly calmer just for the fact of a reply. *"And we don't have sidearms. Blantyre's probably the same. The crews are completely out of control, and the Bagarian officers are bloody useless! Over."*

"All right, Vesey," Daniel said. His fingers stabbed buttons, setting up equations on a pilotry screen. *"Hold what you've got. If they won't listen to spoken orders, then we'll provide them with something they will listen to. Break, Woetjans? Prepare as large a party as you can trust for dismounted action. Over."*

"Aye aye, sir," said the big bosun cheerfully. She and her riggers were all aboard, though some of them still wore the rigging suits they'd need when

the *Ladouceur* set course for home. "*What can you expect from wogs, hey? Rig out.*"

"*Ship,*" Daniel resumed. "*We'll begin our landing approach in thirty, that's three-zero, seconds. We're going to take charge of the situation on the ground. Six out.*"

Tovera was sitting at the station next to Adele's, unused because the *Ladouceur* was so badly undercrewed. She took her little sub-machine gun from its case and slipped it into a shoulder holster, then looked at Rene on the jump seat of Adele's console.

"How good a shot are you, boy?" she asked.

"Mistress?" said Rene, straightening and trying to keep his face expressionless. "I've never used a gun."

He flashed a glance toward Adele, but she remained silent.

"Then you'll have to get close, won't you?" Tovera said. She giggled. "All right, boy. Stay with me, and I'll make sure you get close."

The roar of the thrusters cut off any further discussion.

Mining Compound 73 on Dodd's Throne

Daniel wasn't worried about landing in the sense of being able to get the *Ladouceur* safely onto the ground, but that was only half his problem: to succeed he also had to get his people *out* of the ship. That was going to be very difficult if the plasma thrusters had heated the rock directly beneath the ship white hot.

He'd much rather have been doing this in the *Sissie*, but he wasn't and it still had to be done. And bloody hell, he didn't want to do it in the *Sissie* either.

"Ship, hang on!" he warned. "This is going to be rough!"

Instead of bringing the *Ladouceur* down perpendicular to the surface, Daniel angled two of his eighteen thrusters—One and Nine, the end units on the port side—outboard to induce a slight drift. That in itself wouldn't be enough to do what he wanted, but it meant that he wouldn't have to overcome the resting inertia of thirty-eight hundred tons and change. The nozzles were flared at between seventy-three and seventy-six percent open, greatly reducing their efficiency.

An instant before the cruiser touched, Daniel irised the petals tight in the same motion that he slammed the throttles closed. The reaction mass already in the feed lines continued to flow for a fraction of a second, lifting the ship momentarily as she continued to edge sideways. The bow of the starboard outrigger touched, shrieking like a damned soul. It sprayed a roostertail of white sparks.

The *Ladouceur* landed flat, banging and rattling. *Like a ton of old iron*, Daniel thought, but it was thousands of tons—and they'd landed, safely if not gracefully.

The oleo struts hadn't collapsed. They'd scraped a hole in the starboard outrigger beyond question and the impact might've started seams as well, but the very worst that could mean was that the ship started to sink when they landed in Morning Harbor.

After Daniel took control of matters on the ground, they'd check on the damage, then repair what they could. If quick repairs wouldn't do the job, well, they'd land on firm ground when they returned to Pelosi and sort out the problem at leisure.

But the first order of business was to take charge here.

The *Ladouceur* had entry hatches on both sides, offset toward bow and stern opposite the 4-inch turrets. Daniel switched only the starboard hatch to open, then remembered to wait an interminable thirty seconds to make sure that it *did* start to open. He'd brought them down bloody hard, and the usual cushion of water hadn't been there to spare the plates from torquing.

The dogs withdrew with ringing clangs; hydraulic rams whined as they extended, driving the hatch outward to become a boarding ramp. Once the process was started, there wouldn't be a problem that Woetjans and an emergency crew with jacks and sledges couldn't cure.

Daniel rose from his console. Hogg had slung a stocked impeller and was offering a sub-machine gun; Daniel took it without comment. The weapons were a necessary part of the business. He didn't want a fight, but he knew that when the forces of order arrived heavily armed, the forces of chaos were more likely to choose the peaceful option.

"Six to Ship," he said. For now his commo helmet was able to transmit through the cruiser's PA system; he heard his words echoing from the A Deck corridor and the compartments opening onto it. "Those of you in the landing party, obey your section leaders. Don't shoot unless Woetjans or I order you to, not even if you're shot at. Lieutenant Cory commands during my

absense. For those of you remaining aboard, be ready
for anything, but don't start it. Sun—"

The gunner's mate, now gunnery officer, was controlling all the guns himself. He'd cranked the 6-inch
turret back over the *Ladouceur*'s stern quarter to bear
on the *Sacred Independence*, while the lateral turrets
were aimed at the *Generalissima DeMarce* a quarter
mile off the cruiser's bow.

If the guns fired on their present bearings, they'd
toast half the *Ladouceur*'s rigging and maybe even
damage her hull. Which didn't mean Sun was bluff-
ing, of course.

"—I particularly mean you. Do *not* fire unless I
personally tell you to. Now, Sissies, let's get moving!
Six out."

Adele was starting for the hatch, looking, well,
dissociated. Beside her were Tovera and the Cazelet
boy; Tovera had found full-sized sub-machine guns
for both of them, while her small personal weapon
hung in a shoulder holster.

"Officer Mundy?" Daniel said. He barely caught
the "Adele" that his tongue was starting to form. "I
believe you can handle the communications duties
better from your console here."

Adele shrugged and said, "Yes, perhaps I could.
I'm going to the *DeMarce* with my associates." She
nodded to Tovera and Cazelet. "Vesey's taken over the
bridge of the *Independence*, but it seemed to me that
Blantyre could use some help. Besides, the *DeMarce*'s
commo suite is in better condition."

"Right," said Daniel as they all turned into the
down companionway. It'd be four decks, not three,
to the *Ladouceur*'s entrance hold. Tovera followed

her mistress while Cazelet led. The sub-machine gun banged the boy's ribs because he hadn't snugged up the sling properly, but he was as sure-footed as a rigger on the worn steel treads.

Adele *was* right, of course. Three slightly built people, two of them women, weren't going to impress a mob of spacers who'd probably already broken open the liquor cabinets as the first stage in the process of looting.

These particular women could take charge of a warship's bridge, though, even if they had to shoot the present occupants out of the way. Daniel hoped that wouldn't happen, but he didn't trust the judgment of Captain Seward and his henchmen while they remained in control of the *DeMarce*'s plasma cannon.

Woetjans was forming her teams at the foot of the boarding ramp when the group from the bridge arrived. Adele set off with her companions for the *DeMarce*. She didn't say anything further nor look over her shoulder, though Cazelet did. The boy didn't seem frightened, but he obviously didn't know how to handle a sub-machine gun and the blankness in his eyes was probably a sign of being completely at sea.

Daniel grinned and gave him a thumbs-up. The now-Commander Daniel Leary had been just as lost many times in his life, and he wouldn't pretend he knew how matters were going to work out in the next hour or so. They'd work out better because he had people like Adele and Rene Cazelet supporting him, though. Yes, and Tovera's support too.

"Sir, I put Barnes in charge of the section that sorts out the *Babanguida*," Woetjans said, turning when she heard Daniel's boots on the ramp behind her. "I figured to take the *Carree* myself, all right?"

Daniel eyed the eighty or so spacers in two straggling clumps. Fewer than two-thirds of them were former Sissies, which meant the bosun had more confidence in the Bagarians than Daniel himself might've. Woetjans was closer to the *Ladouceur*'s personnel than her new captain'd had time to become—a truth Daniel regretted, but a truth nonetheless.

There'd be a few Sissies staying on the cruiser. Pasternak, Woetjans' counterpart as Chief of Ship, was notable among them. You could be a first-rate spacer and still not be somebody your captain wanted to take into a fight. That was all right: Sissies were needed to leaven the hundred and fifty Bagarians aboard also.

Each of the landing party carried a sub-machine gun or a stocked impeller, but they had lengths of pipe, rods, and knuckledusters as well. Some, even of the Sissies, couldn't be trusted with firearms; for example, Daniel hoped the impeller which the hulking Skrubas carried was unloaded. But he's seen Skrubas use the *stock* of an impeller, and he couldn't think of a quicker way to end a brawl than that combination.

At least half the personnel carried rolls of cargo tape, intended to snug down objects in the holds when there wasn't time to use more complicated restraints. It had a multitude of uses aboard a starship. One use was to immobilize people who you didn't want wandering around.

"Right," said Daniel, shuttling quickly through the options in his mind. "The country craft can wait. Barnes, Hogg and I will accompany you, if you don't mind. Now let's get going."

He suited his action to his words by striding off in

the direction of the *Babanguida* some three hundred yards away. Half the spacers followed him in a jostling mob; they'd never been taught to march in unison and Daniel didn't imagine it'd make them any more useful to him or to Cinnabar if they could.

He frowned. He really *must* institute firearms training on a more regular basis than the rudiments that Sun and Hogg had been giving interested personnel in the entry hold on long voyages. His crews regularly saw more dismounted action than many Land Forces regiments did.

The ground was a rusty slate, hard enough that thin plates cracked off under Daniel's weight. There was no sign of water or vegetation. Scores of starships had lashed the stone with their plasma thrusters; piles of trash marked the landscape and blew across it. Some pieces of printed cardboard had been here long enough to bleach white.

Though the *Babanguida* was big to be trading out here in the boondocks, it was rigged with only sixteen antennas. It needed only a small crew, but it'd wallow through the Matrix. On a given voyage it'd take half again as long as ships which were better able to shift between bubble universes and take advantage of varying energy gradients.

As Daniel approached the boarding ramp at the head of his band, a spacer carrying a double armload of women's dresses stumbled down it singing, *"Come you lads of great Pelosi, lift the old song once a—"*

Daniel caught the looter by the elbow. "Hold on, my good man," he said, trying to sound cheery but firm. "Carry that back to the hold, if you will. It's the property of the Republic, not ours as individuals."

"Who the bloody hell are you to give me orders,

shithead?" the man said. He'd been drinking something with a mint flavor and enough alcohol content that his breath would've burned.

"Wrong answer, wog," Hogg said as he reversed his impeller. He butt-stroked the looter in the belly. The fellow collapsed on his face, vomiting yellow bile and chunks of undigested meat. The dresses were of some metal-smooth cloth; they spilled across the ground with a sheen as iridescent as an oil slick.

"Now he can't carry the loot back, Hogg," Daniel pointed out mildly.

"Oh, the bugger was too drunk to be any use to us," Hogg said as he continued up the ramp. "Anyway, we can worry about it later."

In the entry hold were three more spacers—all male; on the fringes of civilization women generally weren't considered sturdy enough for the work. One had an armload of entertainment modules, while his companions had piled a score of similar units on a tarpaulin which they were dragging toward the hatch.

"Hold it!" Barnes said, stepping in front of them. "Turn around and take the crap back, boys. You been naughty."

"Hey, who says?" demanded the Bagarian at the leading edge of the tarp.

Dasi grabbed the fellow by the throat left-handed and lifted him off the deck. "Commander Leary says," he said. "Me and my friend say so too."

He tapped the muzzle of his impeller against the looter's mouth. Blood splattered from a cut lip.

The lone Bagarian dropped the modules he was carrying. Daniel pointed to him and said, "Where's the ship's crew?"

"They, they're in the forward hold, s-sir," the Bagarian said. "It was generator sets in there, too big to carry, so we locked the crew out of the way."

Then he said, "Who in bloody hell *are* you?" That wasn't a protest but rather a bleat of amazement.

"All right, take me to the forward hold," Daniel said, ignoring the question. He looked over his shoulder. "Four of you—Asnip, Ward, Bolden, and Suplinski—come with me. Barnes, police up the rest of the looters. Tape who you have to but try not to shoot them."

"Move!" Hogg said to the Bagarian. He poked a finger into the fellow's ribs to make sure he was listening.

Daniel could—any of the spacers with him could—find a freighter's holds in his sleep, but the *Babanguida* was big enough that she might well have them split along her axis as well as transversely. A guide saved searching for the correct hold. Besides, it didn't hurt when they met Bagarians on the way that one of their shipmates was leading the armed strangers.

The guide took them to a locked accessway; half a dozen looters lay taped like chickens along their route. The hatch was stenciled F3, a complex enough designation to make Daniel pleased that he'd played safe.

Hogg pushed hard on the latch plate. It didn't move. He backed away and presented his impeller, saying, "Want me to shoot it open, master?"

"No, I don't think that'll be necessary," said Daniel, twisting the plate ninety degrees and *then* pushing it. The dogs withdrew, ringing like an ill-tuned bell chorus. In the SET position the hatch could've been locked from the bridge so that personnel in the corridor couldn't break in. Daniel had very much—and correctly—doubted that the looters had been that organized.

He'd expected the imprisoned crew to burst into the corridor when the hatch opened, but instead there was silence relieved only by the sound of somebody whimpering in the hold's chill darkness. What in heaven's name was going on?

"Come on out!" Daniel called; his words echoed. The hold was two decks high. The hull-side cargo hatch was on the level below, and a slatted staircase led down from this portal. "This is Commander Daniel Leary of the RCN—"

He figured that was a better claim to make under the circumstances than "Admiral Leary of the Bagarian Republic."

"—and I need to talk to your captain." If he'd been thinking ahead, he'd have asked Adele for the commanding officer's name. It was the sort of thing she learned automatically, rather like breathing.

Nothing happened, except that the whimpering became open sobs.

"Bloody hell!" Daniel said. "I want your captain *now*. Don't make me come in after you!"

"I'm coming out," somebody called from behind one of the fusion bottles. They were electric generators, the sort of thing an outlying farm would need—or, on a fringe world like Pelosi, a rich man's home even if it were in the center of Morning City. "Don't shoot, please! I've done you no harm. Please!"

"Great heavens, man!" Daniel blurted. "We're not going to harm you. I told you, I'm an RCN officer. You're a legitimate prisoner, but I see no reason for you and your crew to be locked up so long as we can come to an agreement. Come on up here!"

He thought for a moment, then added as the first

figure started shuffling up the stairs, "All of you come out. Why in heaven did you think you were going to be shot?"

The captain wore a blue uniform jacket which, like the *Babanguida*, was cheaply made and rather the worse for wear. The pin clipped over his right breast pocket read Robinson or Robertson; the gilt had rubbed off the right side.

"I'm Ian Robertson," he muttered without meeting the eyes of anyone in Daniel's party. Then, "If you're RCN, why're you with pirates?"

"Buck up, Robertson," Daniel said, trying to sound jolly. The merchant captain had the right of his claim, but with luck he could be cajoled to forget the past. "I know how it seems, but a little indiscipline is easily put right. You're a legitimate prize of war. Now, we'll repatriate your crew at the earliest opportunity, but I'm sure that some of your people would rather sign on with me than spend weeks or even years in a prison compound."

He looked down at the figures gathered at the base of the stairs. He could see only a dozen, which meant some were still in hiding.

"How does it strike you?" he called to the spectators. "Who of you'd like liberal pay and the best spacers in the human galaxy for your fellows?"

"What d'ye mean about pay?" called one of the figures below. The voice was cautious, but the concern this time was over money instead of drunken Bagarian pirates planning to cut the throats of their captives.

This was the result Daniel'd hoped for: even the Alliance citizens in the crew were likely to be from conquered planets with no affection for Guarantor Porra.

Treated well, they'd be as happy to join the *Ladouceur*'s complement as they would to continue aboard an Alliance-registered tub like the *Babanguida*.

He leaned over the railing. "Come on up and we'll discuss it like spacers," he said cheerfully. "Regular pay is eighteen ostrads a month, but you'll also take a share in the prize money. You can talk to any of the Sissies who came with me from Cinnabar about what prize money's meant in the past, and you can look at today for proof that it'll keep on in the future. While you've been slaving on this ship, my crews are going to be splitting her value in prize cash!"

He was shading the truth and he knew it, but until these folk signed on, their welfare didn't touch the honor of a Leary of Bantry. It wasn't such a bad offer regardless. Daniel was sure—well, he was hopeful—that he could convince the Navy Minister to raise pay when the squadron returned after this triumph; if he couldn't, he'd enlist the new personnel into the RCN under his authority as commander of the *Princess Cecile*.

Spacers began to shuffle up the stairs; additional figures drifted out from behind the dense lumps of fusion bottles. He'd move them all to the *Ladouceur*, adding those who enlisted to the cruiser's crew and confining the remainder away from temptation to take back control of their own ship. Prize crews for the two Alliance freighters required a tricky balance between Sissies and Bagarians or he'd simply be transferring the looting from Dodd's Throne to the Matrix, but with Woetjans' help it could be worked out.

The smile Daniel gave the Alliance captain was harder than his usual expression. "Now, sir, if you and your officers will come up to the bridge with me, we'll settle details while I get back in communication with my squadron."

"I don't understand this," Captain Robertson muttered. Now that he wasn't terrified, he was willing to complain. "We're just trading with you. If you capture us like this, there won't be any trade!"

"Exactly, my good man," Daniel said. "People in the Bagarian Cluster don't seem to have quite grasped what war means. They're about to learn."

CHAPTER 12

Morning City on Pelosi

Adele hadn't imagined there'd be a parade when the squadron and the two Alliance prizes returned to Pelosi. She hadn't *dreamed* there'd be a parade.

"Mistress?" said Rene Cazelet. He was trying to keep his voice down, which meant he had to lean very close to her ear to have a chance of being heard over the cheering crowd. "How did they learn about the victory in time to do this? It must've taken days to prepare, surely?"

"I was wondering the same thing," said Adele. That was of course true. Because she was Adele Mundy she was already in the process of getting an answer by entering a local database.

Her personal data unit didn't have enough power to transmit more than a quarter mile or so, and Pelosi didn't have a public communications system that was worthy of the name. There were—there had to be—private commercial systems, however. Adele'd tied her data unit and the RCN commo helmets worn

163

by at least one spacer on every parade float into the microwave communications system belonging to Fidelity Mercantile Corporation, Minister Lampert behind a corporate veil.

The ten floats which carried naval officers, whether or not they'd been on Dodd's Throne, were (as before) flatbed trailers covered with bunting and pulled by eight-wheeled tractors. There was nothing complicated in that, though Adele strongly doubted the Bagarian government could've put even so simple a business together in the hour and a half since the squadron reached Pelosi.

Canvas murals hung across the fronts of buildings all the way from the docks to the House of Assembly. They couldn't possibly have been created since the squadron arrived, even if the paint were still wet.

As best Adele could tell, the paint *had* cured properly. Even if it hadn't, the images depicted—though they weren't in any sense realistic—*did* make direct reference to the events on Dodd's Throne.

"Hurrah for Lady Leary!" somebody shouted. The crowd took up the theme raggedly, mixing, "Lady Leary!" and "The Admiral's Lady!" with similar but unintelligible cheers. The result was a sort of muddy good-humor.

Tovera laughed. Rene said in scandalized horror, "Mistress! They mean you!"

"Then they're idiots," Adele said, concentrating on her search. Well, trying to concentrate on her search. *Most* people were idiots, not just this mob of goggle-eyed, garishly dressed, *wogs* shouting in the—

She caught herself and sat bolt-upright in a flush of embarrassment. She'd allowed her anger to control

her; which she never did, which she couldn't afford to
do. She was holding both wands in her right hand so
that her left could reach into her tunic pocket, just
because civilians were happy and foolish.

And what would her mother Evadne have said
about Adele referring to foreigners as wogs, even in
the quiet of her own mind? Adele winced. Her mother
would've been horrified at the disrespect for foreign
cultures which she *knew* were just as valid as that of
a Cinnabar noble.

Adele had seen a great deal more of foreign cultures
than her mother, a very parochial woman despite her
principles, had done. Some of those cultures were
entirely worthy of disrespect.

But Evadne would also have considered the term
"wog" to be common, the sort of word used by untu-
tored spacers and rural louts like Daniel's servant
Hogg. In that she would've been quite correct. By
thinking the word, Adele had disgraced her station
as Mundy of Chatsworth.

She, Tovera, and Rene were on the tenth and last
float. Daniel was at the front, bowing to the crowd,
with Minister Lampert on one side of him and Generalissima DeMarce on the other. Hogg stood behind
them, looking rumpled and thick with his hands in
his pockets.

Hogg *was* rumpled. He wasn't thick, though, and
Adele had a very good notion of what he was holding
in those pockets, ready to use on anybody he thought
was a danger to the young master.

The trailers in between—the quality of bunting
decreased from the front to the back of the procession; that draping Adele's was canvas decorated with

what seemed to be house paint—carried Hoppler and Seward, then apparently everyone on Pelosi who could claim to wear a naval officer's uniform.

Vesey, Blantyre, and Cory rode the ninth float. Vesey seemed uncomfortable but the two midshipmen were in their element. Well-dressed youths were throwing flowers to Blantyre over the Bagarian soldiers lining the parade route, while not only women but some heavily made up men tried to get through to Cory.

"The traders, the country craft we found on Dodd's Throne . . ." Adele said, scrolling through data. She'd started with the files of Fidelity Mercantile. She could've transferred from there to other databases, but Lampert's information provided all she needed. "They arrived back on Pelosi several days before we did. They brought reports about what'd happened."

"Of course!" Rene said. "We couldn't travel any faster than the *Babanguida*, and she'd have been a bucket even with a proper crew. But—"

He looked at Adele with a frown.

"—surely they didn't bring positive reports, did they? They were near as anything, well . . . Except for Commander Leary, they'd have been robbed of everything."

"*Lay*-dee *Lear*-ee!" shrieked at least a dozen spectators. They were better organized than the Bagarian Navy—or for that matter than the clerks of Fidelity Mercantile. Lampert should hire a few of them, assuming they could read and write. "*Lay*-dee *Lear*-ee!"

Adele was smiling; good. That was the right attitude to take toward well-intentioned people who didn't have the advantages of education and intelligence, but who nonetheless insisted on opening their mouths.

"It appears that they took being robbed as a given

if they met Bagarian warships," Adele explained as she reflexively tried to bring order to Lampert's files. "Rather like crashing if your thrusters fail on landing. You hope they don't fail, but if they do the crash is inevitable. When Daniel—"

A mistake. She didn't underline it by trying to correct the personal reference.

"—stopped the business and saw to the return of whatever hadn't been drunk, they were delighted. And of course the citizens here really wanted a—"

The word "citizens" made her look up from the data unit's holographic display. Stretching across two building fronts above the cheering crowd was a painting on a tarpaulin large enough to cover half a dozen cargo pallets. A female figure—the prominent bust made that obvious—in a white uniform (with a scarlet cloak added, but that was a minor license for *this* artist) bestrode, literally, a starship. From the turrets drawn all over the vessel's hull it was no ship ever built, but the legend GENERALISSIMA DEMARCE was painted prominently on the bow.

The figure had a pistol in one hand, a stocked impeller in the other, and with both was shooting at attackers who waved Alliance flags. Because they were more or less in scale with the ship, they barely came up to the ankles of the giantess.

"They wanted a victory," she concluded, but her voice had dropped to a whisper. "By all the *Gods*."

On the figure's left, red letters with an arrow read CAPTAIN ADELE MUNDY. On the right, a similar legend and arrow—in violet—read GRAND ADMIRAL LEARY'S WIFE.

"I don't remember having that much fun when we

took over the *DeMarce*," said Tovera. Her voice was chirpy, though she had to shout to be heard.

"There weren't any Alliance personnel!" Rene said. "Why, this is infamous! And we didn't shoot anyone. We scarcely had to threaten Captain Seward!"

"Right, no fun at all," said Tovera. "Well, better luck next time, boy."

She was baiting Rene, a positive sign. Tovera's sense of humor, grim and deadpan though it was, was a human trait. Adele didn't suppose her servant would ever develop a conscience, but this was a step in the right direction.

"I prefer to think of it as amusing, Rene," Adele said as she sent a text message to the commo helmet Hogg wore; he'd pass it on. The information she'd gleaned from Lampert's files wouldn't surprise Daniel, but he might as well have the details before DeMarce and Lampert spoke to him in private.

Partly because of what she was thinking about the Bagarian government and partly because she found Tovera's sense of humor infectious, Adele added, "I find my trigger finger gets quite enough exercise as it is without me needlessly adding to the list of people I intend to shoot."

Before the door of the conference room in the north wing of the Hall of Assembly had finished closing, Jordan Wiens—the Minister of Trade—snarled, "What possessed you to rob our own merchants that way, Leary? Are you out of your mind?"

"You had no right to do that!" Minister Lampert said, his words stepping on his colleague's. "You lied to us, admit it! You lied to us!"

There was a yelp in the anteroom and the door opened again behind Daniel. He didn't bother looking over his shoulder to see that Hogg had followed him regardless of what the attendant outside thought about the matter. The servant's presence wouldn't be necessary, but it wasn't a bad thing to have him around.

Daniel stepped chest to chest with Lampert and said in a ringing voice, "See here, my good man! I'll thank you to keep a civil tongue in your head when you speak to a Leary!"

He wasn't as near the edge of control as his tone implied, but neither was he merely pretending to be angry. This was a case, Speaker Leary's son had decided, when it was politic to show one's teeth.

Lampert stepped back in surprise; Wiens, his mouth open to resume, instead fell silent. No one spoke for a moment.

The Generalissima herself said plaintively, "This really has caused a difficult situation, Admiral. I know you couldn't have foreseen the problems, but I do wish you'd explained ahead of time what you intended. I don't know how long it'll take us to put matters straight."

Daniel thumped his left leg out to the side and crossed his hands behind his back. Only after he struck the pose did he realize he'd just come to Parade Rest. Well, it'd do. Quite obviously the members of the Bagarian government didn't intend to sit.

The central table would seat a committee of twenty, and there were chairs around the walls for aides and functionaries. Over the long south wall was a railed balcony, though the doors onto it were closed and perhaps locked. The high windows in the other three sides were in alcoves with built-in seats. Bright-colored insectoids fluttered against the inside of the panes, though it was beyond Daniel's ability to imagine why they'd entered if they were so determined on escaping again.

But then, he'd walked into this room also, hadn't he? And he'd known full well what to expect.

"Generalissima, Ministers," Daniel said. "I told you I was taking the squadron for a training cruise, and that's all I did. That we stumbled onto a pair of Alliance prizes was a piece of great good luck but not a violation of orders either explicit or implied. I'm puzzled that you're not as pleased about that as I am, though; and as pleased as the citizens outside clearly are."

"You see, Leary," said Alfred Decker, the Minister of Resources, "if you start seizing civilian property, the Alliance is going to do the same in retaliation. Many—most, in fact—of our substantial citizens have property and accounts receivable within the Alliance. On Pleasaunce even. What's to stop the owners of the ships you've captured from recompensing themselves from our—that is, from the property of Bagarian citizens?"

"Absolutely nothing, I suppose, Minister," Daniel said. He was beginning to find this amusing. He had the trump card and knew it: he didn't mind a public scene over the issue, and the ministers couldn't afford to let that happen. "But you're at war, you'll recall. Guarantor Porra could order such confiscations at any time."

"But he *won't*, Admiral," DeMarce said. "Not unless he's, well, provoked. Capturing civilian ships in the way you did on Dodd's Throne is *exactly* the sort of provocation we want to avoid."

"Why, Your Excellency, gentlemen . . ." Daniel said in a good counterfeit of puzzlement. "I don't believe you've thought this through. You've been chosen—"

How *had* they been chosen? He'd understood that DeMarce was a military strongman, but close contact with the government left him with the suspicion she was the puppet of the wealthy merchants who'd become her ministers.

"—to lead the Bagarian peoples in their struggle for liberty. Surely you see that temporary personal loss is a small price to pay for that liberty. Why—"

He stepped toward the east windows, facing the square which the crowd filled. The cheers were sparser in the absence of anyone present to spark them, but they continued nonetheless.

"—you can hear the people's enthusiasm even now. You see how our good fortune on Dodd's Throne has raised patriotic fervor on your behalf. You wouldn't think of dashing their joy, would you?"

"Bloody hell!" said Nick Bedi, a wizened stick of a man with the Cluster Affairs—that is, internal security—portfolio. "If you tell them that, they'll hang us all! By all the gods, man! And chances are they won't stop with us, either, so watch your tongue for your own sake!"

"With respect, Minister," Daniel said, knowing that if Bedi wanted to find respect in his tone he'd have to listen very hard. "I'm an RCN officer, so of course concern for my personal safety comes a bad second to doing my duty."

Daniel's duty lay to Cinnabar, however, not to the

Bagarian Cluster or even to its common people. Some of the ministers must suspect that by now, though at least DeMarce seemed to think the young Cinnabar advisor was just dangerously naive.

They all knew they had a tiger by the tail, though. Daniel could rouse the mob against them, and if they'd so much as glanced at his record they realized he'd be willing to do that or to do anything else his duty required.

The chances were that a lot of cluster citizens were going to die because the government had called on Cinnabar for help. Daniel deeply regretted that, but Admiral James was depending on him.

"Look, Leary, we're all pleased about the prizes, of course," Lampert lied with a straight face. "But what the Cluster needs now isn't more commerce raiders, it's Churchyard and Conyers. They're daggers to our throat as long as the Alliance continues to hold them."

"That's right," said Kevin Hewett, the Chancellor. "Alliance commerce can be taken care of by the privateers we're commissioning. Our share will be very important to the budget for the coming year."

"Yes, very important," Lampert said. "While *you're* supposed to be attacking Churchyard, Leary. Before the Alliance reinforces it, you see. Not swanning off to Dodd's Throne, which isn't a threat and couldn't ever be a threat!"

If you're worried about your own trade, Daniel thought, *you're out of your collective minds to commission privateers—for which read pirates, in result if not by intention.*

These ministers were too desperately shortsighted

to understand the dangers; Daniel thought it was that rather than ignorance of how lines blurred at the sharp end. Spacers with privateering commissions, few of them Bagarians and some no doubt from Alliance worlds, would be balancing money for themselves against the wishes of a government of strangers. Their own profit would win every time.

But that wasn't the business of Cinnabar nor of Commander Daniel Leary, not right at the moment. Aloud he said, "I'm pleased to have the government's support, sirs and madame. Your Excellency—"

He looked at DeMarce with a bland smile.

"—we discussed troops for the Churchyard expedition when we last spoke. Where are they billeted? And of course I'll need transport and at least a month's rations—"

"That won't be possible, I'm afraid, Admiral," said the plump, balding Terry Dean. He was Minister for the Army and wore a bright green military uniform with scarlet shoulder boards. "The demands on the Army of Freedom are such that we don't have any troops to send off with you. But the oppressor's forces have no bottle. You'll see. When you start bombarding Churchyard, they'll all surrender the way they did on Schumer's World."

That's not the lesson I would've drawn from Schumer's World, thought Daniel. There'd been only a battalion of Cluster Militia on the planet, and the *Victoria Luise*—now *Ladouceur*—had been captured while provisioning as the first act of the revolt. Churchyard, with a major naval base and no more colonists than it had immigrant workers from deeper into the Alliance, would be a very different matter.

"I must say that I regret to hear that there won't be troops available," he said aloud, keeping his tone neutral. "You mentioned bombardment, General Dean. Are the plasma missiles ready for the squadron to load, then?"

"They certainly are, Leary," said Lampert, suddenly cheerful again. "My friend Power delivered the final tranche of the contract just this morning. Bloody fast work, *I* say."

"Delivered and been paid for," said Chancellor Hewett sourly. He was a tall man with soft features, a stoop, and the expression of a dying camel. "Which leaves bugger all in the treasury, I don't mind telling you."

"Well, of course he was paid!" Lampert snapped. "He did the work, didn't he? I'm sure that when Admiral Leary here captures Churchyard, there'll be plenty of loot to plump the treasury up. Isn't that so, Leary?"

"One can certainly hope so," said Daniel. He caught a glimpse of himself in the mirror between the windows. The varnished hardness of his smile disturbed him. But these folk weren't his first responsibility. "At any rate, Minister, the Cluster's share of the captured freighters and their cargoes may be of some help when they're auctioned."

"Just so, Leary, just so," said Lampert. "Now, I'm sure you have a great deal to do before you leave to sweep the oppressors off Churchyard, and we do too. You understand?"

"Perfectly, Minister," Daniel said, bowing. "Oh—and one further thing. I've raised spacer's pay to the usual eighteen ostrads a month with senior ratings in proportion. I trust this meets with your approval, as it's absolutely necessary to retain experienced personnel."

"For heaven's sake man, where do you expect me to find the money for that?" Hewett growled. "No, we don't approve!"

"I believe *I* found the money on Dodd's Throne, Chancellor," Daniel said. "If you require me to, I'll find more in the same place or similar ones; but I'd rather be concentrating on the problem of Churchyard."

Ministers looked at one another. "All right, Admiral," DeMarce said to break the silence. "We'll find the money. You deal with Churchyard."

Hewett grimaced. "All right, all right," he muttered. "But it's wasting money on trash, you know."

"I know many people who feel that way about spacers, Chancellor," Daniel said. He bowed again and backed out of the room respectfully. Hogg slipped out after his master and closed the door.

Daniel turned to put his back to the door. His lips were pursed as though he'd been sucking on a lemon.

As Adele settled onto a stone bench in the entry vestibule of the Hall of Assembly, the heavyset man who'd been leaning against a pillar on the other side straightened and walked toward her. "Excuse me, Lady Mundy," he said. "I'd appreciate a moment—"

Tovera stepped in front of Adele with her hand in her attaché case. Adele knew from experience that the pale woman's face would be blank, as far from threatening as could be imagined, but the man stopped dead. He didn't raise his hands, but he held his arms out to the sides and spread his fingers. He wore a khaki military uniform whose only adornments were rainbow shoulder patches and a rainbow-dyed tuft pinned to the left side of his forage cap.

"Lady Mundy," he said carefully, "my name's Chatterjee. I'd like to speak with you for a moment regarding your, that is the RCN, mission to our cluster."

He smiled. "Here in public is fine," he said. "But I won't raise my voice during some parts of the discussion."

Adele eyed him without bothering to reach into her pocket. A line of soldiers was more or less good-naturedly keeping the celebration in the square from spilling into the Hall proper, but the noise of the crowd would adequately cover normal speech from anyone but an eavesdropper with a parabolic microphone. Because the engaged columns of the vestibule were so deep, that putative microphone would have to be directly across from the people speaking—a circumstance which Adele could deal with very quickly if Tovera didn't do so first.

"All right, Colonel Chatterjee," Adele said. The man's uniform was unfamiliar, but the rank tabs—dragons displayed—were the ones which cluster forces had borrowed from Alliance practice. "I can give you a few minutes while I'm waiting for Admiral Leary to finish his meeting."

Rene Cazelet had been chatting with Vesey near the entrance to the vestibule. His eyes had flicked to Adele when Chatterjee approached; now he stepped toward them, apparently without taking leave of Vesey. She watched him walk away with an expression Adele couldn't describe.

Chatterjee seated himself to Adele's right. He glanced over his shoulder at Rene and said, "It's of course your business how widely you want this information disseminated, milady . . ."

"I appreciate your delicacy," said Adele as she gestured Rene back. She wasn't concerned at what the boy might hear; she'd found him as discreet as Tovera herself. Chatterjee was obviously concerned, though, and it was Adele's duty to gather information.

That was her duty and her whole being.

"I'm the chief military aide to Governor Radetsky of Skye," the colonel said, noticeably more relaxed. "And his friend of long standing, I'm pleased to say."

"Go on," Adele said. She'd taken her data unit out when she sat down. Her wands had been sorting for Chatterjee; now she added Radetsky and Skye as she listened.

"Five years ago Guarantor Porra settled military veterans on the South Continent of Skye," Chatterjee said. Three young men glanced toward the pair as they walked past, but their eyes didn't linger. They were probably clerks who'd decided that the celebrations permitted them to leave the office for the day. "The old settlers are enthusiastic for freedom, but not the new ones. There isn't much fighting, but we independence supporters've raised a division of two thousand men in case South Continent tries to invade."

"Go on," Adele repeated. Chatterjee was a Skye native, but in his youth—he was thirty-nine standard years old now—he'd been a lieutenant in the Alliance Army. Governor Radetsky was officially a general now, but unlike his aide he didn't have previous military experience.

"The Governor offers you a battalion of two hundred and fifty men," Chatterjee said. "They'd be under my command. We have transport as well, a former immigrant ship manned by spacers loyal to the governor. Just tell us when and where you'd like us to be."

Adele's wands stopped moving; she met Chatterjee's eyes. "Why?" she said.

"Conyers and Churchyard aren't a danger to Pelosi," Chatterjee said. "Nor to most of the other worlds that've joined the rebellion. They're a danger to us, though. With ships and troops from them, the colonists in the South can sweep over us. The Governor felt the quickest path to our own safety is to help you capture the Alliance bases before they organize to conquer us."

"To help Admiral Leary, you mean," Adele said, watching to see Chatterjee's expression when he heard the words.

"I believe that when I talk to you, Lady Mundy," he said calmly, "I'm talking to Admiral Leary."

She shrugged. "Near enough, I suppose," she said. "Why do you think we need troops from Skye? Since you're so well informed, you certainly know that the Cluster government has promised us a much larger force already."

Chatterjee laughed bitterly. "The government can promise you Pleasaunce and Blythe," he said, "and you'd have the same chance of getting them. Terry Dean won't let any real number of men out of his immediate control. They're his power base, you see. And if he did, you wouldn't be pleased with what you got. *I've* trained the battalion we're offering Commander Leary, milady."

"I see," Adele said. The words weren't simply a placeholder; she saw a great deal now. "If Admiral

Leary should wish to get in touch with you at some later point, how would he go about it?"

"Send a message to this address," Chatterjee said, offering Adele the printed card he'd been holding in his palm throughout the conversation. "Either I'll be there or they'll contact me."

Tovera reached past with her left hand, flashed the card's face to Adele who continued to hold her wands, and slipped it into the attaché case. It read

SKYE BENEVOLENT SOCIETY
55 Paterson Street East
Morning City

"A courier vessel will get from here to Skye in a day and a half," Chatterjee said. "The men are ready to board. It'll take the transport between four and five days to reach Conyers; perhaps a day longer to Churchyard."

Adele's fingers brought up a map display and highlighted the address. It was in the northern fringe of the city, not far from Morning Lake.

Chatterjee's grin almost split his broad, flat face. "Those are the times they tell me," he said. "I know nothing whatever about starships, Lady Mundy. But I *do* know troops, and mine are good ones."

"Thank you, Colonel," Adele said, nodding to Chatterjee in dismissal. "I'll see to it that the information gets to the proper quarters."

As Chatterjee rose, Adele allowed him a minuscule smile. "Colonel?" she said. "I shouldn't wonder if you got a chance to prove what you say about your soldiers."

CHAPTER 13

En route *to Churchyard*

Daniel rose from the *Ladouceur's* command console. The course was set and the cruiser's systems were operating within parameters. Within fairly reasonable parameters, in fact; the ship was in better condition than there'd been any reason to expect. The Financier Class's design failings seemed to have been mitigated by very solid construction standards. The ships were a peacetime series, of course.

"Captain, this is Dart Six," said Borries, the Chief Missileer. *"I'm in Bay B as in boy. I think you better come look at this, over."*

"On the way, Dart Six," said Daniel. "Break. Lieutenant Liu—"

The *Ladouceur's* current XO, now on duty in the BDC, Wai Liu was a young man from the Cinnabar protectorate of Rochefort. He'd joined the Bagarian service before the *Sissie's* arrival. His astrogation was a trifle better than Cory's, but Daniel wouldn't trust him in a fight till he'd seen a different side of the fellow than he had thus far.

"—I'm going down to the missile bays. You have the conn, but inform me if anything unusual happens. Six out."

Liu's "*Roger, Six*," sounded bored. That was legitimate, though Daniel hoped he'd react quickly enough if anything did crop up.

He grinned. Adele didn't bother to look up as Daniel trotted past the signals console, but an image of his face grinned from the top of her holographic display. Whether or not Liu kept him on top of events, Adele would.

Daniel turned into a Down companionway; the missile bays were on B and C Decks, while the Bridge was on G, the dorsal spine. Hogg was following him for no particular reason; their soft boots syncopated one another; like brushes on a drumhead, they drew whispers up and down the armored tube.

They didn't meet anyone in the companionway; the *Ladouceur* was undercrewed. Daniel wouldn't pretend to have full confidence in the three-quarters of the complement who hadn't served with him before, but he was sure most of them would be all right once they'd had time to work up under an RCN captain and RCN petty officers. He could only hope he'd have that time for working up, but he kept reminding himself that the enemy personnel in this cluster were at any rate no better.

The *Ladouceur*'s squadron-mates consisted not only of the *Independence* and *DeMarce*, but also eleven light vessels of the Bagarian Navy. These last were tramps of the sort that handled intra-cluster trade in peacetime; the largest was 1,000 tons, and two barely displaced 300.

They weren't even sparred heavily enough to serve as fast couriers, so under normal circumstances they had no real military purpose. Each could carry between three and six missiles, however, strapped to the outer hull. Working the sails would be even more difficult than usual, and the smaller vessels had been forced to lift with the missiles' reaction mass tanks empty. They'd been filled in orbit by the *Ladouceur*, whose thrust to weight ratio allowed her to rise from a gravity well carrying much greater incremental mass.

The B Deck hatch was latched open; rust streaked the mating surfaces. Daniel frowned, wondering if Pasternak had found time to check the seal of the cruiser's internal subdivisions. If the hull were damaged in action—hard maneuvering could open seams, let alone the risk from enemy missiles and ions—everybody aboard would have to shift into suits unless the damage could be isolated.

Daniel gave a wry smile. Well, in the event they might have to wear suits. Pasternak had enough on his plate in the Power Room. He couldn't be faulted if he let his duties as Chief of Ship go by the boards for the time being.

B Deck was bulk storage, which included two of the cruiser's four missile magazines. Crew members called to one another in a parallel corridor, their voices gibberish from echoes. The air on this level smelled of old food, old lubricant, and the faint bite of ozone.

Daniel's makeshift missile boats didn't have the targeting capacity or maneuverability to be useful in a ship-to-ship action, but they *could* dip into Churchyard's atmosphere and launch plasma missiles at ships tied to the quays. The base certainly had anti-starship defenses, but only in limited quantity: missiles capable of ripping ships from orbit cost more than these ragged tramps did. The Alliance commander couldn't safely expend them on light craft while three large warships waited just out of range.

The Bagarian squadron was to rendezvous off the unnamed seventh planet of the Churchyard system, a gas giant with no moons to confuse officers who weren't used to trying to identify other ships in vacuum. Daniel would marshal his little flock there, then make the short intra-system hop to Churchyard. His missile craft would bombard the harbor until the Alliance commander either surrendered or sent his warships up to fight.

Daniel grinned. He didn't expect the Alliance ships to fight. If they did, though, he couldn't think of a better way to give his raw squadron a stunning victory that would boost its confidence.

The internal hatch to B Magazine had been slid partly open. It was long enough that thirty-foot missiles could be dollied out and rolled to the aft magazines in event the tubes fed by B Magazine were out of service. Daniel hoped he'd never have to do that, because even with a crack crew it was a recipe for death and injury every time the ship changed the amount or angle of thrust. He'd try if he had to, of course.

The light craft carried a total of forty-six plasma missiles. The squadron's three heavy ships had only partial loads of High Drive missiles, so Daniel had split the remaining twenty-four bombardment weapons among them as reloads—half on the *Ladouceur* and six each on the converted freighters. It seemed to him that he had a good chance of destroying the Cluster Command's remaining ships, and an even better chance of frightening Churchyard Base into surrender.

Except—

"Captain," said Borries, standing in the hatchway and looking down the corridor, "we got a problem."

The Pellegrinian had a long face. He'd look like he was in mourning on the happiest day of his life, but this wasn't that day. "I been looking at these half-assed missiles we took aboard on Pelosi."

"Right, Borries," Daniel said, following as the missileer stepped into the magazine. A Bagarian spacer, originally from Mistral—Daniel couldn't remember his name, Robert Canedo or Caneta he thought—was already inside. "The reloads for the bombardment fleet."

The magazine was a wilderness of steel and hard lines. It'd originally been painted white, but generations of oil film and the friction of missiles, dollies, and spacers in hard suits had left it in layered gray shades picked out by patches of rust.

To its deck was welded a double rank of missile cradles, twelve and twelve, but only the forward set was filled. Borries had removed several plates from the round on the inboard end. Mechanics' lights glared into the openings, and tools littered the deck.

"I didn't realize these missiles had access ports," Daniel said, surprised at this level of effort from David Power. Captain Burke's plans didn't include such refinements, and nothing Daniel had seen on Pelosi would've caused him to complicate a project he was giving to the locals.

"They do if you got a diamond saw," said Borries

grimly. "Now, don't worry, Captain, I'll weld it back neater'n it was. Which won't be hard."

He gestured to the spacer with him. "Go on, Canedo," he said. "Tell the cap'n what you told me."

"Well, it's like this, sir," the fellow said nervously. "Look, I don't want you to think I'm not loyal to the Bagarian Republic, sir?"

Daniel frowned. He wouldn't have spoken, but Canedo had stopped with a statement his tone turned into a question. He obviously wasn't going to proceed without encouragement.

"I don't expect loyalty to the Bagarian Republic, Canedo," Daniel said. "I can assure you that the spacers I brought here in the *Sissie* aren't loyal to the Bagarians."

"Too right, sir," said Borries with an enthusiastic nod.

And true of me as well, spacers, Daniel thought, but it wouldn't do to say that. Aloud he continued, "I do expect you to do your job to my satisfaction and to the satisfaction of my officers. If you can manage that, then the Bagarian Republic is going to get a lot more than its money's worth out of you. Now, tell me what you know."

"Well, you see I'd been a gunner's mate on the *Vickie Lu* when the wogs grabbed her on Schumer's Pisspot," Canedo said. "The wogs let common spacers enlist, but since I had a rating they kept me behind barb wire even though I wasn't an Alliance citizen. After you lot arrived, though, Ship and Rig went through the camp and pulled out folks they figured were okay. And I *am*, sir, I swear it!"

"Go on," Daniel said, smiling faintly. He'd made

Woetjans and Pasternak responsible for crewing the heavy ships of the squadron. He had enough to do himself without worrying about the crew situation unless somebody brought it to him as a problem. His senior warrant officers were too competent and too proud to do that.

"Well, you see," Canedo said, "what the wogs put us prisoners to doing was making these missiles—"

He rang his knuckles on the partially opened round beside him.

"—if you want to call 'em that. And sir, there's some of the crew from the *Vickie Lu* as think the sun rises outa Guarantor Porra's butt every morning. I told Mister Borries that—"

"He's got missile training, Cap'n," Borries said eagerly. "I'd like to make him my striker, if you don't mind."

"Granted," Daniel said. "Go on, Canedo."

"Well, Mister Borries thought we oughta take a look for ourself. And we did."

"Take a look here, Cap'n," Borries said, leaning into the access port and pointing with his right index finger. Canedo reached in through the next opening to the left and lifted the trouble light so that it better illuminated the feed line to which the missileer was pointing. "Just *look* at this!"

The line was extruded from light metal; not as good as copper or the high-density polymer which RCN missiles would use, but adequate for the present purpose. The lines wouldn't have time to fracture from vibration in the intended use.

Somebody'd crushed this one flat in the middle with a pair of heavy pliers. No water would flow through it to feed the thruster.

"I figure they're all like this, sir," Borries said. "This or something else as bad. Only I wanted to tell you before I started taking the rest of 'em apart."

"You did right, Borries," Daniel said. "And you did very well, Canedo."

After a momentary pause he said, "You can fix them? I'll tell Pasternak to give you technicians if you like."

"I guess Canedo and me can do it, Cap'n," the missileer said. His expression didn't look happy so much as it did anguished, but Daniel was willing to bet it was meant for a smile. "I'll tell Ship if we need help, then."

"Then I'll get out of your way, Borries," Daniel said, turning on his heel. As he started back toward the bridge, began whistling, *When I was a young man, young man, young man* . . .

He could either become furious at Master David Power, whose fiddle had saved him a few hundred florins in labor charges and bid fair to cost his nation a major victory; or he could smile cheerfully because his make-do crew was shaping up so nicely.

He was Daniel Leary: he smiled.

Then I met a young girl, young girl, young girl . . . he whistled.

Above Churchyard

Adele sat poised at her console. Because she used her own data unit as an interface, she wasn't handicapped when she changed from the *Sissie*'s recently upgraded electronics to the cruiser's much older systems.

Realistically, differences in displays, input devices, and operating systems never slowed her down when she was on the track of information; not to a degree that any onlooker would've noticed it. Still, she was a conservative person and would rather have things the same than not.

"Preparing to extract from the Matrix in thirty seconds," Liu announced from the BDC.

Adele felt the quiver of charges building as the *Ladouceur* neared the end of its short hop from the outskirts of the Churchyard System. The *Independence* and *DeMarce* had reached the rendezvous without difficulty; that was almost a given with Vesey and Blantyre plotting the courses. Only seven of the eleven light craft had arrived, though Daniel seemed to think they'd be sufficient. She smiled: indeed, he'd said he'd be amazed to find as many as nine.

Adele smiled more broadly; almost as broadly as what an ordinary person would call a smile. One change that she didn't in the least regret was being adopted into the RCN family. There were costs to the association, physical and mental ones both, but Daniel Leary and the RCN had saved her life. More important, they'd given her a reason to live.

"Extracting-g-g . . ." moaned a voice dehumanized by the process of returning to the sidereal universe. The interior lights sharpened, the displays swelled to life now that the *Ladouceur* wasn't in a bubble universe shut off from every other human artifact, and the five turrets squealed as Sun slewed them toward real targets.

Adele didn't care what Sun did or Daniel did, and for that matter she didn't care very much about whether a missile was about to blast the *Ladouceur* into dust and ions. Other people, friends and enemies alike, had duties for which they were responsible; that was fine. Adele Mundy would focus on *her* duty, which right now involved learning everything possible about Alliance ships on and about Churchyard.

The *Ladouceur* was 103,000 miles out from the planet and displaying very little proper motion to it. Daniel had placed them a little east to the perpendicular of Hafn Teobald, the Alliance naval base, so that Churchyard's rotation would keep the target in view for the longest possible time even if the cruiser didn't maneuver.

That was Daniel's problem; Adele's first act was to tap into the planetary network of weather satellites. That gave her day and night coverage of Churchyard's surface at a level of detail that was more than adequate for the present purposes. The system could be shut down but probably wouldn't be, at least not before she'd found another path to continuous surveillance.

With the future provided for, Adele surveyed the ships in harbor below. That hadn't been *her* first priority because she knew it'd be Daniel's. He was better at optical identification than she was anyway. In this case, the electronic signatures would only confirm what the captain'd already learned.

Three freighters, one of them gutted for use as a warehouse and accommodation ship, were anchored parallel to the harbor's northern shore. In two of the six slips on the south side were a large modern destroyer, the *Cesare Rossarol*, and the missile boat *S81*.

The latter was a 300-tonne vessel built to do the job for which Daniel had jury-rigged the lighter vessels in his squadron. It could carry two High Drive missiles on external mountings, and unlike the Bagarian country craft, it had full targeting equipment.

Adele'd seen enough space battles by now to know that a pair of missiles wasn't a threat to a ship which could maneuver normally; doctrine recommended use of missile boats in squadrons of six or twelve, making possible a volley which could in theory overwhelm the defenses even of a battleship. In the present case, *S81*'s missiles weren't mounted. A quick dip into her electronic log suggested that General Auguste, the Commander of Cluster Forces, had been using the ship as a courier to and from Conyers.

The remainder of the Bagarian squadron appeared in bits and pieces—the *Independence* and a moment later the *DeMarce*, then three light craft, followed by two more light craft. Adele focused on entering Hafn Teobald's main database now that she was sure there were no orbiting Alliance warships, but she was glad to note on an inset that Cazelet, using the otherwise-empty console across the compartment, was keeping track of friendly vessels.

Surely the final two ships couldn't have gotten lost in the course of an intrasystem transit, could they?

Of course they could. Some of the Bagarian captains had as little astrogation experience as Signals Officer Mundy did, and they were using hardware which hadn't been checked ahead of time by Commander Leary. But with luck the ships weren't permanently lost; and anyway, Daniel'd make do. Daniel always made do.

Adele found the information she needed and forwarded it to the command console. Over a two-way link she said, "Captain, the base has a triple launcher for anti-starship missiles. There're three more missiles to reload in a bunker attached to the launching pit. The launcher's active, and it's isolated from the headquarters communications system that I can enter. I'm afraid that I'm not able to attack the launcher. Ah, electronically."

She stumbled over the thought, remembering the pit on Dunbar's World that she'd shot her way into. That wouldn't be possible here either, because the *Ladouceur* couldn't land close enough to permit a ground assault.

Razor ribbon singing as bullets cut the tensioned strands.

Osmium pellets ricocheting from posts like streaks of neon light.

Faces framed in her sight picture.

"*Signals, are you all right?*" Daniel's voice was saying. "*I repeat, what's the status of the two warships, over?*"

"S-sorry," Adele said. "Sorry, Daniel, I . . . It doesn't matter, sorry. The *S81* is fully crewed and was scheduled to lift for Conyers within the hour with dispatches. The *Rossarol* has only a skeleton crew though it seems to be fit for operations as soon as it's manned. Over."

She'd remembered to close her speech according to RCN protocol. Good, good . . . but that didn't make up for the way she'd drifted into nightmare when people were depending on her.

Though Adele's left side occasionally knotted where the bullet'd hit her during the assault on Dunbar's World, the physical twinge wasn't the worst damage she'd received that night. Everything has costs, and the benefits of being part of the RCN family were worth everything she'd paid thus far—and everything she'd continue paying to the day she died.

She smiled faintly. She'd heard Sissies bragging about how Mistress Mundy'd cleared the missile pit, putting two rounds through the same eye of every member of the launch crew who'd dared to show himself. That was pretty much true, as a matter of fact.

And no one except possibly Daniel suspected what it cost her in the hours before dawn to have done that. To have done so many things of that nature, because they were part of the job.

Not complaining was part of the job too, at least as she saw it. She was Mundy of Chatsworth.

"Roger, Signals," Daniel said calmly. *"Link me to all ships in the squadron soonest and inform me when you're ready, over."*

Adele frowned. *Does he think I'm too worn out to do my job?* Aloud she said, "You're connected to the whole squadron as soon as you speak the keyword, Captain Leary. Would you prefer that I manually connect you? Out."

She meant, "Over." It was all childish nonsense anyway, boys playing games.

"Squadron, this is Squadron Six," Daniel said instead of—pointlessly—answering her. *"I'm sending the approach information and order of attack to the bombardment force."*

Adele transmitted his words on 15.5 KHz, the frequency to which the whole squadron was supposed to be tuned, as well as via individual laser heads aimed at each of the other vessels. She could guarantee that a modulated laser painted each Bagarian ship, but in her wildest dreams she didn't imagine that all of them had working receivers or that they'd bothered to turn them on if they did.

"*The initial order of attack,*" Daniel continued, "*is* Columbine, *Forsyte 14, and* Stager Brothers. *These leading vessels will rendezvous with the* Ladouceur, Independence, *and* DeMarce *respectively after they've launched their initial loads.* Clinton *and* Burke Trading, *wait for further orders. Are there any questions, over?*"

"*Who the hell do you think you are to be giving me orders, boy?*" said a voice. Adele identified it as Captain Michael Stout of the *Stager Brothers*, a 600-ton tramp whose plating rattled at anchor. She slugged the information to the command console in text. "*I'll go in when I decide I'll go in. Out!*"

"*Stager Six, this is Squadron Six,*" Daniel replied mildly. "*I sincerely hope you'll attack when your orders from the commanding admiral direct you to attack, Captain Stout. Your vessel is within 18,000 miles of the flagship, and our guns are trained on you. Do you understand, over?*"

There was a hiss of static across the shortwave spectrum: the 800-ton *Columbine* was braking hard with her High Drive to drop her into Churchyard's gravity well. Almost simultaneously the squadron's two missing ships reentered the sidereal universe.

Adele fed the information to the command console and went back to eavesdropping on the increasingly panicked Alliance HQ. The personnel on duty were beginning to realize what was happening. It wasn't her place to judge, but Adele allowed herself a tiny smile.

Things seemed to be going according to plan.

CHAPTER 14

Above Churchyard

Adele watched the *Stager Brothers* begin its attack run. Despite Captain Stout's prickliness, his approach through the top levels of the atmosphere was as smooth as that of any starship could be.

She smiled. Perhaps being prickly was a necessary part of being good. There were certainly people who'd found Adele Mundy difficult over the years, and even Daniel ruffled feathers with his focus on accomplishing the mission regardless of proprieties.

Ever since the *Columbine* came alongside, the *Ladouceur* had been ringing like the interior of a steel drum. A warship in action was always noisy, but this time the missiles bumping down the rollerway were being transferred to the smaller ship rather than sliding into the cruiser's own launching tubes. Woetjans had all her riggers on the hull, manhandling the projectiles across the gap separating the ships and clamping them into the *Columbine*'s hull mounts.

Adele didn't imagine the effort was going to be

of any use, though. Certainly none of the previous attacks had been.

"*Adele?*" said Daniel unexpectedly. She'd carefully avoided interrupting him at a time when he had his hands full. Out of squeamishness she hadn't even echoed the command display as she sometimes did from curiosity. Since things were going so badly, it would've felt to her like staring at a friend who'd just upset the table at a formal dinner.

"Yes, Daniel?" she said, replying on the same two-way link and pleased to ignore protocol.

The *Stager Brothers* had made two circuits of Churchyard, cutting progressively deeper as if shaving thin slices from the atmosphere. As Stout started his third orbit, he launched his four plasma missiles. This was no part of Adele's job, but simply as a matter of interest she'd expanded an image of the vessel coming around the curve of the planet.

The only communications that she had to monitor right now were the excited chatter of both the Alliance and Bagarian forces. The Alliance voices were predictably in a better humor, but nothing important was being said by either side.

"*I'm going to be taking charge of the* Columbine *for the next attack,*" Daniel said. "*Can you keep me in direct touch with the entire squadron?*"

One of the *Stager Brothers'* missiles didn't appear to separate until the ship drove up through the atmosphere again on gimbaled thrusters. The missile continued for a few moments on a ballistic course, then began to tumble; it quickly broke up.

"One moment," said Adele, because she didn't give Daniel a certain answer without knowing *everything* about the *Columbine*'s commo suite. She'd never had occasion to learn that information before now—

But she'd gathered it, because it was information and that was what she did, gather information against need. In the particular instance she'd thought knowing the particulars of the Bagarian ships might help her communicate with them, though in the event she'd decided that the 20-meter band was all she could count on.

The thrusters of the *Stager Brothers'* remaining three missiles lighted. One blew up three seconds later, rocking the ship that launched it. The blast didn't appear to do serious damage, but Captain Stout's torrent of profanity was justifiable if pointless.

Adele brought up the data on the *Columbine* and considered it coldly. She smiled: she did everything coldly. Even when others might think that she'd lost her temper, she was really quite cold inside.

In the particular instance, the data were better than she'd feared it might be. She said, "Daniel, the *Columbine* has a working laser communicator. It's a single-head device, but the *Ladouceur* can retransmit to the rest of the squadron without a noticeable lag. Oh!"

"Is there a problem, Signals?" Daniel said. He remained on the private channel, but he'd slipped into formality to jog her out of her silence.

The problem is that I have to be at both ends of the transmission in order to make the relay work.

The thruster of the *Stager Brothers'* third missile cut off abruptly. Without power for its gyroscope, the missile wobbled, swapped ends, and tore itself into a shower of fragments. They blazed white with the friction of their passage through the atmosphere.

Instead of replying to Daniel directly, Adele switched manually to the command channel and said, "Cory, I'll be away from my console for a considerable length of time. Until I return, can you relay laser transmissions from the *Columbine* to the rest of the squadron if I set the system up for you? Over."

"Ah," said Cory. *"I'm sure I can, sir, over."*

"Negative, Officer Mundy," Daniel said. He didn't exactly shout, but he meant to be heard and obeyed. *"Your presence with the* Ladouceur's *sensor and commo suites will be absolutely necessary if something unpredictable occurs. You will* not *be leaving the bridge. If that means a gap in my control of the rest of the squadron, then that's still the better choice, over."*

The *Stager Brothers'* last missile began to describe a slow spiral. Adele was too busy to magnify her image of it, but she'd seen several rounds from the *Columbine* and *Forsyte 14* fail in the same fashion. Exhaust had eaten a hole in the thruster nozzle so that plasma was pushing sideways as well as straight back. As Adele'd learned to expect, the missile carved increasingly wider circles until a gush of flame blew the whole back end away.

All sixteen missiles from the three Bagarian ships had failed before they got within ten miles of the surface of Churchyard. Adele didn't know what Daniel thought he could accomplish since the problem wasn't in the way the rounds had been aimed, but that wasn't her job to determine.

"Captain, I don't think Cory can keep the *Columbine's* sender focused on us, on the *Ladouceur*, if both ships are maneuvering," she said. "He *can* handle the relay, that's automated. I—"

"*Captain Leary?*" Rene Cazelet interrupted. Adele knew Rene'd added himself to the command channel that linked all the commissioned and warrant officers aboard, but she hadn't given the matter any thought when she moved the discussion there to include Cory. "*I can direct the head manually. I don't mean to imply criticism of Mister Cory; your Cinnabar naval equipment is automated, but I trained in the merchant service with apparatus very like what the* Columbine *has. Over.*"

"*Adele?*" Daniel said, back on the two-way link.

Adele looked at the image of Rene Cazelet on her display. She knew that she could meet his eyes directly by just looking up and glancing across the bridge, but she preferred the electronic semblance. His expression was clear and open; and underneath that, afraid. He was afraid that she wouldn't think he was competent.

Which meant that *he* really thought that he could do the job. Well, he had more data on the subject that she did, so she might as well accept his judgment.

"All right," Adele said. "Cazelet, accompany Captain Leary to the *Columbine*. Keep a real-time connection with me, and do everything else he tells you to. Over."

Or did she mean, "Out"?

"*Yes, mistress!*" the boy said as he leaped from his console. He was beaming as he strode to the suit locker in the rotunda beyond the bridge hatch.

"*Lieutenant Liu, you have the conn,*" Daniel said as he rose. Hogg got up also. Daniel added, "*Hogg, you can stay aboard the* Ladouceur. *Space may be tight on the* Columbine's *bridge, and there's nothing for you to do, over.*"

"Sure there is, young master," Hogg said, speaking

loudly over the sound of the air handler. "That wog captain may not want to give you his seat, admiral's pips or no."

As he spoke, Hogg pulled his big folding knife from a pocket. It had a handguard in the form of a knuckleduster.

"I'll come along to reason with him," Hogg concluded, tossing the knife—still closed—in the air and catching it again.

"Captain Julian, gentlemen," said Daniel as he and Hogg stepped out of the airlock. They'd taken their helmets off before the hatch undogged, so he didn't have to struggle with that task while the three men in *Columbine*'s forward compartment stared at him in surprise. He hadn't warned Julian by radio because he shared Hogg's opinion that the Bagarian captain wouldn't be in agreement with his plan.

"What're you doing here?" David Julian demanded. He struggled awkwardly to rise from his console. It was placed in the far bow facing inward, so that the captain seated there could see everybody in the forward compartment.

"I'm going to take the *Columbine* in on this run, Captain Julian," Daniel said cheerily. "I regret the suddenness of this."

In fact Daniel regretted a lot of things, certainly including the fact that he was cutting corners in a fashion that could only be described as discourteous to a fellow spacer. Admiral James and the Bagarian Republic both depended on clearing the cluster of Alliance bases, though, and this seemed to be the only way to do that in a reasonable length of time.

"You'll do nothing of the sort!" Julian said in a scandalized tone. "This is my ship. I own her!"

Daniel stepped around the console, noting with relief that the seat was so oversized that he could use it without stripping off his hard suit. That was a common feature on tramp freighters, since the crew could rarely depend on the climate control system or the vessel remaining airtight either one. If the controls couldn't be operated by people wearing suits, they couldn't be operated at all.

Captain Julian wasn't suited up, but he filled and overflowed the console; Daniel instinctively sucked in his gut. Mentally, he murmured a promise to *really* cut back on his meals. Mind, he'd made the same promise every time he'd put on his Dress Whites during the past six months.

"*He most certainly is* not *the owner of the* Columbine!" Adele's voice rattled from the implant in Daniel's left ear. "*He sold the ship to the government for one point five million ostrads, on the basis of a valuation by Petrus Lascaux. Who appears to be Julian's brother-in-law!*"

"I'm very sorry, Captain," Daniel said. He didn't suppose he sounded any sorrier than he felt. "Nonetheless you knew this might happen when you sold the *Columbine* to the government for one and a half million ostrads."

Because Julian had risen to confront Daniel, the console's empty seat was between them. Daniel set his armored right foot on it, knowing the hard suit trumped the Bagarian's greater bulk.

The information from Adele didn't change anything but the words, though. Daniel would've commandeered a private vessel if he'd had to, counting on his admiral's rank to justify the action; or if not that, then success wiping the slate clean. If he *didn't* succeed, he'd probably be dead and the question of whether he'd committed piracy wouldn't matter.

The airlock cycled again. It only held two suited figures at a time, so Adele's friend Cazelet had to come through after Daniel and Hogg had.

Julian clenched his fist and said, "You can get your Cinnabar ass off this ship, buddy, or—"

"Or what, lard-butt?" Woetjans said. "You're talking to Commander Leary. That means you keep a civil tongue in your head or somebody's likely to pull it out!"

"Who're *you*?" Julian said in a tone of wonderment. He lowered his arm, all bluster vanished.

Daniel half-rotated his body; the rigid suit kept him from glancing over his shoulder as he'd have done in street clothes. Cazelet was there, all right, but the bosun had entered ahead of him. She held the short come-along she'd been using to lever the plasma missiles into their cradles on the hull.

"Six, the kid here—"

She pointed a thumb over her shoulder; Cazelet hopped back. Behind them both, the airlock was cycling again.

"—told us what you were pulling. We sent his riggers onto the *Laddie*, but me'n four a my crew are gonna handle the rig while you're aboard. Or handle any bloody thing at all, right?"

"Right!" said Daniel briskly. "Captain Julian, if you'll make yourself as comfortable as you can on one of the benches, we'll take care of business so that you can have your ship back."

Dasi and Barnes were the next pair of Sissies out of the airlock. Like the bosun, they carried the tools they'd been using out on the hull.

"We cast this tub loose from the *Laddie*, Six," Barnes said cheerfully. "Say, we going to put it to the wogs again?"

Dasi glanced at the two spacers who'd been in the compartment when Daniel arrived. "My buddy means Alliance wogs, not you lot," he said. He pursed his full lips in consideration. "That's right, ain't it, Six?"

"Perfectly correct, Dasi," Daniel said, checking the little freighter's systems. Cazelet settled himself on the console's jump seat; the controls on that side were already live, probably by accident.

The Power Room with the fusion bottle and a crew of three was the *Columbine*'s only other pressurized compartment. The engineer hadn't opened the hatch to see what was going on in the fore cabin and Daniel didn't see any reason to disturb him.

The aft two-thirds of the hull was partitioned into three separate holds, empty now except for crew stores. The total volume was slight. Bulk cargo would be slung externally, much as the missiles were being carried now.

The nozzle of Thruster Three was paper thin; the *Columbine* could make this attack using only the fore and aft pairs, but to lift with a full cargo requiring all six thrusters seemed a recipe for disaster. According to their internal diagnostics the four High Drive motors were fine, but a scan of the log indicated that Starboard Aft didn't develop better than seventy percent of its rated impulse. That could mean the pump was failing, the feed line had a blockage, or for that matter that there was an instrumentation flaw. Again, it didn't matter for now.

Sayer and Braun shambled out of the airlock. Anja Braun, a stocky woman who could kick her heel through a brick wall, looked at Woetjans and asked, "What you want us t'do, Chief?"

"Sit your butts down till I tell you," Woetjans growled. She slapped the come-along into the palm of her left glove. It was an idle gesture, but the two Bagarian spacers winced.

"Look," muttered Captain Julian, staring at his fingers interlaced over his heavy belly. "You can make me the goat if you like, I can't fight you. But it wasn't my approach that screwed the pooch on the first attack. The missiles're bloody useless, it's that simple."

"I agree that you're not to blame, Julian," Daniel said. He spread his hands over the console's virtual keyboard, making sure that he was aware of its subtle differences both from the *Sissie* and from the cruiser he'd been commanding these past few weeks. "It's simply a case of, well—"

He shrunk the display and looked at Julian until the fellow turned and their eyes met.

"—if this attack fails, there'll be a move to crucify the foreigner who planned it, not so? And if I'm going to be hung for failing, then it's bloody well going to be *me* who fails."

In the air before him COMMUNICATION ESTABLISHED pulsed in green letters. Daniel brought up his display and said, "*Ladouceur*, this is Columbine Six. Can you hear me, over?"

"*Of course I can hear you, Columbine Six,*" Adele's voice rasped from the console's speakers. "*If you want

*to address the squadron, just verbally key them and
the relay will work automatically. Otherwise, you'll
be speaking through me. As usual. Over."*

"Roger, Signals," Daniel said, grinning as he so often
did when dealing with Adele. "Ship, prepare to attack."

He cleared his throat, then said, "Squadron, this
is Squadron Six. *Columbine* is taking the place of
Heartsease in the attack rota. *Heartsease*, set up your
attack to follow that of *Columbine*. Six out."

Daniel pressed the EXECUTE button; the High Drive
motors fired on preset angles, dropping the *Columbine*
toward the surface of Churchyard. *Let's see how long
the Alliance garrison continues to laugh . . .*

Freighters didn't have true attack boards; Daniel'd
adapted the pilotry display as if he were setting up a
landing. That was basically what he was doing, except
that if things worked out it'd be six plasma missiles landing in Hafn Teobald instead of the *Columbine* herself.

The vessel began to slide into the atmosphere. The
air wasn't thick enough to buffet the hull yet, but Daniel
heard the *ping*s of antimatter in the exhaust disintegrating gas molecules in the throats of the motors. He
didn't switch out of High Drive yet because he didn't
trust the plasma thrusters.

Daniel expected Captain Julian to complain, but
the Bagarian simply sat with a glum expression. He
might also stay long in High Drive on his approaches,
for the same reason.

When the pinging increased in frequency to that of
water coming to a boil, Daniel shut down the High
Drive, waited three seconds on a ballistic course, and
finally lit the thrusters. They came on line raggedly,
as he'd more or less expected.

He'd been afraid of a late power blip from one of the motors. If by bad luck only one thruster was making power at the moment when a High Drive motor fired late, the combined impulse could rotate a small vessel like the *Columbine* on her axis. Better a long freefall than to take that needless risk.

"*Columbine Six, the antiship battery at Hafn Teobald is tracking you,*" Adele said in a cool tone. "*This was the battery's practice with earlier runs as well. None of the Alliance communications indicate an intention to launch this time either.*" A pause. "*Ah, Ladouceur out.*"

Daniel smiled. It no longer struck him as odd that in the middle of an attack he was getting reports on the enemy's internal communications.

The *Columbine* was well into the first circuit of her attack and was rocking noticeably. The choppiness wasn't as bad as he'd have expected on the *Princess Cecile*, though the corvette was a somewhat heavier vessel; the outboard-mounted missiles acted as roll dampers.

What would Admiral Vocaine say if I recommended that he recruit librarians for signals duty in all RCN vessels?

Daniel began to laugh. Julian spluttered something which Daniel couldn't make out over the snarl of air jumbling about the rigging. The sound may not have been words at all, of course, just generalized amazement. Woetjans clapped the Bagarian on the shoulder and looked smug.

They'd completed their second circuit and started into a third, going deeper than the previous runs. The *Columbine* was slowing, so the roughness wasn't noticeably worse despite the thicker atmosphere.

"*Columbine Six, Command Headquarters has put the*

missile battery on launch warning but haven't directed them to launch." Adele's voice trembled. *"Under current protocols they won't launch unless the target drops beneath three thousand meters. Over."*

"Roger, Signals," Daniel said as his fingers adjusted flow to Thrusters One and Two, raising the bow slightly. "We're not going to come close to that, over."

The warble in Adele's voice was an artifact of atmospheric distortion on the laser signal. An RCN warship's software would've reshaped the signal into its original form, but the *Columbine* had nothing so sophisticated. Well, she didn't need it; at least with Cazelet handling commo duties, the freighter's rig was more than adequate.

"Ship," Daniel said, "prepare to launch. Launching one—"

The ship bucked into a roll to port as the lower starboard missile separated.

"Launching two—"

Two was the upper port missile, thrown clear by the ship's rotation.

"Three—

"Four—

"Five—

"Six—

"Ship, we're pulling up!" Daniel cried as he slammed keys to activate the preset course. "RCN forever!"

His Sissies cheered over the roaring thrusters. Maybe some of the Bagarians did too, though it wasn't the most politic thing to have shouted now that Daniel had time to think about it.

Bloody hell, they were in the middle of a battle. The six missiles they'd just launched were running straight and true as the *Columbine* lifted back out of Churchyard's atmosphere.

"RCN forever!" Daniel repeated. This time he was sure the Bagarian spacers were cheering along with his own.

Adele noticed the next of the Bagarian ships dropping into the atmosphere while the *Columbine* was only beginning her ascent. She didn't know whether or not that was a problem, so she said, "Columbine Six, the *Heartsease* is attacking already. Over."

"*Thank you*, Ladouceur," Daniel said, his voice a little strained. He was accelerating hard, of course. "*I've got them on my display. I didn't intend such close separations, but I guess it's all right so long as one of us knows what he's doing. Six out.*"

The jabbering on the ground wasn't quite as boastfully contented as it'd been an hour earlier, but the Alliance garrison wasn't really worried. The *Columbine* had driven deeper into the atmosphere than the five runs that'd preceded this one, and now the *Heartsease* was coming in immediately on the *Columbine*'s heels.

Neither was a threat on the face of it, given the complete failure of the attack to this point. They were changes, though, and nobody likes to see a change when everything's been going well. Especially when the situation involves other people shooting at you.

Since the *Columbine* was out of the battle until it reloaded, the antiship battery shifted its tracking to the *Heartsease*. The latter was one of the smaller Bagarian vessels and carried only three missiles. It'd been a late arrival, and though it appeared to receive signals, it hadn't emitted any since the seventh-planet rendezvous.

In past years Adele would've assumed the ship's transmitter had gone out, but she'd seen enough of fringe-world navies to realize that the captain might be in a snit and refusing to respond verbally. That would be insane, of course, but it was by no means impossible.

The *Columbine*'s six rounds had been tracking smoothly, but the second one launched slowly diverged from the path of the others. There wasn't anything obviously wrong with it; perhaps its gyrocompass had gone awry. Still, if the others—

The fifth missile dived straight downward, splashing into the ocean half the planetary circumference short of Hafn Teobald. Adele felt a wash of disappointment.

Daniel had done all he could. Nobody was successful all the time, not even the most brilliant officer in the RCN. There'd be another way to overcome the Alliance forces, there was always another way. Daniel wouldn't stop—they'd none of them stop—until they'd found a way to—

The *Columbine*'s first missile plunged into the Alliance base, striking the *S81* amidships. There was a huge white flash, the friction of steel hitting steel at high velocity. The boat's hull sank, dragging the outriggers with it. An underwater blast emptied the slip momentarily of water and demolished one of the concrete piers.

The sea gushed back; an outrigger bobbed to the surface. Steam drifted across the harbor on the light breeze, the cloud expanding slowly.

Adele smiled in self-mockery. She should've given Daniel more credit. Though assuming failure as she'd just done wasn't a problem so long as she went ahead with her tasks regardless. As, of course, she always did.

High Drive missiles were expected to be on a ballistic course at impact, so they didn't have guidance systems. Despite their relative simplicity, the Bagarian plasma missiles *did* have sensor-activated controls. They homed on modulated laser signals reflecting from the target. In this case the laser designators were on the *Ladouceur*, not on the ships launching the missiles.

Given how crude the missiles were, Adele had wondered if the guidance system could possibly work well enough to matter. Apparently it would.

The third missile—the second was off-course, thirty miles to the west of Hafn Teobald—had been aimed at the antiship battery. Instead it slammed into the center of the tidal pond behind the site. Reflection from the water must've confused the homing system.

Adele's smile twitched. The shrieking terror of the battery captain talking to Alliance HQ was worth something, though.

The fourth missile hit Alliance Headquarters; the center of the sprawling, U-shaped building, unfortunately, since Adele by now knew that the real command center was in a bunker under the north wing. Nonetheless, it was very satisfying to watch the magnified image of the walls shattering in a pall of pulverized concrete. The roof of plastic sheeting fell in and began to burn.

The final missile was aimed at the *Cesare Rossarol*; likely one or both of those which failed had targeted the vessel also. The cloud from the *S81*'s ruptured fusion bottle drifted over the destroyer, not concealing it but providing a medium to reflect the laser illuminator. The incoming missile spiked the center of the false bull's-eye and plunged into the far wall of the slip beyond the *Rossarol*'s.

Chunks of concrete flew in all directions. The destroyer pitched and bucked, but apart from the shaking it must be unharmed.

The *Heartsease* was starting her second circuit. Adele's interest in the attack had always been secondary to her duty of listening to intercepted Alliance communications. Now she manually keyed the 20-meter transmitter and shouted, "*Heartsease*, change direction! They're about to launch at you. Stop your attack now, stop!"

A plasma missile separated from the *Heartsease*. The ship rocked and threw off a second missile.

"*Heartsease*, pull up or do something! They're going to—"

The blast of an antiship missile ripped a huge divot from the ground behind the rotating launcher. The projectile itself was a needle glinting in the sunlight; shock diamonds formed in back of its triple nozzles, and far behind swelled a white blanket as the borate exhaust plume absorbed moisture from the air.

"Pull up, you fools!" Adele screamed. "Dodge, do something!"

She wasn't sure that the *Heartsease* would be able to do anything that'd help it survive. Inertia and air resistance might be binding it into a practically fixed course. But the crew ought to try instead of going on with what was effectively a march to the scaffold.

The third plasma missile dropped away from the

Bagarian ship which shuddered as its captain started to pull up at the end of his attack run. The Alliance missile spitted it like an ice pick through an egg. The round depended on velocity, not an explosive warhead; it continued to scream upward into the stratosphere as a thin silver streak.

The *Heartsease* flew apart, wrecked by its own speed once it'd been gutted. Chunks of hull and rigging battered each other to fragments that rained toward the surface. The initial impact had probably killed the whole crew; regardless, nothing human—even wearing a hard suit—could survive the hundred-thousand-foot fall.

Adele's face was grim. She'd tried to warn them, but they hadn't listened. It wasn't her fault, not as anybody else would judge blame.

Besides, people die in wars. She'd killed a lot of them herself. . . .

One of the missiles from the *Heartsease* dropped; its thruster hadn't lighted. The second blew up after thirty seconds of operation. The third curved into a helical course that'd probably be twenty miles in diameter by the time it landed somewhere in the ocean west of Hafn Teobald.

"*Squadron, this is Squadron Six,*" Daniel said crisply. "*Well done, spacers, we've got their measure now. One more attack will do the job, but this time the entire bombardment flotilla will go in together and swamp the defenses. At the same time, the* Ladouceur, *Independence and* DeMarce *will approach at low level. The garrison'll panic, I expect, and if they don't we'll burn them out with plasma cannon regardless of what the bombardment missiles—*"

"Like hell we will, you bloody Cinnabar madman!"
Captain Seward shouted in fury. *"You're just trying to
get us all killed so that we can't tell the government
that your notion of shooting down at Churchyard
was a waste of time. I'm going back to Pelosi, and
when I get there I'll call for you to be removed for
unfitness. Out!"*

The *Stager Brothers* had reloaded with plasma
missiles from the *Sacred Independence* while Daniel
was attacking with the *Columbine*. Now it began to
accelerate, its High Drive motors stabbing blue-white
sparks into vacuum.

"Stager Six, this is Squadron Six," Daniel said
sharply. The *Columbine* was on what the Plot Position
Indicator predicted to be an approach course with the
Ladouceur. *"Shut down your motors soonest, Captain
Stout. We'll be attacking all together after I work out
courses, over."*

Stout didn't answer; instead the bead marking
Stager Brothers faded off the PPI. Stout had fled
from the sidereal universe.

The other small ships were vanishing also. Adele had
seen how long it took their captains to plot a course;
it seemed likely that all they were doing was getting
out of the immediate vicinity of the *Ladouceur*'s heavy
cannon. None of them directly addressed Daniel or
the cruiser; they were simply leaving.

"Admiral Leary," said Hoppler of the *Independence*.
It and the *DeMarce* were accelerating to gain use-
ful velocity that they could multiply in the Matrix.
*"Because of a serious leak in my reaction mass tanks,
I'm forced to return to Pelosi for repairs. I hope to
greet you there soon on your arrival so that we can*

plan further operations against the common enemy. Hoppler out."

Sun turned from his console with a look of anguish on his face. "Mistress!" he said to Adele. "They're rats, they're running out on us! Can I ring their bell while they're still this side of the Matrix?"

"You may not," Adele said sharply. She didn't bother to say that the question was beyond her authority: it *wasn't* beyond her authority, her real authority at least. There wasn't a Sissie who wouldn't do as Mistress Mundy ordered, Daniel included. "We'll serve them out later, Sun, but not in that fashion."

She wasn't sure precisely how they'd even the score. Daniel wasn't the sort to send Hogg and Tovera to assassinate the captains who'd ignored his orders and fled. He wouldn't ask Lady Mundy to challenge the cowards to duels, either; but if he did ask that, she'd shoot Hoppler, Seward, and the rest of them down with as little compunction as she'd killed a hundred other men and women in the course of her duty.

It didn't bother her in the least while she was doing it: she saw only a blur in her sight picture. The features didn't appear until late into the darkness, when the dead came to speak with her again.

The *DeMarce* faded from the PPI; the *Independence* was already gone and so were most of the light craft. The *Forsyte 14* suddenly reappeared within the display, but that was simply because it hadn't had enough velocity in the sidereal universe to get any distance even with the help of the Matrix. It was accelerating at what appeared to be its maximum rate, now, and it didn't reply to Adele's attempts to raise it on short wave and laser. She didn't imagine that any response the captain made would be a useful one, of course, but she thought she ought to try.

"Ladouceur, *this is Squadron Six*," Daniel said. Adele thought he sounded weary, but that could be an artifact of the freighter's commo system. "*The* Columbine *is coming alongside. Mister Liu, have Captain Julian's riggers ready to transfer back aboard, if you will. Six out.*"

Adele's algorithms caught the disruption of a ship extracting from the Matrix before the cruiser's own did, but only moments before: the *Ladouceur* might be old, but she was a warship which'd been constructed and equipped to serve in the foremost navy of the human universe. Software had improved since then, but the real question has always been the skill of the person using the apparatus rather than the apparatus itself.

"Squadron Six!" Adele said. The *Columbine* certainly didn't have the sort of electronics Daniel would need to deal with this, and she didn't imagine there'd be time for him to reboard the cruiser. Could she transfer the necessary data to him using the freighter's single-head laser transceiver? "A heavy ship's entered sidereal space three hundred . . . and six thousand miles from Churchyard. It's not one of our squadron. It's—oh."

She paused for a moment as she crosschecked the data cascading in from the new arrival; her data were entirely consistent. There hadn't been time yet for an optical identification, but Adele trusted her signals intelligence farther anyway.

"Daniel," she said, her voice clipped from embarrassment at having given a needless alarm, "the ship is the *Zwiedam*, a former immigrant transport now owned by the Free State of Skye. I believe this is—"

"Skye Defender *calling Admiral Leary*," announced the new arrival over tight-beam microwave. Adele relayed the message to the *Columbine* over the laser link. "*This is Colonel Raymond Chatterjee reporting as ordered, over.*"

"*Colonel, this is Squadron Six,*" Daniel replied with a cheerful bounce that hadn't been in his voice a moment before. "*I'll be aboard my flagship inside half an hour. We'll shape course to some place we can discuss matters in greater comfort than I suspect you and your troops find in vacuum. Hold what you've got till then, if you don't mind.*"

In an even more ebullient tone he added, "*I'm very glad of your arrival, Colonel. I think we'll now be able to turn the present bag of lemons into lemonade! Six out.*"

CHAPTER 15

Dansant

The bush above Colonel Chatterjee's head shrilled like a steam whistle. He spun around, holding his briefcase in front of himself reflexively. His troops and the spacers mixing in the dry scrub weren't carrying sidearms, but quite a number of them reached into pockets or under floppy jackets.

"Ah, very good!" Daniel said, stepping forward. He took a large checked handkerchief from the hip pocket of his utilities and spread it between his hands. With his attention focused wholly on the bush, he added, "I saw it this time."

He snatched, enveloping a thin branch in the handkerchief, and pulled it carefully away. A lump in the fabric was kicking, and one of the shoots which'd angled from the branch a moment ago was missing.

"See?" Daniel said, carefully opening his makeshift capture net. A brown creature no bigger than his little finger writhed for a moment, then stood upright on the four tiny legs on its broader end. He could feel

216

them gripping the palm of his hand beneath the cloth. "My, I don't suppose there's been a proper zoological survey of this place, has there?"

"There has not," Adele said from where she was sitting twenty feet away. Her personal data unit was on the table; the air above it quivered with imagery that Daniel couldn't make out from his angle. "Not that I can find, at any rate. I don't even swear that the planet's name is Dansant, since the Kostroman who located the place may not have been the original discoverer as he believed he was."

"Surely that doesn't matter, does it?" Colonel Chatterjee said with a slight frown. "It hasn't been colonized and there doesn't appear to be any reason it should be colonized. I thought we were just landing here to have firm ground under our feet while we held discussions?"

Yes, thought Daniel. *And also so that Woetjans and Sun can assess how good your troops really are.*

"Quite right," he said aloud, returning the creature to its branch. He had to rub his handkerchief against the bark to get the little fellow to release and hop back where it belonged. There were times he wished he could put all his efforts into natural history; there were such wonders here among the stars!

But that'd mean giving up all that it meant to be a member of the RCN. No number of branch-hoppers and six-winged flyers and carnivorous flowers that crept onto their prey could make up for the thrill of seeing your missiles on a course converging with that of an enemy ship.

Several of Pasternak's people had tack-welded an interior partition to a pair of empty cable spools to make a table. They'd brought three chairs out of the *Laddie's* wardroom and set them all along one long side as Daniel had directed. Overhead, riggers had strung an awning of sailcloth between sections of beryllium shroud. Untensioned, the rigging would flex, but it was more than stiff enough to stand upright while supporting something as light as the microns-thin fabric.

"Take the chair to the right of Officer Mundy, Colonel," Daniel directed, "and we'll get down to business."

Dansant, if that was really its name, wasn't a very prepossessing place; that was no doubt why it hadn't been colonized. The atmosphere was breathable but very arid. There was no standing water and no rainfall; the local plants used their fibrous bark to absorb minuscule amounts of condensate during the night, then closed up tightly at dawn to avoid drying out again.

That much from the discoverer's notes which Adele had copied in the Kostroman archives while she was employed there. She'd brought the data out now, years later, because Daniel had needed a habitable world within twenty-four hours' distance of Churchyard.

The *Sailing Directions* issued by Navy House didn't have the information, but Commander Daniel Leary did. And not even Adele had known there was animal life on Dansant; that was Daniel's own discovery.

He grinned as he seated himself to Adele's left. The little branch hopper wouldn't be what history remembered him for, but perhaps in a better universe it would be.

"I considered making a landing on Churchyard with your troops," Daniel said as Adele threw up an omnidirectional image of Hafn Teobald from an apparent vantage point of a thousand feet in the air. "If we'd disabled the *Rossarol* or destroyed the missile launcher either one, I think that would've been a very workable plan. As it is, with a destroyer able to use its plasma cannon against us on the ground and ourselves unable to reply in kind, it doesn't appear practical."

"You're not planning to return to Pelosi, are you?" said Chatterjee with a deep frown. "I won't lecture you on Bagarian politics, Admiral, but the enemies you made when you raided Dodd's Throne will crucify you if you do. It's no good saying that a missile boat for a missile boat is a fair exchange; they'll call it a disaster."

"You're right, Colonel," Daniel said, feeling the curves of his smile become minusculely harder. "You shouldn't lecture Speaker Leary's son on politics. And no, I don't propose to return to Pelosi until we've achieved what the meanest intelligence will regard as a major stroke against the enemy. If we act quickly and don't slow down once we've committed, I believe we can capture the Cluster Headquarters on Conyers."

Adele switched to imagery of the Conyers complex, a pentagonal enclosure with a surface area of twenty-three acres. Sloped concrete ramparts fronted by a broad ditch formed the boundaries. An expanded cross-section showed shuttered firing slits and a double monorail system inside for shifting the garrison quickly.

The angles of the pentagon were self-contained strongpoints. Two held antiship missile launchers, two had turrets equipped with twin 13-cm plasma cannon, and the turret on the fifth point sheltered a pair of 20-cm howitzers whose explosive shells could blast targets concealed from direct fire weapons.

"That's the Cluster HQ?" Chatterjee said, leaning closer to the display. "There's a thousand troops in the garrison. Aren't there?"

"More than twelve hundred according to the pay records," Adele said coolly as her wands rotated the image. "I've learned not to trust those, however, especially the farther one gets from the center, and this cluster is very far from Pleasaunce."

She sniffed with displeasure. "It's not a great deal better in Cinnabar service, I'm afraid," she added.

The rectangular headquarters building was constructed of precast concrete slabs. Each of the three levels was stepped back from the one below it, making the structure look like a crude pyramid from the side. On top was a landing stage for aircars; armored cupolas holding automatic impellers were placed at the corners of the next level down.

There was room for small starships to land between the HQ Building and the northwest facet of the pentagon. A missile boat—perhaps the *S81* that they'd destroyed on Churchyard—had been on the ground when the image was captured. Larger vessels, the freighters that supplied the garrison and the occasional warship visiting the planet, used a river-fed artificial lagoon half a mile to the west of the complex. A fence with guard towers surrounded that harbor, but it had no defenses capable of withstanding determined attack.

"It appears to me," Chatterjee said, "that the base is stronger than that on Churchyard. A great deal stronger, as a matter of fact."

He looked at Daniel and raised an eyebrow.

Daniel laughed. "Yes, I quite agree," he said. He was pleased that Chatterjee'd noted the problems instead of spluttering that the odds were impossible. "The great difference is that Churchyard is expecting us, and Conyers is not. I assume that Governor Platt knows most of what's happening on Pelosi?"

Chatterjee snorted. "You're certainly right about that," he said. "Governor Radetsky and I sometimes speculate on which members of the Council of Ministers are selling intelligence to Platt. Personally, I'd give even money that all of them are."

"So Platt knew that we were going to Churchyard," Daniel said. "The corollary is that we *weren't* going to attack Conyers. Furthermore, he's expecting reinforcements to his garrison from Maintenon."

"He is?" said Chatterjee, frowning. "How do you know that?"

"From the data banks on the *S81*," said Adele. Her wands threw up a sidebar, though Daniel couldn't have read it without squinting. The little data unit's display was clear enough, but there were tricks to reading airformed holograms against a natural background. Adele'd had occasion to learn those tricks; he hadn't.

"I wouldn't have been able to decrypt it if the ship'd been a real courier vessel with isolated storage for the messages being carried," she went on, "but in this case they were simply held within the *S81*'s main computer. Which wasn't shielded at all, at least from someone who knows what she's doing."

Daniel said, "I believe Officer Mundy can make the *Skye Defender* appear to be the ship from Maintenon—"

He nodded to Adele beside him.

"—can you not, Mundy?"

"Yes," she said, bringing up three-dimensional images of four ships. At this scale they appeared to be identical even to Daniel's eyes. "The *Zwiedam* and her sister were regarded as a successful design, so the *Zaandam* and *Westerdam* were built on slightly enlarged lines. The Alliance's using the *Westerdam* as a transport at the moment. Though in the Ribbon Stars, nowhere near here."

"I don't think the Conyers' garrison will be able to tell that a ship they've never seen before is three hundred tonnes smaller than the records say she should be," said Daniel, letting his smile spread. "Not if the markings and especially the electronic signature is correct. The tricky part is that there's a picket boat, and you'll be boarded in orbit before you're allowed to land. Colonel, can you convince the inspectors that you're a militia battalion from Maintenon?"

Chatterjee frowned. He took out his own personal data unit but simply glowered at it instead of turning it on.

A burst of gunfire ripped the morning, thin and echoless in the dry air. Daniel jumped to his feet. Instead of reaching for her pocket pistol, Adele's wands moved rapidly. That startled Daniel until he realized that she'd switched her display to the targeting screen of the *Ladouceur*'s dorsal turret. It gave her a much better vantage point than he had standing.

"Please, it's all right," said Colonel Chatterjee in obvious concern. "Please, I'm very sorry, Admiral. I told my officers to arrange a marksmanship demonstration while we were on the ground here. I felt that your spacers would be more comfortable if they could trust the infantry that was supporting them. But I should've spoken to you about my plans."

Daniel forced a smile and settled onto his chair

again. "That would've been helpful, yes," he said mildly, "but I'm sure it's good for me to get my heart rate up. Now, as for the inspection party, Chatterjee?"

"I'm sure we can do that," Chatterjee said. "Yes, I'm sure. I used to be an Alliance officer, you see?"

He paused on a rising note, lifting an eyebrow in synchrony. He obviously thought the information would be a surprise—and feared it'd be an unwelcome one.

"Yes, we were aware of that," Daniel said, smiling internally. "We," meaning Adele had learned that and had immediately passed it on because it was potentially important. "But you're a native of Skye. If Governor Radetsky trusts you, that's good enough for me."

"Ah!" said Chatterjee. "Well, there isn't much uniformity among the planetary militias in Alliance service. If we *were* Alliance militia, we'd look about the same. It'll just be a matter of making sure the troops the inspectors are allowed to see all have patches saying Maintenon."

He snorted. "Or at least that they don't say Skye Volunteers. Though I don't think many of the men got around to having patches embroidered on their uniforms before we lifted for Churchyard. We boarded in haste, you see."

A branch hopper—not the one Daniel had caught— shrieked nearby. A third little creature answered it from much farther away. The high-pitched sound traveled well.

"Are we to assault the headquarters complex when we've landed?" Chatterjee said, frowning at the image of the fortress again. "I suppose if we have surprise, that should be possible. Surprise and a way to cross the ditch and climb the wall, that is."

"Yes," said Daniel, "surprise of course. And as for the rest, we'll be landing inside the compound."

"What?" said Chatterjee. "Leary, Admiral, that is—there's no room! Look at that little boat in the picture. The *Defender* isn't huge, I don't mean that, but she's far too large to land there."

"The *Westerdam*, as we'll be calling her, is 381 feet between perpendiculars," Daniel said. He flexed his spread fingers as he considered the approaching test. "If I keep her centered between the headquarters building and the rampart, I'll have over five hundred feet to settle onto. The 53-foot beam is no problem. Now, it'll be tricky because it's concrete and not water, but I don't foresee serious problems."

He beamed, a wholesome, cheery expression that he figured was the best way to give a lie the gloss of truth. The combination of angles and hard verticals would reflect the transport's exhaust in unpredictable fashions. The *Ladouceur*'s landing simulation program didn't have software to mimic such terrain: it was too far beyond what the designers had imagined anyone would want to do.

Granted, missile boats and couriers obviously managed it, but the task was going to be an order of magnitude more difficult for a vessel the size of the, well, *Skye Defender*. On the other hand—

Daniel's smile became completely real.

On the other hand, he figured he was an order of magnitude better than the captains of minor elements of an Alliance cluster command.

"Ah, one thing that I've only implied, Colonel," he said. "I'll be taking charge of the *Skye Defender* myself. I've landed ships her size on dry ground, of course."

Daniel'd landed *one* ship that size on dry ground, and that'd been a controlled crash which wrote off the vessel. This had to look like a real landing, not the vertical assault it really was, if it had a prayer of succeeding. Well, he'd manage it.

Chatterjee shook his head in amazement, but he was grinning broadly. "All the stories we heard were true then, Admiral," he said. "We'll do as you wish, of course; what else can we do when so famed an officer leads?"

His expression became speculative. "And you will be leading, of course?" Chatterjee said. "You will be putting your life on the line with ours?"

"Not only my life, Colonel," Daniel said, nodding to Adele, "but the life of the finest signals officer in the RCN. I assure you that I wouldn't be risking Officer Mundy if I weren't confident of success."

Adele looked at him without expression; Daniel laughed to make a joke out of it. It wasn't a joke, not really. All he was really confident of was that they wouldn't have a prayer of succeeding if Adele *weren't* in the ship that made the landing.

"So," he said, "if you'll call your officers together in half an hour in the entry hold of the *Ladouceur*, I'll go over the detailed assignments for the assault."

"Very good," said Chatterjee, rising. "A bold plan is the best plan, I agree."

He bowed and strode off to where the target practice was taking place. The rattle of shots and the howl of ricochets from stone had been continuous since they began.

"Well, Adele," Daniel said quietly. "What do you think?"

"I think that if I can't take control of the fire control

computer for the plasma cannon on the wall," Adele said, "that they'll destroy us as soon as they realize we're hostile. I'll try to accomplish that."

"Yes," said Daniel. "I expected that you would."

A branch hopper called very close to them. Daniel jerked his head around, but he wasn't able to pinpoint the creature this time.

"I think they're more active than they'd usually be," he said, "because of our breath. Five hundred people exhaling in a close compass like this is going to raise the humidity a great deal in this climate. I think it's a good omen, don't you?"

"I'll search under 'Omens, finger-sized animals on Dansant,' shall I?" said Adele with a deadpan expression. "But I'll be frank, I don't believe I'm going to be able to support your belief there."

She didn't laugh with him, but her smile was as broad as he'd seen it in a long time.

En route *to Conyers*

Adele heard the voices pausing outside her room. When she realized one of those speaking was Woetjans, she noticed where her left hand was. Grimacing in self-disgust, she removed it and smoothed the pocket before calling, "Yes? Come in."

The *Zwiedam* had carried six hundred immigrants at a time on long voyages. Adele couldn't imagine where they'd all fitted, but regardless there was plenty of room for half that number of the soldiers and armed spacers who'd make up the assault force.

Adele and the other officers had private rooms—of a sort. What'd been a barracks for fifty in five-high hammock towers had been broken up into ceilingless compartments made from sail fabric stretched on tubing. The fabric was perfectly opaque: when energized, it reflected even Casimir radiation. It didn't do anything about sound, though, so the voices, music, dice games, and snoring from the other nine cubicles came through unhindered.

The room was noisy, dank, and adorned only by chipping paint. At that, it was better than most of the places where Adele had roomed during the fifteen years between when her family was massacred and her joining the RCN. She didn't care much about her physical surroundings anyway.

Woetjans opened the door panel by turning the double pivot that served as a latch. Instead of entering, she remained in the corridor with a Bagarian spacer whom Adele didn't know by name.

Tovera and Rene Cazelet stood just behind the spacers. They had the cubicles to either side of Adele's, and they appeared to've dropped whatever they were doing to join the party.

"Ramage found something back on Dansant, mistress," the bosun said. "I told him we needed to bring it to you because you'd know what it was."

She nudged Ramage. "Go on, show it to her, buddy," she said. "You don't have to be scared. We're on *her* side. Right, mistress?"

"I usually don't shoot people for asking me questions, Woetjans," Adele said dryly. "Even when they're not shipmates."

She took the little pyramid which Ramage held

out to her. It was about an inch high from any base to its apex and remarkably heavy for its size. There were carvings on all four faces, though Adele couldn't tell the detail in this light. She moved it above the data unit and focused the display into a bar of white light.

Adele used to think that the spacers she served with considered her a monster; the thought had disturbed her. After a time she realized that people who'd just heard the stories might think she was a monster, but to the Sissies themselves she was a guard dog: very dangerous, but *their* dog.

That didn't bother her as much. She basically agreed with the assessment.

"It was where we were shooting, mistress," Ramage said. She'd heard the Bagarians call him Andy. "The Skyes'd painted targets on rocks. They'd shoot and we'd shoot, and after the paint'd been blasted off we'd go paint 'em back again. I was helping paint, you know, and I saw this so I picked it up."

"He thought it was a slug, you see, stuck in the rock," Woetjans said. "But we scraped the rock away and it wasn't."

"Anyway, it was too big," Ramage said. He'd loosened up a good deal in the course of this short conversation.

"No, it's not a bullet," Adele said, hefting the pyramid in her palm. It was as *dense* as the osmium and iridium projectiles which heavy impellers shot, though. Her little pocket pistol fired ceramic pellets which lost most of their velocity in the first fifty yards.

Each face of the pyramid had an image; the edges were sharp, apparently carved instead of being cast. The base was marked with a symbol, a figure-8 or perhaps an analemma, beside two slanted diagonals. It meant nothing to Adele or to her personal data unit.

The other three facets showed heads in left profile. One was birdlike, though the beak was vestigial; the next was clearly reptilian, but the jaw was shorter than that of any reptile Adele had seen and the forehead bulged almost like a man's; and the third *was* a slope-browed man, or at least something manlike.

Daniel will be interested in this.

"Where'd it come from, mistress?" Woetjans asked.

Adele stood, closed her data unit, and handed the pyramid back to Ramage. She'd started to put it in her pocket, but she realized the spacers would think she was appropriating it. They'd accept that, of course: she was Lady Adele Mundy, the Captain's friend, and they were the dirt beneath her feet.

They thought that; she did not. She winced to imagine reinforcing their belief by accident.

"I'm not sure we'll be able to tell, Woetjans," Adele said, "but come with me to the Medicomp and we'll analyze the thing in more detail than we can here."

She strode down the corridor between fabric cubicles and then through the open hatch to C Deck's central passage. In warships the automated diagnosis and care facility was usually on A Deck, but the builders of this immigrant ship placed it in the middle of the three decks given over to barracks. It was within fifty yards of Adele's compartment.

No one was in the Medicomp at the moment, so Adele simply used the cabinet itself instead of everting one of the arms. When there were many to treat at the same time, the unit did so externally. After the assault on Mandlefarne Island, Adele had been one of half a dozen casualties in the corridor of the *Princess Cecile*.

She could easily have died there; but she hadn't, so she was here to answer questions for Woetjans and Ramage. The spacers were pleased that she'd lived, and at the moment Adele supposed that she was glad also.

"The object, please," Adele said, but Ramage was already holding it out to her. The cylinder would hold a large human lying flat. She set the pyramid in the center and closed the cabinet again.

"Why, that's brilliant, Adele!" Cazelet said as he watched her program the Medicomp. "I never would've thought of that. Of course, it has full-spectrum analysis capability, but I just considered it a, well, a Medicomp."

"One gets used to field expedients in the RCN," Adele said, smiling faintly. "For example, a large wrench makes a very good club. Doesn't it, Woetjans?"

"Yes, ma'am," said the bosun. "Though I prefer a length of high-pressure tubing."

Adele scrolled the readout, using the Medicomp's vernier control. She hadn't coupled her personal data unit to it, and doing so now would be more effort than it was worth. The integral controls and menus were clear and simple, as befitted equipment intended for use by common spacers who might themselves be injured.

"It's pure platinum," Adele said. "Chemically pure, that is; it'd have to have been refined to achieve that degree of purity. And the angles are all within microns of 120 degrees, which also means it wasn't bashed into shape by a savage with a rock."

Not that she'd imagined it had been. She wasn't sure of the temperature required to smelt platinum, but—

Adele settled cross-legged on the deck and brought out her data unit. A few twitches with the wands gave her the figure: 3164.3 degrees. No, not a temperature you got from a wood fire, even with three of your cousins blowing on it through cane tubes.

"Ah, Mistress Mundy?" Rene said, carefully circumspect. He'd embarrassed himself by blurting "Adele" a moment ago in front of the spacers. "If the object was really set in the limestone outcrop rather than dirt—"

"Hey, it was rock!" Woetjans said. "You think I don't know what rock is, kid? When Ramage here showed me what was sticking out, I cracked it loose with my impeller's butt that I'd been shooting."

"Yes, Chief Woetjans," Cazelet, stiffening his back and clipping his syllables slightly into an upper-class Pleasaunce accent. "If it was limestone, as I said, then it should be possible to use radiation dating on the particles still caught in the grooves of the carving. Should it not?"

"Can one carbon date stone?" Adele said, but she was already typing the commands into the Medicomp's keyboard.

"Limestone's carbonate rock formed by living creatures," Cazelet said. "In the sea. Use the ratio of oxygen isotopes."

"If there was a sea there, it was the gods' own time ago," said Ramage with a puzzled frown. "I never been no place so dry as that."

"Yes, it was a long time ago," Adele said, staring impassively at the readout. Her fingers typed. "Sixty-two thousand years before present, plus or minus seven thousand. That seems an excessive range of error, but I don't suppose it matters from our viewpoint."

"Mistress, that must be wrong," Rene said. "Try another facet. The sample must be contaminated."

"I don't see how it can be correct either," said Adele, intent on her work. "And I am sampling another side, of course. But I'm less sure than you are that it *has* to be wrong."

She cleared her throat. "This time it's reading sixty-two thousand, plus or minus five point five," she added.

Adele opened the cabinet and removed the little pyramid. After bouncing it twice in her palm, she handed it to Ramage again.

"I think Commander Leary would like to see this," she said. "Perhaps he'll be able to offer a better explanation than I can."

"Mistress?" said Woetjans. A frown furrowed her brow like a freshly-turned field. "There weren't people that far back, was there? I mean, sixty-odd thousand years?"

Adele reached for her data unit. Before she could call up an answer, Cazelet said, "There were people of a sort, Bosun, but they weren't making art from platinum. And they weren't *here*."

"There's no reason to assume humans created this little thing anyway," Adele pointed out. "Just that someone who'd seen humans did it."

Cazelet looked at Adele and said harshly, "Mistress, for this to be true would require a star-traveling race sixty thousand years ago. There's no evidence of that!"

Adele gestured toward the pyramid in Ramage's

hand. "No previous evidence that you'd seen, you mean, Rene," she said with a faint smile. "I've seen some odd things since I began traveling widely."

She was always puzzled to learn that the most avowedly skeptical people took things on faith. Adele believed data, but only until better data appeared; as for analyses and explanations, they were no better than the intellect of the person making them. Rene's certainty was a matter of blind faith.

"Do you mean there was?" Rene said, raising his voice without intending to. "That there was a race that was sailing the stars when human beings thought fire was high technology?"

"I mean that Ramage found a platinum pyramid on Dansant," Adele said calmly. She let a slow smile spread a little wider than was normal for her. "I won't speculate about it or about most things; I don't care for the paths my mind sometimes takes when I speculate."

"Guess I'll show this to Six," Ramage decided aloud. "That all right, Chief?"

Woetjans nodded without expression.

"He might want to buy it, d'ye think, mistress?" Ramage said. Before she could nod agreement, he added, "But you know, I might give it to him anyways. Tell the truth, it makes me feel kinda funny."

"Yes," said Rene Cazelet, "I understand perfectly, spacer."

He looked at Adele, shook his head, and said, "What does it mean, mistress?"

"It means we were on Dansant and Ramage found a platinum pyramid," Adele repeated. "If you mean that question in a broader sense—"

She smiled again.

"—I'm *really* the wrong person to discuss the meaning of life, Master Cazelet. Because you see, I don't think life has any meaning."

After a pause Adele added, "Though Commander Leary would disagree, I suspect. And anyone who's served with Commander Leary will tell you that he's generally right."

CHAPTER 16

Above Conyers

"I can't get it to work," said the senior inspector. He withdrew the chip from his translator, rotated it end for end—which shouldn't make any difference—and inserted it again. His junior colleague watched with his mouth slightly open, an expression which Adele thought made him look like an imbecile.

It *didn't* make any difference. "It still doesn't work," the fellow said.

"It's the manifest we were given on Maintenon," Adele said, trying to sound bored. In order to impersonate the mate of a contract transport, she'd borrowed clothes from Tedesco, a small-framed Sissie. Because he was a motorman, the loose tunic and trousers were indelibly stained though clean in the sense that they'd been washed since their last wearing. "If you can't read it, that's your problem, not ours."

"But don't you have the paper copy that's supposed to come with it?" the senior man said. "Look, I've got to certify that the manifest checks before we allow you to land. This may be listed as a cluster capital but it's really a hardship posting. We'd be under attack here if the clodhoppers had any weapons, you know."

Adele'd thought the clothes might be a problem—why would the *Westerdam*'s first mate have oil-blotched garments?—but the inspectors who boarded from the picket boat didn't appear to notice. The coveralls under their translucent airsuits weren't in any better condition.

"Well, certify it, then!" growled Daniel from the command console. "You can read it on this display if you can't on your own."

"Paper copies aren't controlling," Adele said. She spoke in an upper-class Blythe accent. It might cause speculation coming from the mate of a transport, but it wasn't suspicious. "Anyway, they didn't give us one. Do what he says, read it on our console."

She'd had no difficulty mocking up a format for the manifest the *Westerdam* should be carrying. Unfortunately, the nearest equipment to burn that information to a chip was on Pelosi. It wasn't exotic, but it simply wasn't the sort of thing that ships normally carried themselves.

Adele could wipe the *Skye Defender*'s manifest, though. She could program the command console's database to throw the correct information onto the display when a blank chip was inserted into its reader.

"Or you can send us back to Maintenon where we belong," Colonel Chatterjee growled. "We're militia. We should never have been taken away from our home planet. That's for emergencies only, and you can't tell me that holding the hand of some provincial governor is an emergency!"

"Better not let Governor Platt hear you talk that way," the junior inspector said.

"Or what?" Chatterjee said. "Or he'll send us to West Bumfuck in the Bagarian Cluster? I'm an important man on Maintenon, I'll have you know!"

"Nothing on bloody Maintenon is important," muttered the official, but to his partner he said, "All right, Booth, we'll run it on theirs. But get that bloody reader over to the shop when we come in, right?"

"Dunno why it don't work," Booth said as his senior handed the chip to Daniel, who in turn inserted it into the slot on his console. Unless his looks belied him, there were many things that Booth didn't know.

Both inspectors leaned forward to stare at the information glowing on Daniel's display. The manifests of the Alliance's Transport Auxiliary Command were mauve, a strikingly ugly color for air-formed holograms and difficult to read besides. Adele had precisely duplicated the hue.

"All right, you guys can land," the senior inspector said as he straightened. "But you better be careful when you open your hatches. The clodhoppers've been known to take shots at ships in Grand Harbor. This is a hardship posting, I tell you!"

The Alliance officials sauntered back into the airlock, refastening the fittings of their air suits. When the hatch had closed behind them, Adele rose and strode for the companionway where Rene and Tovera waited. Tovera was carrying a full-sized sub-machine gun.

"Adele?" called Daniel from the bridge. She turned.

"Good luck," he said with a smile. "I wish we had an aircar, but the box should work well enough."

"Yes," Adele said. "Good luck to all of us."

A starship was merely a steel box, after all. Leaving a starship in a smaller steel box on wheels was unusual, but perhaps it was fitting. A coffin was just a box too, after all.

"Ship," said Daniel. "All right—"

His tongue caught momentarily. Great heavens, what to call them! Certainly not Sissies, not least because he wasn't going to cheapen that name by applying it to a battalion of pongoes, and foreign pongoes as well.

"—comrades, we're going in. Remember your orders, obey your officers, and above all—when it starts, *don't* slow down till you've finished it. Six out."

The *Skye Defender*'s thrusters roared, squeezing Daniel back into the command console. Starships never had a high enough thrust to weight ratio to accelerate quickly. More power would be pointless, because hard acceleration would strip off the antennas and yards that the ship required to maneuver in the Matrix.

During the landing approach, the transport was a sitting duck for the pods of ship-killing missiles in Fort Douaumont. Well, if the Alliance garrison figured out they were hostile, it wouldn't require missiles to turn the assault into a massacre of the would-be attackers. A missile would have the virtue of being quick.

The Spring is come! Daniel whistled, *I hear the birds—*

The mate's position had a flat-screen display rather than a holographic tank, though it should be possible to carry out all the functions of star flight from it. Captain Chris Salmon, the officer who'd commanded the *Skye Defender* until Daniel took over, sat there now. He seemed an adequate officer, but Daniel would much rather've had Vesey—or even Blantyre—on that couch. He knew how people he'd trained would react after the shooting started.

Indeed, Daniel'd thought of making Cory his XO, despite the implied insult to Salmon, but Cory was probably better off handling signals from the minimal controls in the captain's office just astern of the bridge. Cory was a brave officer who never gave less than his best, but ham-handed would've been a generous description of his piloting skills.

—that sing from bush to bush, Daniel whistled.

Captain Salmon hadn't complained when Daniel supplanted him. Chatterjee backed Daniel's plan. Besides being of higher rank in the Skye service and a friend of the Governor, the Colonel had two hundred and fifty armed soldiers to enforce his orders. Nobody'd mentioned that, but Salmon was certainly aware of it.

The violence of the descent increased as the *Skye Defender* carved deeper into Conyers' atmosphere. The navigation laser was focused on the misnamed Grand Harbor, the fenced lagoon to the west, but Daniel had keyed in an offset so that the transport was really landing in the interior of Fort Douaumont. He doubted that the garrison would've noticed the laser beam—it was below the optical range—but he preferred not to take unnecessary risks. The necessary ones were bad enough.

Hark! Hark! I hear them sing.

He wished Adele was sitting in the adjacent console to update him on what the fort's defenses were doing, though she'd have to use the transport's electronics.

There hadn't been time to transfer high quality naval hardware from the *Ladouceur*. He was sure she'd have managed, though; she always did.

Daniel grinned. Well, so had Daniel Leary, if it came to that. And Adele had a much more critical task to perform than to warn the captain that a missile he couldn't avoid was aimed at the ship.

There was a blat of static as someone tried to call the transport using short wave. The thrusters' exhaust, oxygen and hydrogen ions roaring across the RF spectrum as they changed state, smothered the attempt at communication. Adele wouldn't have let the white noise through to him, but Cory caught it quickly enough. Cleverness wasn't required in an RCN officer, but steadiness was; Cory was steady.

"*Westerdam*, *this is Conyers Control!*" snarled a female voice who'd belatedly switched to laser communication. "*What in the bloody hell are you playing at, you fool! Sheer off, you're supposed to be landing in Grand Harbor, over!*"

"Roger, Conyers Control," Daniel said, trusting Cory to route the transmission properly. He had enough on his plate to fight the controls through the thickening atmosphere. "This is *Westerdam*, Captain Schaffer speaking. Your orbital control, Officers Isaac Richards and Lloyd Booth, warned us that Grand Harbor is under attack. We're landing within the fort to disembark our troops, over."

"*You bloody fool, Schaffer!*" screamed Conyers Control. "*Sheer off! Sheer off now! You can't fit a ship that size on the courier pad! You'll wreck and do the devil's own damage to us! Sheer off now, damn you, over!*"

"Conyers Control, this is Schaffer," Daniel said in a tone of mindless insouciance. "We cannot change angle now, we are committed. Don't worry, little missie, this will all be all right. I, Schaffer, promise you, over."

He was grinning as he spoke. His words and tone would send the control officer right around the bend, he figured, but she wouldn't imagine that he was a threat.

Daniel wasn't worried about the controller warning of an attack, though she should be sending out a landing alert to keep people from sauntering across the courtyard while a ship was coming in. At worst a ground control officer wouldn't have authority to order the batteries into action. By the time she contacted someone who *did* have that authority, the ship would be cooling on the pad.

At a hundred and thirty feet in the air the *Skye Defender*, temporarily *Westerdam*, slowed its descent to the rate of molasses dripping. Daniel had never controlled the ship on landing before; to his pleased surprise, she was remarkably well-balanced and responded smoothly to throttle inputs.

He dropped lower. Reflected thrust pummeled the hull, but even that was in the form of twenty-Hertz vibrations rather than the violent surges he'd been afraid of. He'd cut the complementary angles of the central building and the rampart's inner face so perfectly that the transport only drifted outward slowly instead of pivoting around her vertical axis.

A nice job if I do say so myself.

"*Ship, prepare for landing!*" Captain Salmon announced.

The *Skye Defender* touched down along the length of her starboard outrigger, dead level axially but with a half degree of yaw. The ship rang like a steel drum, every plate and bulkhead at a slightly different frequency. Daniel kept a firm grip on the controls, neither adding nor reducing thrust.

The port outrigger touched and the main hull squealed on the oleo struts. Daniel flared his thruster nozzles and only then chopped the mass flow to zero.

The *Skye Defender/Westerdam* was down. Outside the concrete and soil—the transport was far too big to fit on a pad poured for vessels a quarter of her size—shimmered with heat they'd absorbed from the flaring ions. Metal pinged as it cooled.

A port clanged open. Not the main hatch; that'd remain closed for ten minutes even after a landing on water which dissipated the thrusters' impulse much more quickly than solid ground did. This was the Power Room access port in the far stern. It was designed so that a crane could swing the fusion bottle off its bed and onto a waiting barge or lowboy.

Daniel's console was rattling with the fury of Conyers Control and several levels of officialdom above her. Hogg offered a sub-machine gun; as usual, he carried a stocked impeller himself.

"Handle the discussion if you would, Captain Salmon," Daniel said. "I have other duties. I'm going to join Colonel Chatterjee in the entry hold right now."

His face was settled into sterner lines that it usually wore. Adele needed to be in one of the distributed command centers of Fort Douaumont in order to take control of the heavy weapons. Her skill with protected information systems was critical to the success of this mission.

But she and her companions would probably have to shoot their way into that command center. Again, Adele's remarkable skill would be required. . . .

It seemed to Adele that the roar and vibration of landing were concentrated in the aft companionway. The tube around the helical stairs wasn't armored the way it would've been on a warship, but it was nonetheless heavy-gauge steel. The cylinder, the treads, and the square-section stringers rang at different frequencies. Occasionally they struck a harmonic which made her teeth hum.

The G Deck rotunda was dim. When she followed Tovera through the Power Room's heavy hatch—open now; she wondered if it should have been—she found the long compartment was hot, muggy and darker yet because of the fog swirling around the catwalks and machinery.

She paused for a moment. Rene muttered something from close behind; he must've nearly walked into her when she stopped abruptly.

The hiss of escaping steam was a pervasive background. Adele supposed it was coolant from the fusion bottle or its auxiliaries, though she restrained the urge to pull out her data unit and check.

She smiled slightly. Or she could ask Pasternak, watching from his upper-level office in a blister cantilevered from the forward bulkhead; he waved when he saw her look up. Instead of being glazed, the windows were guarded by heavy mesh.

That's not what I'm here for, thought Adele, nodding in reply as she walked on. Why was she here? Well, she could give an answer to that for the short term: to penetrate Fort Douaumont and disable its heavy armament, enabling a combination of Cinnabar and Bagarian forces to capture the bastion. In the more general sense, as she'd told Rene on the voyage out, she was the wrong person to ask.

She wondered if the steam was radioactive, then smiled. It would have to blaze like the blue heart of a sun before it was likely to reduce her present life expectancy.

Three spacers in rigging suits waited beside a battered nickel steel container; their helmets were slung. The box was about six feet by four; it was thirty inches high, but it'd been mounted on a missile trolley that lifted it a foot off the ground. The lid was open.

Adele stepped close to the bosun and said in a loud voice so she could be heard, "Woetjans, I told you *two* spacers only, you and one other. We can't afford to let this look like an attack."

"Yes ma'am," Woetjans agreed. "But I'm bringing Barnes and Dasi both."

The riggers must have heard their names; maybe they'd learned to read lips while working on the hull? They nodded, smiling like a pair of clowns.

"This waste can's going to be a pig to maneuver even if the ground's hard," Woetjans said, banging the container with her gauntlet. It was intended for wiping rags and other solid trash, but the strong smell of lubricant suggested that oil had been dumped into it at some point. "And besides, mistress . . ."

The bosun grimaced with embarrassment, an unfamiliar expression and one that made her craggy face look even more grotesque than it usually did.

"Well, it's like this. Six'd never forgive me if something happened to you, and he'd be right. I see where you're coming from, but I'm still taking Barnes and Dasi both to back me. That's how it is."

"Thank you for your honesty, Woetjans," Adele said. She wouldn't know who was present as soon as the lid closed over her, so the bosun could have offered a *fatt accompli*. It wasn't as though Adele could prevent the riggers from doing anything they pleased, even now that they'd explained their intention. Short of shooting them, she had no means of compulsion.

Adele stepped onto the trolley and gripped the sides of the box to swing herself in. It already held two sub-machine guns, a stocked impeller, and packets of plastic explosive in slick green wrappers.

"Here you go, ma'am," Dasi said. He took Adele's waist in his gauntlets and lifted her; when she kicked her legs out, the rigger lowered her into the container. His grip was as firm as a vise but he didn't squeeze enough to cause discomfort. His size and strength belied that degree of delicacy.

Tovera swung herself in and looked coldly at Rene. "It's going to be tight with him too," she said. "He's scarcely necessary."

Instead of snarling a reply, Rene used the length of his legs to step into the container. Nothing in his expression suggested that he'd heard. He had a sub-machine gun, but the sling bound it so tightly across his chest that he'd have to detach it from one of the swivels to use it.

He wore one-piece coveralls of dark gray-green fabric. It struck Adele for the first time that the garment might have been a uniform of some kind: the color was similar to that of Alliance infantry utilities.

She squatted in the box. Her head was above the rim, so she lay down on her side, ignoring the slick filth which coated the bottom. She still had Tedesco's jerkin on, but she'd changed into a pair of RCN fatigue trousers. The cargo pockets of the motorman's slops had tie fasteners; Adele wanted the familiar ease of press-seals over her personal data unit.

Tovera and Rene curled up beside her. The boy's boots bumped her neck; he tried to draw his legs up more tightly, but that wouldn't—couldn't—last through the landing and what would come after.

"Just relax, Rene," she said sharply. "This is going to be uncomfortable no matter what we do, but there's no reason to contort ourselves into worse shape."

"Mistress?" said Woetjans, looking down in concern. "It's going to be a couple minutes before we land, but I can't rig the hoist without the lid's on. I mean, not if we're going to put the lid on ever, if you see what I mean. Is it all right I put the lid on?"

"Yes, of course," Adele snapped. "For heaven's sake, Woetjans, we're not crystal figurines! Do what's necessary!"

The lid clanged over them. The sudden darkness made her cramped posture worse. A hoist squealed; loops of chain clanked and rattled against the sides of the box.

Adele felt Rene shifting. *He's trying to keep the submachine gun from jabbing him now that he's lying on his side*, she thought. Instead a light winked on, only a tiny penlight but enough to show the whole glistening interior. She relaxed and found herself smiling.

The ship's vibration changed note. "We'll be on the ground in thirty-five seconds," Rene said unexpectedly. "Judging from Captain Leary's previous landings. He's as regular as an automated system, but he does it by being very smooth instead of by switching the thrusters on and off quickly the way the computer does."

The roar redoubled. Adele tried to brace herself against the container, but the ship crashed down in a chorus of deafening clangs and the shriek of meter-thick struts compressing. The box lurched to the right, then banged back to the left when the other outrigger touched. The lift chains jangled against the sides.

The box jerked again and swung freely. Adele heard a deep ringing sound, followed by the squeal of hinges: that would be the access port pivoting out from the hull. The container with her and her companions crawled sideways, swinging back and forth on the short loop from the hoist.

Adele wanted to take out her data unit. *How long is the crane? If I knew that, I could determine the number of seconds at the present rate it'll take us to reach the end and—*

They banged to the end of the run-out. Almost at once the hoist began to clank downward. Adele found herself anticipating the trolley ringing against the bottom long before it actually happened. She'd forgotten that the transport was on solid ground instead of floating on the yielding surface of a slip.

They hit concrete in a lesser edition of the landing itself, the wheels on one side clanging momentarily before those on the other. The chain loops fell away in cheerful dissonance, though the trolley bumped over them as the suited riggers began to shove the container forward.

Even in the enclosed box, the air became noticeably hotter and laced with ions of several distinct tangs. Adele's nose quivered and Tovera began to sneeze violently. She muffled each one, but Adele knew her servant well enough to imagine her boiling fury at being unable to control her body.

Adele stroked the pocket holding her personal data unit; she'd need it soon.

She was already gripping her little pistol. She might need that even sooner.

CHAPTER 17

Fort Douaumont, Conyers

The trolley roared on the short apron of concrete. When the six-inch steel wheels got onto the unsurfaced soil, the noise wasn't as bad but the box rocked as first one side, then the other, slipped into low spots.

I'll apologize to Woetjans after it's over, Adele thought. It *did* require three people to roll the container beyond the area so hot from the *Skye Defender*'s landing that no one could walk across it without the protection of a rigging suit. Besides the person pushing from behind—a hard job, but within the strength of each of this trio of spacers—there had to be people to both left and right to prevent the heavy container from toppling over.

Had Woetjans known that? Perhaps; the bosun had more experience with moving heavy objects than all members of the Mundy family from time immemorial. In any case, Woetjans'd been right and Adele was wrong.

The trolley bumped onto concrete again, then stopped. Rene lifted the lid a hand's breadth with one arm; the air that curled in through the gap was hot but not searing. Adele straightened, but Tovera had already flung the lid clear and vaulted out.

The riggers had halted at the base of the rampart. Woetjans had already taken off her helmet; Barnes and Harned were following her lead.

Behind, the *Skye Defender* was a huge presence which shut off sight of the headquarters building. The courtyard throbbed with heat from the landing, but it was no worse than midday in a desert. They'd only be out in it for a short time.

A three-step base rose to a platform which ran the length of the rampart to the left, but Adele and her companions were beside a bunker built out squarely from the back-slope. There were no openings on the inner face, but stairs protected by a blast shield ran along the side to a steel door on an upper level.

Tovera, holding a sub-machine gun in her right hand and a satchel of plastic explosive in her left, climbed to the door, taking the steps two at a time. Rene was right behind her.

"Get away from here, you puppy!" Tovera said as she peeled the backing off a 20-ounce block of plastic explosive. "Or you'll be blown to mush."

She molded a comfortable handful of the doughy white explosive over the upper hinge. Giggling, she added, "But if you want to stay, I shouldn't get in your way, should I?"

"Let's try this first, old girl," Rene said. The armored door had a bar latch that pivoted on one end. From the handle's length and sturdiness, it was meant to withdraw two or more heavy bolts when the door was unlocked.

unlocked now. The bolts squealed, though

Rene had to shift to put his full weight on the bar before he racked them clear.

Tovera stepped back on the landing, her face expressionless. She looked at the portion of the explosive still in her hand and threw it onto the concrete.

"I'll go first," Adele said, trotting up the steps. Working in the stacks of a major library was good training for a starship's companionways—or for this.

"*No*, mistress," Tovera said. She gripped the submachine gun in both hands.

"Yes, Tovera," Adele said. "Remember your place!"

Rene had started the door groaning open, but Woetjans speeded the process by reaching past Adele to grab the edge of the panel. The bosun tugged. She'd slung a sub-machine gun, but she couldn't have used it without removing her gauntlets. Apparently she'd decided her armored hands were to be her weapon of choice for this business.

Adele took her left hand out of her pocket and slipped through the portal. The interior was pleasantly cool after the ion-baked courtyard, though it'd probably seem dank if she had to spend long in it. Beyond was a corridor whose walls, floor and ceiling were concrete, splotched frequently with rust leaching from the reinforcing rods.

Adele turned right and strode toward Command Center Barbonnet, the post controlling this facet of the rampart. Her fingers itched to take out her data unit, but she had no need of it. She'd memorized not only the floor plan of this sector but also that of the one to the immediate south; until they'd reached Conyers orbit, Daniel hadn't been certain about where he'd land within Fort Douaumont.

Adele's entourage strode or stomped along behind her. Tovera and Rene were side by side. Adele risked a quick glance over her shoulder. The pair were glaring at one another, though they jerked their eyes ahead again when they realized she was watching them.

Woetjans was a step ahead of Barnes and Dasi. They'd taken their gauntlets off so that they could use their weapons, though the guns looked like toys in the hands of big men wearing rigging suits. Despite the weight and sweaty bulk of their gear, they matched Adele's quick pace.

To the left were short staircases up to a gallery. From it opened embrasures in the outer face, intended for automatic impellers or small plasma cannon. From the records she had available Adele hadn't been able to tell how many weapons were mounted. It wouldn't matter if things went as they should, but—

A weedy young man stepped into the corridor. He saw the group of strangers and started to duck back up the stairs from which he'd come.

"Hold it right there, soldier!" Adele called in her most sneeringly upper-class Blythe accent. "Don't you bother to salute here on Conyers?"

It'd be better if she weren't wearing ill-sorted, oil-soaked utilities, but you use what you have. Tone and audacity would get her some way; she hoped they would get her far enough.

The man—soldier? civilian technician?—stopped, then slowly returned to the corridor. He started to salute, then fully absorbed the motley group of strangers and lowered his arm. "Mistress?" he said doubtfully.

"I'm Colonel Adele Mundy of the Fifth Bureau,"

Adele said sharply. *I say most things sharply, I suppose.* "I'm here to investigate corruption in the government of the Bagarian Cluster. I expect answers and I expect them *now*."

She paused. The local's mouth dropped at the mention of the Fifth Bureau, Guarantor Porra's personal enforcement organization. His face went pale and he began to pant.

"Who's the officer in charge of Command Center Barbonnet?" Adele snapped. She'd be perfectly happy if the fellow hyperventilated and fainted, but there was also the risk that he'd run off in a screaming panic. It'd be easy to shoot him down—as Tovera, who'd been a member of the Fifth Bureau, would certainly do—but the sub-machine gun's chatter risked giving the alarm also.

"What?" the fellow said. "Who?"

He swallowed. "Sir!" he chirped. "That's Captain Cleggs, but I don't think he'll be there so it'll be Chief Belmont. Sir!"

"All right, come along with us," Adele said with a nod. "Corporal Barnes, take the fellow in charge but don't hurt him unless he tries to warn the traitors."

She strode down the corridor. The command post was on the other side of a pair of right-angle turns, intended as blast traps in case the fortifications were penetrated. A glance to the side showed her the local—what ever was his name?—following obediently, behind Woetjans and just ahead of Barnes and Dasi.

The door to the post hinged inward; it was halfway open. No one was on guard in the corridor, but a soldier in the outer section was seated so that he could watch through the gap.

He got up when saw Adele approaching. "Yes?" he called. He gripped the barrel of the sub-machine gun leaning against his chair and cradled it in his arms.

"I'm Colonel Mundy—" Adele said.

The soldier saw the armed group behind her. He slammed the steel door with his foot as he groped for the charging handle of his sub-machine gun.

Adele shoved against the door, jouncing it off the jamb but recoiling herself; the soldier outweighed her considerably. Woetjans stepped past and slammed her shoulder into the panel. The door flew open, bouncing the soldier into the partition separating the guard room from command center beyond. Another soldier was reaching for her sub-machine gun. The first man shot Woetjans in the chest.

Adele fired, hitting the shooter at the hairline. He lurched against the partition, then sprawled sideways. She took the pistol from her smoldering pocket and shot him twice more through the base of the skull as she entered the outer office.

The second soldier screamed and dropped her sub-machine gun. Tovera killed her anyway, a three-shot burst at the top of the breastbone which destroyed all the major blood vessels connected to the heart.

"Don't hurt the equipment!" Adele shouted as she pulled open the door of the inner office.

An overweight woman in rumpled khakis sat at a U-shaped console with her back to the left-hand wall. Three younger male clerks in utilities had been at smaller electronic desks which faced hers. They'd started to get up when the door flew open, but the nearest threw his hands in the air and cried, "I surrender! I surrender!"

The woman in khaki snarled, "You bastards!" and opened a drawer in the right-hand pillar of her console. Adele shot her through the right eye; the bone behind the sockets was thin. She didn't trust the ceramic pellets of her pocket pistol to penetrate the solid portions of the cranial vault.

The woman's legs spasmed, throwing her out of her integral chair. She lay on the floor, thrashing and battering her head against the concrete wall. She'd voided her bladder and bowels when she died.

Adele stepped over the body, setting her pistol on top of the console. She needed both hands to bring up her data unit, and the gun barrel glowing from the quick sequence of shots would melt into the synthetic fabric of her tunic if she dropped it back in her pocket.

A sub-machine gun slammed the three captured clerks against the back wall and pinned them there for the length of the burst. Fifty rounds pulped their chests, splashing the room with osmium ricochets and powdered concrete.

"Tovera!" Adele screamed, but of course the shooter wasn't Tovera, a sociopath but also a craftsman of slaughter. Tovera would never have wasted a full magazine like that when precise three-round bursts would do the job as well.

Barnes stood in the doorway, reaching for a reload from the pouch hanging from his hard suit. The barrel of his sub-machine gun was white-hot. The dusty gray air shimmered with ozone and aluminum ionized from the projectiles' driving bands.

Tovera grabbed Barnes' weapon by the receiver. When he wouldn't let go, she cracked his knuckles with the butt of her own sub-machine gun and jerked it away.

"Help Dasi with Woetjans!" Tovera said. "Quick! Do you want her to die?"

Barnes' mouth dropped open. He turned and slipped back into the outer office, moving as easily as if he weren't wearing the rigging suit.

"Mistress?" said Tovera. "He was upset. He's a good man."

Adele nodded as she synched her personal data unit with the console. She needed secure communications with the transport as well as to be able to access both Fort Douaumont's systems, so she couldn't simply use the console.

She wondered if the bosun was still alive. The hard suit wouldn't stop projectiles, but being shot in the chest wasn't necessarily fatal. As Adele knew.

Tovera returned to the outer office; Rene sat at the end desk and began shuffling through the display. At the moment, Adele was too busy to check what he was doing.

The boy looked greenish and his face was set. That might simply be in reaction to the smell. Smells, rather. The dry sharpness of lime laced with ions could only tinge the effluvium of bodies ripped apart while alive.

Adele found the controls quickly enough. First she changed the password and authentication sequence for all five batteries to a pair of eight-character strings of her own choosing. Next she switched the input option so that the password and authentication had to be entered through her personal data unit in order to be valid. Only when that background was in place did she shift the batteries to director fire so that they couldn't be controlled by the battery officer.

Adele leaned back and closed her eyes for a moment, then opened them. Her wands twitched, using Fort Douaumont's own systems to open communications with the *Skye Defender*. As she did so, Rene rose from his desk and started for the door.

"Cazelet?" she said. Her eyes were watering from the dust, and the back of her throat was raw. The sound came out as a croak.

"I found a Medicomp in the next bay," Rene said in a harsh voice. His eyes were watering; tears streaked his cheeks. "Maybe if we get the Chief to it. . . . The riggers and me, I mean. You'll be all right with Tovera."

Adele nodded curtly. "Yes," she said, "I will."

Had Tovera really feared that she'd punish Barnes for killing someone who perhaps didn't need to be killed? That was a matter between Barnes and those who visited him in the night.

Adele focused on her display again and connected with the transport.

"Captain, this is Signals," said Daniel's commo helmet as he stood in the transport's forward entry bay. It was Adele's voice, but she sounded odd. Well, goodness knows what sort of rigmarole she'd had to go through to send the signal. *"The artillery positions are neutralized. That's the missiles too, I mean. And there hasn't been an alarm yet, but there may be at any moment. Over."*

"Roger, Signals," Daniel said. As he spoke, he pointed his finger across the bay toward Michael Sayer, the engineer's mate at the hatch controls—he was a

Sissie, of course—and chopped it down in a short arc while nodding to the hatch. "Break. *Ladouceur*, this is Squadron Six. Come down now and land in Grand Harbor according to plan. Nothing fancy, Mister Liu, just bring her down. Over."

The hatch dogs withdrew like a bell chorus. Pumps whined, building pressure in the hydraulic jacks that forced the ramp down. Chatterjee hadn't seen Daniel gesture to Sayer. He looked up, startled; at Daniel's calm nod, he spoke into the mike flexed to his epaulet.

"*Roger, Six*," Lieutenant Liu replied from the cruiser. "*We're approaching the window. We'll begin our descent in ninety seconds.* Ladouceur *out.*"

Daniel didn't remark, but if it'd been him at the cruiser's command console he'd have started his descent immediately and recalculated the details on the way down. He grinned. That, of course, was why Liu was in orbit now instead of being here where serious work was in progress.

The *Ladouceur*'s plasma cannon could've come in handy, but using them would require the cruiser to hover close to Fort Douaumont. Lieutenant Liu's shiphandling ranged from good to better than good; certainly he was skilled enough to hold the cruiser in a safe hover under normal circumstances.

The kicker was the definition of "normal." Being shot at had become normal—or at least not abnormal—for Daniel and his Sissies; that wasn't true for Liu. Daniel couldn't risk learning that an impeller slug clanging from the hull made the fellow throw up his hands and send the cruiser plunging into the ground.

The air roiling in as the hatch lowered was hot and stank of ozone. Daniel slitted his eyes reflexively.

He was opening up the ship earlier than he normally would've done following a landing on dry ground, but he hadn't considered that it might be a problem. He realized he was wrong when he heard shouts of fear and anger from the platoon of Skye infantry waiting in the bay with him and forty armed spacers.

"Admiral!" Chatterjee said. "What's happened? Are we on fire?"

"It's all right!" Daniel said: "The ground's hot from the exhaust, but it isn't dangerous. We probably don't have much time before an alarm goes off, so we need to cross to the headquarters building as soon as the ramp's down."

Which would be another minute or more. The boarding hatch weighed twenty tons, far too great a mass to fling around without regard for inertia.

"Admiral, I don't know that we can!" Chatterjee said. "We're not trained for this! Please, cannot we wait till it's cooler, a few minutes at least?"

Daniel thought, his face blank. He should've realized that what spacers took more or less for granted might be impossible to soldiers who weren't familiar with the searing violence of a starship's landing. On the other hand, the reasons for getting into the Alliance HQ as quickly as possible were valid regardless of how unpleasant the process was. Hot, curling ozone wasn't lethal at the concentrations outside, but the automatic impellers which might start firing at any moment would be.

"Right," he said. "I'll take my spacers in now, and you'll follow as soon as you're able to. But don't waste time, Colonel, *please* don't waste time."

Chatterjee bent over his mike and gave a series of

orders. Daniel didn't really care what the colonel was saying, though he realized with a smile that Adele would've been coupled into the Bagarian net as a matter of course.

His smile faded. *I hope you're all right, my friend,* he thought.

The ramp thumped down. "Spacers with me!" Daniel said. The hold's PA system boomed his voice out from speakers in the upper molding. Cory wasn't Adele, but he was doing bloody well. "We're not attacking, we're simply marching to our new billets. Until I say different or *they* shoot at us!"

"Aw, Six, we gotta march?" Kris Dehaes called, her voice an alto as cracked as a crow's. "You know we're no good at that!"

"Pipe down, Dehaes!" ordered Sun, leading the contingent because Woetjans was off with Adele. "If we keep cool and listen to Six, it'll go just fine."

Well, I don't know about that, thought Daniel, but he stepped off on his left foot. As expected, the spacers clumped down the ramp with him. They looked more like a mob rushing for the jakes between innings than a military unit.

What he *hadn't* expected was that Colonel Chatterjee would still be at his side. The Bagarian'd tied a kerchief over the lower half of his face and seemed to have squeezed his eyes shut. Maybe he was squinting, but it didn't look that way.

Chatterjee touched Daniel's arm, for balance or maybe just to be guided. "I told Major Zaring to bring the men along ASAP," he said, his words making the kerchief puff and flap. "I'm going with you, Admiral!"

Dust and stray ions eddied in the heat shimmering from the ground. The air felt hotter with each step down the ramp, and by the third stride onto the concrete Daniel was thinking that he should've worn something heavier than the soft-soled spacer's boots he had on.

He grinned, wondering if the dry heat was going to make his lips crack. And here he'd been mentally chiding the pongoes for not being up to crossing this little bit of hot ground. . . .

Daniel stepped from the pad onto bare earth. It wasn't so bad, now. They were farther from the thrusters, there'd been a little longer for the whole courtyard to cool, and dirt didn't store heat as well as reinforced concrete. Even so, the bare skin of his face and hands felt crisp.

The main entrance to the headquarters building had monumental double doors, armored and now closed. They were reached by a ramp instead of a flight of steps; Daniel wondered if dignitaries expected to be driven in. Walking at a measured pace—he didn't want his assault force to look like an assault force—he started up the slope.

The door valves were decorated in low relief with scenes of happy laborers, farming on the left panel and assembling machinery on an assembly line to the right. Despite the embellishments, the doors were a very real barrier. Sun carried a satchel of explosives, but the upper hinges were ten feet above the door sill.

Daniel supposed they could form a human pyramid to allow someone to climb high enough to place a wad of explosive there, but that presupposed that the Alliance garrison would sit on its collective hands during the preparations. That didn't seem the most likely scenario.

A pedestrian door opened inward from the left panel. A head wearing a bicorn hat full of gold braid peered out.

"You!" the Alliance official called angrily. "Whoever's in charge of this shambles, get over here *now*."

"*Daniel!*" Adele's voice snapped on his commo helmet through a 50-hertz hum. "*Claim to be the political officer accompanying the battalion from Maintenon. The man in the door has cluster-command major's insignia, though I don't know his name.*"

The officers of a real Maintenon battalion wouldn't know the fellow's name either, Daniel thought, *but of course it wouldn't bother them. It wouldn't bother anybody but Adele, to whom information was life. And thank heavens she's with me!*

"I suppose that's me, then, Major," said Daniel, who'd reached the apron before the door alcove. The stone facing was pleasantly cool through his thin soles. "I'm Commissioner Leary, the battalion's political officer. Colonel Chatterjee here will handle the purely military decisions, but he defers to me in, shall we say, intra-Alliance matters."

He stepped through the doorway. It was designed like the hatch of a starship, and the valve in which it was set was as thick as a starship's hull plating.

Hogg entered also. He swung the door fully back as Chatterjee followed.

"Here!" protested the major. His gaudy uniform made Daniel think of doormen at expensive Xenos hotels, though a doorman's garb wouldn't have been so worn and dingy. "They can't come in here! I have to shut the door to keep the stink out! And what*ever* possessed you to land here?"

"Well, I can scarcely leave them out in the heat, can I?" said Daniel cheerfully. He eased forward with Chatterjee at his side. Their presence moved the major back, allowing the spacers room to enter and spread along the front of the hall. "And as for where we landed, you'd have to ask Captain Salmon. I will say, though, that we were informed in orbit that you were under attack, so the decision seemed reasonable to me."

The entrance hall was sixty feet long, forty wide to the square pillars framing it, and thirty feet high to the top of a barrel-vaulted ceiling which was decorated with mythological scenes.

Daniel supposed they were mythological; at any rate, the figures wore flowing robes and some of them had feathered wings. From the outside the HQ Building seemed a fortress or the ritual center of a brutal religion; within, however, the Cluster Governor lived in a palace.

"We're not being attacked!" the major cried. With him were three civilian clerks—two were women—and a young male warrant officer who looked as sharp as Hogg's knife. The warrant officer carried a personal data unit hooked to his belt; it was projecting a display before him, but he was also keeping an eye on the present discussion. "What blithering idiot said that we were?"

"With respect, Major . . ." Daniel said, drawing out the other man's rank. Commissioners, like warrant officers, came in various grades, but the major would know that it was normal for the commissioner to be senior to the line officer whom he accompanied. "It was your blithering idiot, not mine. Now, where is Governor Platt?"

"He can't see you," the major muttered. He still hadn't bothered to identify himself. "Anyway, there's no reason to see him. You'll need billets and—did you bring your own rations?"

He looked up hopefully, his eyes sliding from Daniel to Chatterjee. The warrant officer's face had gotten very still, but the three clerks were chattering to one another beside a pillar. There was nobody else in the hallway, though the door to the left marked AUTHORIZED PERSONNEL ONLY had the look of a guardroom. It was ajar.

"We have—" Chatterjee said and paused to hack up phlegm. He continued, "We have nine days' rations left, but we're on your strength from the moment we touched down. You'll have to reimburse the Government of Maintenon for anything I issue to my troops until we're released from Conyers' control."

Perfect, absolutely perfect . . . Daniel thought. All his spacers were in the building. While Chatterjee and the major wrangled over administrative costs, Daniel sidled over to Sayer and murmured, "I want to make sure our pongo friends can get inside fast when they decide to join us. Can you open the main doors here?"

"Does a rat shit in the sewer, Six?" replied the engineer's mate with a big grin. He was obviously a city boy.

"Governor Platt is in his suite on the top level," Adele said in a tone of cold detachment. *"There don't appear to be any combat troops billeted in the*

*building itself, but there're gun crews on the second
level and there's supposed to be a platoon dispersed
to guard the entrances. Over."*

Sun had already detached a squad under Jo Ashburn,
his striker, to drift toward the guardroom. Ashburn
pulled a Bagarian grenade from her cargo pocket,
though she didn't appear to have armed it yet.

"Right," said Daniel. "Open the doors, spacer."

He walked back toward the major. Sayer thrust a
short prybar into a crack Daniel hadn't noticed in the
surface of a doorpost. He gave it a quick twist to pop
the latch and swing out a panel, displaying the set of
control buttons beneath.

The warrant officer said, "I'll get right on that, sir," in
a cheery voice and turned, striding quickly in the direction of a doorway entering the hall from the right.

"Hey!" cried the major. He bustled toward Sayer
with his features set in an expression of outrage. "What
are you doing? What are you *doing*?"

The main doors began to crawl apart. Their pained
squeals were louder than those of the transport's
hatch; they may not have been opened in years or
decades.

Chatterjee's ear-clip speaker chirped at him. He
looked at Daniel and said, "Jon, that's Major Zaring,
is on the way, Commissioner."

"Hold it, soldier!" Hogg said. "You're not faster
than this is!"

The warrant officer froze in mid-step and threw
his hands in the air. Only then did he turn toward
the impeller pointed at the middle of his back. In
other hands, a long-arm held at the waist wouldn't
be a real danger; this fellow had correctly estimated

the likelihood that Hogg would hit his target even if he closed his eyes before shooting.

The Alliance major grabbed Sayer by the arm. A rigger lifted off the major's bicorn and clocked him over the head with a length of pipe; he went down like a shower of sand.

One of the civilians squealed and put her clenched fists to her mouth. The warrant officer turned his head and snarled, "Shut your face, you stupid cow! Do you want to get us all killed?"

Daniel looked through the doorway to make sure that the Bagarian soldiers really were coming as announced. The detached squad placed themselves against the wall to either side of the guardroom door.

"Colonel Chatterjee," Daniel said, "secure the lower floors with your troops while—"

Ashburn cocked her right arm back with the grenade poised to throw. A member of her squad jerked the guardroom door fully open and dived out of the way. The remaining six spacers pointed impellers and sub-machine guns into the doorway.

"Freeze!" Ashburn shouted. "Freeze or you're for it, pongoes!"

Half a dozen soldiers, two in their undershirts, were playing poker. The man with the deck let it get away from him; cards fluttered through the air like mayflies in a mating dance. There were guns leaning against the back wall, but nobody was foolish enough to try to grab one.

"Very good," Daniel said. "As I was saying, Colonel, I'm taking my detachment to the Governor on the top floor where I hope to end this business without bloodshed."

He cleared his throat and added, "We've kept it relatively peaceful thus far. I'd like that to continue."

Chatterjee nodded curtly, watching Ashburn' squad bind the guards with cargo tape. "I've been a real estate lawyer for the past fifteen years, Admiral," he said. "I hope to go back to that profession. If I *never* hear a shot fired in anger, it'll be too soon."

Daniel clapped him on the shoulder. "Sissies to me!" he called. "Up three floors to the Governor's suite, spacers. The pongoes can take care of things on the ground, right?"

There was a broad staircase of polished gneiss at the far end of the hall. Halfway up it split into a Y and reversed direction onto both sides of a mezzanine; it didn't appear to go higher. Hogg had located a spiral staircase in the alcove to the left of the entrance door, however. He stood at the foot of it.

"Follow me!" Daniel said, waving his sub-machine gun as he strode toward his servant. "Sun, bring up the rear!"

"Trade me!" said Hogg, tossing his stocked impeller to Daniel, who handed over the sub-machine gun without pointless argument. The man in the lead in these close quarters should have the automatic weapon. Hogg was the proper person to lead because decades of poaching had honed his senses to react to the slightest sound or movement. Daniel was good, but he knew he wasn't in the same league as his servant.

Besides, Hogg was *going* to lead in a situation like this, even if that meant clubbing his master down and tying him to keep him out of the way. Relationships generally, not just political ones, were the art of the possible. Daniel'd had his whole life to learn what was—and wasn't—possible in dealing with his old servant.

Their soft-soled boots *whisk*ed on the cast concrete stairs. Hogg and Daniel both kept their faces turned up instead of looking down at their feet. The muzzles of their weapons pointed to the left, the direction of the doors off the clockwise spiral staircase, but that to the mezzanine was closed.

The detachment following banged and rattled like a busy day in a bucket shop. The spacers were all sure-footed: quite apart from the riggers, the wear-polished steel treads of the companionways that the Power Room crews negotiated many times a day were slicker and trickier than this.

On the other hand, though all his Sissies'd had firearms training, they *weren't* ideal people to have running behind you with guns in their hands. The spiral was some protection; and anyway, if Daniel'd made personal safety a priority, he wouldn't be in the RCN.

The door to the second level was closed also, but as Hogg reached it a siren outside began to wind up and hooters—one of them in the stair tower—blatted. Almost at once an automatic impeller on the first-level plaza began to fire. The clang of heavy slugs ricocheting from steel indicated the gunner was shooting at the transport.

"*Sector Two, that's northwest, has given the alarm,*" said Adele as dispassionately as if she were ordering lunch. "*I've rung down the barriers between sectors, but troops can get out through the courtyard doors if they care to, over.*"

Hogg paused and glanced at Daniel. Daniel looked back in turn and found—not surprisingly—that the spacer directly behind him was Sayer.

"You!" Daniel said. One petty officer was as good as another in a crisis, and the engineer's mate had proved he was a quick thinker. "Take half the detachment and clear this side of the plaza. Tell Sun to take the other half and clear the west side. Hogg and I'll take care of the Governor."

"Come on, Sissies!" Sayer shouted down the staircase. "We got wogs to teach what's what!"

"*I've relayed your order to Sun*," Adele said, as primly as a senior professor. "*The captain on duty in Sector Three has informed Governor Platt that the building is under attack. Over.*"

"We're on our way, Signals," Daniel said. He followed Hogg up the stairs as the spacers clumped through the door onto the second floor.

His spacers'd be hitting the gun crews from an unexpected direction. He'd have liked to be leading them. He'd have liked to be bringing the *Ladouceur* down—and to be sitting at the cruiser's gunnery console, demonstrating what a 6-inch plasma bolt did to reinforced concrete.

He'd have liked to be doing a lot of things, but he was an RCN officer so the job nobody else could do became his priority. Admiral Daniel Leary was in command of the Bagarian assault force, so he would treat with the Alliance commander.

The door at the stair head was open; the heavy automatic weapon had stopped firing, but bursts from sub-machine guns and individual *whang*s from stocked impellers came up from the plaza. There were shouts, screams, and frequently the ringing growl of projectiles ricocheting off gun mountings.

Daniel followed Hogg into the corner of a garden

twenty feet on a side. Sparkling gravel walks wound between rough stone planters set with colorful flowers from several planets including Earth. Boxwood hedges enclosed three sides. The polarizing screen overhead let light through but from above appeared to extend the roof of the penthouse whose end wall—with a door flanked by bay windows—formed the garden's fourth side.

Hogg headed for the door between a planter of flowers streaming like red flags and one of blue, purple and violet cups. Even in haste he planted his feet with such delicacy that his fur-lined poaching boots barely disturbed the gravel path.

He twisted the latch with his left hand, pointing the sub-machine gun in his right like a pistol; the outward-opening door didn't move. He backed, tensing his right leg to kick.

"Get back," Daniel snapped, raising the impeller to his shoulder. The door panel was wood-grained metal. The wide troughs in which the clear panels of the casements were set implied that the windows were armored also.

Hogg stepped aside, reflexively careful not to cross in front of the gun muzzle. Daniel fired, blasting the latch into shards. The door itself jounced barely ajar.

Checking to see that Daniel still had the impeller leveled, Hogg stuck his sub-machine gun's muzzle into the hole where the latch had been and levered the door open. He couldn't use his bare hand, because the opening was white-hot and as sharp as a jumble of razor blades.

Beyond was a sitting room with a malachite table on which a vase of roses had been recently overset;

water still dripped to the carpeted floor. The chairs had ornate frames of gilt wood and upholstery which matched the tabletop, picked out with stylized gold stars. *It costs a great deal of money to buy things so tastelessly ugly*, Daniel thought.

"I'm in!" Hogg said. He slanted through the doorway in a crouch that kept him below the line of Daniel's impeller.

"I'm in!" Daniel said. He followed at the opposite angle.

To the right was a well-appointed office. It could be closed off from the drawing room, but the slatted door made from mirror-finished synthetic was collapsed against the wall. There was no one in either room.

Straight ahead was an archway made shimmeringly opaque by holographic distortion; Daniel guessed that there'd be a band of active noise cancellation at the same point to provide complete privacy for those inside. The trouble was, the only way to tell what was on the other side of the curtain of light was to go through it into whatever was waiting—

Hogg lifted the muzzle of his sub-machine gun and raked the transom. Bits of cast synthetic flew in all directions. Sparks popped as the burst slashed away several projectors; strips amounting to half the screen vanished, showing a huge bed. Its rumpled duvet was in the same hideous gold-on-malachite pattern as the chairs in the drawing room.

The bed was empty. On the far wall between built-in bookcases—false ones, Daniel suspected—was another armored door, this one slowly swinging to. Beyond, the powerful fans of an aircar whined, then bogged as the driver tried to bring them up to speed too quickly.

"No you don't!" said Hogg. He leaped into the bedroom, ignoring the risk that a shooter waited in ambush.

Daniel turned and ran back through the garden. The hedge was dense and the sculptured boxwood branches raked him like so many fingernails, but he'd hunted in brush before. He forced his way between trunks, holding the impeller vertical before him.

If necessary he'd have run on the lip of the planter in which the boxwoods were set, but there was a good five feet between the hedge and the second level's roof coping. Daniel sprinted around the penthouse to reach the back, just as an open aircar roared out of the garage housed in the rear half of the suite.

Hogg fired a burst, pocking the quarter panel. Where the sub-machine gun's light projectiles hit, they stressed the black thermoplastic skin to gray-white.

The driver hauled his vehicle into a tight spiral as he gained altitude. The car banked, fifty yards out from the garage and ten or a dozen feet above the level of Daniel's head.

He fired twice. The impeller's heavy recoil woke nostalgic memories of his childhood. He'd actually become a better wing shot than Hogg, who took the reasonable attitude that birds shot off a branch tasted the same as those he'd shot out of the air. The aircar was just a bigger bird, and the buttplate's punch against his shoulder was much the same as that of a shotgun using full charges.

Daniel saw a tiny spark in the car's rear fan housing. For a moment the vehicle continued to spiral upward, its fans howling.

Hogg stepped out of the garage, pointing his

sub-machine gun. "Don't shoot!" Daniel shouted. He kept his cheek weld on the stock but he'd lifted his finger from the trigger.

"Shoot, you pup!" Hogg shouted. "You bloody missed it, you did!"

The car howled. There was a *Blang!* and the rear fan blasted shreds of itself out of the housing.

Daniel heard shrill cries from the cabin. He lowered his impeller.

"Sorry, master," Hogg muttered in embarrassment. "Shoulda knowed you wouldn't miss a clout shot like that."

"I put holes in a couple blades instead of shooting out the motor," Daniel explained quietly. "I want them to have a chance to set down. Remember, I'm trying to capture the Governor alive."

The driver—a woman in uniform, Daniel saw as the car came around—fought her controls as the unbalanced rear fan shook itself increasingly to ruin. With the nose continuing to rise despite anything the driver could do, the aircar slanted toward the pad from which it'd lifted.

Daniel and Hogg flattened themselves against the wall in case the vehicle landed *be*side rather than *in*side the garage, but the driver managed to hold it straight as it slid down. The nose cleared the transom by no more than a hair. There was a crash, screaming metal, and a second crash which shook the wall that Daniel was leaning against.

The fan motors shut off. *They're not all dead.* Somebody was sobbing. Holding his impeller at port arms, Daniel walked around the end of the building and looked into the garage.

The car's bow was wedged against the back wall; the frame had bent enough to crack. The driver climbed out of the front seat. Her mouth was open and, though she was moving, there was nothing behind her eyes.

All three men in the rear compartment were bloodied, but they didn't appear to be seriously injured. The two chubby youths were nude except for rings and other piercings; one's penis stud had tufts of feather at both ends.

The male in his sixties was even fatter than his catamites. He'd thrown on a shimmering robe before running to the car, but it didn't cover as much as Daniel wished it did. His blubbering made tracks down the blood oozing from his nose.

"Governor Platt," Daniel said, "I'm Admiral Daniel Leary. I'm here to demand your capitulation to the Independent Republic of Bagaria."

Hogg began to laugh. He was laughing so hard that he had to kneel on the plaza to keep from falling over.

Adele switched to the last of the six intercom channels and grimaced: no matter what she did, she couldn't get rid of the 50-cycle hum. Fort Douaumont had an excellent communications system as installed, but it apparently hadn't received maintenance *since* that installation.

She supposed the background interference resulted from moisture and failing insulation in a distribution node which also contained a lighting circuit. Now that four of the fort's five sectors had surrendered to the Bagarians, she might escape the problem by going to another command center.

She'd decided not to move, at least for the time being. Something could go wrong with the process, and anyway—they'd paid for this location. She wondered if Woetjans was still alive.

"*Captain Ringo . . .*" Daniel said to the commander of Sector Two. "*You've proved yourself to be a brave and loyal soldier. It's time to lay down your arms as Governor Platt has ordered and spare your own life and the lives of your troops. I give you my word as an officer of Cinnabar that you'll be treated with full military courtesy after your surrender, over.*"

Adele was channeling all communications through her position, though it was obviously possible for Daniel in the Governor's suite to speak directly to the Sector Two command center or anywhere else in Fort Douaumont. She felt better believing that she knew everything that was going on, and it allowed Daniel to use his RCN commo helmet instead of fumbling with Alliance equipment.

"*Fuck you Cinnabar monkeys and fuck that pansy Platt!*" Ringo replied. A burst from an automatic impeller rang off the *Skye Defender*'s hull. His troops must've manhandled the gun from its emplacement on the outer wall and aligned it to fire through one of the small-arms ports on the courtyard side of the rampart.

Most units of the Conyers garrison were nationalized planetary militia like the Maintenon battalion which the Bagarians had impersonated. There was one company of Home Office troops, however, sent to enforce discipline generally and Guarantor Porra's will in particular. Ringo commanded them. It was Adele's good fortune that she and her team had entered the fortress in Sector Three, not Two, though it might not've made any difference. Tovera was ruthless and a dead shot, and so was Tovera's mistress.

An alarm sounded from Station B, the artillery emplacement above Ringo's sector. Adele expanded the visual link to the site, a pair of 10-cm plasma cannon on a disappearing carriage which nestled behind an armored breastwork while they were at rest.

Though the weapons were fully automated, the designers had provided for manual control in an emergency. They hadn't expected the emergency to be that a command post would be captured by a Cinnabar intelligence officer who understood the system better than the Alliance garrison had, though.

Six soldiers in field gray had come through the floor hatch and were trying to put the guns in action. They'd figured out that the Bagarians had taken electronic control of the installation, so two of them with chisels and heavy hammers were trying to cut the conduit. That wouldn't actually free the guns as they hoped, but it showed a degree of imagination which couldn't be permitted in an enemy.

"Daniel," Adele said. "Captain, that is, there're Alliance soldiers in Station B, trying to free the cannon. I don't think they can unless they're more skilled than I'd expect, but I thought you should be aware of what's going on. Over."

"*Hold one, Signals,*" Daniel said. After a few seconds' pause, he resumed, "*Roger, now link me to both the command group and the* Ladouceur *on the same circuit. Can you do that, over?*"

"Yes, Daniel," Adele said, too startled by the absurdity of the question to feel insulted. "I can do that."

Rene Cazelet returned to the command post and sat at the desk

"*Officers, this is Squadron Six,*" Daniel said briskly. He probably didn't realize he'd been out of line. "*Lieutenant Liu, land in Grand Harbor as planned. When the* Ladouceur's *down, Officer Sun and I will transfer to her. We'll have to hike the half mile unless there's another aircar that I haven't found, but I guess we can handle that. A group of political troops're dug into a section of the fort and won't give up, so I'm going to let them die bravely.*"

He paused without signing off, then continued, "*Woetjans, I gather there's a lot of unrest on Conyers. Since I don't expect the rebels to introduce themselves and ask for our identification, Sun and I'll need an escort of twenty or so Sissies. Over.*"

"Captain . . ." Adele said. Her lips twisted as though she were sucking on a lemon, but the words were coming out all right. "Chief Woetjans has been wounded. You'll need another detachment commander. Over."

"*Understood, Signals,*" Daniel said calmly. "*Break. Ashburn, alert twenty spacers as an escort. You can pick anybody you want. Six out.*"

Adele rubbed her eyes, letting the chatter of the many detachments flow through her. She was as tired as if she'd been carrying another person on her back. She wondered if a drink would help her relax.

"Adele?" Rene said.

She looked up. He flinched from her unintended expression, but he seemed calm as he continued, "We got Woetjans to the Medicomp and she's stable now. Barnes wanted to transfer her to the *Ladouceur,* but I'm familiar with the units installed here in the fortress.

They're quite satisfactory, a little different from the RCN type but of the first quality. And they're newer than the cruiser's."

The image of Station B still held a quarter of Adele's display. One of the men trying to cut the conduit leaped to his feet, flinging his hammer and chisel in opposite directions. Before his body'd collapsed, his partner lurched into the gun carriage and sprawled in a flag of blood. On the other side of his body, the projectile that'd killed him ricocheted as a bright purple streak from a trunnion.

"Thank you for taking care of that, Cazelet," Adele said. She didn't mean to sound so formal! "I wouldn't have gotten around to it in time."

She cleared her throat. "That is, if it's in time now. I didn't get much of a look at the wounds, but it's clear the Chief was, ah, badly wounded."

Another Alliance soldier dropped. Two more ran for the hatch and died in a tangle across it. The sixth man, rather than trying to outrun impeller projectiles fired from the roof of the HQ Building, huddled behind the plasma cannon. Hogg must be smiling . . .

"She's stable, mistress," Rene said with a lopsided smile. "It's been my experience that if you get them to the Medicomp, you'll probably be all right. Except for brain and spinal injuries. Shock kills more than trauma does, and she won't slip off that way now that she's hooked up."

"Ladouceur *Six-two to Squadron Six-four*," said a voice Adele didn't identify instantly. "*Mundy, this is Borries. Please reply, over.*"

The Pellegrinian was using the laser communicator, not the microwave link through the planetary comsat system by which Adele'd netted the cruiser with the detachment on the ground. Because the *Ladouceur* was landing in a descending spiral, for part of the time she'd have been out of line-of-sight with the fort's laser transceiver heads.

"Mundy to Borries," she said. "Go ahead, over."

"Mistress?" said Borries. He sounded tense. *"Can you highlight where the holdouts are on a map of the fort for me, over?"*

Adele frowned. "Borries," she said, "there're friendly troops holding the sections to either side of the target. I know that Captain Leary intends to displace them himself, over."

"Mistress, I can do this," Borries said in a tone of frustrated despair. *"Six won't let me but I can. Let me do my bloody job, mistress, over!"*

Adele pursed her lips again. She'd already prepared the schematic with Sector Two in red and a pulsing cursor over the gun emplacement still in Alliance hands. "Borries," she said, "I'm transferring the data now, out."

Her wands flicked.

In her experience there were very few people who wanted to do their jobs. If the Pellegrinian missileer badly missed his aim, well, there weren't many friendly personnel closer to the target area than Signals Officer Adele Mundy.

"Captain Ringo," Daniel said, *"I'm speaking to you as Commander Daniel Leary, RCN. Please, you have a last chance to surrender on honorable terms. You can see that with only small arms at your disposal, you can't resist for more than an hour or two. Surrender and—"*

A low-frequency rumble from the east was beginning to shake the fort. Dust which Barnes' burst had smashed from the walls quivered in the air.

"*Bugger you, Leary!*" Ringo screamed. He must be spraying spittle into the microphone; perhaps he too had watched his men shot down. "*Didn't you hear me the first time? Bugger all of you bloody Cinnabar faggots!*"

The sound of the cruiser in its final landing approach built to thunder. Through it Adele heard a shriller sound.

"Adele," said Cazelet as he slid out of the seat built into his desk. "I think we'd better get down—"

The CRACK! was earsplitting. The Alliance warrant officer's corpse bounced from the floor at Adele's feet, spun on its axis, and flopped back face down.

Adele's display went monochrome for an instant, but the console had its own power supply. Dust lifting from the floor interfered with the projections and blurred the images, but there was nothing wrong with the computer itself. The quadrant showing the gun position went blank because the sending unit had vanished.

"Adele, get down!" Rene screamed. He started toward her but sprawled headlong when the second missile dealt the fort another hammer blow.

Adele strapped herself in and switched her display to a video pickup on the exterior wall of the HQ Building's penthouse. It provided a 90-degree panorama of the rampart, including Sector Two. The gun emplacement was a smoldering crater where a few strands of wreckage poked out of the smoke. The angle beneath it, the precise middle of the sector, had taken the second hit. Blue sparks snapped and sparkled through the bitter gray whorls, showing that the missile had punched deep enough to cut power lines.

The third missile hit twenty yards to the right of the second, delivering the worst shock of all to Adele's CP. Concrete shattered and steel—the missile's nose, cast from a nickel-iron asteroid, and the wall's reinforcing rods—burned white from the friction of impact. The fourth missile drove into the rampart on the left of the angle, a perfect pairing with the third.

The *Ladouceur* roared overhead as it dropped into Grand Harbor. Its magazines still carried two plasma missiles which hadn't been launched on Churchyard, but Adele supposed Borries hadn't had time to program them during the cruiser's landing approach.

He hadn't needed them, either. There was no question about that.

Smoke shot up from scores of gunports and ventilation shafts; occasionally a streamer of red flame licked like a snake's tongue before sinking back into the foul blackness that was settling over the gutted angle. The barriers were already down, cutting the late Captain Ringo's sector off from those which had surrendered to the Bagarians. The deepest bunkers may've survived, but all passages from them to the surface had been filled with rubble.

"*Squadron, this is Squadron Six,*" said Daniel. "*Fellow spacers, don't get cocky quite yet, but I believe we've completed the conquest of Conyers. Ashburn, I won't need your escort after all. And Chief Missileer Borries—*"

He paused, then resumed, "*Mister Borries, I have some quibbles about your judgment, but your professional skill is on a par with that of the best people*

I've ever seen in action—myself very definitely among them. Congratulations, my fellow spacers, I'm proud to serve with you. Hip hip—"

"Hooray!" shouted Rene Cazelet. And Adele found herself shouting also.

CHAPTER 18

Fort Douaumont, Conyers

When the *Skye Defender* had lifted thirty feet or so above the courtyard, the echoes hammering from the fort's inner walls no longer multiplied the thruster roar. Though the noise was only *just* short of deafening, Hogg put his mouth close to Daniel's ear and said, "I'm surprised you let the wog take it up himself, master. I thought you'd want to do that."

"Oh, Captain Salmon's quite competent," Daniel said, turning his head sideways to follow the freighter through the bay window of the penthouse office. "Anyway, there's no great trick to liftoff, even from hard ground. So long as you're continually adding power instead of reducing it, a few coughs and stumbles from the thrusters aren't going to do real harm."

Salmon'd been trying to rise vertically, but there was enough wind to drift the transport west as soon as she'd risen out of the shelter of Fort Douaumont. That was all right: she was high enough that her plasma exhaust wasn't a danger to those on the ground.

"Besides, I have other business to tend to," Daniel muttered, embarrassed at his sudden desire to snatch the controls out of Salmon's hands. He wanted to be in control of everything himself, which wasn't proper. Most people did a perfectly adequate job of whatever they were doing, and a few—Borries for example—were exceptionally good.

The *Skye Defender* began to settle into Grand Harbor where she belonged. Troops came out of Douaumont's bunkers where they'd sheltered during liftoff and crossed the courtyard, going about their business. Daniel turned away from the window just as Ashburn rapped on the jamb of the open door.

"We got everybody down in the second-floor conference room, sir," Ashburn said. She'd been acting as chief of the ground detachment in place of Woetjans. "You want me to bring 'em up here? It's gonna be tight, but I guess that's their lookout."

"No, I'll come down," Daniel said. He looked around the room to see if he was leaving anything behind.

And who'd replace Woetjans as the *Ladouceur*'s bosun? Riley, he supposed, though he suspected Woetjans herself would say Harrison. Daniel was almost of a mind to give the job against his better judgment to Harrison—who'd twice been broken back to ordinary spacer for being drunk on duty—in deference to the opinion of a comrade who was comatose and might not recover.

Hogg offered the sub-machine gun, keeping the heavy impeller for himself; Daniel brushed the suggestion aside more harshly than it deserved. Hogg functioned quite well in civilized society by acting like a dimwitted rube, but he wasn't really a part of that milieu. Daniel could get along in a state of nature better than most could, but he wasn't comfortable in it. He treated even battle as a civilized contest.

He preceded Hogg down the stairs; Ashburn had gone on ahead. Governor Platt had an elevator behind a curving door in a corner of his bedroom. It was keyed by his retinal pattern, but that would've been child's play for Adele to modify. Daniel hadn't asked her to do so; stairs weren't a hardship for him, and the less he had to do with a pig like Platt, the more comfortable he was.

His boots whisked on the treads. Ashburn opened the door and a babble of voices echoed in the polished stone corridor beyond. "Clear the bloody way, will you?" Ashburn snarled. "Make way for Six!"

Hogg belonged in the natural world, his master belonged in a civilized one. And Lady Adele Mundy? Adele was Adele, no more part of any world than a pearl was part of the oyster which formed it. She was a pearl beyond price, no doubt about that . . . but it must be a very lonely place to be. As her friend, Daniel wished he had a better existence to offer her.

The conference room had seats for twenty-five but at least a dozen additional people were standing. Colonel Chatterjee sat at the foot of the long table opposite the empty chair left for Daniel. He started to rise at Ashburn's announcement, but Daniel waved him down and strode quickly through the milling standees.

Adele and Cazelet were on chairs in the corner nearest the door; her servant stood in front of them with her miniature sub-machine gun in her hand instead of being discreetly concealed in her attaché case. When a stranger—one of Chatterjee's aides—backed too close, Tovera pinched his earlobe between her thumb and forefinger and pulled his head around so that the muzzle of the little gun was within an inch of the fellow's right eye.

He squealed; Tovera let him jerk away. Daniel didn't exactly approve, but the Bagarian *had* been discourteous to a lightly built woman. And he had to smile at the sheer professionalism of Tovera's response: an amateur would've prodded with the gun and might've lost it if the fellow were well trained and very fast.

Though it was unlikely that anybody in this room was fast enough to disarm Tovera.

"Ladies . . ." Daniel said, nodding to the heavyset woman seated to his right. She was Lee Brandt—Ma Brandt. Her past year of imprisonment in a bunker under Sector Four had left her hard as the stone walls of her cell.

"And gentlemen," nodding this time to Colonel Chatterjee. "As the highest-ranking official of the Independent Republic of Bagaria who's now present on Conyers, I've gathered you to discuss the settlement I propose."

"Who are you to be discussing anything?" Brandt said. "And what's the Independent Republic of Bagaria when it's at home?"

"I'm Admiral Daniel Leary, mistress," Daniel said mildly. "And since we're doing introductions—Colonel Chatterjee, Mistress Brandt was Chairman of the United Grange of Conyers until her arrest for sedition. She led the opposition to Governor Platt's autocracy. Mistress, Colonel Chatterjee commands the troops which captured the fort here to free you and your fellow prisoners. He's an officer of the worlds which've rebelled successfully against Alliance misrule in the Bagarian Cluster."

"I'm an officer of Skye," Chatterjee said. His words were a trifle too forceful for the pleasant tone. "Which is a member of the Bagarian Republic, yes."

"There are delegations from all over the planet on the way here, Mistress Brandt," Daniel said, settling back in his seat to look less threatening than he would if he weren't careful. "Some of them are here now—"

He gestured to a pair of men whose clothing had been cut out of canvas. They leaned forward to look past the people between them and Brandt.

"Hi, Ma," one of them said, waving his hand side to side. "This is Bob Casey. I think he's after your time—"

"Ma'am, I'm honored," the second man said. They were both in their mid-thirties, as much alike as one sand perch to another.

"—but he's got a battalion of two hundred militia in the Northanger District."

"Right, only no guns," Casey said. "Until just now, right, Leary?"

Daniel nodded pleasantly. He was structuring this discussion carefully, the way he'd conduct a battle. He'd get to the guns in good time.

"Fort Douaumont is the key to Conyers," Daniel said. "If the Alliance recaptures it, your Grangers won't be able to take it back, mistress. And—"

"We won't let them recapture it!" Brandt said. "No fear on that score. Now that we've got it, we'll keep it!"

"With respect, mistress," Chatterjee said. "*My* troops have the fort, not yours."

"Look here, Colonel!" Brandt said. "If you've got the notion your lot's going to waltz in here and take over where Platt left off, I'm telling you you're wrong! We—"

"Silence, if you please!" Daniel said.

"—can run our own—" Brandt said at a rising volume.

The aide seated to Chatterjee's left started to get up, his face already crimson. Ashburn put her hand on the fellow's shoulder and slammed him back in his seat.

"—government and collect our own—"

Daniel was poised to grip Ma Brandt and turn her forcibly to face him, but that had a danger of leading to real problems. Still—

Hogg gestured upward. Tovera nodded, grinned like a serpent, and fired a single round into the ceiling over Brandt's head. The ceramic pellet punched through the molded plaster and pulverized itself against the concrete underlayer.

"What?" Brandt shouted, looking up just in time for a mist of finely divided paint, plaster, glass, and concrete to cover her eyes and open mouth. She lurched forward, trying to sneeze and cough at the same time.

"Thank you," Daniel said calmly. "I believe that if we all remain courteous, we can arrive at a generally acceptable solution."

He smiled. He wondered if Hogg and Tovera had planned this ahead of time or if they were just so much in tune with one another's mind-set that a crooked finger was all the communication they needed.

Hogg's stocked impeller was a very powerful weapon.

Its discharge inside a room would've sounded like a bomb going off, and the osmium projectiles it fired would've ricocheted lethally instead of disintegrating.

Nobody tried to speak, though several people were sneezing. Daniel tightened his diaphragm to smother a sneeze of his own.

"The fort depends for its safety in the first place on its missile batteries," Daniel said. "Unless they're operational, the Alliance can reduce the position as easily as my cruiser destroyed the sector which refused to surrender to Colonel Chatterjee's forces. Mistress Brandt—"

He nodded to the Grange leader again. She held a hand over her mouth, but that seemed to be a precautionary measure.

"—your personnel don't have the skills to operate the missile system."

"We could learn," Brandt said, glancing toward Chatterjee with a wary look. She didn't raise her voice, and she only partially lowered her hand.

"Mistress," Daniel said before Chatterjee stepped in. "I've very frequently led forces into battle. If I were a man who lied about his own resources, I'd have been killed long since. Your farmers, properly armed and led, may well become the best infantry in the Bagarian Cluster, but they won't learn to operate shipkilling missiles in your lifetime or mine."

Brandt muttered something inaudible. Daniel turned to Chatterjee, who wasn't perfectly successful in controlling his pleased smile, and continued, "Which brings me to the next problem. Colonel, your battalion can't prevent the Alliance from landing out of the fort's range and bringing anti-ship missiles close enough to blockade you. To be safe from being starved out, you need to control the planet, not just Fort Douaumont."

He paused. "Go on," Chatterjee said, wary also but smart enough to wait to hear the complete proposal.

"Because Conyers was a Cluster Headquarters," Daniel said, "the bunkers beneath us here contained more than just Mistress Brandt and other prisoners. There are over ten thousand—"

"Over twelve thousand, if the inventory records are correct, Admiral," Adele interjected.

"Over twelve thousand, that is," Daniel said with a spreading smile, "stand of arms. That's small arms, no automatic impellers even, but sufficient to make Conyers a deathtrap for any force landing on the planet without the good will of the local populace. My people—"

"My people" was precisely true, Sissies whom Daniel was certain he could trust completely.

"—are distributing those arms to members of the United Grange of Conyers even as we speak."

Chatterjee started to jump up, then started to speak. He restrained himself both times, but the smile he gave Daniel was at best wry.

"With the military aspects of planetary defense settled," Daniel went on, "I've fulfilled my obligations with one exception—making arrangements for command of the defenses. I'm appointing Colonel Chatterjee as Military Governor of—"

"Now just—" Brandt said.

Hogg pointed his left arm, index finger extended, toward her face. He held the heavy impeller like a pistol, its butt resting on his right hip.

"If you'll please wait, mistress," Daniel said crisply in the renewed silence. "Military Governor, as I said, to coordinate with the civilian government through the mechanism of a Council of Twelve chosen by the citizens of Conyers."

He nodded toward the local men down the table from Brandt.

"Masters LaPlant and Casey inform me that this corresponds to the subdivisions of the United Grange."

"That's right, Leary," Bill LaPlant said. "And let me tell you, if Platt and his pansies think they can take things over now we've got guns, we'll teach him different!"

"I don't believe Governor Platt will be in a place where what he thinks affects anybody else, Master LaPlant," Daniel said. "But I agree with your larger point: So long as the Skye troops and the United Grange cooperate, there's no chance at all of Guarantor Porra reconquering Conyers."

Dasi and Barnes stood against the wall on either side of Adele; they grinned at one another over her head. There was no need to make a point of it, but either man could've convinced the Granger that who you screw has nothing to do with how well you fight.

"Right," said Daniel, rising from his chair. "My spacers and I will leave you here to work out the details for the government of Conyers. I very much hope you all understand that this requires consensus among the parties, but—"

He smiled around the room. From the tightness he felt in his facial muscles, he suspected his expression was merely a broader version of Tovera's before she shot into the ceiling.

"—when all's said and done, I'm an RCN officer. My responsibilities don't include the governance of planets which aren't enrolled in the Friends of Cinnabar. Good luck to you all, ladies and gentlemen."

As Daniel spoke, he strode toward the door on the other side of the room. Hogg, his impeller slanted across his body, made sure the path was open. As they stepped through the door, Adele leaned close and murmured, "How long do you think this will last?"

Daniel shrugged. "I give it a good chance," he said as they walked toward the stairs. His next order of business was to go aboard the *Ladouceur* and see to matters there again. That meant a hike, but at least they wouldn't need an escort.

"Ma Brandt herself may be a problem, but I think the people who've been running the Grange since her imprisonment are reasonable. As is Chatterjee."

He grinned. "And anyway, speaking as Commander Daniel Leary, RCN," he concluded, "I think it'll last long enough to take the pressure off Admiral James. The rest isn't really any of my business, right?"

Daniel laughed. Shortly he'd be back in command of a warship, where he belonged. What could be better than that?

Pasternak lit the first pair of thrusters. The *Ladouceur* rocked gently, not from the negligible lift but because the rhythmic pulses of ions rippled waves in the surface of Grand Harbor. Adele began to recheck her display.

"*Mistress?*" said Rene on a two-way link from the console beside the one she was using. "*I'd thought of Commander Leary as a, well, a fighting naval officer.*

After watching him settle the government of Conyers, well . . . he's really a politician, isn't he? Over."

Adele smiled wryly. "I assure you, Rene," she said, "Captain Leary *is* a fighting naval officer. Any Alliance commander who's faced him will vouch for that. The survivors will, that is."

She expanded the inset of Daniel's face on her screen. Another person might've turned around instead, but Adele had an instinctive preference for information recorded and therefore distanced from her.

"But yes," she said, "he's a politician too. He comes by that honestly, of course. His father was—is—a very successful politician."

"Lighting Three and Four," Pasternak's voice rumbled on the command channel. When discussing the ship's propulsion system, he always spoke with the gloomy assurance that something was going to go wrong.

"Do you suppose he could take over the Bagarian Cluster, Adele?" Rene asked. His face had a taut lack of expression, like that of a tennis player awaiting his opponent's serve. *"Give them a real government, I mean?"*

Adele let the question tumble in her mind for a few moments. She called up a series of data fields in quick succession, not really to view them but to remind herself of their contents and to revisit the questions they'd raised when she compiled them.

"He . . . might be able to do that," Adele said slowly. She frowned and went on, "I'm not putting it that way to be mealymouthed, I'm honestly not sure that anyone could unite the cluster without a powerful fleet behind him. But if it were possible, Daniel would certainly be the one to do it."

The *Ladouceur* had come fully alive. All sixteen thrusters were alight, though their nozzles were flared to keep lift to a minimum. A pump was running at full capacity to replenish reaction mass through a hose lowered into the harbor. Hatches were sealed, necessary systems were running in the green or—because this was the reality of a starship in service, not an ideal from a training manual—the operators had found satisfactory workarounds.

One of Adele's stern quadrant of microwave dishes no longer sent or received, but she'd found that at full extension the installations on either side could provide coverage for any target more than two hundred feet out from the cruiser's hull. That'd do till Pasternak had leisure to assign a team to trace the fault.

"The *Ladouceur*'s the most powerful ship in the cluster," Adele said, musing aloud. "The only real warship, barring that Alliance destroyer whose captain apparently isn't willing to fight."

"*They were badly outnumbered, Adele,*" Rene objected quietly.

Adele sniffed. "Imagine the odds were reversed," she said. "Ask Vesey what she'd do. Or Blantyre, or Cory. Or Sun for that matter, though I'm not sure that he'd be able to program a course on the astrogation computer. They'd still fight. The only difference between them and Commander Leary is that he'd do a better job of it."

She called up the lists of military organizations in the cluster: the Presidential Guard, individual planetary forces, the private militias in the pay of a local merchant or landowner. Numbers and quality, both slippery fish to pull out of the morass of corruption and incompetence which underlay every revolutionary movement Adele had seen. You wondered how any of them succeeded, until you looked at the governments they opposed.

"The spacers would support him," Adele said. "We'd have to arrange to pay them, but that could be done by nationalizing a bank. Nationalizing all the banks, perhaps. The present government doesn't do that because the ministers either own the banks or are in the pay of those who do. Daniel wouldn't be constrained. Further—"

She pursed her lips. She was speculating in a fashion she normally did only in the silence of her mind. She could argue that if Rene was smart enough to understand what she was about to say, he was smart enough to figure it out for himself . . . but the truth was that she *felt* like telling him. Adele didn't pretend that she fully understood the workings of her own mind, but she didn't lie to herself.

"—I think it's probable that he could float a loan from Cinnabar sources to enable him to become overlord of the cluster."

Daniel could obtain money from the Shippers' and Merchants' Treasury, owned by his father and sister; or from the Chancellery itself, with his father pulling the necessary strings in the Senate. Oh, yes: Speaker Leary was a *very* effective politician.

"*Ship, thirty seconds to liftoff,*" Daniel said. He sounded pleased. He had every reason to be, of course: he'd successfully completed his mission on Conyers, and he was going back into space. To Daniel, either was cause for celebration.

"With control of the navy, it'd just be a matter of

finding allies on the individual worlds who'd support him for leadership of the cluster. That wouldn't be difficult."

Adele smiled faintly. "He has me, after all," she said. "If there's a data bank in the Bagarian cluster that I can't enter more or less at will, it's kept itself well concealed thus far."

Was that bragging? Perhaps, but it was also part of a dispassionate analysis of the question. And besides, she felt like saying it. To Rene.

"The present government is a cabal of Pelosian magnates," Adele said. "They aren't really united, and with the exception of Madame DeMarce, they don't have any real support outside of Pelosi. Overthrowing them wouldn't be a problem, but uniting the separate worlds afterward would take considerable skill."

The thruster note changed from an omnipresent *hoosh* to a snarl which built to thunder as the petals sphinctered down. The rocking motion stilled, replaced by a purposeful hammering. The *Ladouceur* started to lift.

"*The sort of skill Commander Leary showed on Conyers, you mean?*" Rene said. Commo helmets had active sound cancellation, and the thrust rising quickly to 3 g didn't show in his voice. He had more experience of space travel than the Bagarians in the crew, after all. "*Over.*"

"Putting the cluster together would require an order of magnitude greater ability than the settlement on Conyers did," Adele said, watching data cascade past her. A real-time panorama of Grand Harbor showed at the top of her screen, but the roiling, rainbow-shot mist was by now too familiar to be interesting. "But I don't believe Daniel considered Conyers a serious test of his capacity. So, as for your initial question . . ."

Adele weighed probabilities with her lips pursed. She knew what she felt, but she didn't trust feelings—though she'd acted on the basis of feelings and might do so again. The answer to a question asked by someone else had to be based on data and reason.

"I believe Commander Leary would have a reasonable chance, a better than even chance, of taking control of the Bagarian Cluster by coup," she said. "I don't gamble, but I assure you that the spacers who've served with Daniel in the past would certainly bet on that outcome. Bet their lives."

The noise softened as the *Ladouceur* rose into thinner levels of the atmosphere, but the thrusters' vibration was worse for lack of air to dampen it. Daniel would be switching to the High Drive shortly, Adele supposed.

"*Adele*," said Rene. "*Will he do that? Take over? He must know that the cluster would be better off under his leadership than under the present government, over.*"

"I'm sure even the current ministers know that Daniel would rule the cluster better than they do," Adele said, feeling a smile quirk her lips. "They won't offer him the position, though, because the well-being of the cluster isn't their primary concern. And Daniel won't take the position by force, because the cluster isn't his primary concern either. Remember, he's an officer of the Republic of *Cinnabar* Navy."

"*Ship, we'll be switching to High Drive in fifteen seconds*," said a half-familiar voice. Adele checked: Ashburn was speaking. She'd forgotten she was a Power Room tech. "*Switching now.*"

The thrusters cut out. For several seconds the *Ladouceur* was in free fall save for a late burp from a nozzle toward the stern; then the ship quivered with the harder, higher frequency note of matter-antimatter conversion. Renewed acceleration kicked Adele back into her couch.

"*Mistress,*" Rene said, "*when the present ministers— when people of their sort—are afraid, they could do anything. And they'll never believe that Commander Leary doesn't plan a coup, because they'd plan a coup in his position. He . . . I'm sure he knows that, over?*"

"Yes, Commander Leary knows that," Adele said. Daniel would've known that even if she hadn't warned him herself. He was, after all, Corder Leary's son. "I'm sure he's factoring that probability into his plans."

Daniel reduced thrust to one gravity now that the *Ladouceur* was clear of Conyers' gravity well. People were moving in the corridor outside the bridge, riggers preparing to go out on the hull and set the sails.

"*I don't see what he can do if he doesn't launch a coup,*" Rene said softly. "*I just don't see what other choice there is, except giving up.*"

He coughed and as an afterthought added, "*Over.*"

Adele almost laughed. "Daniel will do what he believes is best for Cinnabar," she said primly. "And I very much doubt that means giving up."

The forward airlock sighed open for the riggers to enter. In a few days the *Ladouceur*'d be back on Pelosi. Things would happen then.

Adele absently patted the left pocket of her tunic. She didn't know what those things would be; but like Daniel, she'd deal with anything that arose.

CHAPTER 19

Morning City on Pelosi

Daniel closed the office door behind him, then saluted Minister Lampert as best he could. He said, "I called to see if you have any questions regarding the report on the liberation of Conyers which I transmitted from orbit, Minister."

The frame of Lampert's desk was bronze cast in floral designs reminiscent of carved wood, and the desktop was a sheet of Blue John. The whorls of blue, indigo and violet picked out by inclusions of white calcite might've been attractive, but use had chipped and scarred the soft stone.

There'd been vandalism as well. Several yahoos had carved their names, and at least one had attempted a pornographic drawing.

"Questions, Leary?" Lampert said in a heavily ironic tone. He didn't rise. Behind him was a hammered-glass panel, an allegory in which a half-draped woman bestowed bounty on uncertain figures; half the panel's backlighting had failed. "I wouldn't know where to start. Perhaps with the fact you turned all the resources of the Alliance headquarters over to a traitor to the Republic? Yes, let's start with that. *Why* did you give Conyers to General Radetsky?"

"I did nothing of the sort, sir," Daniel said, searching for a place to let his eyes rest so that he wouldn't seem to be glaring at the Navy Minister. "Troops from Skye participated in the capture of the planet. I left them as a garrison, but the citizens are now armed. Even if Skye weren't a loyal member of the Bagarian Republic, which to the best of my knowledge it is—"

"It is not!" Lampert said. The potted plants at both sides of his huge desk were yellowing, though their stiff fronds hadn't shriveled or drooped. Maybe they were supposed to be yellow. "Radetsky is planning to revolt."

"Be that as it may, sir," Daniel continued with an appearance of calm. "I assure you that the citizens of Conyers won't permit their planet to be given to Governor Radetsky or anybody else."

The government had ignored his return from Conyers. He hadn't even been sure Lampert was going to allow him this meeting.

"I don't know whether you're really that stupid, Leary," Lampert said, knuckling his forehead with his right hand, "or if this isn't just another example of the dumb insolence we've had from you in the past. Well, what's done is done, I suppose."

He nodded toward the door behind Daniel. "You can leave now," he said.

"There's one further matter, sir," Daniel said, clasping his hands behind his back. He'd given considerable thought to what he'd wear to this meeting with the minister after returning from Conyers. He'd finally decided on RCN utilities, but with the solid rectangle of a Commander's insignia on his forage cap in bright silver instead of the proper subdued form. "Payment for the crews, that is. Would you care to be present at the pay parade, or will you simply deliver the money to me for disbursement?"

"Neither, I'm afraid, Leary," Lampert said. He was ostentatiously giving his attention to the flat-screen display on his desk return. While Daniel couldn't be completely sure from this angle, he suspected that the minister was playing a game that involved swirls of color. "There isn't money in the treasury for the purpose. As soon as there is, I'm sure Chancellor Hewett will inform me and I in turn will inform you."

"Sir," said Daniel, a trifle more harshly. "There's the prize money from the *Babanguida* and the *Vieux Carree* captured on Dodd's Throne, you'll recall."

Matters were proceeding in the fashion he'd expected; indeed, they were proceeding in the fashion that he'd intended. Nonetheless, Daniel found himself getting angry—not only as an RCN officer with duties to the spacers under his command, but also as a Leary of Bantry who—whatever else he might do, and at one time and another Learys had done many reprehensible things—always paid his gambling debts and always protected his retainers.

"There was a problem with that, Leary," Lampert said, turning with a theatrical frown. "The prize court found that those ships were owned by merchants here in Morning City—Master David Power and Minister Bedi. I shouldn't wonder if you find yourself on the wrong end of a lawsuit for the expenses they were put to to recover their property."

"With respect, sir!" Daniel said in a tone of incredulous contempt. "Those ships were both owned and registered on Pleasaunce itself. As shown in the ships' documentation and confirmed by the Navy House List, which the *Princess Cecile* carries as updated to the day we lifted from Xenos!"

"You'll watch your tongue, Leary," said Lampert with a rising inflexion. "Cinnabar file clerks don't rule us here in Bagaria, our courts do!"

His hand had slipped under the desk for either a pistol or a call button. The call button, Daniel supposed. Lampert wasn't the sort to stomach violence, even if he were the one offering it.

Daniel took a deep breath. He'd been out of line. If he'd behaved that way to a superior in the RCN, he'd have lost his commission instantly—even if Admiral Anston were still Chief of the Navy Board.

"Sir, I apologize for my clumsy choice of words," he said. "But it's my duty to say that I believe the Republic is making a serious mistake in not remaining current with pay to the spacers who've risked their lives to preserve that Republic. Noblesse oblige, you see, sir."

"I see my duty to the republic, Leary," Lampert said. He'd relaxed slightly, but his hand was still under his desk. "Now, I have work to do. You're *dismissed*."

Daniel saluted again and left, closing the door gently behind him. He allowed himself a bitter smile as he strode past the clerks in the outer office. As bad as he was at drill and ceremony, he couldn't have found a more pointed insult than that inept second salute had been.

Hogg rose from the bench by the door, folding his knife and slipping it away into a pocket. He'd been whittling a thumb-thick branch which he must've clipped from one of the ornamental trees lining the boulevard, forming a chain. Each link was separate from the two to which it was connected.

He grinned broadly at Daniel. There was no great trick to the work, but Hogg had been using the main blade instead of the little one which opened out from the pommel. From the horrified way the clerks were staring at him, he'd gotten the effect for which he'd obviously been striving.

"There's a couple ladies want to chat with you, young master," Hogg said, holding the door open for Daniel to step through. "They figured they'd wait for you in the bar next door, though. One stuck her head in here and told me to pass you the word when you come out."

The main victory celebration was in front of the Council Hall three blocks away, but a clot of happy drunks were staggering back in the middle of the street shouting, "Bagaria forever!" and "Drown the oppressors in blood!"

Daniel heard shots, but they were the random pop-pop-pop of revelers shooting in the air instead of the rolling volleys of riot suppression. Though the government was pointedly separating itself from the victory, the general populace of Morning City was deliriously triumphant.

"I ought to be getting back to the *Ladouceur*," Daniel said. It wasn't like him not to talk with a woman, but the interview with Minister Lampert had left him with a distaste for civilian companionship just at the moment. "Look, I don't mean to be unsociable, but—"

"Nor shall you be," said Hogg, gesturing toward the swinging double doors of a tavern. It really *was* adjacent to the three-story office building which'd become the Bagarian Ministry of the Navy. "Come in or I'll grab you by the ear and tow you, like I done when you were a snotty five-year-old."

Hogg grinned. "Besides, you could use a drink," he said. "And me, I could *always* use a drink."

A bar of polished wood on a leather-padded pedestal ran the length of the narrow room. A spray of cut flowers stood on the return; the clear vase displayed colored gravel into which the stems were thrust. The bartender, a middle-aged fellow who affected a white shirt and a narrow black ascot, raised his sad eyes.

Down an aisle past the ten stools was a back room; its door had been stopped open with a crate of empty bottles. Daniel looked through the doorway and saw Vesey seated with Blantyre at a table, both dressed in civilian clothes.

"Thank you, Benno," said Hogg, passing what was clearly scrip rather than a coin across the bar in the hollow of his palm. "Here's the other half. And a pair of rums for me and my friend, all right?"

He glanced toward Daniel, who was already striding toward the back past the three men on barstools. "I think the rum's better'n the whiskey on Pelosi, but if you want the other . . . ?"

"I'll trust your palate, Hogg," Daniel said. The women were getting up. He waved them back into their chairs and kicked the crate out of the way as he entered.

He didn't ask what he owed his servant for arranging the use of the back room. Hogg would make himself whole one way or another—and Daniel wouldn't ask about that either.

The back room held two tables of laminated wood, each with four leather-upholstered chairs. The women had tumblers of clear liquor which they didn't seem to have touched. Their faces were taut.

"Sir, we didn't want to hang around Navy House—well, you know, the Ministry," Blantyre said. "More than we had to, till you got back."

"What's happened?" Daniel said, keeping his voice calm. He sat, but Hogg, who came in a moment later, remained standing by the closed door after setting a squat glass on the table. The rum was the color of kerosene.

"It's more 'in case,' sir," Vesey said, looking down at her glass. She grimaced and blurted, "I couldn't stop them from running, sir. I—"

She looked up with an anguished expression. "Sir, I know you'd have done something, but I didn't . . . I couldn't. I protested when Captain Hoppler gave the orders to shape course back to Pelosi, but he ordered a couple spacers to tie me to my bunk if I opened my mouth again."

"Me too, sir," said Blantyre. "I told Seward that when there were two sides, only a fool would line up against Mister Leary, but I didn't fight. And he ignored me."

Daniel sipped his rum. It was smooth going down despite having a proof close to that of industrial alcohol.

"I don't know what you expect I'd have done, Vesey," he said. "Shot it out with a crew of two hundred, perhaps? Though of course that'd require that I be wearing a sidearm, which neither I nor you normally do. And I rather think—"

Daniel paused, realizing that this wasn't as much of a joke as he'd intended. Still, he'd started to say it.

"I rather think that even Officer Mundy would find that long odds, don't you?" he concluded. He shook his head, smiling.

The rum had an oily aftertaste initially, but it'd gone away. Maybe his mouth'd been numbed.

"No blame attaches to either of you," he added. "Though I don't mind saying that I wished I'd had you with me on Conyers. Things worked out there too, in the end."

"When we landed in Morning Harbor . . ." said Vesey. She seemed to have loosened up a trifle once she'd apologized. "There wasn't anything said. But then some of the crew told us there was going to be a pay parade the next morning."

"But nobody'd told us," Blantyre said. She paused to take a healthy swig. From the way the liquor shifted in the glass, she was probably drinking gin. "Well, that didn't mean anything for certain, but we went back aboard the *Princess Cecile*. And we took the Sissies who'd been aboard the *Independence* and *DeMarce* too. If they wanted to come, I mean, and they all did."

"We weren't running away, sir," Vesey said earnestly. "But—well, I'm sorry, but I don't really trust the people we're dealing with in the dockyard and the supply branch. I know, there's always a difference in attitude between the ground establishment and the space establishment, but . . ."

Daniel laughed, which he shouldn't have done,

because he sucked rum down his windpipe. He hacked violently against the back of his hand.

"My goodness," he whispered in apology. "Next time I'll just breathe lava so it won't hurt as much. Goodness."

He coughed again, clearing his throat, and said, "Vesey, if you *did* trust the ministry, I'd worry about your sanity. You did well to stay out of sight until the *Ladouceur* landed."

He meant "until I landed," but the cruiser's heavy guns were a factor also.

"We watched the pay parade," Blantyre said.

"We had a good angle," said Vesey, "and the *Sissie's* optics put us right at the table."

"And Lampert really paid the crews?" Daniel said, deliberately lowering his glass this time before he spoke. "What percentage of the arrears?"

"Sir, I believe all of it," Vesey said. "And they were using Alliance notes, not the Cluster currency the Chancellery's been printing."

"Only it wasn't Lampert," Blantyre said, "or Hewett either, though they were both watching. It was one of the ministers and a local merchant, the fellow who built those plasma missiles that didn't work—"

"That would be the Cluster Affairs Minister, Master Bedi," Daniel said, "and Master Power?"

"Yes sir," said Vesey. "Those two sat at the pay table, each with clerks and guards. But they paid out the money themselves, one paying and the other making a note, then they traded off. While the Navy minister and Chancellor Hewett watched."

"I see," said Daniel without inflexion. That was showing a better long-term strategy than he'd have given the government credit for. The ministers had robbed him and his crew of the prize money owed them, but they'd spent a portion of what they'd stolen in attaching common spacers to their party.

Whereas the crew of the *Ladouceur* would not be paid. The original Sissies wouldn't desert, but spacers who were simply serving for money—which is why most people, not merely spacers, did *any* kind of work, of course—would leave a ship where they weren't being paid, in order to serve on one where they were.

"I can enlist the *Ladouceur*'s crew in the RCN . . ." Daniel said, thinking out loud. He took a large drink of rum and swirled the liquor in his mouth while he mused. "But that doesn't give me money to pay them with. If there were Cinnabar merchants here I could get loans, but this was Alliance territory before the revolution. . . ."

"Ah, sir?" said Vesey. "I was wondering where Master Cazelet might be?"

Daniel frowned despite himself: the question had broken him out of a productive reverie, and as far as he could see there was no reason whatever for it. Aloud, though, he said, "The civilian? I suppose he's with Officer Mundy aboard the *Ladouceur*."

"No sir," Vesey said. "Neither of them's on the *Ladouceur*. We were there before we followed you here, and we thought they might be with you."

"I didn't think that," said Blantyre, mildly incensed. "I didn't think anything at all about them, I was just looking for Six. But—"

She turned to Daniel with an expression of concern. Perhaps she thought she'd sounded too emphatic.

"—it's true that they must've gone off too, sir. Do you think there's a problem?"

"Well, Vesey . . ." Daniel said in mild puzzlement. "I think Officer Mundy is capable of handling her own affairs, so unless I receive some serious evidence of a problem I'm not going to worry about her."

He drank the rest of his rum with a frown. Part of him wanted another drink; but then again, part of him wanted to lead a party of Sissies to the Navy Ministry, turn the place upside down, and paint Minister Lampert green before dangling him out a window.

Daniel grinned. He could flip a coin to choose between those alternatives; or he could carry on, as of course he would do, by adapting his plans to existing conditions until he'd found a combination that'd permit him to achieve his mission.

Vesey lowered her glass. Great heavens, she'd tossed off half of it in a gulp! "Sorry, sir," she said in a raspy whisper. Couldn't blame her for a husky voice if the gin was as strong as the rum. "I didn't mean to suggest otherwise. Of course."

"Right . . ." said Daniel, a placeholder while his brain worked out the details of his decision. "Blantyre, you'll return to the *Ladouceur* with me. Vesey, I want you to continue in command of the *Sissie* with your present personnel."

He thought for a moment, licking his lips. The rum had dried them. "I'm going to transfer Woetjans to the *Sissie* also," he went on after consideration. "She's not really fit for duty, but there's no way I or the Gods Assembled can keep her on bed rest. I think there'll be less stress on the *Sissie*, because I don't want you to do anything except keep close in case I need you."

Daniel smiled to make the next words sound lighter than they were in fact. "You may have to act without orders at some point, Vesey," he said. "I'm counting on you to get word back to Cinnabar if things go badly wrong here. Do you understand?"

"Yes sir," Vesey said, grimacing. She lifted her glass, then lowered it untasted. "Sir?" she said. "I was wondering how Master Cazelet was working out. I was very impressed with the skill he showed in my astrogation classes."

Daniel blinked again. "I suppose Officer Mundy would've dealt with any deficiencies she found in his behavior, Vesey," he said. "Passengers aren't any of my business, after all, so long as they don't interfere with the workings of the ship. Cazelet has been quite satisfactory from that standpoint."

"Yes sir, quite right," Vesey said. Blantyre was looking at her blank-faced as well. Vesey finished her gin and banged the tumbler down. She was flushed and her eyes began to water.

"We'll head back to the ship now," Daniel said, scraping his chair legs as he rose. "The ships, that is. I know this is a difficult situation, Vesey, but I trust your judgment. And there isn't a great deal of choice."

The immediate problem was to find money to pay the *Ladouceur*'s crew and keep the Bagarians aboard. He hoped Adele would return soon, because she might have a suggestion.

Which would be good, because apart from turning pirate, Daniel didn't have any ideas of his own.

"You see, Mistress Hu . . ." Adele said to the angry fat woman across the desk from her. "Admiral Leary needs a loan to meet the wage bills of the spacers in his squadron. I hope—"

"You can go away now," Esther Hu said. She'd taken public control of Binturan Brothers Trading on the death of her husband, but according to the records he'd been only the public face of the business run before her by her father and uncle—Kostroman citizens. "I've paid my taxes to the government—and if you think you can pressure me, I've got the protection of Chancellor Hewett!"

"We know you've paid your taxes, Mistress Hu," said Rene Cazelet. Like Adele, he had his personal data unit live on his lap. "And I assure you, Admiral Leary isn't the sort of man who'd use your Kostroman citizenry to rouse the population against you if things begin to go badly on the naval front—as they certainly will if the crews aren't paid."

They were in a real working office at the back of one of Binturan Brothers' three warehouses. In the vast room outside, fork lifts snorted as they shifted pallets and bales; diesel fumes drifted under the office door. There were two calendars on the wall to the right, a local one with religious art and another with images of Pleasaunce City and Alliance holidays marked.

"This is a real loan," said Adele. It was useful to have Rene present to counterpoint the sales talk—or the extortion threats, if one preferred. Sometimes Tovera provided a useful foil, but she'd have been wrong for this negotiation. She stood now, watching sardonically with her back to a steel filing cabinet. "You'll get the money back with interest as soon as the Admiral is in a position to redeem it."

"I'm not interested in getting the money back!" Hu said. "I'm not giving you an ostrad! Are you deaf?"

"We'd considered asking you for three hundred and

twelve thousand Alliance marks," Adele said calmly, her eyes on Mistress Hu's.

"I can't—" Hu said in a changed tone. She flushed, then went white and slumped back in a swivel chair whose leather upholstery leaked stuffing.

"You sons of bitches," she muttered. "This *is* a shakedown."

The amount Adele'd named was Binturan Brothers' exact profit on thirty tonnes of wheat shipped from Islandia in the Bagarian Cluster to the Alliance Fleet on Formentera, as listed in the set of books which Hu kept personally. No one else—except Adele, as of the previous week—had access to the figure.

"No, mistress," Adele said with a dry forcefulness. "It is not. It is a request that you go the extra mile in support of the naval forces of the state in which you are resident."

"We realize that you have many expenses beyond those appearing on any single transaction," said Rene with a sympathetic smile. "My family's in the shipping business also—on Pleasaunce. In fact, last month we were involved in transshipping wheat from Formentera to Pleasaunce."

"You're from the Alliance?" said Hu, looking from Rene to Adele in blank surprise. "I thought—"

"Both my colleague and I are acting in behalf of the naval forces of the Bagarian Republic," Adele said. "As I'm sure you would do in similar need. As you will do, I'm confident."

"As I said, that full amount would be unreasonable," Rene put in, jerking the shipper's head back around. Adele had located the transaction when searching the files of Binturan Brothers, but only the connection with Phoenix Starfreight made it significant. "But a hundred thousand marks, paid over a period of four days beginning the day after tomorrow—that's quite possible. And necessary."

"As a loan," Adele repeated. Hu wouldn't believe her, but it was true: when the money became available to repay Binturan Brothers, Daniel would pay it over instantly. "Because you realize the importance of keeping the Cluster's warships crewed and effective."

Mind, Daniel wouldn't have authorized even this approach. It did have the hallmarks of extortion rather than business—but the Mundy family had tended to lump business and extortion together as activities unbefitting to a noble house. Adele could console herself that her parents, at least, would be no more upset by the present negotiations than they would be—for example—at the fact their daughter was a warrant officer in the RCN.

"Look, you've got me over a barrel, I see that," Mistress Hu said. She tried to glare, but anger quickly melted to miserable resignation. "But I can't come up with that much, not half that much, after fitting out all six of my ships for the Skye expedition. Sure, I've got Chancellery pay warrants, but what're they good for? And I don't know when I'll see my ships again. Can't you understand that? When or *if* I'll see them again."

Adele's face didn't show anything, but she immediately changed the search she was performing as she sat in the dusty office. "Admiral Leary has no wish to cripple Binturan Brothers. He understood—"

This was a complete lie. Adele noted that it didn't bother her to lie when it was necessary as part of her duties to Mistress Sand or to the RCN. Odd; she hadn't been aware of her skill at deceit until her job changed a few years before in a burst of gunfire.

"—that the demands of the expedition were being spread more widely among the shipping companies in Morning City."

"Did he?" Hu said bitterly. "Well, you can tell him that he's not the only one who noticed that my family's not from Pelosi and that I don't have citizenship. It didn't matter while the Alliance was in charge—oh, the governors were all crooks, but they robbed everybody! It's our new *Bagarian* ministers, Hewett and Dean, who put it to me that the only way I could prove I was loyal was to offer my whole fleet!"

"I see," said Adele calmly. She shut down her data unit; she'd gathered more information than she could process quickly, and this wasn't the time to spend in processing anyway. Without quick action, there'd be no need for analysis.

She rose nodding to Hu. "Mistress," she said, "I'll inform the Admiral of the present situation. If he finds you've been telling the truth—"

"By the Gods, I wish it *wasn't* the bloody truth!" the shipper snarled with the first animation she'd shown since Adele unmasked the fact of her transaction with the Fleet.

"If that's the case," Adele continued stolidly, "I'm confident he'll direct us to find some other arrangement for protecting the independence of the cluster. Good day to you."

She twitched her right index finger to the door. Tovera opened it, looked hard at Mistress Hu, and preceded Rene into the warehouse proper. Adele brought up the rear and closed the door behind them.

"Adele?" Rene said.

She nodded curtly and said, "Outside, if you will."

Binturan Brothers wasn't the sort of business which put eavesdropping apparatus in the light fixtures—indeed, the cavernous warehouse was noticeably *short* of light fixtures—but it might have been. Adele did things properly not so much for practical reasons but rather because she preferred to be proper. She felt more comfortable.

One of the three sliding doors in the front of the warehouse was open; a turbine was rocking slowly along an overhead trackway toward the ten-wheeled truck waiting to take it. Workers in dungarees made from coarse local fibers turned to watch Adele and her companions stride past and out the door.

Tovera rotated her head toward the workmen and outside, back and forth. Adele's lips tightened momentarily, but there was nothing to say that'd change the situation. Expecting attack from every quarter wasn't paranoia in Tovera; it was a part of life, like breathing.

And every once in a while, Tovera was right.

The warehouse faced Morning Harbor across the broad but unpaved seafront boulevard. Similar warehouses were scattered among spacers' hotels, taverns, and shops specializing in cheap clothing. Motorized buses—three or more open cars pulled by a tractor with a diesel or electric motor—ran a schedule of sorts throughout Morning City, but the four-wheeled taxi Adele had hired to bring them to Binturan Brothers was waiting down the street as directed.

The problem was that it couldn't go in two opposite directions at once.

"Rene," Adele said. She'd made the decision simply

by laying out the choices in neat mental columns. There wasn't a perfect solution; there wasn't even a good solution. Therefore she picked the least bad option. "You'll take the taxi—"

She nodded.

"—to the *Ladouceur* immediately and warn Admiral Leary that the ministry is about to move on Skye. This is too major a policy decision not to affect us, though at present I don't know in what way."

She'd been too busy with financial questions since their return from Conyers to keep abreast of the government's activities. That was a mistake: during the time she and Daniel were off Pelosi, the government had turned on an internal rival with a speed and ruthlessness it was incapable of displaying toward the common enemy.

Adele had made a mistake; but it would've been a mistake to put off raising funds to pay the *Ladouceur*'s crew. Time would probably show that she'd failed to deal with other absolutely critical matters as well, every one of which had been necessary for the successful completion of the mission. They would fail because Adele Mundy hadn't done her job adequately.

She'd go on, of course. She'd known from as far back as she could remember that she'd never be good enough to meet her own standards. But she'd go on.

"Tovera and I will find another taxi—"

"Mistress, that may be difficult around here," Tovera protested.

"Then we'll walk until we find one!" Adele said, letting her self-loathing flare out at her servant. "We'll find one and take it to the Skye Benevolent Society offices."

"Adele, we could call," Rene said, hefting his personal data unit. "I've linked into several commercial repeater grids."

"Do you trust the person who'll take the call either on the *Ladouceur* or in the Skye offices not to be an agent of the ministers?" Adele sneered. "*I* don't. And if you do, you're a fool."

"Mistress, sorry," Rene muttered.

"But the boy could deal with the other business while we return to the ship," Tovera said quietly.

"They wouldn't believe him," Adele said. "The permanent secretary knows me. He'll get word to Radetsky, I think in time."

She took a deep breath; her mouth worked, trying to squeeze out a sour taste. "We owe Radetsky something. We can't save him—Dean and Hewett are in league with the Alliance forces on West Continent. Between them they'll crush the present Skye government. But Radetsky can get himself and his family off-planet to Conyers. They'll be safe there with Chatterjee."

A red haze covered Adele's eyes momentarily. It cleared; Rene was still looking at her with concern.

"Get on with it, boy!" she said. "How much time do you think there is?"

Rene nodded and got into the taxi. It pulled off almost immediately.

"Let's go, Tovera," Adele said. All the emotion was burned out of her. "The sooner we take care of this, the sooner we return to the ship ourselves."

How much time is there? had been a good question. Probably not enough, the way things seemed to be going. She'd made mistakes. . . .

But she'd go on. Until she died.

CHAPTER 20

Morning City on Pelosi

The call plate beside Daniel's bunk buzzed. He slapped it and said, "Six, go ahead, over."

The room was dark. Daniel didn't know where he was, and he wasn't really awake: his conscious mind was watching from an indefinite distance as his body communicated by rote with whoever was on the other end of the circuit. He was already wearing utility trousers and an undershirt; he began pulling on his boots by reflex as he spoke.

"Sir, this is Liu on the bridge," the plate said.

Lieutenant Liu is officer of the watch. I'm in my space cabin, dead tired and catching a few minutes' sleep before Adele returns and the watch awakens me according to my instructions so that I can talk with her.

"Captain Hoppler's here and he's got orders from the Ministry, he says, over," Liu said. He sounded concerned, probably afraid that he was mixed up in something too big for him. More likely it was a request

318

that Admiral Leary turn in the ammunition expenditure forms that were by now so badly overdue . . . but it was just possible that Hoppler was bringing at least a portion of the crew's back pay.

"Roger, Liu," Daniel said. "I'm on my way."

He'd gotten his boots on the correct feet; now he pulled a utility jacket over the undershirt and sealed its closure also. He hoped it was presentable, but he didn't have time to check. It'd be good enough for Hoppler regardless, but if the Newbernian were coming with pay, Daniel would like to display a reasonable regard for the proprieties.

He grabbed his forage cap from the small desk and put it on; it still had his commander's square on the peak rather than the four wreaths of a Bagarian admiral, but it'd do. An RCN commander ranked a wog admiral any day of the week . . . and he hoped he wasn't so logy that he'd say that aloud.

Daniel opened the hatch and stepped into a corridor full of soldiers. A hundred or more armed spacers were milling about, fingering impellers and chemical rifles. Those near the hatch stared at him.

"Let me by, if you will," Daniel said sharply. "I'm the captain, and I need to get to the bridge!"

He'd had a momentary urge to duck back into the space cabin, but he couldn't do any good there and there was more than a little chance of precipitating something if he tried. Dogs instinctively chase when they see something running, and this lot were mangy curs or he much missed his bet. There were a lot of them, unfortunately.

The spacers made way at the tone of command. He recognized some as crewmen of the *Independence* and

DeMarce. Though armed with projectile weapons, many were barefoot and those with rifles wore bandoliers with only a few extra rounds thrust through the cartridge loops. Daniel didn't doubt they'd be able to control the *Ladouceur*, however. Clearly, that's why they were here.

The bridge hatch was open. Daniel strode through and swept those present with his eyes. Liu was the only member of the cruiser's crew, but half a dozen officers who'd been assigned to the *DeMarce* or the *Independence* had accompanied Hoppler and Seward.

"Welcome aboard, gentlemen," Daniel said with a bent smile. "If you'd told me you were coming, I'd have been more ready to entertain you."

Liu wasn't stupid, but neither was he sufficiently imaginative when faced with the unexpected. If any of the former Sissies'd been on watch, they'd have closed the hatches and summoned Six when they saw a body of armed men approaching.

"That's what we thought too, Leary," said Hoppler with a toss of his chin; his goatee wobbled. "That's why we didn't warn you."

He glanced at the girlishly slim Seward. "Give him the documents, Captain," he said. "It's only polite to let him read them."

Daniel took the rolled sheaf of hardcopy from the smirking Seward and untied the tape holding it. The document on top was engraved with:

INDEPENDENT REPUBLIC OF BAGARIA
OFFICE OF THE GENERALISSIMA

The remainder of the text was offset printed and the registration was skewed:

> *By virtue of the powers vested in me as
> head of state, I hereby rescind all offices and
> appointments of the Independent Republic
> of Bagaria previously granted to Daniel
> Orville Leary, a Cinnabar citizen.*

It was signed *DeMarce, Generalissima,* and countersigned *Douglas Lampert, Minister of the Navy.*

Daniel felt a smile twitch the corner of his mouth. *I wonder if I can appeal the order on the grounds they got my middle name wrong?* He didn't let the thought reach his lips. That was probably a good thing, given the glares of frightened anger which even the tiny smile drew from the Bagarian captains.

Correction: the captain and the admiral. The second document in the group appointed Andreas Hoppler as Admiral of the Navy of the Independent Republic of Bagaria, while the third—

Daniel shuffled the hardcopy, still smiling faintly

—transferred command of the cruiser *Ladouceur* to Captain Ronald Seward.

"Well, gentlemen," Daniel said, returning the documents to Seward, "these appear to be in order. I'll instruct my servant to collect my personal belongings and be off shortly."

He nodded politely.

"Don't play us for fools, Leary!" said Hoppler harshly. "You'll stay right here—in your space cabin until everything's settled. I don't mind telling you that that may take a few months."

"You've been subverting discipline in the squadron for too long for loyal officers to be safe if you were loose to pursue your schemes," said Seward. His anger was probably a reaction to being frightened when Daniel smiled. "Planning a coup, I shouldn't wonder! Well, Bagarians are going to run their own affairs now without foreign meddling."

An odd thing to hear from a Kostroman citizen, Daniel thought; but that, like so many things, could pass for now. Aloud he said, "Gentlemen, I see that I won't be able to convince you that I neither had nor have any designs on the government of the cluster. I hope, however, that you'll accept my parole as an RCN officer on my oath that I will in no way harm or act against the interests of the Republic or her officials?"

He did hope that, but with rather less belief than he had for the salvation of his soul. A promise of honorable conduct only works with people who conduct themselves honorably.

"Dream on, Leary," Seward sneered. "Just stay quiet until we've put paid to the rebels on Skye and you'll be all right. And if you're wondering, we're replacing the *Ladouceur*'s crew with spacers we can trust from the *Independence* and *the DeMarce*."

"And I'll only warn you once," said Hoppler. "If you continue to connive with traitors, you'll regret it—briefly! Even Cinnabar citizens have accidents, you know."

Daniel nodded calmly. He was worried about Hogg, but not very worried. Hogg had the instincts of a poacher, not a wild boar. If they hadn't picked Hogg up when they filed aboard—which they weren't sophisticated enough to have done—he'd be lying low and making plans which probably included wire nooses.

"Well, gentlemen," Daniel said, "I regret that you won't accept my parole."

That wasn't entirely true: if they'd been willing to treat him as an honorable man, he'd have acted as one. By making him a prisoner . . . well, it greatly extended the range of options open to an RCN officer.

"*Admiral Leary,*" rasped the command console. The voice was Vesey's, though flattened almost beyond personality by compression and expansion. Her words were being repeated on the speakers in the roofs of the corridors and compartments. "*This is Sissie Five. Please report on your situation, over.*"

A Bagarian aide drew his sidearm and pointed it at Daniel. Another aide more usefully jumped to the console. His face was grim.

"Gentlemen, let me handle this!" Daniel said. "I don't want any trouble, especially not trouble for my friends."

Daniel wasn't sure how Vesey'd been able to access the cruiser's public address system from the *Princess Cecile.* Adele could've done it, of course; but Daniel himself couldn't have. Vesey was a very sharp officer, but in this case it seemed likely that Midshipman Cory was again demonstrating his talent for communications. Cory'd never make an astrogator, but the RCN had more good astrogators than it did officers who could handle a warship's electronics.

But that was a matter for another time.

The aide looked back at his seniors. Seward shrugged. "He knows what'll happen to him if he says the wrong thing," he said to Hoppler.

"All right, Leary," said the new-made admiral. "But remember what I said about accidents!"

Daniel stepped to the console, smiled at the Bagarian beside it, and sat down. The fellow who'd drawn his pistol kept the muzzle following Daniel. His marksmanship probably wasn't any better than his judgment, but projectiles ricocheting around the steel bulkheads might accomplish what skill would not.

"Sissie Five, this is Six," Daniel said, trying to sound reassuringly bored. He wasn't worried about Vesey reacting badly, but inadvertently frightening the Bagarian officers might lead to all manner of problems. "All's well here. There's been a change of command. I'll remain aboard the *Ladouceur* to work out the details, but this doesn't affect you as commander of an RCN naval unit. Remain as you are until I return or you receive orders from a higher authority, over."

There was what seemed a long silence. Daniel really wanted to ask if Vesey'd had word from Adele, but he couldn't risk calling her to the Bagarians' attention. Things weren't immediately dangerous, so he'd gather information before he acted.

"*Roger, Six,*" Vesey said. This time her voice really was flat, quite apart from the effect of transmission. "*We'll wait in Security State One until further notice. Sissie Five out.*"

Daniel rose from the console, giving the Bagarian officers a friendly smile. "There, gentlemen," he said. "There's no need for trouble, you see."

But there *would* be trouble, as soon as Daniel knew more about the situation. And he didn't think it'd take long to learn all he needed.

"I won't wait to send the courier," said Secretary Yager, a wild-haired man in his mid-fifties. "But there are citizens on Pelosi I need to warn also. Bloody *hell*!"

His fingers hammered commands into the integral

computer. It had a flat-plate display rather than a holo-tank and a mechanical rather than virtual keyboard, but the Skye Commission's electronic security was better than usual in Morning City. Adele had made her initial link through a disused microwave port which would've been difficult to access outside Yager's office.

"I wish you and your principals the best," Adele said to the Skye official. She started to shut down her little data unit, preparing to leave.

She knew that other people would've said something about regretting the situation or commenting on the injustice, but that was simply a waste of words. She'd delivered her warning and she didn't expect to see Secretary James Yager ever again.

If they were together again, it was likely to be in a Bagarian prison. Too much was happening for her to predict events beyond the moment she stepped outside the Commission building.

As her holographic screen collapsed, it flashed red. She brought her unit live again to receive the urgent message that she'd almost missed.

"Lady Mundy?" Yager asked as she settled back in her chair.

Adele ignored him. Her mouth quirked in a wry smile: she couldn't predict as much as she'd thought. She hadn't gotten as far as the door.

The message, voice sent as text, was from Rene Cazelet: *As I arrived at the harbor, I saw over two hundred armed spacers boarding the* Ladouceur. *I diverted to the* Princess Cecile *and informed Lieutenant Vesey, who has sealed the ship. Over.*

"Lady Mundy, is there something wrong?" someone nattered. "Can I help you?"

Adele entered the *Ladouceur's* command console. She ran the visuals live but voices as a text crawl at the bottom of her display. . . . *no need for trouble, you see,* Daniel was saying.

"She's busy," replied a dry voice. It was like hearing a wasp speak. "Shut up or leave the room. Or I'll kill you."

Adele split her screen and imported the bridge record from ten minutes back, then scrolled forward to the point Daniel had entered the compartment. He looked calm, but he usually looked either calm or cheerful. Actually, he seemed rather cheerful also.

Daniel turned and left the bridge unmolested. Adele shrank the real-time display to a thumbnail while the record was still running, then searched for Minister Lampert's present location. She knew she was taking a chance, but time was limited and she had to set priorities.

Lampert was in his townhouse. He wasn't married. Three servants and four guards recruited from his company's security force were in the building with him. Adele did a quick background check on the guards. All were from off-planet and had military experience either with the Alliance or Cinnabar.

"All right," she said, shutting the data unit down again. There might be more to learn, but there was always more to learn. Now she had to act. "Tovera, leave all your weapons here. We're going to visit Minister Lampert at home. We have no chance of getting through his security if we're armed."

As she spoke, she took out her small pistol and set it on the desk. Secretary Yager goggled at it.

"Mistress, that's not a good idea," Tovera said. Her

hands squeezed the attaché case minusculely closer to her chest, probably unconsciously.

"Do it!" Adele said. "Hoppler and Seward have arrested Daniel under Lampert's orders. We have to get Lampert to change his mind."

Tovera grimaced but didn't otherwise move. "Do it or stay here!" Adele said.

"Mistress," Tovera said without expression. She set the case on the floor beside her, took a knife from either sleeve, and bent to do something with her half-boots.

"Lady Mundy," Yager said softly. He didn't seem to have moved since Tovera offered to kill him. "I know Lampert. He'll never change his mind once he's committed himself."

Adele looked at the secretary and smiled faintly. "It's always a matter of the argument one offers," she said. "I think I know one that will convince him."

Tovera was taking off her belt. She looked up, saw Adele's expression, and smiled also.

"Sorry, mistress," Tovera said, again a wasp speaking through human lips. "I should've known better."

CHAPTER 21

Morning City on Pelosi

Adele rapped the street door of the narrow, four-story townhouse with her knuckles. She wished she had something hard to make a sharper sound, but though her personal data unit shouldn't have been harmed, she wasn't willing to disgrace it by such a use.

She stepped out of the door alcove, looked up the ornate brick facade, and cried "Minister Lampert! You're being robbed and I'm being robbed too! Let me in to explain while there's still time to get our shares!"

The second-story window moldings were ornate, but the living quarters were on the third story just beneath the mansard roof. The small balcony there had a wrought-iron railing and was supported by caryatids of ivory-glazed terra cotta. Engaged columns and what looked like the entablature of an ancient temple framed the double-width window which opened onto the balcony.

Tovera stood on the other side of the street where she had a better view of the building. She'd crossed her arms; she didn't seem to know what to do with them when she didn't have the attaché case to hold.

"The curtains of the balcony door moved," she said. There hadn't been any traffic on the narrow street since the taxi dropped them off. Two vehicles had started to turn in but thought better of it when they saw Adele shouting. "And a servant looked out from the second floor but ducked away when I looked at him."

Adele knocked again. She half-wished she'd kept her pistol so she could use the butt as a gavel, but—she smiled—that *really* would've sent the wrong signal.

"Minister Lampert, do you have any idea how much money you're walking away from?" she called. "There was a king's ransom on Conyers, a *cluster's* ransom, and we won't get a trissie of it if you don't listen to me!"

"Somebody's coming onto the balcony!" Tovera said. Then, "It's not the honorable Minister Lampert."

Adele backed a little further from the door. The tunic of the man leaning over the railing had puffed sleeves with a white sash over one shoulder, business dress here on Pelosi. His sub-machine gun made his real function clear.

"What do you want?" he called.

"To speak with the minister," Adele replied. "He and I are being robbed, but there's still time to get our shares."

Under the circumstances she had to raise her voice;

she was speaking to Lampert inside the building, after all. She regretted doing that both because raised voices always read as anger in a human's mind and because she was making a spectacle of herself. That wasn't behavior she expected of a Mundy of Chatsworth.

Her mother would've been horrified. There was a great deal in Adele's life in the past seventeen years that would've horrified Evadne Mundy, if she hadn't been murdered and beheaded in the Proscriptions following the Three Circles Conspiracy.

The guard had straightened to hear instructions muttered from the room behind him. Now he leaned over the railing again and said, "All right, but you'll be body-searched before you come in. And that secretary of yours! We've heard about her."

"Yes, all right, get on with it!" Adele said. "If we don't hurry, they'll split the treasure among themselves and we won't get any. Tovera, come over here."

The street door opened outward. Beyond was a narrow anteroom in which stood two more guards. Their sub-machine guns were aimed at her.

"Come in here and lie flat on your backs!" said the older, balding one. There was another door behind him, just as sturdy as the outer one. Adele wasn't sure *what* Lampert had heard about her and Tovera, but he obviously wasn't taking chances.

Adele took the data unit from its pocket and set it on the floor of the anteroom, then obeyed the command. Tovera walked across the street and lay down also. She'd protested in Secretary Yager's office, but when she accepted Adele's judgment she accepted it without reservation.

Tovera knew that she was a sociopath, lacking some

of the pieces that real human beings have. She couldn't grow a conscience, so she let her mistress supply its absence. She'd realized from the first that Adele's conscience didn't bar her from doing the quick, lethal things that were Tovera's only pleasures in life.

The search was complete and professional. Adele's mind was in another place. That was no great trick for her; this was just one more incident in a life filled with indignity and unpleasantness.

The younger guard's right arm had been burned from wrist to throat. The scarring was bright pink but flashed white when the muscles moved. *It must be very painful still . . .*

"All right, they're clean!" the older guard said.

The younger man gave Adele a final prod and straightened, grinning. "Hell, Bill, I thought we was getting a couple women. Better luck next time, hey?"

"Shut up, Darrell," the older guard muttered. Another guard with a sub-machine gun opened the inner door.

Adele stood and tucked in her tunic. "May I have my personal data unit, please?" she said to the older man. "I may need it for my presentation."

"You'll do without it," said the guard. He stepped in front of the unit and twitched his sub-machine gun meaningfully.

The third guard said, "The other one stays out here with you guys. I take Mundy up to see the boss."

"Yes, all right," Adele said. She walked past the guard, ignoring his weapon, and started up the stairs. They were wood and meant to be impressive, though there were limits to what was practical on a lot with a twenty-five-foot frontage.

The runner had been ornate. It remained colorful

on the edges where the wear of years hadn't worn
it to the nap.

The last guard looked over the second floor railing. When Adele reached the landing midway, he
gestured—with his weapon, as usual—and said, "Minister Lampert'll see you in the conference room here."

"And make sure you don't try anything!" said the
man following Adele.

There was nothing about his voice that Adele found
attractive, but he seemed to like the sound of it well
enough. She thought of asking him what he imagined
she could try, but that would've been a waste of breath.
The best thing to do with people of his sort was to
ignore them. Though—

Adele smiled slightly.

—there was a certain attraction in the alternative
Tovera would probably suggest.

Douglas Lampert was wearing a dark blue uniform
with a great deal of gold piping. His cloth-of-gold sash
displayed even more medals than graced the breasts
of his jacket. Its shoulders were padded to half again
the width of the man within; the effect unfortunately
accented pudginess that might've gone unremarked in
a less closely tailored garment.

"Your Excellency," Adele said. She made a formal
curtsey that would've pleased her mother. She'd been
raised to be a lady. This was one more proof that
there is no useless knowledge.

"I appreciate your seeing me without an appointment," Adele continued, as smoothly agreeable as
though this man's thugs hadn't just been groping
her, "and—"

She made a deprecating gesture.

"—under difficult circumstances. The meeting is in both our interests, however. The Conyers treasure is huge. I can't even estimate the value of the jewelry, but Governor Platt's inventory listed it as three milliards of Alliance marks."

"*What?*" said Lampert, his mouth gaping.

"And the credit chips amounted to an additional two milliards," Adele continued. "Colonel Chatterjee took a one-third share, but Commander Leary and I secreted the remainder on the *Ladouceur* to divide it between us. Captains Hoppler and Seward arrived while I was away from the ship, and they struck a deal with Leary which excluded me. Unless I'm very much mistaken—"

She gave Lampert a tight, cruel smile. He'd mistake the reason, but the expression was quite natural to Adele under the circumstances. Lampert would learn the reality soon enough.

"—your subordinates haven't informed you of the treasure. I propose that we confront them before they're able to get that wealth off-planet."

"No, they certainly *hadn't* informed me," the minister said. He flushed, and his breath came in deep snorts. "So those foreign *monkeys* think they're going to rob me!"

He gestured to the guard who'd brought Adele into this conference room. "McClelland, bring the car around. I'm going to pay a visit to the *Ladouceur*, and I want all four of you with me. There may be trouble."

The guard who'd stayed with Lampert all the while laughed. He was about fifty but extremely fit. "If there is, sir," he said in a Pleasaunce accent, "we'll finish it."

"Tovera and I will accompany you, your Excellency," Adele said calmly. "Oh, for our own reasons, of course, but you'll need us to locate the treasure if the conspirators don't cooperate."

She smiled again when Lampert seemed to hesitate. "Besides," she said, "they may have already started to move the treasure off the ship. Tovera has special skills which will be useful in making the thieves *wish* to cooperate. For that matter—"

Adele's expression was quite real, but the image in her mind was not of Hoppler and Seward but of the scarred young soldier who'd searched her.

"—you might be as amused as I will to watch her work on the men who robbed us."

Lampert made a moue and looked aside for a moment. "Right, there's room for the two of you in the aircar," he said as he started for the stairs. "Come along, Brodsky, I'm going to end this right now!"

The creature was the size of Daniel's thumbnail and had ten legs, but the front pair had been modified into tentacles with spiky hairs on the inside to help it grasp prey. Daniel didn't know what planet it was native to; perhaps Schumer's World, where the cruiser'd been captured, but it could be from anywhere in the Alliance or even farther.

He didn't think it was from Pelosi, though. Equivalent life-forms here had exoskeletons, while this little fellow's tough, rubbery hide was like that of a mollusk.

The guard outside Daniel's de facto cell was talking with another spacer. There was no provision for locking anybody into the compartment, so Hoppler'd had a sliding bolt and hasp welded on the corridor side of the hatch. The guard was to prevent anybody from releasing the prisoner; though the bolt was simple, it was an inch thick—Daniel'd examined it when guards brought in food—and beyond his strength to force.

The little predator stood on the edge of the desk, facing Daniel's left hand. Daniel extended his index and middle fingers toward it, keeping the others curled into his palm. He twitched the index finger up and down twice, then twitched the middle finger.

The creature twitched its right tentacle twice, then its left. Its body had been a dull mauve; it now flushed crimson in bands moving slowly from its head backward.

Hoppler had disconnected the cabin display from the *Ladouceur*'s communications system. The cruiser didn't have a large natural history database, and Daniel couldn't access the one loaded into the *Princess Cecile* now. He was sure that Adele would've been able to circumvent the block, but that was Adele.

He grinned. She wouldn't have been able to set up a missile attack, though. Which, unfortunately, wasn't a skill he needed at the moment.

The creature rotated ninety degrees to face the flat-plate display; its tentacles twitched again. *Am I supposed to turn with it or against it . . . ?*

The display itself worked. On the screen was a series of images and calculations involving the Castle System, the governmental hub of the Alliance. Pleasaunce was Castle Three, but Daniel's interest was centered on the unnamed fourth planet.

Well, now his interest was on the creature which shared his captivity; he had operations against Castle

Four planned as well as he could at his present stage of knowledge. Daniel turned his hand so that his fingers pointed the same direction as its tentacles.

The diameter of Castle Four was over 6,900 miles, but the gravity was only about half standard because it didn't have a metallic core. Despite the thin atmosphere being low in oxygen, vast quantities of water ice were locked beneath the surface crust.

The creature hopped almost an inch straight up, changing direction 180 degrees while in the air. It settled and its tentacles tapped, twice and twice as before. Daniel pondered, then tapped in answer but without moving his palm.

Hundreds of ships were on or above Castle Four at any one time. It was easier to get landing rights on Four than on Pleasaunce, making it an ideal emporium for high-bulk goods which could be stored cheaply in a near vacuum until they were purchased and transshipped. Most ores and grains were carried to Pleasaunce by intra-system lighters. Tariffs on such items were rigged to favor the practice. Not coincidentally, the monopoly on such transit was in the hands of a favorite of Guarantor Porra.

The creature hopped around, then hopped back and repeated its tapping. *All right, I was supposed to turn with it*, Daniel thought. He rotated his hand accordingly.

He assumed this was a courtship ritual, but it was possible he was in the midst of a dominance battle. If so, the creature who'd challenged him was insanely brave. It would make a good mascot for the *Sissie. . . .*

"All personnel on the IBS Ladouceur," roared the

ceiling speaker. Even through the sealed hatch, Daniel could hear the command rumbling in the corridor and from other compartments. *"This is the Minister of the Navy, his Excellency Douglas Lampert. Captains Hoppler, Seward, and Leary are to report to the* Ladouceur's *bridge immediately to confer with me. There can be no excuses!"*

The voice said it was Lampert, but there was no question that Adele was speaking the words. Daniel grinned and straightened his uniform, then checked the set of his cap. The RCN insignia gleamed neatly.

"I repeat!" said the speakers. *"Hoppler, Seward, and Leary will meet me as soon as I arrive or face immediate justice as traitors to the Republic!"*

How in the world was Adele able to do that from outside the ship? It wasn't a surprise—she'd taken over the PA systems of hostile vessels and forts a number of times in the past—but to Daniel it was like spring or a sunrise: it didn't become less magical by repetition.

"You heard your orders!" Hogg said from the corridor, his voice harsh and forceful. He wasn't shouting, but he clearly meant business. "What do they do to traitors on this anthill of a planet? On Cinnabar it's the high jump, then your head nailed up on the Pentacrest, but here I'd guess they just shoot you. That what you want them to do to you?"

"I can't let him out!" whined the guard's unfamiliar voice. "Look, if the minister wants him out, that's fine, the minister can let him out. Right? I—look, here's Lieutenant Blyth, talk to him. Lieutenant, this guy wants to let the Cinnabar admiral out!"

"Well, let him out!" snarled the aide who'd drawn

his gun on Daniel when Vesey called from the *Princess Cecile*. "And he's not an admiral, you bloody fool!"

The hatch swung back. David Blyth was toying with the flap of his holster again, but he hadn't drawn the pistol. He was a trim little man with a pencil moustache and a nervous tic in his left cheek.

"Good evening, Lieutenant Blyth," Daniel said pleasantly. He was glad that the guard—standing aside and holding his carbine by the muzzle end—had used the officer's name or he'd have had to peer at the corroded nametag to recall it. "What's going on?"

Daniel thought of the creature he'd left on the desk behind him. He felt a pang of regret, but he could tell the little fellow from personal experience that romance was a tricky business. Less so now that he was the famous Commander Leary with a chestful of medals—which he *wasn't* above using in his dealings with the fair sex; but even so, he too had disappointments.

"Look, just get . . ." Blyth said. He made a sour face; he must've realized that the situation had just changed and he didn't know what was happening. He resumed, "C-Captain Leary, will you come with me to the bridge, please?"

"I'd be pleased to, Lieutenant," Daniel said, stepping toward the bridge; it was adjacent to the space cabin, after all.

An aircar flew low over the cruiser. The whine of fans and downdrafts from shifting directions bounced through the many open hatches.

"Master," said Hogg, matching Daniel step for step, "you need to change into your Whites. It's not proper to meet the minister—"

An armed spacer stood at the bridge hatch, goggling at the procession. Daniel entered. Hogg followed.

"—dressed like that."

"There's no time!" Lieutenant Blyth said, his voice becoming shriller with each syllable.

The poacher's pockets sewn into Hogg's baggy clothing could conceal a whole covey of game birds—or an arsenal. He'd just entered the bridge unchallenged.

"Leary, you're behind this!" said Hoppler, standing arms-akimbo beside the command console. He'd obviously noticed that Minister Lampert had called him "Captain Hoppler" instead of "Admiral" and he wasn't sure what that implied.

Seward and two aides were between the signals and gunnery consoles to starboard of the perhaps-admiral Hoppler. They glanced keenly from him to Daniel and back. They appeared concerned, but they weren't showing the degree of anger that Hoppler was. They hadn't been verbally demoted, after all.

"With respect, Admiral," Daniel said cheerfully, "I don't know what you're talking about. I've been locked in my cabin, you'll recall. What *is* going on?"

"Which, is a, *bloody* good, question!" Minister Lampert said between wheezes as he clomped out of the companionway. He must've run all the way from the entrance ramp, five decks below. A guard with a sub-machine gun preceded him; Adele, Tovera, and three more armed guards followed him out of the armored tube.

"And you're going to, *answer* it," Lampert continued as he entered the bridge. His medals jangled with his gasping breaths. "Right now!"

"Of course, Your Excellency," Daniel said, walking

between Hoppler and Seward before turning to face the minister. "Whatever you'd like to know."

Hogg was wearing a glove of metal mesh on his left hand; Tovera took a writing stylus from her breast pocket. Behind them, Adele gestured Lieutenant Blyth aside and closed the bridge hatch.

"For myself . . ." Daniel said, putting his arms around the shoulders of the two Bagarian captains. "I'd like to discuss my plans for an attack on Castle Four."

While everybody—all the Bagarians, that is—stared at Daniel, Adele stepped to her right so that Lieutenant Blyth could move past her to see better. Seward grimaced and reached toward Daniel's hand to remove it like a piece of lint from his shoulder.

"Leary, have you gone insane?" Minister Lampert said, his tone that of a real question rather than an insult.

Adele nodded. Daniel banged Hoppler's and Seward's heads together with a hollow *thwock!* Adele had seen him demonstrate his strength before, but this was a remarkable reminder. She drew Blyth's electromotive pistol left-handed and pushed the safety at the front of the trigger guard forward, off-safe.

Lampert's young guard staggered forward. His mouth was open but the pain was too great for him to force words out. The last inch or so of a writing stylus projected from his lower back; it slanted upward, so most of it had been rammed through his kidney. Tovera twitched the sub-machine gun from his nerveless hands.

The flicker of light to the starboard side of the compartment was a length of beryllium monocrystal—

deep-sea fishing line—snaking out on the end of a two-ounce sinker to wrap the neck of the chief guard. Hogg jerked back hard, cutting the man's throat to the cartilage. Bright blood sprayed for yards. If it weren't for the protective glove, the thin line would've severed Hogg's fingers as well.

Adele shot the guard to her left; Lampert had called him "Darrell." The borrowed pistol was a full-sized service weapon; she hit him in the temple as she intended, but the butt recoiled hard into the web of her hand and the slug—osmium instead of the light ceramic beads she was used to—punched through the skull and whanged into the hull plating beyond.

The last guard, "Bill," grabbed for the charging handle of his sub-machine gun; he hadn't switched the weapon live when he came aboard. That'd probably been a safety measure, since an accidental burst of gunfire in a spaceship—a series of steel boxes—could kill a dozen people in a heartbeat.

Adele swung the pistol onto the new target. The pistol's unfamiliar weight meant she'd overcompensated to bring the muzzle back after the initial heavy recoil. Her shot hit the sub-machine gun's receiver, blasting out a spray of aluminum, copper, and the transformer's iron core. The slug wobbled through to take the guard at the top of the breastbone as blue sparks flared, melting the remainder of the receiver stamping.

A scoring computer in Adele's head sneered, *Center of mass, not a safe stopper on a real opponent.* It'd been good enough. As Bill lurched against the bulkhead behind him, she shot him again. His head was tilted back, so the slug took him in the throat and exited through the top of his skull.

All the aides wore sidearms, but only one besides Blyth seemed to be aware of the fact. He dabbed his hand down toward his holster, his eyes wide and staring.

Adele swung. Tovera's sub-machine gun ripped a burst and another burst, toppling the spacers in the corridor. Hogg saved the aide's life by kicking him in the crotch and, as the fellow doubled up, chopping him on the back of the skull with the pommel of the knife in his right hand.

"What?" said Lampert. "What? Wha—"

The minister dropped to his knees. He gulped, then spewed vomit over the corpse of the guard thrashing at the end of Hogg's fish line. Adele couldn't tell whether Lampert was still trying to speak or if his grunts were simply those of mindless nausea.

Adele looked at the pistol she held. The pressed-steel barrel shroud had faded back to the dull gray of its phosphate coating, but heat still made air passing through the ventilation slots tremble.

"Cease fire!" said Daniel, rubbing his knuckles. Lieutenant Blyth lay faceup on the deck. The side of the aide's jaw was angry red and already beginning to swell. He hadn't been a threat, so Adele hadn't been aware of his presence after she took his pistol.

The aide who remained standing was trying to unbuckle his pistol belt, but his fingers fumbled as uselessly as so many sausages. His face was blank and he couldn't look away from the muzzle of Tovera's sub-machine gun. He'd lost control of his bowels, but he didn't seem to be aware of the fact.

Daniel slid onto the command console and switched fields with forceful keystrokes nothing like Adele's dancing wands but every bit as precise. The ship trembled as machinery worked, though Adele didn't understand what was happening until hatches began to clang shut.

Adele's first shot had blown a bright divot out of the bulkhead beyond the guard; a film of osmium drew a soft luster over the cratered steel. Around it was splashed a much wider circle of blood and brains.

She rotated the power switch, turning the pistol off instead of merely putting it on safe; then she dropped it onto the guard's corpse. At point-blank range, the powerful slug had scooped out his skull like the remains of a soft-boiled egg.

"*Ship, this is Admiral Leary,*" Daniel said over the PA system. "*All personnel, prepare for liftoff in one hour's time. All leave is canceled. All personnel should be at their stations. Six out.*"

Hoppler and Seward were coming around, though the former's pupils weren't the same size. He'd need the Medicomp or there'd be danger of coma and death. Lampert had taken off his gold sash and was using the back of it to wipe his mouth.

Two spacers sprawled in the corridor. One lay on his carbine and the other, face-up on the deck, gripped his weapon to his chest like a funeral lily. They probably wouldn't have interfered, but they'd been armed and Tovera had decided not to take a chance. Adele would've made the same decision if she hadn't been busy killing other people at the time.

She walked over to the communications console. Hogg was carefully cleaning his razor-thin line on the jacket of the guard he'd nearly decapitated. She stepped around him. It was time for Signals Officer Adele Mundy to resume her duties.

✦　　　✦　　　✦

Daniel started to connect with the *Princess Cecile* himself, then realized he needed to talk to Vesey privately and didn't know how to be certain he'd really locked out everyone else. He didn't want even the veteran Sissies to know everything about the present situation. Besides, his right hand hurt from the punch that'd decked Lieutenant Blyth.

And besides that, he was trembling. A lot of it was adrenaline that he hadn't burned off but, well, his eyes'd happened to be on one of the fellows with sub-machine guns when Adele blew his head off. He'd seen that sort of thing before, but not quite so close or so clearly.

He flicked a blob of something off his left sleeve. Very close indeed.

"Officer Mundy," he said, pleased that he sounded unconcerned. The cruiser's systems were on standby, so he didn't need to use the intercom to be heard without raising his voice. "Connect me with Captain Vesey personally, if you will. Ah, privately, that is."

"All right," said Adele, though Daniel was guessing at what the faint words were. Her wands flickered; though in truth, that was a regular thing when Adele had her data unit out, and having the data unit out was a regular thing when Adele was awake.

"Hogg, lend me your knife," Tovera said. Hogg thrust his right hand into his pocket and tossed her the weapon, then resumed coiling his line.

Daniel couldn't pretend he liked Adele's servant or even liked to be around her, but at times like the one just past Tovera was more valuable than a squad of armed spacers. And she was perfectly loyal to Adele, a virtue that by itself would justify even a poisonous reptile in Daniel's mind.

He'd feel better when the wounded were taken to the Medicomp and the bodies—including the parts of bodies—had been removed. He didn't want to do that until he had a cadre he could trust aboard the *Ladouceur*, though.

"Six," Vesey said. "*This is Sissie Five. Go ahead.*"

Daniel smiled. Vesey was the *Princess Cecile*'s captain in fact as well as by title, but she insisted on using the call sign of a first lieutenant. That was a completely unnecessary display of humility, and if it'd been any other ship Daniel would've put a prompt end to it.

It was the *Sissie*, though, Daniel's first command and the foundation of his present success. He wouldn't insist on that deference, but under the circumstances he wouldn't protest Vesey's behavior either.

"Vesey, I want you to send me twenty of your top people, strikers and leading spacers," Daniel said. "Especially send Harrison to me as bosun."

Tovera was kneeling beside the gunman she'd stabbed with a stylus. He'd fallen on his back. His eyes stared upward; his mouth opened and closed without any words coming from it. He might recover if they got him to the Medicomp, though.

Daniel continued, "As soon as we're off-planet I'll trade you a dozen ordinary spacers to make up the watches, but I need people who can put some backbone into—"

Tovera cut the injured man's belt and started to slip his trousers down. Was she going to give him first aid?

"—the *Ladouceur*'s present company. They came off both the *Independence* and *DeMarce*, so I've got enough—"

Tovera gripped the Bagarian's member with her left hand. She gelded him with a quick slash of the knife in her right.

"Bloody hell!" Daniel shouted, bounding to his feet. Hogg shifted sideways and body checked him back onto the console.

"It's not her, master!" Hogg said. "It's for Her Ladyship! It's not our place to interfere."

Tovera stuffed the severed genitals into her victim's gaping mouth. He stiffened and fainted; his eyes were still wide open.

Adele rose from her console and looked at the carnage with eyes as cold as the hull in deep space. "Tovera," she said without raising her voice. "You and Hogg get this man—"

She gestured with her toe.

"—to the Medicomp. *Now*. It should be able to save him."

"I'd rather wait to open the bridge hatch till a draft from the *Sissie* boards, Officer Mundy," Daniel said.

Adele looked at him. He wasn't sure he'd ever before seen an expression as bleak as hers.

"I'd rather a lot of things, Daniel," Adele said. Then to Tovera in a voice like a whiplash, "Get moving! If he doesn't recover, I'll have you whipped out of my sight if I have to hire an army to do it!"

Tovera wiped the blade on the Bagarian's tunic, then flipped the knife to Hogg to close and pocket again. She took the guard's shoulders and lifted; he moaned softly. Hogg undogged the hatch and tugged it open before bending to take the ankles.

Adele settled back onto her console. "I'm going to call the Skye Benevolent Society," she said, "and request that Secretary Yager return to us the items Tovera and I left there. I'll feel more comfortable with my own tools. I don't know that Tovera cares—"

She glanced down the corridor as Hogg and Tovera disappeared into the Medicomp amidships. The cruiser had two, here in officers' country and on Level C where the enlisted personnel bunked.

"—but she's a loyal retainer of the House of Mundy. I'll not cause her to lose her possessions if I can avoid it."

"Yes, all right," Daniel said. "I'd like to lift within the hour, but realistically it'll take longer than that to organize matters here. And if we had to wait a few minutes longer yet, the delay wouldn't be critical."

"Where are you going?" Lampert said. He remained kneeling with his eyes closed. The lids quivered upward minusculely, then squeezed firmly shut again. Tears dripped slowly down his cheeks.

"We're going to raid Castle Four," Daniel said cheerfully. He was setting up the courses, a task he found familiar and congenial. With astrogation to occupy his mind, he could ignore the mingled smells of blood, feces, and the bite of ozone from the coil-gun discharges. "The *Ladouceur* in company with the *Princess Cecile*, that is."

"Let me go," Lampert whispered. "I'll pay you. I'll pay you anything you ask. Don't take me off to be killed, *please*."

"Oh, it'll be dangerous, I grant," said Daniel, "but scarcely a suicide mission. The Alliance isn't expecting a raid into their home system. If we make a quick job of it, I think there's a very high likelihood of not only getting in but also getting out with twenty or so prizes. Think of the value of twenty prizes, Your Excellency! And the Ministry's share is an eighth, remember."

Seward was awake, but when Daniel glanced at him he closed his eyes and pretended still to be unconscious. Hoppler groaned softly.

"The crew doesn't seem disposed to show itself, let alone make trouble," Daniel said, speaking to Adele but perfectly willing to be overheard by the Bagarians present. "When Hogg and Tovera return, I'll have them carry Captain Hoppler to the Medicomp also. We'll need him fit when we get to Castle Four."

"Why?" said Lampert. His voice sounded like leaves rattling through a graveyard.

"We'll need everyone we've got who can program an astrogational computer," Daniel explained. "We'll have enough personnel to form crews for twenty prizes, but that's no good unless they can navigate the ships back to Pelosi, you see?"

He grinned broadly. It was absolutely necessary that the captured vessels all start back toward the Bagarian Cluster. Most of them wouldn't make it, of course, not if they were relying on computer solutions which would be completely predictable to the Alliance forces who responded to the raid.

But Daniel, as Minister Lampert's orders made clear, no longer had a position in or duties toward the Independent Republic of Bagaria. He was an RCN officer, pure and simple, and he very definitely had duties to Cinnabar.

CHAPTER 22

Above Castle Four

"Ship, preparing to extract," announced Blantyre from the Battle Direction Center. Adele went over her prepared screens once more. At the moment they had a pearly blankness because they were being fed by a universe whose physical constants were utterly different from those of the human universe where the equipment was built. *"Extracting!"*

Adele felt her bone marrow vanish, then spread itself on the outside of her skin. Her body was cold, *beyond* cold, and she was seeing Blantyre's words as a pattern of light varying from bronze to muddy brown.

The *Ladouceur* reentered the sidereal universe. Her body felt normal—she hadn't been able to move for a moment—and her display lit segment by segment as the hull sensors came live.

Nobody liked the process of extraction from the Matrix, and Adele probably disliked it as much as anyone. She'd found, however, that so long as she concentrated on her work, nothing else really touched her. Extraction was merely a subset of life itself for her.

The *Ladouceur* had initially dipped into sidereal space forty-five light-minutes down-sun from Castle Four. That allowed Daniel to plot his approach on the basis of orbital traffic above the planet and Adele to preset her instruments. They'd then reinserted for a short hop, knowing that the cruiser would arrive well before the light from its previous appearance reached Castle Control—and more particularly, before it reached the guardship *Siegfried* in planetary orbit.

Astrogation, even over short intra-system distances, was partly a matter of chance even for Daniel. Still, the *Ladouceur* had arrived within ten thousand miles of where she was supposed to be: 142,000 miles above the dun surface of Castle Four, curving past from east to west in contrast with the *Siegfried*.

Adele adjusted one of her laser transceivers to bear directly on the guardship. "AFS *Siegfried*," she said, using the accent to which she'd been exposed during the decade she'd lived on Blythe, studying and then working in the Academic Collections following her family's massacre. "This is AFS *Victoria Luise* requesting landing clearance, over."

She'd thought of doubling the message on the 20-meter frequency, but that'd be read—correctly—as an insult if the *Siegfried*'s crew was halfway competent. Adele would be saying that she didn't trust them to have reliable tight-beam capability on a major—if very old—Fleet asset. If she had to repeat the call on short wave, she would, but for now she was assuming that the signals section knew its business.

"Victoria Luise, *this is Four Control*," said a female voice. "*State your business on Four, over.*"

The *Ladouceur*'s sensors were scanning the ships on the planetary surface. There were over three hundred vessels concentrated around three ice mines—two near the poles and the third at 71 degrees of north latitude. The cluster at the north pole contained more than half the total number of vessels.

"Four Control, this is the *Victoria Luise*," Adele said. She was keeping the exchange boringly formal, hoping that would lull any concerns of the *Siegfried*'s crew. "We were directed here from Tadzhik where the *Hildebrandt* replaced us as guardship. We're to be surveyed preparatory to sale or salvage, over."

Adele had set up the search for targets on the ground, but Rene was running it from the console to her right. She watched the results as a sidebar inset onto her main display, but she found no need to interfere or even comment. Rene was grading ships according to their state of readiness; those coded red were capable of lifting off in thirty minutes. There were forty in that category in the northern cluster, three at the south pole, and none in the mid-latitude grouping.

"Victoria Luise, *hold one*," the duty signaler said.

The lengthening pause suited Adele's—Daniel's—purposes even better than empty conversation. The *Victoria Luise* had been stationed on Tadzhik briefly, but that'd been eighteen standard years earlier. If the *Siegfried*'s officers searched the records, they'd learn that just as Adele had done. It'd confuse them, but the natural assumption would be that the records were wrong.

"Victoria Luise," said a forceful male voice, *"this is Castle Four Control. We have no record of you being authorized to land here. Hold in orbit until we receive instructions from Pleasaunce Control, over."*

The cruiser's rig was coming down in a chorus of metallic shrieks, rattles and clangs. There was more noise than usual so far as Adele's experience went, since the *Ladouceur* had twelve rings of antennas instead of the corvette's six. Even a thin atmosphere like that of Castle Four would strip away the rigging unless it'd been furled, folded, and locked to the hull before the vessel started its descent.

Raising and lowering the sails was a completely automated process if everything worked as it was supposed to—which of course it never did. The riggers were outside to splice broken cables, free frozen joints, and all the thousand other ways machinery that'd been exposed to vacuum and the rigors of alien universes might choose to fail. Normally both watches would be on the hull to get the rig in quickly in preparation for landing.

Though the *Ladouceur* had a full crew of nearly four hundred on this voyage, only a short crew of riggers was at work. The remainder of the personnel waited in the three entry holds, formed into boarding parties. After the cruiser landed, they'd capture Alliance-flag vessels and sail them back to Pelosi.

"Four Control, please," said Adele. Daniel had briefed her on what to say at this juncture; she hoped she could rattle it off in a believable fashion. "That'll take *hours* with the planets in opposition like this. We don't have enough reaction mass to hold a powered orbit for that long, not and land besides. Can't you give us clearance and we can work the details out later, over?"

Besides the racket the antennas and yards made, Adele felt a low rumble of quite different character. Sun was at the gunnery console, swinging the dorsal turret and elevating the 6-inch guns. According to plan, the Port Three main course would remain set to hide the turret from the guard ship's view until it was time for the guns to go into action.

"*Negative*, Victoria Luise!" thundered the battleship's spokesman. He was obvious a senior officer. "*You are not, I repeat not, cleared to land. If you're short of reaction mass, that's nobody's fault but your own. A few hours of weightlessness isn't going to kill you. Four Control over!*"

Daniel had split his screen. The left half was an attack board, while on the right he oversaw the boarding party assignments. Rene passed to Blantyre information on the cargoes of the ships ready to lift on short notice; Blantyre then chose and briefed the section that would capture the vessel, usually half a dozen spacers under a petty officer who at least in theory could program an astrogational computer.

"Four Control," Adele said primly, "I must protest. This is mere harassment. I demand to speak to your superior officer, over!"

"*You dickheaded landsman, you're speaking to Captain William Dunn!*" the voice snarled. "*I have no superior this side of Pleasaunce, and it's for Pleasaunce to respond that you're bloody well going to wait. Four Control out!*"

Blantyre had assigned the last of the intended prizes: the ten-thousand-tonne grain ship *Star of Acapulco*.

Captain Hoppler himself, with twenty-four spacers whom he'd commanded on the *Sacred Independence,* was to capture and sail the big ship home.

Daniel straightened, shrank down the assignments board, and grinned broadly toward Adele. She nodded to his miniature image in the upper register of her display.

"*Ship,*" called Daniel over the intercom. "*Prepare to launch missiles!*"

"Firing four!" said Daniel, mashing his thumb down on the EXECUTE button. On the *Ladouceur* the switch itself was virtual but the cage over it was physical and spring-loaded; it flopped back when it was released.

As a jet of live steam hammered the first missile out of its tube, Daniel used his left hand to furl the Port Three main course and rotate the yard in line with the antenna. If the sail jammed instead of furling, he'd fold the antenna anyway rather than wait for riggers to clear the problem: all the riggers were supposed to be within the hull.

If the antenna jammed also, the first plasma bolt would clear a path for the second and future rounds. The *Ladouceur* could suffer much worse damage than losing a single antenna and he'd still consider it a cheap victory.

The second missile banged out five seconds after the first. That was a shorter separation than he'd have allowed in the *Princess Cecile* or a converted freighter like the *Sacred Independence*, but the cruiser's mass and the stiffness of a warship's hull meant the launch of five tons of steel and reaction mass didn't seriously twist the vessel.

He glanced toward Sun at the gunnery console, his right hand poised over the Execute key. "Officer Sun, you may fire when you bear," he said. It was barely possible that nobody aboard the *Siegfried* had noticed that the *"Victoria Luise"* was launching missiles, but they *would* notice six-inch plasma bolts even if they were sound asleep.

Daniel'd planned to bring the *Ladouceur* from Pelosi to the Castle System in six days, and he'd believed that the *Sissie* could've done it in five. The latter was probably true, but the cruiser'd taken seven.

Now that he had a moment to consider, he decided that they'd made a pretty good run at that. Not only was the whole crew new to the ship, always a recipe for error and confusion, the *Ladouceur's* folding antennas were like nothing most of the riggers would've ever seen before.

The ship rang with the third missile's launch. Additional missiles were rumbling down the tracks from the magazine. It normally took forty-five seconds to reload, but Daniel was shaving time by starting rounds on the way before the tubes were empty. That'd mean a serious problem if he had to abort the launch; there was no mechanism for returning missiles to the magazine except by chocking them, unclamping the harness, and levering the massive weapons back up the rollers with prybars.

On the other hand, he'd only abort the launch if there was a serious problem to begin with. Being able to send out a follow-up salvo thirty seconds sooner could be well worth that risk.

The fourth missile launched with the same hammer-on-anvil crash as the others. The whole process, beginning to end, had taken only thirty seconds. Daniel knew that, but it felt like a day spent at Navy House, waiting for a clerk to *maybe, please the Gods*, call the number of his chit.

The dorsal turret fired, a spaced *CLANG! CLANG!* much sharper than the missile launches, though a layman might not've made a distinction. Adele'd high-lighted the communications antennas that the guard ship was using, a cluster near the bow. That was Sun's aiming point. The range was too long for even six-inch bolts to penetrate a battleship's plating, but scouring off the antennas would delay the *Siegfried*'s report to Pleasaunce Control.

Because the *Victoria Luise* had been a Cluster Command vessel instead of a unit of the Fleet proper, she carried single-converter missiles, none of which had been manufactured on the advanced planets of the Alliance. They'd reach the same terminal velocity as first-line missiles which had dual antimatter converters feeding twin High Drives, but they accelerated at only half the rate. At the short range from which Daniel'd launched at the guard ship, that was a significant handicap—

But not a crippling one. Besides, the *Ladouceur*'s closing velocity with the battleship added something to the kinetic energy. Daniel's first missile struck a little below the *Siegfried*'s center of mass, on Deck G instead of E. The flash of rending metal preceded by an instant the fireball of friction-heated steel burning in the gush of escaping atmosphere. It dwarfed the yellow-white lash of Sun's plasma bolts licking the bow.

Daniel ran the *Ladouceur*'s High Drive motors up to

full thrust, braking her toward the planet's surface. The cruiser's old 6-inch guns required a minute between discharges, so the dorsal turret was silent; the 4-inch turrets were now whining to life, however. Daniel was sure they wouldn't bear on the *Siegfried* soon enough to be of any service, but he was equally sure that Sun was going to fire them anyway.

The second missile slammed into the *Siegfried* forward, scalloping away the bridge in another flash and flare. Captain Dunn had been wrong about there being no authority higher than his in Four orbit.

"Sun, cease fire!" Daniel said. "This is Six. Cease fire or I'll break you back to wiper, I swear I will, over!"

The third missile struck the Power Room. Like the previous two, it punched a hole through the plating instead of vaporizing a thousand tonnes of hull the way it'd have done if it'd been at terminal velocity.

The difference wasn't noticeable this time. When the fusion bottle ruptured, the stern third of the *Siegfried* vanished in a scintillating ball of gas.

"Sun, you heard me!" Daniel shouted. "Acknowledge or I'll *break* you, I swear I will. Cease fire! Cease fire!"

He thought the last missile was going to miss because the Power Room explosion had devoured the part of the battleship it was aimed at, but the blast shoved what remained of the hull into the projectile's path. The impact was almost delicate in comparison to the fusion bottle's rupture, but it'd certainly killed another hundred or so spacers.

It was war, and Commander Daniel Leary hadn't gotten his reputation by being unwilling to go for an enemy's throat. Even so, if Daniel could've been certain that his first three missiles would eliminate all danger from the *Siegfried*, he'd never have launched the fourth. His bellowing fury toward Sun wasn't because he knew the gunner was so focused on the chance to use his weapons that he didn't care that his bolts'd be killing harmless spacers who might otherwise survive; it was because Commander Leary himself had just killed all but a handful of the six hundred or so human beings aboard the *Siegfried*.

It was war, and it'd been necessary; but it was regrettable nonetheless.

The *Siegfried*, debris tumbling in a gas cloud, drifted overhead as the *Ladouceur* plunged toward Four's surface. Plumes of sparkling ions made the wreckage look as though it were burning.

The cruiser's motors began to ping. "Ship, shutting down High Drive," Daniel said. It was all rote and reflex, now; he could probably land a starship in his sleep, so ingrained were his responses to sensory inputs. "Lighting thrusters . . . *light*."

Because Four's atmosphere was so thin, they were closer to the surface than they'd have been on a fully habitable planet. In only a few minutes the *Ladouceur* would be on the ground. Very likely more people were going to die in the process of capturing a score of Alliance prizes and destroying others by gunfire.

"Ship, prepare for landing!" Daniel ordered.

It was war, and it was necessary.

But it was also regrettable.

CHAPTER 23

Minehead North on Castle Four

"IBS *Ladouceur* to *Die Ehre Muenchens*," Adele said. Normally she ignored the external world while she was heavily involved in message traffic, but of present necessity one quadrant of her console showed a real-time view of a new-looking Alliance freighter. Plasma and Four's friable soil rose in a shroud as the vessel ran up its thrusters preparatory to lifting. "Shut down immediately. If you attempt to lift off, we will destroy you. Over."

Her voice was as dry as the plain outside. She felt a degree of exasperation at the *Ehre*'s captain for being a pigheaded fool, but she'd learned not to let that concern her. So *many* people were pigheaded fools.

Rene was at the console beside hers. It was intended for the sailing master, but the closest any crew of Daniel's had ever had to that senior warrant officer was a common spacer being trained to handle the ship's boats.

He'd been echoing Adele's display while she kept track of the boarding parties and channeled relevant information to Blantyre in the Battle Direction Center.

He was handling those duties alone, now, while she dealt with the freighter which was trying to escape.

The *Ehre* started to lift. Her shining hull rose, free for the moment of the plume of dust. The captain herself must own the vessel; surely no hireling would risk her life to avoid a mere monetary loss for an absentee owner?

"*Ehre*, this is your last chance," Adele said. Would she be more effective if she sounded excited? Surely the words were clear enough in themselves. "Shut down or we will destroy—"

The freighter was half a mile away, and there was a score of other grounded vessels between it and the *Ladouceur*. It'd now risen twenty feet in the air, however, which meant Sun had a direct line of sight to it from the cruiser's dorsal turret.

"—you certainly."

The freighter continued to rise. Sun stabbed his gun switch. The 6-inch guns fired, right tube and then left. The miniature thermonuclear explosions seemed to echo; weight anchored the *Ladouceur* firmly to the ground through the outriggers, so the hull didn't flex as it would while under way.

The streaks of plasma lifted vortices of dust through the thin air; if boarding parties were outside in the vicinity of the track, they'd be cursing the gunner. The Bagarians were wearing suits, however, so they shouldn't be in real danger.

The first bolt stuck the *Ehre* on A Deck, a little forward of the midpoint. Telescoped masts flew up in a geyser of steel. The vessel started to roll away from the thrust of her own vaporized fabric, so the second round struck a little farther down.

The *Ehre's* bow tilted; Adele couldn't tell whether that was a direct result of damage or if the captain had simply jerked her controls in shock. The stern slammed into the ground. When the thrusters shut off or failed a moment later, the bow dropped with a terrible crash. The freighter bounced upward, rolled onto its port side when one outrigger collapsed, and hit the ground again.

"*Six, I shoulda let her get a little higher and used the lateral turrets on her,*" Sun crowed happily. "*I mean, we don't know that the four-inchers even work, right? But praise the* Gods, *didn't the big boys do a job on that dumb sucker, over?*"

Adele blocked the transmission; the gunner was just chattering in his joy at the destruction he'd achieved. Daniel was busy programming courses for the merchant vessels which boarding parties from the *Ladouceur* were capturing all across Four's northern port area.

Adele had been amazed at how quickly the Bagarians spread out on their mission, given that on the voyage from Pelosi they hadn't shown anything like the spirit she'd been accustomed to in crews under Daniel's command. After a moment's reflection, though, she saw that these spacers understood they were in the home system of the Alliance. They were simply trying to get away.

They might think that if they were captured, Guarantor Porra would have them all shot out of hand in retaliation for the raid. Adele smiled faintly. She suspected that their concern was well founded.

"*Mission Control,*" said a breathless voice on 3625kHz. "*This is Blackwell! We've got the* Jabez Croft *and we're buttoning up for liftoff! Over!*"

Adele's wands danced. David Blackwell, an engineer's mate from Thuer, had experience as watch officer on tramps in the Viscount Region though no formal astrogation training. In charge of six spacers, Unit 17 in Blantyre's terminology, directed to the 2,300-tonne freighter *Jabez Croft* out of Wakeland, over a half mile to the west of where Daniel'd brought the *Ladouceur* down.

"I'm transferring your data to Control Six, Blackwell," Adele said. She sent it to Daniel with a dip of her left wand and copied Blantyre as well, since the midshipman was coordinating the boarding parties. "Prepare for liftoff, but don't leave the ground until Control Six has given you clearance."

One of the prizes lifted in the next row over from the *Ladouceur*. Half a dozen other ships—

She checked herself out of habit: *nine* ships had already lifted, and this one made ten. The number didn't matter, but the fact that she'd been so far out in her mental tally was disquieting.

Ten prizes were already away, and two more were running up their thrusters. The operation was on schedule, though of course nobody knew how much time they really had before Alliance forces on Pleasaunce reacted. In an ideal universe it might even be days.

The universe had rarely shown itself to be ideal in Adele's experience, but the present raid was so audaciously unlikely that there wouldn't be mechanisms in place to counter it. A smile lifted the left corner of her mouth again. Daniel made rather a habit of that sort of stroke.

A plasma cannon fired in the mid distance. Adele had closed the electronic window in which she'd viewed the *Die Ehre Muenchens*; now she opened it again and began to hopscotch through real-time imagery from captured ships, searching for one which would show her where the shooting had occurred. It seemed to be to the northwest of the *Ladouceur*.

The ground thumped to an explosion; a piece of something banged against the cruiser's hull. It could've simply been an impeller slug, but it sounded heavier than that. Adele'd heard a lot of impeller slugs and sub-machine gun slugs and pistol slugs in the two years since she met Daniel Leary. . . .

"Signals, it's all right," said Rene over the intercom. *"It's Rasmussen and Harned, using the gun on the* Scarlett *to make the* MP5052 *open up. They called while you were talking to the* Ehre, *over."*

An icon pulsed in the window Adele'd opened; she expanded it with a click. Most ships trading on the fringes of the settled universe carried light armament to discourage pirates. The *Scarlett*, a three-thousand-tonne Kostroman vessel, had an old 10-cm plasma cannon in a nose blister.

"Signals, the Scarlett's *deadlined because her climate control's shot,"* Rene explained. *"Her other systems still work, though, so when the* MP5052 *wouldn't open up to the boarders, I told Blantyre. She sent Rasmussen and Harned to her. They got the gun working, over."*

"I see," said Adele. Beth Rasmussen and Richard Harned were a Power Room tech cross trained as a gunner and a very tough rigger. Perhaps the Bagarian boarding party could've handled the job, but at best they hadn't come up with the plan themselves.

Adele didn't see the expected cratering of a plasma

bolt on the *MP5052*'s hull, but a chemical explosion had blown antennas Dorsal Two and Dorsal Three off the hull. She selected memory and ran the imagery back to before the gun'd fired.

As expected, she found that the *MP5052* had mounted a basket of free-flight rockets on her spine for defensive armament instead of a gun. They'd exploded when Rasmussen put a bolt into them. Though the blast hadn't seriously damaged the hull, the ears of everybody on the freighter's A Deck would ring for a month.

Adele checked her apparatus, then made a pair of adjustments. The *MP5052*'s commo system was wide open, so it was no great trick to take control of it.

"Freighter *MP5052*, this is the IBS *Ladouceur*," Adele said. Her voice would be thundering through the PA system as well as on the main console. "You saw what happened to the *Ehre* when they refused to surrender. You've had your only warning. Open your main hatch to a boarding party from the Bagarian Republic in thirty seconds, or we'll melt you to slag, over."

Could they melt a freighter to slag? Not with a low-powered 4-inch gun, certainly, but she supposed Sun would find a way if she gave him his head on the subject. Regardless, it was a permissible part of her job to exaggerate for effect while speaking to an enemy.

"*Mistress, they're opening up,*" said Rene. "*Break.*"

He shifted circuits for the next portion of the call, informing Blantyre that the operation had been successful so she could recall Rasmussen and her bodyguard. They discussed whether the freighter was too badly damaged to lift—decided it wasn't—and shifted their attention to the *Antipodes* out of Carnera; the prize crew said that vessel was missing two thruster nozzles.

Adele listened to the conversation long enough to determine it was none of her concern, then returned to panicked messages from the boarding parties. She was acting as Port Control, a task well beyond her rank and rating, but Daniel was busy writing astrogation programs for the prizes.

Two more ships lifted from opposite sides of the large harbor. According to Daniel, Castle Four's loess soil didn't reflect thrust the way most dry land did. Each liftoff and landing was in a curtain of dust, but that was no worse a problem than the steam that blasted up from normal water operations.

Though it didn't impede operations, the dust coated everything instead of draining off the way condensate would. That was simply unpleasant, though, and there was very little about star travel which *wasn't* unpleasant in Adele's estimation. It didn't matter, because she wasn't going to be on Four long.

Only a handful of the Bagarians would bother to use Daniel's complex programs. For the most part they'd let the computer take them toward Pelosi by the simplest route, pleased not to have officers aboard to roust them onto the hull to make manual adjustments. But Daniel would've tried to keep them clear of Alliance pursuers, would've done his duty and gone well beyond it. That shared attitude was why Adele found him such a congenial friend.

"Ladouceur, *this is Sissie Five*," said Vesey's clipped voice. "*We're on station. There's no sign of unusual activity in the vicinity of Pleasaunce, over.*"

Adele ran the message as text at the bottom of Daniel's display. While it didn't interfere with his computations, he'd notice it there.

How very typical of Vesey that she'd give two critical pieces of information and not ask any questions. Most people, even most RCN officers, acted as though their excitement and nervousness were more important than whatever the party they were jabbering at was doing.

Another prize lifted. The initial vibration was as violent as that on water, but the sound through Four's thin atmosphere was only a shrill whisper. The plasma flare was so bright, however, that the display dimmed it with a ten percent mask.

"Acknowledged, Sissie Five," Adele said. "The operation appears to be proceeding well. Over."

The *Antipodes* lifted while the immediately previous prize was still in mid-sky. Clearly Blantyre and Rene had made the right decision. The cargo—Adele's wands flicked—was Carnera brocades; they'd be quite valuable if they reached Pelosi.

Daniel transmitted the latest course data—to the *MP5052*, Adele noticed—and switched to the still-open channel with the *Princess Cecile*. He winked at Adele.

"*Sissie Five, this is Six,*" Daniel said, stretching his arms to the sides. He arched his shoulders backward to loosen those big muscles too. "*We'll be lifting in the* Agave *as soon as the last of the prizes has lifted, which I judge to be within the next half hour. We'll get a light hour distant before we exchange personnel, though, over.*"

Daniel was grinning with satisfaction; Adele found

herself smiling back at his image. He had reason to look satisfied. Even if things went badly from here on out, Commander Daniel Leary, RCN, had singed the beard of Guarantor Porra. Nothing would take that away.

"*Roger, Six,*" Vesey said. Despite the compression, there was more animation in the lieutenant's voice than Adele'd heard since the day Midshipman Dorst had died in battle. "*I'm looking forward to relinquishing command. Five out.*"

"*Six out,*" Daniel replied. He rose from his console. Adele turned when his image blurred from her display.

There were only five of them on the bridge. Daniel grinned and said, "I'm going to offer my resignation to Minister Lampert in the BDC now, I believe. Would any of you like to come along? We'll leave for the *Agave* in ten minutes."

"I'll wait," said Sun, intent on his display. "Somebody might try t'lift, you know?"

He really loves those heavy guns, Adele thought. Well, he was a gunner; he should. Sun didn't think of the result as ruin and charred corpses. Rather, it was the meaning in his life.

"Adele?" Daniel said.

She shook her head. "I'll stay at the equipment here until we leave the ship," she said. "Just in case."

Sun would understand. And of course Daniel understood also.

"Here you go, master," said Hogg, handing a submachine gun to Daniel. He took the weapon but frowned in surprise.

Hogg hefted his impeller. "Most of who's aboard

isn't Sissies," he said, "and they been issued guns for the business out there. Just in case, you keep that with you."

He nodded at Adele and added with a touch of challenge, "Tovera's in the BDC. I told her I'd take care of things on the bridge so she could watch the wogs there. Understood?"

"I do indeed," said Daniel with a spreading smile. "And I assure you, Tovera isn't any more concerned about Officer Mundy's safety than I am."

Adele grimaced, but she didn't speak. Daniel strode off the bridge, cradling the sub-machine gun. He was whistling.

Whistling "The Handsome Cabin Boy," Daniel sauntered toward the Battle Direction Center at the end of the A Deck corridor. Tovera stood in the hatchway; she gave him a glance and a cold smile, then returned her attention to the interior of the compartment.

Her cheeks appeared like roses . . . Daniel whistled as he stepped past her. Tovera lifted the muzzle of her sub-machine gun politely so that it didn't point at the middle of his back, but she didn't bother to greet him.

Daniel grinned. He preferred Tovera's silence to her speech. When she spoke, he felt as though he were talking with a viper sunning itself on a rock; albeit a very useful viper.

"Well, I'll tell you, Duncan!" said Blantyre, sitting at one of the star of five consoles in the center of the BDC. "If you don't think you can handle a ship that big with six men, then you've got a choice. You can get some of the Alliance crew to sign on with you, or you can bloody walk back to Pelosi! Now, make up your mind in the next three minutes or stay here and rot. Control Two out!"

James Shearman, a Power Room tech who'd been learning the rudiments of astrogation, sat at another of the consoles. He nodded awareness to Daniel but didn't speak. Seward was at the console nearest the hatch, but Lampert sat hunched on a bench folded down from the starboard bulkhead. When he looked up at Daniel's entry, his eyes were dull as mud.

Blantyre caught the motion in the corner of her eye and turned also. "Sorry, sir," she said. "I had to redirect Team Twelve to the *Cimmerian Queen* because the *Swordsmith*'s High Drive motors had all been taken off. Not a bloody thing on record about it, but they were!"

"I'll send a strongly worded protest to the Harbormaster's Office, Blantyre," Daniel said dryly.

"What?" said Blantyre, blinking. She was a stocky woman, perhaps a hair too forceful but shaping into a very good officer. "Oh, sorry sir. Sorry. Anyway, the *Cimmerian*'s nine thousand tonnes where the *Swordsmith* was twenty-three hundred, so Matt Duncan wants somebody to hold his hand. There's no time for that now, *I* figure."

"As do I," Daniel agreed. Changing tone slightly, he went on, "You and Shearman are ready to transfer to the *Agave* in a few minutes?"

"Yes sir," said Blantyre. "The forward party shifted our gear with their own."

"Roger that, Six!" said Shearman. He had straight black hair and was cultivating a thin moustache to make himself look older than his twenty standard years. It actually made him look more like a rat, but a very keen rat. "Ready and willing!"

Minister Lampert stared at Daniel, wringing his hands but saying nothing. Seward turned but didn't get up from his console. He said, "Are you going to let us go, Leary?"

When Seward moved, Daniel noticed that he was watching looped imagery of the attack on the *Siegfried*. Daniel found it odd to view a record of what he'd given only passing attention to after the first missile hit. At that point the guard ship was out of the war; the additional destruction was more a matter of embarrassment than pride. He couldn't have afforded to take a chance, though.

Daniel turned toward Lampert and made a slight bow. "I'm here to resign my commission," he said, "if that's what you mean. And—"

He returned to Seward.

"—surrender command of the *Ladouceur* to you, Captain," he said with a smile. "I'm leaving you with a crew of two hundred and fourteen. That should be more than sufficient for your return to Pelosi, though I'll admit the prize crews have left you short of leading spacers and riggers more generally."

"That's not a proper crew for a light cruiser!" Seward said. "That's not half a proper crew."

"It's more than sufficient to work ship," said Daniel. "You'll want to avoid combat, of course, but—not to be pointed, Captain, but I'd have expected you to avoid combat regardless."

"You can't resign," said Lampert. He straightened on the bench and his voice grew stronger with each word. "You were dismissed. You're a pirate!"

The Minister was wearing clothing from the ship's stores, a coarse tunic and trousers with soft-soled boots. The dress uniform he'd boarded in was unsuitable for general use, even if it hadn't been soaked in blood and other matter when authority was transferred back to Daniel. Spacers' slops were unflattering garments at best, but Lampert looked like a burlap sack half-filled with beans.

"Well, that's one for the lawyers, I suppose, Your Excellency," Daniel said with a bright smile. "In any case, the *Ladouceur* will be in your hands, yours and Captain Seward's, just as soon as the last of the prizes have lifted. I brought those crews into the situation, so I feel responsible until they've gotten out again. Then I'll leave with my cadre, the Cinnabar contingent—"

He'd almost said "my Sissies." The Bagarians might've misunderstood.

"—on another captured freighter. I wish you and the Bagarian Republic all deserved fortune." Daniel coughed, then added, "I programmed a course back to Pelosi by way of the Heart Stars, Captain, but that was just a courtesy. I have no desire to influence your actions after the moment I relinquish control."

"Sir," said Blantyre, "Duncan's closed up the *Cimmerian Queen*. They'll be lifting in five."

"Ten, I suspect, Blantyre," Daniel said with a grin, "but I like to see optimism in my officers."

His face hardened, though his cheerful smile remained. He looked from Seward to Lampert.

"Captain, Your Excellency?" he said. "I told you that I don't wish to influence your actions. I think I should mention, though, that while I'll be leaving the

Ladouceur's guns in fully operable condition, it might be better if no one goes near that console until after my cadre and I have lifted on the *Agave*. You see, if there were an accident, well.. . . . The *Princess Cecile*'s in orbit and Captain Vesey—for all her other virtues—is notoriously without a sense of humor."

Daniel gestured to Seward. "Captain," he said, "you might want to explain to His Excellency precisely what it means to try to climb out of a gravity well with a hostile vessel in orbit above you."

Seward scowled. "Just leave, Leary," he said. "Nobody's asking more than that. Just leave."

"Quite," said Daniel, nodding. "I regret that matters didn't work out better between us, and I certainly understand your attitude. But one thing, Captain?"

He cleared his throat, then dipped his left index finger toward the imagery on Seward's display. It'd cycled around to the *Siegfried*'s fusion bottle venting again.

"You'll recall your guard ship ignoring the *Princess Cecile* when we arrived above Pelosi," Daniel said. "Your colleague Captain Hoppler said something to the effect that the corvette was too small to be of concern, even if she'd been hostile. I led the way here in the *Ladouceur* because she was already in the Alliance books with her authentications in place, but I assure you that the *Sissie*'s two missiles per salvo would've been quite sufficient to eliminate any guard-ship. They certainly would've eliminated a converted transport like the *Independence*."

Seward glowered. Daniel smiled more broadly and said, "A word to the wise, is all."

"Sir," said Blantyre with a touch of urgency. "The

Cimmerian's running up her thrusters and they all read in the green."

"Thank you, Blantyre," said Daniel. "Inform the bridge crew that we're transferring to the *Agave* immediately, and inform the *Agave* that we're coming."

"Done, Six!" said Shearman, rising from the console.

"Then let's move, Sissies!" Daniel said, striding toward the hatch. He glanced over his shoulder and added, "Your Excellency? I wish the best of luck to you and the Cluster, but you're in a real war now. If you ever forget that, it will go very badly for you all."

"It'd be kinder for me to shoot them now than leave them for the Guarantor's amusement," Tovera murmured as she followed Daniel out of the BDC. "Besides, I'd *like* to do it."

The bridge party was on its way down the corridor from the other direction. Sun led, and Hogg was chivying along Adele and the civilian.

"I'm sure both those things are true, mistress," Daniel said. "Just the same, we're going to leave matters in the hands of the parties involved. Sometimes they'll surprise you in a good way."

But not this time, Daniel thought. Not Lampert and Seward. But he'd still leave it to them.

CHAPTER 24

One Light-Hour to the Solar North of Jewel

"Admiral Guphill's exercising his squadron off Zmargadine," said Daniel as he viewed the Jewel System on the *Sissie's* command console. The volume of space involved meant that even a gas giant like Zmargadine was an icon rather than a scaled image. "The ability to do that may be a bigger advantage to the Alliance than the numbers are, over."

He was speaking on the command channel so that all the commissioned and senior warrant officers could hear, but it was basically a tutorial for the midshipmen.

With the exception of Vesey, the others on the push didn't know or care about fleet tactics, and Vesey already knew this lesson.

Adele was listening also, in fact if not by right. When Daniel came to think, he realized that she might be interested in knowing simply because it *was* knowledge. Adele was less likely to be directing a

374

fleet in battle than even Woetjans was, but if it ever happened she'd already know the theory.

Daniel shrank his field of observation by orders of magnitude. The Alliance ships became beads with three-letter designators: PLE and FOR for the battleships *Pleasaunce* and *Formentera*, with similar abbreviations for the fourteen lesser vessels exercising with them. They were several light-minutes from Zmargadine, using the bulk of the giant planet to conceal their activities from observers on Diamondia. As Daniel watched—more accurately, an hour before Daniel's observation—the squadron vanished raggedly into the Matrix.

Daniel expanded his field of observation again, but for the time being he couldn't tell where the Alliance ships had gone. Guphill had probably taken them out in a wide sweep, making several doglegs a few light-days out from their base. The exercise would keep his crews sharp, and Admiral James' squadron wouldn't be able to take advantage of the brief Alliance absence. By the time the data'd been recorded and analyzed on Diamondia, Guphill's ships would've returned.

A pair of Alliance destroyers cruised in powered orbits at a comfortable distance from Diamondia while the minesweeping flotilla ground inexorably away at the planetary defense array. Nothing had changed there since the *Princess Cecile* lifted for Pelosi, except that there were fewer mines. The deterioration wasn't significant yet, but its slope led inexorably toward the capture of Diamondia by Alliance forces.

Daniel shrank his field of view again, this time focusing on Zmargadine, its rings, and its dozen moons. The Alliance base was on Z3, an ice moon with standard gravity and easily obtained reaction mass for the squadron. It was at present on the opposite side of its primary from Diamondia, so RCN observers there couldn't tell when ships lifted or set down.

"Signals," Daniel said. He considered shifting to a two-way link with Adele but decided this was legitimately business for the whole command group. "Do you have equipment which would punch a laser signal from Zmargadine's rings back to Diamondia? That is, equipment that could be used from an escape capsule, over?"

"*Yes, of course,*" said Adele with her usual disregard for protocol. Perhaps she felt that the question touched her professional abilities. The Mundys of Chatsworth were—Daniel grinned—notably punctilious of their honor. "*For it to work from a capsule, I'd have to operate it myself, though. What do you want me to do? Over.*"

"Signals, I can't afford to lose you from the *Sissie's* complement," Daniel said, nailing down the important part of the exchange first. "I'd like to put an observer in Zmargadine orbit, though. A capsule with everything but basic life support shut down could hide in the rings for months. That'd give us detailed information on how Admiral Guphill reacts when he gets orders from Pleasaunce."

He cleared his throat without closing, then said, "Might Cory be able to handle the equipment, over?"

"*No,*" said Adele. The edge was certainly there this time. "*I told you, I'd have to do it myself.*"

"*Mistress, I'd try, over,*" said Cory quickly.

"*Yes, of course you'd try,*" Adele snapped. "*And I'd try to land a starship if I had to. But I'd fail and you'd fail at this, Cory, so stop making a fool of yourself!*"

"*Officer Mundy,*" a new voice said with a hint of tremolo. "*This is Cazelet. I can keep the laser head manually aligned with Diamondia. Ah—what I can't do, though, is maneuver the escape capsule. I have some basic shiphandling, but keeping station and a line of sight to Diamondia within a ring system is realistically beyond me. If Midshipman Cory can pilot the capsule, though, I don't see a problem, over.*"

"Bloody Hell, Cazelet, this is the *Princess Cecile*!" Daniel said. "Half the crew can plotz about in Zmargadine's rings without dinging anything badly. Woetjans, take care of it! Over."

"*Roger, Six,*" said the bosun. She'd lost twenty pounds while hooked to the Medicomp, but her voice was strong and she'd made it clear that she was still the *Sissie*'s bosun. "*And it's more'n half I'd say. All my riggers anyhow, over.*"

"Officer Mundy," Daniel said. "Do you agree with the plan, over?"

There was a pause. Then Adele said, "*Yes, I suppose I do. I . . . can vouch for Master Cazelet's skill with the equipment. Ah, over.*"

"Very good, then," said Daniel, feeling his cheeks crinkle with the breadth of his grin. By all the Gods, he had a crew here! And Cazelet too, it seemed: as surely as Hogg and Tovera were Sissies, so was this boy of Adele's. "Break. Ship, this is Six. We'll be making a quick side jaunt into Zmargadine orbit to discharge cargo, then jumping straight to Diamondia since we've already got the codes for the defense array this time. It'll be a little hairy, fellow spacers, but nothing to us Sissies, right? Six out!"

He started programming the short insertion that'd

take the *Princess Cecile* into the third of Zmargadine's four belts of debris. It was the sort of maneuver that'd make most spacers blanch.

But as the cheers he'd deliberately provoked rang through the corvette's compartments, Daniel grinned. What he'd said was the truth, after all: it wasn't an unusual task for the crew of the *Princess Cecile*.

"*Mistress Mundy . . . ?*" said Cory over a two-way link. "*Ah, this is Cory, mistress. Ah. I'm watching the sensor display. If you'd like to see your, ah, assistant off, I'm . . . well, I'm watching the sensors. And we won't be in normal space long, over.*"

Adele frowned. The fact that Cory'd asked meant he thought it was what she should do. Rene had, after all, taken on a task that was rightly hers. The capsule would be quite uncomfortable, not that a corvette was a luxury liner either, and the job was dangerous.

Likewise staying aboard the *Princess Cecile* was dangerous, of course. Still.

"All right, Cory, thank you," Adele said. She rose from her console. Over the command channel she continued, "Commander Leary, I'm going down to the missile bay to see Cazelet before he, ah, leaves. If that's all right? Mister Cory will be on the board in my absence."

"*Roger, Signals,*" said Daniel, turning his head from his display to look at her directly. "*We'll be extracting from the Matrix in eight minutes, forty seconds. Over.*"

Tovera led the way off the bridge; she'd been listening to the exchange. Tovera's technical skills didn't permit her to circumvent the software blocks that protected Adele's console, but she'd put a transponder under the fascia which rebroadcast to her all conversations. Adele was aware of the bug, of course, but there was no reason Tovera shouldn't have complete access to her conversations.

The missile bays were on D Deck but well forward, so when Adele stepped into the corridor she had only a short further walk to the double-width hatch. Her footsteps and those of Tovera continued to whisper up and down the armored companionway like distant surf.

Inside the bay, the squat, blunt-nosed cylinder of an escape capsule waited to be inserted in the launch tube. The hatch was open, but Rene and the spacer who'd do the shiphandling were already aboard. Beside it stood Chief Missileer Borries, three technicians from his section, and to Adele's amazement Woetjans and Lieutenant Vesey.

Both rigging watches were on the hull, poised to react if anything malfunctioned while the corvette maneuvered in the Matrix. The two short transits that remained—into Zmargadine's ring system and from there into the planetary defense array protecting Diamondia—both required a great deal of precision. Adele'd expected Woetjans to be out with her riggers.

The bosun must've understood Adele's blink of startlement because she replied with an embarrassed smile. "Mistress," Woetjans said, "Six said Riley and Harrison'd do on the hull between them, but he wanted me to make sure the capsule gets away clean. Maybe he thinks there's still a stitch in my side from the slugs but, well, that's not what he said."

"Commander Leary's generally correct," Adele said coolly. *Certainly he's right about Woetjans not straining herself on the hull in her present condition*, though of course she didn't say that aloud. "I'm glad you and Officer Borries are both here."

Which left the question of what in heaven Vesey was doing in the missile bay instead of being in the BDC. Vesey flushed, but instead of answering the obvious question, she said, "Officer Mundy, I didn't know you'd be seeing Master Cazelet off."

"Cory said he'd handle the signals duties," Adele said. Vesey's non sequitur seemed to require some sort of response, but the whole situation was baffling. "We'll only be in this location for a matter of minutes, after all. I can examine any new data while we're in the Matrix again."

"Mistress Mundy, I'm honored!" Rene said as he stuck his torso through the low-fitted hatch. He was wearing an air suit with the helmet off for the present. Escape capsules—Adele'd been transported in one above Kostroma—were pressurized, but they were so flimsy that passengers were safer wearing suits despite the discomfort that entailed.

"You're satisfied with the installation, then?" Adele said, kneeling so that she and Cazelet could look at one another without contortions on his part. She resisted an impulse to frown. What did the boy think she'd done to honor him or anyone else?

"Yes, mistress," he said. He stuck his arm outside and gestured toward the bow. "The antenna's welded on a stub mast to the nose. It'd be a problem in an atmosphere, but we won't be in one. And the controls—"

Rene backed so that Adele could see through the small hatch; he pointed to the panel clamped to a rack welded to the curved starboard bulkhead. The capsule's interior was spartan even by the standards of a prison.

"—are here. I've made sure everything moves, and if a joint binds after we're deployed, Matthews assures me we'll be able to go out and clear it."

The spacer sharing the capsule, a stocky woman, gave Adele a flat stare. She wore a rigging suit, again without the helmet. The three parallel scars on her right cheek appeared to be a result of ritual rather than injury.

"Very good," said Adele, straightening. She'd thought she was done speaking, but another point struck her.

"Ah, Cazelet," she said, kneeling again. "I don't expect the Alliance squadron to be keeping close watch for a boat like yours, but there are more than thirty ships including the minesweepers. If only one of them has a signals officer who's doing her job, there's a chance that your transmissions will be observed."

"Mistress, it's low-power laser," Rene protested with a frown. "Unless they're virtually in line, I don't see how anyone could intercept my signals."

"You're in a ring system," Adele snapped. "That means there's a great deal of dust, which will scatter your signals to a degree no matter how tight they are at the sending head. It'll be faint, I grant you, but *I* would notice it. Don't ever assume that your opponent is incompetent."

She paused, then added in a softer tone, "Though

goodness knows, that's where the balance of the probabilities lies. And not just your opponents."

"Yes, mistress," Rene said. "I apologize."

"Use your own judgment," Adele said, "of course. But I recommend you transmit only when you have something which won't appear to careful observers on Diamondia. I know it'll be difficult to seem to be doing nothing, but you may only get one chance to send information. Make sure it's the information we need."

Rene sucked in his lips and nodded.

"*Ship*," said Blantyre's voice over the PA system, "*we'll extract from the Matrix in sixty, that's six-zero, seconds from—now!*"

"Mistress, time to button up," Woetjans said. Adele scrambled back.

As Woetjans started to swing the hatch closed, the spacer inside the capsule called, "Don't worry, mistress. I'll bring your boy back to you!"

"Very good," Adele muttered, though she doubted anyone heard her over the clang of the hatch. It was simply polite chattering, after all, the sort of thing one said in a social situation. The Sissies were her family, so she made an effort to behave the way people were expected to behave in society.

The capsule rattled down its track, then vanished into the launching tube. Borries himself threw the switch for the hydraulic ram that closed the breech.

"I figured they'd be cooped up bugger knows how long," Woetjans said quietly to Adele. "That's why I left the hatch open to the last, you know? Besides for you, I mean."

"Very thoughtful, Bosun," Adele said. She knew

there were RCN bosuns with a reputation for knocking a spacer down to make sure he listened to the order that followed, but Woetjans clearly cared about her personnel. Not that she was slow to knock somebody down if she thought the circumstances called for it.

"*Extracting . . .*" Blantyre said. "*Now!*"

Adele's body vanished and her eyeballs turned inside out to engulf a whole universe of frozen crystal. Why did Blantyre think she had to inform anybody of the hell of extraction?

"*Stand by to launch,*" Daniel said. "*Launching.*"

With the word, the bay rang loudly. Adele had never been standing near a launch tube when a jet of live steam shoved an object out of the ship. From that standpoint, an escape capsule was no different from a missile.

"*Preparing to insert into the Matrix,*" Daniel announced. "*We will insert in three minutes thirty seconds. Repeat, we will insert in three minutes thirty seconds, out.*"

"We'll return to the bridge, Tovera," Adele said. She really had no idea of where the capsule had been placed, nor what was around it. Her instrumentation would have stored that information for her.

Vesey was staring at the launch tube. She didn't move. Adele couldn't see the lieutenant's face, but her hunched posture made her look anguished. Adele frowned, but it was none of her business unless Vesey brought a problem to her.

"Ah, mistress?" Woetjans said. "I know what you're maybe thinking with your friend and Matthews cooped up for so long, but you don't have to worry. Bird ain't going to get ideas, and if your friend maybe does—I'm not saying anything, but you know what men are like—Bird'll convince him otherwise. And likely without breaking anything major."

"I don't—" Adele said, the creases of her frown tightening. Then suddenly she *did* understand. "By the Gods, Woetjans, you don't think . . . ?"

She couldn't go on. She stared in openmouthed horror at the bosun.

Tovera giggled and touched Adele's sleeve. "Come along, mistress," she said. "You've business on the bridge."

Tovera was still giggling when they reached the companionway.

CHAPTER 25

Port Delacroix on Diamondia

"Here, Leary," said Admiral James, preceding Daniel into the captain's cabin of the heavy cruiser *Alcubiere*. "I told Bussom to unlock his console before he vacated, so we've got it if you need file access."

The admiral was wearing utilities; he'd been making a Power Room inspection when Daniel signaled from the just-landed *Princess Cecile* that he needed to report as soon as possible. The greasy-looking blur on James' left shoulder blade was finely divided heavy metal sublimed from the thruster nozzles. Instead of being expelled, it'd been trapped on the surface of the petals until the admiral touched them.

To get that smudge, James had to've been sticking his head up the throat of a nozzle. His inspection hadn't been a cursory one focusing on how well the brightwork on the control panel was polished.

"Sir, I didn't intend to disturb Captain Bussom," Daniel said. He'd changed into Whites during the minutes before the slip had cooled enough to open

385

the *Sissie*'s hatches. Now that he'd seen James, the difference in their uniforms was one more thing to make him uncomfortable.

Because he *certainly* didn't want to offend Richard Bussom. The *Alcubiere*'s captain was skilled, senior—senior enough to have commanded a battleship if he hadn't preferred the relative freedom of a cruiser—and notably irascible even in a service which put more of a premium on aggressiveness than on genteel manners.

"You're not, Commander," James grunted as he settled onto one of the chairs around the small table in the center of the compartment instead of behind the desk. "I am, and borrowing his cabin won't disturb him nearly as much as the rocket I was going to give him about the condition of Thruster Port Three. Which—"

He scowled at Daniel and gestured to the chair across from him. "Sit, man!" he snapped. "Do you think I want a crick in my neck from looking at you?"

Daniel seated himself carefully. The chairs and table were made from the red heartwood of Vickery firetops. Vickery had been settled early from Pleasaunce and was a core planet of the Alliance.

"Which, just between us," James resumed, "wasn't really that bad. A flaw in the casting that'd ruptured, I shouldn't wonder, and Bussom's bad luck that I checked when I did. But when we're trapped in port like this, I can't afford to let the crews get slack."

"Yes sir," said Daniel. "Perhaps you won't be trapped for very much longer. Ships of the Independent Republic of Bagaria raided Castle Four a week ago. Besides taking prizes, the raiders destroyed the old battleship on guard duty above the planet. There's no end of evidence remaining on Four to prove that it was a Bagarian raid, quite apart from the fact that Alliance forces have probably recaptured half the prizes by now. I expect Guarantor Porra to be very angry."

James slammed the heel his hand on the table. "By my hope of salvation!" he said. "Angry, you say? I'd judge he was! You may well have given him a stroke and ended the bloody war, Leary!"

He cocked his head and looked straight at Daniel. "It was you, wasn't it?" he said. "That business about the Bagarians is just window dressing, isn't it?"

Daniel glanced aside. Captain Bussom'd had the bulkheads painted a smooth cream color with gilt moldings. On them hung sporting prints in gilt frames, and there was even an imitation fireplace. The decor was closer to that of the office in Speaker Leary's townhouse than to a warship.

"Sir," said Daniel, "I've transmitted an Eyes Only report to your headquarters with full details, but the short version is . . . the major element involved was a Bagarian cruiser with a mostly Bagarian crew, and the Bagarian minister of the navy was aboard throughout the raid. But yes, I was present also."

"By the *Gods*, Leary," James said, his face hard and his eyes focused on something at a distance in time. "Guphill's squadron's the only Alliance force within three weeks' transit of the Bagarian Cluster. If Porra orders them off to swat the rebels back into the stone age, we can destroy the base on Z3 before he gets back. By the Gods, we can!"

"Yes sir," Daniel said. "Unless they strip the Castle System of warships and send them to the cluster instead, of course."

James snorted. "Which is about the last thing they're likely to do after you've shot up Four the way you say you have," he said. "Why, they'd be afraid you'd do the same thing to the Guarantor's Pool on Pleasaunce!"

He looked at Daniel and added sharply, "You were thinking of doing that, weren't you, Leary? Tell me the truth!"

"Well, sir," Daniel said. "The possibility had crossed my mind, yes."

"Well, it's not going to happen," James said, returning Daniel's smile with a harder one of his own. "Not least because I don't think destroying half a dozen Alliance merchant ships would be worth losing you to Cinnabar."

He sobered and added, "Admiral Anston spoke very highly of you, you know."

Daniel touched his lips with his tongue. "Sir," he said, "I'm very glad to have the respect of Admiral Anston. He's a great man. A very great man."

He felt a pang as he spoke. Anston's heart attack and retirement had caused career difficulties for Commander Daniel Leary, but he could honestly say that he didn't regret that at all compared with how he felt about the RCN's loss.

"We'll keep our fingers crossed," James said. He waved a hand at Daniel. "Don't think I'm devaluing what you've accomplished, Leary, I'm not doing that at all. But Guphill's an able man, as I know to my cost. I couldn't have handled the blockade of Diamondia any better myself."

He smiled ruefully.

"Unless Porra gives absurdly detailed orders," he continued, "I don't see Guphill sending off more than a couple cruisers and their accompanying destroyers. That won't crush the rebellion, but it'll give him a month or so before Porra notices. And that's long enough for him to finish reducing our defenses here, I'm afraid."

"Ah, sir?" Daniel said very carefully. "My signals officer has a great deal of skill in deception. She—"

"That's Lady Mundy, you mean?" James said, his eyes narrowing.

"Yes sir, Signals Officer Mundy," Daniel said. "She suggested that there are ways to make Alliance observers believe that your major units aren't operational. If that were the case, it'd be much more likely that Guphill would take away his whole squadron or at least detach a major portion of it. Rather than appear to disregard the Guarantor's order, that is. The Guarantor is known to behave very intemperately when he's angry."

James burst out with a laugh. "He shot his Ambassador to Kostroma dead after the debacle there, didn't he?" he said. "And I take your point, because I don't in the least doubt that he's livid about this raid of yours. All right, shall I summon Lady Mundy or can you give me the gist of the plan yourself?"

Daniel rose. "I think you and I are the people to go over the details," he said, "and here in the harbor is the best place to do it. But I'd appreciate it if any report on the operation would give full credit to Officer Mundy."

James rose also. "If this works, Leary," he said, "there'll be plenty of credit to go around, I assure you. And by the *Gods*, I hope it works!"

Above Diamondia

Adele pored over the images the *Princess Cecile* was capturing during its powered orbits. The Alliance destroyers had equally good optics and perhaps comparable anti-distortion software as well, but they were 200,000 miles out from the planetary surface to avoid the mines. Adele could be confident that they wouldn't be seeing anything which she didn't.

"Good day, Commander Leary," said Tovera from the jumpseat at the back of the signals console. Adele glanced at the miniature image of Daniel at his console inset onto the top of her display; it was empty. When she turned her head, she found him beginning to squat beside her.

"Good day, Tovera," Daniel said mildly. "And good day, Officer Mundy. I decided to walk over for a visit. Call it the whim of an eccentric captain."

Adele looked at him. The command console was eight feet away from her at signals. If Daniel wanted privacy, an intercom link from his console with active sound canceling engaged would've been completely inaudible to anyone but the two parties involved. His behavior *was* eccentric, and besides that Adele herself preferred to communicate through an electronic separation.

But he was also captain.

She gave Daniel a wry smile. "Yes, Captain Leary," she said. "Welcome to my—"

What to call it?

"—work space."

Sun pointedly got up from the gunnery console and announced, "I'm going to the head."

"Want me to shake it for you, buddy?" called Borries from the Attack console on the port side of the bridge. The new Chief Missileer was fitting in well with the original Sissies.

Because the High Drive buzzed as it provided the illusion of gravity, no one was likely to overhear them. Well, Tovera would, but that was like saying a passing meteorite might listen in. Not, of course, that it mattered aboard the *Sissie* to begin with.

"I won't take you away from your work," Daniel said, nodding toward the display. The hologram was focused for her eyes, so from his angle it would be a jumble of light as meaningless as the clouds at sunrise.

"There's no rush," Adele said, adjusting the display to make it omnidirectional. "Or more accurately, what I saw at a quick glance is the important thing—and it passes."

Daniel gave the image his attention while Adele watched him. He wasn't an imagery specialist, but he was a very observant officer who knew warships as well as anyone on the RCN list.

"There's no question she's the *Zeno*," he said judiciously. "She's fifty feet longer than the *Lao-tze* and even in her own class she's the only one with the docking bridge between frames 65 and 68 instead of 32 and 35. And she's got a serious refit under way. Three sections of Power Room plating have been removed. The only reason you'd do that would be to replace the fusion bottle. Besides which I think—"

He gestured. Adele used his index finger as a pointer and increased magnification by one step, then another, on the barge moored to the battleship's starboard side.

"That's enough," said Daniel. "Can you increase the shadow detail, over?"

"Yes," said Adele, making the adjustment. She smiled faintly. Daniel was so used to getting this sort of information over the intercom that he'd lapsed into single-channel communications protocol.

"No question, they're thruster nozzles in the barge's hold," he said approvingly. He looked up at Adele and grinned. "Two and a half visible, and probably twelve aboard if there's as many as could be under the tarps where they can't be seen. And they're real?"

"Yes," said Adele, "but there *are* only three of them, and they came from the freighter *Hollandia* in the Outer Harbor."

"Switch back to the missing plates," Daniel said with a wave, "but keep the magnification. If you please."

Adele made the adjustment without comment. Daniel squinted, which of course didn't help, then looked at her again. "I swear I can see the rails that they slid the bottle out on. How in heaven did they do *that*?"

Adele ran the image back so that the display area contained the whole battleship. "I'm told they underpainted the details in dark blue on the canvas," she said. "Then they covered the whole surface with dark gray to simulate the shadowed interior seen through the missing plates."

She pursed her lips, afraid that she'd just taken credit which belonged to someone else. "One of the *Zeno*'s officers, Lieutenant Bainbridge, turns out to be an amateur artist of some note. The underpainting was her idea. Also mixing purple with the dark gray; I simply said black."

Daniel shook his head in delighted amazement. "I certainly wouldn't doubt that the plating was off," he said. "That's quite remarkable. *Remarkable*."

Adele liked to think—she wouldn't say it aloud, of course—that other people's opinions didn't matter: she'd either done a good job or she hadn't. Realistically that wasn't true: she *was* human, and however well she concealed her feelings from others, she couldn't deny that she did feel.

Now she smiled a little wider than usual and said, "They glued the underside of the canvas to the hull so that it wouldn't ripple in the wind. I think movement would be assumed to be an artifact of atmospheric disturbance, but I was pleased at the care with which the work was executed."

She cleared her throat. "Daniel," she said. "I'm pleased to be a member of the RCN."

He looked at her. "Speaking as the ranking member of the organization present," he said, "the RCN is very pleased to have you, Officer Mundy."

For an instant Adele thought he was going to say something else; then he gestured toward the imagery and said, "The question I'd have if I were Admiral Guphill is, 'How did they manage to do all that work overnight?' Because I don't care how many personnel you have available, there's limited space to work in."

"I considered that," Adele said. Was this bragging? But she *had* considered it, and the fact was germane to the discussion. "My expectation, my *hope*, is that the analysts on Guphill's staff will first suspect that the destroyers on station haven't been keeping as close a watch on Port Delacroix as they should be. In other words, that the work was done over the course of two days or even longer. That's the first point."

She looked at the image, wishing that they were having this conversation electronically. There were far too many variables for certainty, and it would be easier to keep her tone of dry detachment if she weren't side by side with one of the many people who would die if her assumptions had been faulty.

"Competent people are very conscious of their own failures, their own mistakes," Adele said. "What they—"

She turned and met Daniel's eyes directly.

"What tends to escape *us* is the fact that our opponents have human limitations also. Daniel, what would you think if I told you that the crew of the Alliance flagship, the *Pleasaunce*, had removed twelve thrusters and all the starboard plating from the Power Room overnight?"

Daniel grimaced, then smiled broadly. "I'd think that Admiral Guphill had a crack crew," he said. "Yes, I take your point."

Daniel was bracing himself with his right hand on Adele's console. He drummed his index and middle fingers momentarily, then said, "It recently occurred to me that I regretted Admiral Anston's illness for the RCN's sake, not my own. You can understand that, I'm sure."

She frowned. "Of course I can," she said. "Daniel, your worst enemy wouldn't suggest that you'd put personal gain ahead of your duty."

"Yes," Daniel said. "But now, sitting here—"

He grinned.

"—squatting here, better, I realized that I most

of all wish Admiral Anston were healthy for his own sake."

His smile faded. "I didn't know Anston well, but I knew him well enough to like him a great deal. The RCN will manage, just as I'm managing. I wish the same were true for him. Which brings me to another point."

Adele waited without comment, without expression. She didn't need to prod Daniel to speak, so she didn't prod.

"I said the RCN was pleased to have you, Adele," Daniel said. He rose to his feet. "But not nearly as pleased as I am personally."

Daniel strode back to his console. Adele resumed her examination of the seemingly out-of-service *Zeno*. A very neat piece of work by the RCN, if she did say so herself.

Above Diamondia

Daniel had split his main display between the Plot-Position Indicator centered around the *Princess Cecile* in Diamondia orbit and a large-scale equivalent which covered the region surrounding the Alliance base on Z3. The latter was as much conjecture as fact: distance and the enormous bulk of Zmargadine denied certainty, despite the specious confidence that the image instilled. A hologram looked the same whether or not it represented more than a computer's imagination.

Though imperfect, the display gave Daniel some information on what was happening near the Alliance base. A bright orange caret winked, highlighting the ship that'd just extracted from the Matrix almost 600,000 miles in-system from Zmargadine. It was too far for the corvette's sensors to have registered the precursors of an extraction, the distortions to the fabric of sidereal space-time caused when a portion of another bubble universe intrudes. It was too far as well for Daniel to identify the incoming vessel even by class.

He had a pretty good idea, though. He felt his palms start to sweat with anticipation.

"Signals, this is Six," Daniel said. He started to say, "A ship has extracted near Zmargadine." That'd be comparable to Adele telling him that the *Sissie's* thrusters had lighted. While she probably wouldn't say that in so many words, he'd heard the dry sneer in her voice often enough that he didn't have any difficulty imagining it again.

Instead he continued, "Will our outpost send us details of the visitor in the neighborhood of Zmargadine? I can't come closer than a rough idea of the tonnage, and even that's going to be a guess, over."

"I don't expect a report, no," Adele said. Her wands twinkled as she spoke; she was carrying on the conversation with a very small portion of her attention, which explained and even justified the way she ignored protocol. *"I told Rene not to risk revealing himself unless there was something we needed him to tell us. Which the arrival of a courier at the Z3 base is not, to my mind. Here, this is a sixty-three percent probability."*

A pulsing red icon appeared on Daniel's display where the two screens met. Adele's skill would've

permitted her to squelch the existing content in favor
of the information she was forwarding, but though she
was brusque, Daniel'd never found her discourteous
by accident.

He opened the icon to an image of an Alliance aviso
of the Hela class. Adele's processing algorithms were
obviously more subtle than those the RCN provided
to the captains of its warships.

"*The supply ships* Balrum *and* Hiddensee *keep a
three-week rotation from the Fleet base on Eisern-
berg*," Adele said, anticipating Daniel's next question.
"*Presumably they carry normal communications as
well as replacement personnel and food. This is the
first time a courier ship has been sent to Admiral
Guphill.*"

The caret marking the aviso faded from Daniel's
display as the vessel itself reentered the Matrix. Now
that her captain had oriented himself in the sidereal
universe, he'd bring his vessel as close as possible to
Z3 before making his final approach on High Drive
and finally thrusters. If he judged his distance properly,
he'd extract the next time with Zmargadine between
him and RCN observers on Diamondia.

Daniel checked his PPI. The destroyers *Echo* and
Eclipse were in orbit with the *Princess Cecile*.

"Signals," he said, "have our fellow friendlies noticed
the courier's arrival? They don't show any sign of it,
but then I suppose we don't either, over."

"*The destroyers have only basic reconnaissance
software*," Adele said. "*Even if they had something
more advanced, they don't have specialists to use it
properly. They'll have gathered the data, but it won't
be processed till they're replaced on station in nine*

hours and download their logs to the Staff computer at Port Delacroix. I very much doubt their officers are concerned with anything beyond the space immediately neighboring Diamondia. Over."

Daniel considered the situation for a moment. Strictly speaking, the *Princess Cecile* wasn't part of the Diamondia Squadron. She was operating under the orders of Navy House, which took precedence to those of the theater commander.

In more specific terms, the captains of the two destroyers were lieutenant commanders, junior in rank if not length of service to Commander Daniel Leary. Nevertheless, it was politic as well as courteous to tell them what he intended to do. So—

"Signals, please make immediate landing arrangements with Diamondia Control," Daniel said. "Break. Poultice Two, Poultice Three—"

The *Eclipse* and *Echo* respectively.

"—this is Rascal."

The *Princess Cecile*'s designator while operating with the Diamondia Squadron.

"We are setting down to refill with reaction mass. Good hunting, spacers. Rascal out."

The *Echo* simply acknowledged. From the *Eclipse* came, "*Roger, Rascal. If you can scare up something to hunt, we could use the exercise, out.*"

Daniel believed it was the voice of Captain Gibbs, who'd been a Senior when Daniel entered the Academy. They'd chatted in friendly fashion earlier when they met in Squadron HQ. Jennifer Gibbs hadn't been unduly harsh to Entrant Leary at the Academy, and she seemed to regard their present reversal of status philosophically.

So did Daniel: the fortunes of war. But he couldn't help smiling.

"*Captain, you're cleared to Berth Twelve in the Main Harbor,*" Adele announced crisply. An icon clicked alive at the bottom of Daniel's display; he expanded it into a half-screen schematic of both harbors, with Berth 12 highlighted.

"Ship," Daniel said, "this is Six. We'll commence our landing approach in three minutes."

He could probably have sent the message down safely with a coded microwave signal, but he was pretty sure that an Alliance signals officer of Adele's quality would be able to read that message in real-time. The Alliance probably didn't have an officer of Adele's quality—and the RCN probably didn't have another—but this wasn't the time to take chances.

Besides, there was no rush. The courier was arriving nine days after the Bagarian raid on Castle Four, exactly when Daniel had calculated it would. Even if it brought the expected orders, though, it'd take Admiral Guphill a minimum of twelve hours to put ships in condition for a voyage to Pelosi. Landing with the message rather than signaling from orbit would add no more than half an hour to the time the word got to Admiral James.

Daniel hadn't closed the transmission to the crew. He grinned broadly: they were his Sissies. They'd been the point of the RCN's spear often enough that they deserved to get the news now rather than when the rest of the squadron did.

"We'll be filling our reaction mass tanks, Sissies," he continued, "but we'll be returning to orbit as soon as I get back from a visit to Admiral James, because

I don't trust any other ship to keep as close a watch on the Alliance squadron as we will. And I strongly suspect that before the day's out we'll be giving the signal for the fleet action that kicks the Alliance out of the Jewel System with their tails between their legs! Six out."

The cheers were spontaneous. Daniel's grin spread wider yet.

Above Diamondia

The signal from Rene threw a red wash over Adele's display. She shut down what she was doing and began processing the imagery seeping back to the *Princess Cecile* from Zmargadine orbit.

She'd been compiling crew lists for the entire Diamondia Squadron. It had no obvious value, but no information was completely valueless.

"Captain to the bridge!" she announced over the PA system. "Daniel, we have a signal. Get here at once."

Daniel'd gone to his space cabin adjacent to the bridge for a couple hours sleep. In the event he was getting less than a full hour: Admiral Guphill was lifting with his squadron barely ten hours after the courier vessel arrived, not the twelve Daniel'd considered a minimum.

Adele smiled coldly. Guarantor Porra must've been *very* angry.

If Adele hadn't been at her console, her personal data unit would've pinged sharply at her. She disliked audible signals, but there'd been slight risk of her not being at the console under these circumstances. Daniel reasonably thought he should get some sleep, but Adele had decided that she'd relax better if she was working.

Sleep had never been a priority with her. It was even less attractive now that so many faces were likely to visit her in the night.

Often she hadn't really seen them when she was squeezing the trigger; they'd merely been pale blurs against which her sights were silhouetted. There was plenty of time in the night for her to stare at the details, though: the pores, the broken veins, and the gasps of surprise. Flesh deformed around the bullet like a pond hit by the first drop of a rainstorm.

Daniel strode onto the bridge. He was fully clothed, but his boots weren't sealed. He'd kept his clothes on while he napped, but he'd loosened his boots; otherwise blood would've pooled in his feet.

Rene's transmission was encrypted with a pattern generated by cosmic ray impacts. It was common only to the transceiver in the escape capsule and to the signals console of the *Princess Cecile*. If something had happened to either Adele or the corvette, no one in the greater universe could read the information Rene was sending.

That wasn't arrogant confidence on Adele's part. It'd be better that Admiral James not get the information than that he get it and the Alliance forces know what he had. In the latter instance, James would sortie against the Alliance base, and Guphill would be in a position to ambush him by shifting his forces in the Matrix and returning in full strength after the RCN squadron was committed.

That said, whatever decision Adele made was a gamble whose probabilities she couldn't really assess. This way if she guessed wrong, no one would be complaining to her personally.

Daniel settled onto his console and brought up the imagery Rene was transmitting. Because of the low-power sending head and interference from debris over the long distance, there was a noticeable delay for even an astrogation computer to process the data into meaningful results.

There was no voice with the transmission, though speech would've absorbed infinitesimal bandwidth compared to the imagery. The images meant more to an expert than they would to Rene Cazelet; Commander Leary was an expert, arguably *the* expert, so Rene simply kept his mouth shut. He consistently demonstrated good judgment for a young man.

Adele frowned at herself. Rene showed good judgment, period; regardless of age or gender.

"*Ship, this is Six,*" Daniel announced. "*Condition Two, I repeat, Condition Two. Section chiefs, issue energy rations. Get your area squared away, spacers, but we won't be going to Action Stations for another half hour or more. Six out.*"

Despite the excited bustle all over the ship, there was no sign of haste or concern. Sun had been at the gunnery console. To Adele's surprise, he got up and left the bridge. Moments later he reappeared, lugging a rigging suit.

There was an air suit in the cushion of each console, but Sun preferred a hard suit despite its bulk and awkwardness. The equipment wasn't authorized for his specialty, but Adele had learned during her first days with the RCN that old spacers could not only find anything, they could find a place to stash it despite the limited room on a corvette.

Data continued to stream from the distant escape capsule as more ships rose from Z3. They tried to use Zmargadine to shield them from RCN observation, but a number came into view as they accelerated and spread their sails. Even so only a third of the vessels were directly visible, though that would've been enough to indicate a large-scale operation was under way.

"*Signals, we've got them!*" Daniel said. He glanced toward her, putting his broad smile in profile on her display. "*Transmit to Admiral James, Most Urgent: Anston. That's the code word we chose for the operation. And let me know when he acknowledges in person, out.*"

Adele nodded and waited ten seconds for the *Princess Cecile* to come far enough over the horizon to have a line of sight to Port Delacroix. She could've relayed through the *Eclipse*—and done so without the destroyer's crew knowing about it, very probably—but ten seconds wasn't long to wait.

"Diamondia Control," she said. She transmitted a text message simultaneously, but the verbal would reach Admiral James more quickly if his staff was properly trained. "This is Rascal for Pitcher Six, Most Urgent, Anston. I repeat, for Pitcher Six, Most Urgent, Anston. Pitcher Six will acknowledge receipt, over."

"*Roger, Rascal,*" the controller said. Hers was the same crisp female voice which'd cleared the *Sissie* into Port Delacroix on their first arrival. "*The message is on the way, Most Urgent. Diamondia out.*"

Daniel wore a look of glee as he manipulated images. Figures scrolled and transmuted in a box on the lower left quadrant, but the bulk of his display rotated images of the Alliance squadron one ship at a time. When the figures reached a solution and froze, pulsing, he shifted to a different vessel and began again.

At last he stopped and leaned back in the console. Rene continued to send imagery, but no additional ships were lifting from Z3.

The Alliance squadron was forming down-system from Zmargadine. Save for a single light cruiser, all the ships the size of a sloop or larger had lifted. It was reasonable that at least one ship out of twenty-odd would be unable to lift with so little time to prepare.

Adele wondered if the Alliance destroyers observing Diamondia knew what their main force was doing. She suspected they did not. There'd been no signal from Zmargadine orbit that she'd noticed—which realistically meant no signal. Nor had Admiral Guphill sent a vessel in-system to alert his pickets. The latter would've been quicker than relying on light-speed communication over such a distance, but the Alliance admiral might've feared that a *de facto* courier would also alert the RCN.

Adele smiled again. His concerns would've been valid, had the RCN not gotten much better information by other means.

"Captain," she said. "I've transmitted your message. I'll inform you when we have a response from Pitcher Six. Over."

She was a little embarrassed at the informal way

she'd summoned Daniel from his sleep, though she knew that nobody—least of all Daniel—would complain or even refer to it. Still, in RCN terms she'd behaved unprofessionally. She'd do better now that time wasn't pressing.

"*Thank you, Adele,*" Daniel said, using her first name in subtly crafted absolution. "*Master Cazelet has earned himself a medal. Unfortunately, he's not a member of the RCN so I can't recommend him for one. Ah—*"

He gestured to his display. Information still fed in from the escape capsule. It refined the holographic ships, providing details which fleshed out what'd been conjecture.

"*I have all the data I need, I believe. I'm concerned that if he continues to transmit to us, an Alliance ship will spot him. And there's no longer any need, over.*"

"Unfortunately," Adele said, pleased but a little surprised to find that her voice remained dispassionate, "I'm afraid that if I contact Master Cazelet from here, I'll make his detection almost certain. A signal from Diamondia, even a laser beam, will be scattered significantly by the time it reaches Zmargadine orbit seventy-one light-minutes away. It'll paint Alliance ships at the same amplitude as it does the capsule, and I don't believe that *all* Guphill's signals officers will be asleep. Over."

"*Ah,*" said Daniel. "*Yes.*"

Adele thought that he might say they were all sharing the danger or something else pointless, but in her concern . . . in her *anger*, anger at the situation and at herself for allowing Rene to put himself into the situation; and anger at Daniel, because he'd quite correctly said that it should be done. In her concern and anger, she'd done a disservice to Daniel's intelligence.

"*We're going to crush Guphill, you know, Adele,*" he said instead. His voice was calm, but she heard the excitement underlying it; he was already trembling with the urge to drive in, to strike, and to keep on striking so long as there was an enemy standing.

As she'd watched Daniel do, and helped Daniel do, many times in the past.

The Alliance squadron was beginning to vanish from the imagery Rene sent back. The ships, singly and in pairs, were inserting into the Matrix. It appeared that they were too intent on their own activities to notice that they were under observation by an RCN outpost. Rene might come through this safely after all.

Coughing as much to clear her mind as her throat, Adele said, "Do you mean that because he's taking his entire force to the Bagarian Cluster—presumably, that is—that we can destroy the base on Z3 and effectively end the blockade? Over."

"*Ah, but that's* not *what's happening,*" Daniel said with the enthusiasm of a man who was enthusiastic about just about everything: an insect, a planet, or a thought. And very often enthusiastic about a bimbo, of course, though there seemed to have been a change since he met Miranda Dorst. "*Look here, Adele. Look at the sail plans of the* Pleasaunce *and the* Eitel Friedrich. *Notice the differences, over.*"

Adele was ready to say that she was no more competent to discuss sail plans than she was to plot a course through the Matrix. That was true, of course, but because she didn't dismiss things without examining them, she looked at the images Daniel had forwarded to her: a battleship and a battle cruiser respectively at the moment they inserted into the Matrix.

And she did see the difference; it required no more specialized expertise than telling a bull from a cow. "Captain," Adele said, "the battle cruiser has almost all its sails set. The battleship has only eight—"

Of forty-eight.

"—antennas raised, and only a portion of their sails have been unfurled."

She cleared her throat again and added, "I don't know what that means, however. Over."

As Adele spoke, her wands sorted the imagery according to the pattern Daniel had just pointed out. She was embarrassed not to have seen it for herself. Intellectually she knew that no one, no matter how careful, could notice everything; emotionally she felt that she herself should be the exception.

"*A portion of the squadron headed by the battle cruisers is rigged for a long voyage,*" Daniel said. "*These are generally the faster, more maneuverable vessels. The remaining ships, roughly half the total—*"

Without interrupting verbally, Adele transmitted the sort she'd just completed to the command console. The two battle cruisers, one of the three light cruisers which had lifted from Z3, the four destroyers—all members of that class in the squadron save the pair on picket around Diamondia—and six sloops had shaken out most of their sails. The two battleships, the four heavy cruisers, and the two remaining light cruisers were only partially rigged.

Daniel chuckled, then continued, "*As I say, half the total is planning to insert into the Matrix, then*"

*extract almost immediately. They're going out purely
to provide cover for the force being sent to gut the
Bagarian Cluster like a fish. Guphill's counting on the
fact that Admiral James can't be certain what may
have happened behind the screen of Zmargadine."*

He paused. *"But Guphill's wrong,"* he said, *"because
of our outpost in the rings. I assure you that I'll jump
Matthews a rate for this, and if Master Cazelet would
care to become a midshipman backdated to the day
he boarded the* Sissie, *it's a done deal. I don't have
the clout to arrange that, but Navy House'll grant
Admiral James any favor he asks if he breaks the
siege of Diamondia."*

"I see," said Adele. But because she didn't trust
any news until she'd confirmed it and didn't trust
good news even then, she said nothing more for a
moment while she manipulated a different two columns of data.

"Daniel," she said. After hesitating a moment, she
echoed her present display onto the command console.
She resumed, "Daniel, you're very confident in victory, so I realize there's something that I'm missing.
It appears to me, however, that even with half his
strength sent to the Cluster, Admiral Guphill has a
far stronger fleet than Admiral James does. Where's
my mistake, over?"

*"I'm afraid that this tabular comparison is quite
correct,"* Daniel said. He snorted. *"Of course it's correct, it came from Signals Officer Mundy. In terms
of tonnage, throw weight, crew size—any quantifiable
measure of value—the remaining Alliance squadron
is greatly superior to ours. Each of their four heavy
cruisers is individually stronger than the* Alcubiere,

and the Lao-tze's *older than my father. She's scarcely comparable to brand new battleships like the* Pleasaunce *and* Formentera *which she'll be facing. But.*"

Daniel adjusted the display. Adele wasn't sure he was acting consciously rather than letting his fingers act by rote while he gathered his thought, but the tabular arrays sorted themselves into opposing fleets formed in three dimensions within the holographic volume.

"*First,*" Daniel said, "*the Alliance squadron will return from its feint without any expectation of fighting, while our ships are at action stations even now as they lift from Diamondia. That's a very considerable benefit to the RCN. And second—*"

He looked at Adele and grinned.

"*The second advantage is even less tangible, Adele,*" he said, "*but it's more important. It's the fact we are the RCN. We know it and they know it. Every Alliance spacer from Guphill to the Landsmen in Training knows that no matter how many ships they have, they've always got to expect us to go for their throats. Deep in their hearts, they're afraid and they know we aren't. We're the RCN.*"

"I see your point," said Adele. She wiped the lopsided tables of ships and missiles, of matériel. "More to the point, Daniel, I feel it. Signals out."

"*Six, this is Five!*" Vesey announced over the command push. Her voice was rarely excited, but this time was an exception. "*Nine ships are lifting together from Port Delacroix. The squadron's coming up, over!*"

"*Ship, this is Six,*" said Daniel. "*Action stations, Sissies. We're very shortly going to get stuck into an Alliance squadron again. Up Cinnabar!*"

"Up Cinnabar!" Adele shouted with the rest of the crew. She felt a little silly shouting patriotic nonsense, but she'd have felt even sillier not shouting at a time like this. Her adoptive family, the RCN, was very patriotic.

CHAPTER 26

Above Diamondia

The Alliance destroyers on station above Diamondia
were the *T65* and *T72*. Adele was waiting for their
panicked interchanges when one or the other watch
officer realized that their entire squadron had sallied
from Z3 and they were for the moment alone in the
Jewel System.

That didn't happen. Though the two ships exchanged
desultory signals, neither was paying the least attention
to their base. A pair of lieutenants who'd been in the
same class at the Fleet Gymnasium were discussing
their chances of returning to Pleasaunce in time to
attend the wedding of a third classmate.

The Alliance destroyers had been holding the usual
1 g acceleration to mimic gravity while they patrolled
safely outside the planetary defense array. They'd
normally be replaced on station by another pair of
destroyers after thirty hours or so, more because of
the tedium of the job than because they needed to
replace reaction mass. Even though destroyers had

relatively small tanks, Adele knew from her database that T-class vessels could easily have held station for eight or nine days at that level of consumption.

The sight of the Diamondia Squadron lifting in unison from Port Delacroix got their attention, though. Though the alarm bells on the destroyers weren't audible through vacuum—of course—the rhythmic sound made the hulls themselves vibrate, and that in turn registered on the *Sissie*'s rangefinding lasers.

"Captain, the Alliance pickets have spotted Admiral James," Adele reported calmly. "They're not aware as yet of Admiral Guphill's movements, however. Over."

"*Roger, Signals,*" Daniel said. "*Keep me informed, out.*"

Adele peeped at his display: he was working on attack plans involving the *Princess Cecile* alone engaging the Alliance destroyers and also the *Princess Cecile* engaging them in company with the *Eclipse* and *Echo*. RCN picket destroyers might well have launched long-distance missile attacks on an enemy squadron rising into orbit. There wasn't much chance of a hit under the circumstances, but it could disrupt what was presumably a careful enemy plan.

Adele smiled coldly. She'd learned a great deal while she served with Daniel Leary; one of the things she'd learned was what it meant to be RCN. There was very little chance of the Alliance destroyers reacting as their RCN counterparts would, but if they did, the *Princess Cecile* and her fellows were ready to give them something more immediate to think about than Admiral James' squadron.

Both pickets began to accelerate. Adele couldn't

overhear their internal communications at this range and she didn't have the expertise to judge the details of what was happening. Even she could tell from the iridescent plume streaming from the *T65* that it was using not only High Drive but its less efficient plasma thrusters as well to get up to speed as quickly as possible. The combined thrust not only would make movement and even breathing uncomfortable for the destroyer's crew, it created greater strains than the vessel's rigging was braced to withstand.

It didn't take an expert to realize that, either. One of *T65*'s starboard antennas carried away, followed moments later by the ventral antenna of the same ring. Adele guessed that the second'd been fouled by lines from the first to go, but the details didn't really matter.

The Alliance destroyers began to chatter to one another, using microwave links. These were directional, but at this distance the *Sissie*'s sensors picked up reflections from the vessels' hulls. The *T72* was using the squadron's current code, but Adele's equipment converted the signals as quickly as they could be read on the *T65*; and as for the *T65*, she was transmitting in clear.

The *Princess Cecile*'s bridge personnel were furiously busy; indeed, the whole crew probably was, though the bridge hatch was closed and dogged to limit damage if the corvette was hit. Daniel was projecting courses both through the Matrix and in sidereal space.

Adele had started to pipe the Alliance communications directly to the command console—that's the way she'd have wanted the information—but she realized in time that the captain of a warship in action had more on his mind than his signals officer did. She instead sent her own summaries as a voice message transfigured into a text crawl across the top of his screen:

THE CAPTAIN OF T72 IS SENIOR. SHE HAS ORDERED T65 TO HOLD STATION NEAR DIAMONDIA WHILE T72 RETURNS TO Z3 TO REPORT. T65 PROTESTS.

Moments later the image of the *T72* began to blur and fade into the Matrix. The process took nearly forty-five seconds, a matter of perfectly neutralizing the ship's electrical charge. It had to cease to be a part of the sidereal universe so that it could shift into the Matrix, becoming a miniature universe of its own.

To Adele's brief amazement, the *T65* started to shift also, even before its consort was gone. The junior captain had been more than intemperate in his discussions with his senior officer; in the RCN, at least, there'd have to be a duel after the battle if both captains survived.

She hadn't expected the junior officer to simply ignore a direct order, however. He might believe that it was properly the job of the *T72* to remain behind rather than running to safety with a message, but surely he could see that one of them should stay, couldn't he?

Adele's lips bent in a hard smile. There was a great deal of contempt among Cinnabar civilians for the quality of the Alliance Fleet's personnel. RCN officers were much more reserved in what they said about their enemies: no, the Fleet wasn't the RCN, but neither was it a collection of farmers and cowards who lacked both skill and courage.

Sometimes, however, you ran into examples that went a distance toward justifying civilian prejudices. This was a good time for that to happen. It would be nice if the rot had penetrated to the officers of Admiral Guphill's battleships as well.

Red light flushed Adele's display momentarily; she opened the incoming message, a resumption of the data stream from Zmargadine orbit. Rene had ceased transmitting when the last of the Alliance squadron inserted into the Matrix. . . .

Adele's wands flashed. She didn't take control of the command console, just inset a pulsing red icon as before, but this time she added verbally, "Captain, this is Signals. Alliance warships are extracting in the vicinity of Z3 base. I repeat, Alliance warships are extracting."

Then she drew in a deep breath and added, "Daniel, Admiral Guphill is back."

Daniel's PPI quivered as the Diamondia Squadron sorted itself in orbit. The *Lao tzo* was still climbing out of the gravity well. Her class had been marginal for thruster power when they were built, and rebuilds since that distant date had inevitably increased her mass without adding power. In sidereal space she was no more sluggish than a later battleship, though, and she had the reputation of being notably handy in the Matrix.

He moved the icon from Adele to the lower right quadrant of his screen and opened it. High resolution images of the Alliance squadron began to cycle in his display. They were marvelously sharp: that was the *Pleasaunce*, because her outriggers were shorter by three frames than those of her near sister the *Formentera*; the *Formentera* extracted only thirty seconds later.

"Command," Daniel said, verbally keying the channel which linked the officers. His orders were to Adele, but the information would please everybody aboard. "Signals, copy the raw data to all the *Sissie's* consoles and also transmit them to the flagship, attention CinC. When you've done that—"

At the bottom of the quadrant where Cazelet's imagery cascaded appeared the legend DATA TRANSMITTED. The letters were in glowing puce, a disgusting color which he suspected Adele had chosen deliberately.

Daniel choked to keep from laughing. *A good thing I wasn't taking a sip of water, as I was about to*. He continued, "Yes, and please restructure the data into a PPI layout centered on Z3 Base if you will. Distribute that in the same way, over."

"*Yes*," said Adele. He glanced to his side to see her wands dancing; it was like watching a machine, a very intelligent machine. "*Shall I transmit the data to the other ships of the squadron also?*"

After a minuscule pause she added, "*Over.*"

Daniel winced. He was afraid one of the junior officers would blurt something, but nobody did. He suspected that it wasn't just that they made allowances for Adele's lack of familiarity with naval protocol: they respected her so greatly that there lurked at the backs of their minds the possibility that Lady Mundy was right again.

She wasn't right. Admiral James would react as

though Commander Leary had walked into the Admiral's Bridge and taken a dump on his console.

"Negative, Signals," Daniel said mildly. "The Commander in Chief would regard that as an attempt to usurp his authority, particularly since the *Princess Cecile* is technically not a member of the Diamondia Squadron. Six out."

The destroyers had their antennas raised and were shaking their sails out. Most of the heavy cruiser *Alcubiere*'s antennas were up, and the flagship *Zeno* had begun the process. The light cruiser *Antigone* was almost as old as the *Lao-tze* and like her was underpowered for operations in an atmosphere, but she'd be joining momentarily.

"*Squadron*," said a voice slugged as coming in through the laser communicator. Admiral James himself was speaking, not his signals lieutenant. "*We will operate in two elements, Foxhunt and Barnyard. Orders will follow presently—*"

An icon winked at the bottom of the command display; the orders had already arrived. Daniel restrained his urge to open them until the admiral had finished speaking.

"*We'll be taking the fight to the enemy, fellow officers*," the admiral continued, "*of course. Because the enemy is superior in force, I expect rigid discipline and prompt obedience to my orders. I do not say that I expect courage and professional shiphandling, because you wouldn't be in the RCN at all if you didn't display those qualities. Squadron Command out.*"

Daniel nodded approvingly. The admiral's words were perfectly appropriate, though none of the captains had needed to hear them to understand the situation inside and out. He opened the Orders icon, but before he could begin going over the contents his console flashed an incoming message warning.

"*Rascal,*" said Admiral James again in a harsher voice than before, "*this is Squadron Command. You're Foxhunt Ten for the duration of this operation. You'll obey the orders of Foxhunt Command, that's Captain Bussom, without hesitation. Do you understand that, Leary, over?*"

Daniel stiffened at the console as though he'd been slapped. *Does the admiral think I'm going to hare off on my own in the middle of a fleet action?*

"Squadron Command, this is Foxhunt Ten-six," he said as formally as he could manage. "Aye aye, sir. Ten-six over."

Obviously James did think that, and it was most unfair. Daniel'd *always* obeyed orders in the past.

Well, almost always. And anyway, he respected both James and Bussom.

"*Sorry, Leary,*" James said in a much softer tone. "*I thought I needed to say that. We've got bloody little margin on this one, and if anybody gets creative it'll confuse everybody else. No matter how clever a notion it might've been on its own, over.*"

"Aye aye, sir," Daniel repeated. His mouth was open to close the transmission—he needed to look at the orders and he was sure the admiral had something better to do than chat with the captain of the least powerful ship in his squadron.

Before he could do so, James said, "*Bloody hell, Leary! Where did you get this imagery? It's not real, is it? It's a computer simulation, right, over?*"

"Squadron," said Daniel, opening the file which Adele

must've forwarded to him and the admiral simultaneously, "the imagery and the derived PPI are real-time, transmitted from Zmargadine orbit some seventy-one minutes ago. You can take it to the bank, sir, over."

Admiral Guphill's reduced force had extracted in the vicinity of Zmargadine; now they'd begun striking their sails to set down on Z3. If they were keeping anything approaching a proper watch, they'd become aware when light from Diamondia reached the gas giant within the next few minutes that the RCN squadron had sallied.

"*By the Gods, Leary,*" James said in a reverential whisper, "*they've laid their balls on an anvil and we're holding the hammer. Judging by their sail plans, a visit from Guarantor Porra wouldn't surprise them as much as we're about to.*"

The admiral paused, then went on, "*Foxhunt Ten-six, head this material 'On behalf of Squadron Command' and distribute it yourself. I want everybody to know it came from you, just in case I'm not around to tell them myself after things settle out. Squadron out.*"

"Aye aye, *sir!*" Daniel said. "Foxhunt Ten-six out!"

He didn't need the bright pink TRANSMITTED legend to tell him Adele would've sent it even before Admiral James finished speaking. The legend nonetheless flashed.

He looked for the first time at the orders which the Squadron staff had sent at the same time Admiral James himself was reading Commander Leary the riot act. They were headed CAPTAIN'S EYES ONLY.

Daniel realized his lips had squeezed together into what he'd have called a pout if he'd seen the expression on someone else's face. Chuckling, he forwarded the orders to the BDC before he started going over them in detail.

"Captain's eyes only" was the sort of nonsense which staff officers came up with. Did they think a Sissie was going to send the plans on to Admiral Guphill? And didn't it occur to them that the whole purpose of the separated Battle Direction Center was to provide a backup command structure in case a missile sliced off the corvette's bridge?

The two battleships formed Barnyard, under Captain Clinton of the *Zeno*. Admiral James was aboard the *Zeno*, but he commanded the whole squadron rather than just the Barnyard element. The remaining vessels—*Alcubiere*, *Antigone*, seven E-class destroyers, and the *Princess Cecile*—were Foxhunt.

Breaking the squadron into a heavy element and a screening element gave James a degree of flexibility, but the orders directed they stay together at least through the initial maneuvering. When all the ships were ready, they were to insert into the Matrix and extract in line ahead, heavy vessels leading, thirty light-minutes in-system of Zmargadine.

They were to be offset ten degrees system west of the line connecting the gas giant with Diamondia. Daniel nodded approvingly. If Admiral Guphill made his initial jump in a direct line toward Diamondia, the RCN squadron would be positioned to rake the Alliance ships with all missile tubes.

It'd take the *Lao-tze* about ten more minutes to complete her rigging. The squadron was to spend seventeen sidereal minutes in the Matrix. Daniel was sure the *Sissie* could make the run in less; the *Alcubiere*, a heavily sparred vessel under Captain Bussom, who—like Daniel—had been trained in shiphandling by Commander Stacy Bergen, might be able to do it in twelve minutes or less. They'd both extract in seventeen, because synchrony was important and absolute speed was not.

VICEROY ADELBERT HAS REPORTED RCN MOVEMENTS, announced a text at the bottom of the quadrant in which the Alliance ships maneuvered for landing. Daniel's screen indicated that Vesey and Blantyre were both trying to call him—with the same news, he had no doubt, and Adele must not doubt it either because she was blocking their interruptions until Six decided he had time to talk to his subordinates.

Daniel checked the full message, then manually cut in the PA system. "Squadron," he said, his voice booming through the speakers in every compartment. "Foxhunt Ten-six. Cruiser *Viceroy Adelbert* has observed RCN movements and reported us to Alliance Command. Ten-six out."

Blantyre immediately withdrew her summons. Vesey did not, so Daniel touched that icon with his cursor and said, "Six, go ahead. Over."

"*Sir, I have a series of solutions for the Alliance squadron,*" Vesey said. "*Over.*"

"Do you bloody indeed!" said Daniel. *By the Gods, I did train this lady well!* "Forward them, if you will, Vesey, over."

He'd expected her to say that she'd done a course plot which would bring the *Princess Cecile* into her place at the tail end of the RCN line after their jump. Of course she did; so did Blantyre and Cory, and Shearman, the spacer who was striking for a master's rating.

But Daniel'd assumed he was the only person aboard the *Sissie* who was calculating what the enemy would or might do. Two of James' lieutenants on the *Zeno* would be doing that, cursing it as an empty exercise because there were too many variables for prediction. That was true, of course: you couldn't really predict an enemy's movements unless you had his sail plan at the moment he entered the Matrix, and even then you had to be both good and lucky.

But the exercise forced you to think *like* the enemy, and that wasn't empty at all. Getting into the enemy's head was more important than predicting his next move in detail.

Vesey'd never be a real fighting officer; frankly, she didn't have the instinct to go for the throat. Vesey had to think through her attacks, and though her solutions would always be proper ones, she'd never have the flair of her late fiancé, Midshipman Dorst. Everything that effort and study could do, however, she *would* do.

Daniel opened her three solutions. The first showed the Alliance squadron reforming forty light-minutes out from Z3 but offset at fifteen degrees to the Zmargadine/Diamondia axis, putting them equidistant from the two bases. The second showed Guphill's squadron in a line anchored at one end by Z3 and at the other by the two battleships. At the scale of the holographic display the ships looked close to their present locations, but they'd still have to maneuver through the Matrix to achieve the formation in less than a week.

The final solution was the most interesting of all: Admiral Guphill's ten ships formed a loose globe just outside Diamondia's planetary defense array. Daniel highlighted this one and said, "Vesey, explain the purpose behind this plan, over."

"*Sir!*" replied Vesey, her voice suddenly without character but half an octave higher than it normally was. "*The enemy will believe he's cut us off from our base by encircling Diamondia. He'll realize that we can extract within our own array, but when we brake to land we'll become predictable targets for missiles even though they're launched from the minimum safe distance. Over.*"

"All right, Vesey," Daniel said. "But why will the enemy assume we're going to run for our base, over?"

"*Sir,*" she said, "*they'll project their own motivations onto us, sir! Over.*"

She's so very clever, Daniel thought. *But she has no instinct for this at all. Well, neither did Uncle Stacy, and there was never born a better astrogator.*

Midshipman Dorst would've said, "Sir, they'll be afraid to go far from their own base. Likely they'll ball up around it. Let's us come at them from one side and grind them all to hell, eh?"

He'd have been wrong too, but he'd have understood what was possible. Vesey was so good an astrogator herself that the idea of ten ships englobing a planet in perfect formation didn't strike her as absurd. Dorst, who couldn't have managed even that modest intra-system distance in less than three sequences of insertion and extraction, had a better grasp of normal human capacity.

"I think he'll do this, Vesey, over," Daniel said, forwarding his solution to her console in the BDC. He didn't need the image inset on his display to imagine her frowning in frustration.

"*But sir, why would he divide his squadron?*" Vesey said. "*That allows us to concentrate superior force on either one, doesn't it, over?*"

Daniel showed the Alliance squadron forming initially ten light-minutes in-system from Z3 because Guphill knew his ships would scatter widely if their initial jump was of any length. They were split into two wings of equal strength, each led by one of the battleships.

"Vesey, Guphill'll do this because he's commanded in four engagements and he's split his force every time," Daniel said. "I think if asked to justify the formation, he'd say that it permits him to catch his enemy between two fires. In reality I don't think he's comfortable with a single large force, but it worked out well for him when he fought a fleet from Novy Sverdlovsk while commodore of a squadron in the Sponsor Stars, over."

"*But sir!*" Vesey said despairingly. "*That was Novy Sverdlovsk. Surely he doesn't think he can do that with the RCN, over?*"

"We've caught him off balance," Daniel said. "I don't believe he *is* thinking; he's reacting because he doesn't have time to think. And Vesey?"

He paused, flashing through several ways to phrase what she needed to understand.

"If a missile's well-aimed, the target's planet of origin doesn't matter. Admiral Guphill started as a missile officer and a very good one; his ships got seventeen direct hits during that fight in the Sponsor Stars. We don't have seventeen ships today. Out."

"*Squadron, this is Command,*" said Admiral James. "*Prepare to insert in five seconds.*"

Daniel's finger poised over the EXECUTE button.

"*Insert!*"

He pressed the button. The *Princess Cecile* began to shudder out of sidereal space, heading again for the enemy.

CHAPTER 27

Jewel System

Some people saw things in the Matrix; ghosts, if you will, and not always human ghosts. Adele merely felt queasy when she wasn't concentrating on something; therefore she concentrated on things, which was what she ought to be doing anyway.

At present she was using her time to review communications among the ships of the Alliance squadron, which Rene had intercepted and transmitted to her. She'd been busy with the imagery while the *Princess Cecile* was in sidereal space, and cursory dips into the commo chatter had convinced her that it wouldn't be of importance.

She'd been correct about the lack of importance, but it was interesting to see that the Alliance's initial reaction had been something close to panic. Adele got the impression of people who'd started to enter their house and found a ravening monster striding down the hall toward them.

She was also distressed by their lack of communications security, though none of the heavy ships were so distraught that they broadcast in clear the way the *T65* had done. The Alliance officers were the enemy, so she knew she ought to be pleased when they seemed incompetent. The truth appeared to be that she felt much more angry about bad craftsmanship than she did about people trying to kill her.

Adele smiled faintly. Daniel would probably understand that, though it was unlikely that he felt that way himself.

Antennas and the bitts to which the rigging was fastened creaked, transmitting strains through the double hulls. Sounds and light were different, flatter, in the Matrix. Some scientists claimed that was an illusion: instrument readings demonstrated that frequency rates and amplitude across the electro-optical spectrum remained the same whether the ship was in sidereal space or in a discrete bubble of the Matrix.

Adele sniffed; it was amazing how foolish highly educated people could be. Sight and sound were artifacts of the brain which processed neural signals. Though the signals might be identical, the processing wasn't—as anybody who'd been in the Matrix could have told them.

She closed the file of Alliance intership communication; there was nothing she needed to pass on to Daniel. That negative knowledge was useful, though.

They had the information because of Rene Cazelet's skill. And courage, of course, but—

Adele grinned in self-mockery . . . though it was true.

—in the RCN one took courage as a given. Guarantor Porra had hurt himself worse than he could possibly have imagined when he drove that young man into the service of the Alliance's enemies.

Adele hoped it'd be possible to retrieve the escape capsule after the battle. Frowning, she realized that only the Sissies knew of the capsule's existence, so a single Alliance missile could doom Rene and his boat handler to a lingering death. Adele quickly composed a message stating the capsule's purpose and location. She set her equipment to transmit the data to all ships of the squadron as soon as they returned to sidereal space.

It'd be extremely bad luck if the corvette was destroyed in the instant of extraction. Regardless, Rene and Matthews were subject to the same fortunes of war as the other members of the crew.

The rig groaned again; an icy knife slid between the hemispheres of Adele's brain and then down the length of her spine. Presumably the *Princess Cecile* had passed from one bubble universe to another.

Vesey had gone out onto the hull where she could make minute changes to the sail plan based on her reading of the Matrix. Daniel said she had a real talent for it, judging energy gradients with a delicacy and precision that the *Sailing Directions*—compiled from averages—and an astrogation computer could never equal.

Thought of Vesey caused Adele to play back the lieutenant's discussion with Daniel regarding attack plans. Again, Adele'd listened to snatches of the conversation at the time, but she'd decided that other matters were more pressing. It still wasn't important, but now that she had leisure she found a great deal of interest—not so much in the words as in the insights to be gleaned from the interchange.

Adele looked at the image of Daniel, now poring

over further course projections. She'd sent him a full dossier on Admiral Guphill and on all the captains in the Alliance squadron. Indeed, she'd provided the same information on all the RCN captains as well; she didn't believe in the concept of too much information.

She hadn't sent Vesey that data—but she'd have been glad to do so if Vesey'd asked. And Daniel *would* have asked if his signals officer hadn't volunteered it. For that matter, the *Princess Cecile*'s regular database had information on all Alliance admirals which Vesey could easily've retrieved on her own.

That didn't mean Vesey was stupid. Rather, it meant that Vesey viewed human beings as interchangeable data points. She had an instinct for the nuances of the Matrix, but she was trying to predict people in large classes.

There was no humor in Adele's smile. Vesey was a smart, decent, *normal* human being. She couldn't look on people with the dispassionate precision which Adele directed toward them.

Elspeth Vesey wouldn't kill unless she were in a rage, and even then she'd probably twitch the muzzle to the side in the instant before the trigger released. She'd loved and been loved by a fine young man, just as young women were supposed to do. She had not only a good mind but all the human attributes that Adele Mundy so signally lacked—

But she didn't seem happy or anything remotely approaching happy. Of course Vesey probably didn't have as many dead people visiting her in the early hours of the morning as Adele did; but perhaps she saw Timothy Dorst, and that might be as bad.

Adele minimized her screen and looked across the

console at Tovera. Tovera raised an eyebrow in query, but Adele brought the holographic display back up without speaking.

Tovera had no conscience, so she slept soundly every night. Though . . . Adele had seen hints that by closely observing her mistress, Tovera was starting to internalize the concept of friendship. From there it was only a series of short steps to regret, remorse, and misery. As best Adele could tell, that was what it meant to be fully human.

She was audibly chuckling when Daniel announced, *"Extracting from the Matrix in thirty, I say again three-zero, seconds!"*

There was so much adrenaline coursing through Daniel's system that he didn't feel the shimmering discomfort of extraction. *We ought to go into battle more often*, he thought; and he was laughing as the corvette slipped back into the sidereal universe.

The *Alcubiere* had extracted within a fraction of a second of the *Princess Cecile*; it was easy to tell by the energetic debris streaming from each High Drive motor. There was none in the case of the heavy cruiser, whereas the destroyers *Escapade* and *Express* must've arrived thirty seconds ahead of schedule to have left the trail they did.

The two battleships arrived to head the line less than fifteen seconds later, with the remaining five destroyers appearing in the next fifteen seconds and the *Antigone* staggering in a few heartbeats after that. Admiral James wouldn't be thrilled about the sloppy timing on a short intra-system hop, but the eleven vessels of his squadron were in notably good line.

Which put them strikingly at variance with the Alliance ships. If Daniel didn't know they had to be in formation, he wouldn't have been able to guess what that formation was: two reverse echelons spreading like the strokes of a ninety-degree V with its implied base at Z3. There was a battleship in either line, but the four heavy cruisers were in the right wing and the two light cruisers in the left; Guphill had apparently decided to keep the cruisers' divisional structures intact instead of splitting them to balance his wings as Daniel had theorized.

Other than that, Guphill's formation—raggedness aside, though there was quite a lot of raggedness *to* put aside—was exactly as Daniel had theorized it'd be, save that it was only five light-minutes out from Z3 and the huge green ball of Zmargadine itself. Full marks to the late Midshipman Dorst, who'd have expected that. The boy couldn't navigate his way to the latrine, but he'd had an instinct for an enemy's weaknesses.

The *T65* and *T72* were the only destroyers remaining to Guphill since he'd sent the others with his sloops off to the Bagarian Cluster. They were wallowing between the squadron's wings while signals flashed in both directions.

The destroyer captains knew less about the Alliance situation than the RCN officers did. Guphill hadn't informed the Diamondia pickets that he intended to send half his force out of the Jewel System, so they were probably expecting the battle cruisers and the remainder of the screening forces either to extract or to lift from Z3 momentarily.

Daniel studied the sail plan of the Alliance vessels.

If you knew the present conditions in the Matrix—as he did—and you had experience as a hands-on astrogator—which again he did; a bloody good astrogator, not to be modest—you could get a fair notion of the enemy's intentions by seeing how his sails were arrayed.

Oh, certainly, there were as many different ways to accomplish a trip from point to point in the Matrix as there were to go from the bridge to the BDC; but you didn't make the latter journey by stepping out onto the hull and back in through the after airlock unless there was a very good reason. Likewise the *Sissie*'s astrogation computer could reverse analyze the *Pleasaunce*'s sail plan to determine the course they'd been adjusted to solve.

Though close by astronomical standards, the opposing squadrons remained over three hundred million miles apart—well beyond the range of missiles, let alone plasma cannon. That also meant that the schematic of the enemy array on Daniel's command console, though perfectly accurate, showed the situation twenty-five minutes in the past. A great deal can happen in twenty-five minutes. . . .

The wings of the Alliance formation were separated by one and a half light-seconds at the wide end and about half that as they tapered toward Z3. The ships were accelerating at nearly 2 gs, but that seemed to be to straighten out the lines in the sidereal universe instead of dipping back into the Matrix to do the job more efficiently. Perhaps Guphill trusted his officers' pilotage farther than he did their astrogation.

The only vessels which began adjusting their sails for reinsertion were the two startled destroyers. Daniel didn't need the summary of communications intercepts from Adele to know that they were being directed to take their place in the left wing ahead of the light cruisers *Bat Durston* and *Rip Waechter*. Unlike Admiral James' dispositions, the Alliance dreadnoughts were farthest from the enemy.

Laser backed with microwave flashed orders from the *Zeno*. Daniel opened the kernel instantly, then forwarded the data to the other bridge consoles and the BDC. He wondered if Admiral Guphill had anyone on his staff who could decode RCN signals as quickly as Adele did those of the Alliance. Perhaps, but it didn't really matter; at this stage of the engagement, Guphill was going to learn about the RCN's plans more quickly than signals would propagate over the intervening distance.

The *Sissie* vibrated in a familiar fashion; Sun was rotating his turrets and running the paired 4-inch plasma cannon from minimum to maximum elevation to be sure that they moved freely. They did, of course, just as they had when the corvette reached orbit initially.

The entire squadron was to insert into the Matrix in seven minutes from arrival of the order. The Foxhunt element would extract between the arms of the Alliance formation, launch a single salvo of missiles at the ships of the right wing, and reenter the Matrix. Because there wouldn't be time to adjust their sails before this second insertion, they'd carry on to the orbit of Samphire—though that barren rock would itself be on the other side of Jewel for the next seventeen months—and re-form.

A lot of assumptions would have to work out for

there to be anything left of Foxhunt to re-form. Well, nobody'd told them that enlisting in the RCN would guarantee that they'd die in bed.

Daniel plotted the course that would put the *Princess Cecile* in the middle of the enemy squadron. Borries was laying out missile attacks, Sun was determining the best angles at which to deflect incoming missiles with his cannon—which was a grim joke to anybody who'd calculated the flux density required to affect a five-tonne missile over such a short range—and the midshipmen were figuring the escape sequence following the attack.

Somewhere out on the hull, Vesey was looking at the orders relayed to her by hydromechanical semaphore and frowning; at any rate, Daniel would be frowning if it were him, as he much wished it were. But Vesey could read the Matrix almost as well as he could, and nobody could lay out a detailed attack as well as Commander Daniel Leary.

"Ship," Daniel said, "prepare for insertion in thirty, I say again three-zero, seconds."

And may the Gods have mercy on our souls.

The *Princess Cecile* shuddered into the Matrix again. Adele leaned back against the cushions and lifted her commo helmet with her fingertips so that she could massage her temples. Quick in-and-out transitions were uncomfortable, though long periods in the Matrix were uncomfortable also and led to hallucinations. Or hauntings, Adele supposed; it didn't matter, since in her judgment one irrational experience was as bad as the next.

She noticed that Daniel had called the riggers in

from the hull. Only the genesis of the signal was electronic: the crew received it by hydromechanical semaphores placed at bow and stern, dorsal and ventral. On Adele's display the recall was a boxed translation; on the hull, the six semaphore arms rose vertically, then swung equidistant around the circle.

The riggers used hand signals to communicate among themselves. When the corvette was under way, the hull was a jungle of antennas, cables, and the shimmer of Casimir radiation impinging on the sails spread above. Inevitably not all the crew would see a semaphore, but those who did passed the signal to their fellows. The bosun's mates were responsible for bringing in all members of the sections they took out.

Everybody on the bridge with Adele was busy with preparations for the attack. Well, Tovera and Hogg weren't; they sat on the jumpseats behind the signals and command consoles, blank-eyed and as tense as trigger springs. Neither was a person with whom Adele could imagine having a restful conversation.

Grinning minusculely, Adele returned to the most recent Alliance intercepts to have something to occupy her mind. As she did so, a green telltale winked on her display. Cory's voice from the BDC said, "*Sissie Five-two to Signals, over.*"

Frowning because she couldn't imagine what the midshipman wanted, Adele said, "Go ahead, Cory."

It was a two-way link so she didn't bother with protocol. They could talk over one another's words just as easily as they could if they were face to face, since their voices were on separate channels.

The midshipmen were under Vesey, Sissie Five, the First Lieutenant, in the table of organization. Cory was junior—by accident of name—to Blantyre, so he became Five-two while she was Five-one. It all seemed ludicrously complicated to Adele, though she could see it'd be necessary on a battleship with a crew of a thousand. Since the RCN arranged everything on the basis of the lowest common denominator, the same rules applied to an undercrewed corvette.

Well, they didn't apply to Adele Mundy unless she chose that they should. She'd been concentrating on the minute details of decoding; now she ached and had nothing to do, putting her in even less than usual of a mood to mouth nonsense when plain words would do.

"Ah, yes, mistress," said Cory. *"I've copied the internal ship traffic for you so you can review my decisions now that we're in the Matrix, ov—that is, ma'am."*

Adele's face softened slightly. While she'd been busy with external signals—those from other RCN vessels as well as Alliance intercepts—she'd made Cory the human filter between Daniel and the yammering that always filled the *Sissie's* intercom circuits when they were on the verge of action.

She'd tested Cory on recordings of earlier actions where she herself had made the decisions. He'd done quite well—surprisingly well, she'd have said a year earlier; since then she'd realized that though the midshipman was lucky to have graduated from the Academy, he had a real flair for communications. He hadn't blocked any signals that Adele had let through, and even initially he'd filtered about eighty percent of what she'd deemed to be pointless chatter. Further, he'd gotten better.

"Thank you, Cory," she said. "I'll go over the material, but I have every confidence in your ability."

From somebody else, those would be mere words. Adele spoke them because they were an accurate statement of her belief. She'd never fathomed why people generally danced around the truth instead of saving time and effort by stating it bluntly.

"*Mistress?*" said Cory. "*There's another thing I wanted to say, while, you know, there's time.*"

"Then you'd better say it or there *won't* be time," Adele said. She hoped she'd kept her tone polite, but this was more nonsense in place of plain speaking. The part of her that would always be Mundy of Chatsworth twitched toward a riding crop to bring Cory to what would obviously turn out to be the only real point of his call.

A whipping wouldn't really have gotten the information out sooner, of course, but it'd have given her pleasure to administer it. Though—since Adele had just been wishing she had a useful way in which to spend the next few minutes—she was being foolish as well as uncharitable.

"*Yes, mistress,*" contritely muttered Cory, who must've heard the lash in her voice. "*I, well, I want to thank you for the guidance you've given me since you came to the* Hermes. *I know I'd never have gotten to be as good as you are, but, well, I don't think many signals lieutenants in the RCN know their jobs better than you've taught me. I think bloody few do!*"

Adele frowned. "You're welcome, Cory," she said. "You were willing to learn, and you've learned very well. Very few midshipmen would've recognized that there was anything to the job besides watching the software route signals."

And from what she'd seen over the past several

years, very few signals officers had any greater interest, despite having the rating.

She cleared her throat. "If I may ask, Cory," she went on, "why did you bring this up now?"

The *Sissie* shook as the inner airlock door opened in the forward rotunda. Though the bridge hatch was closed, stiction made the airlock's mating surfaces release with a high *cling!* recognizable to anybody who'd heard it once.

The riggers were coming in. Both watches had been on the hull, so it required a double cycle of the airlocks to complete the business.

"*Well, mistress,*" Cory said in embarrassment. "*I thought you'd seen the battle plan. Ah, I don't . . . I mean, I'm not afraid, and I know Six'll bring us through as well as anybody could. But you know, the formation . . .*"

Adele imported the battle plan from the command console. Daniel was busy with the third in a series of projected attack boards, but the initial layout from Squadron Six was there, wedged into a sidebar on the screen.

She stared at it. "All right, Cory," she said. "I see the battle plan but I don't see the problem with it. We'll be placed between the two enemy formations. They won't be able to launch missiles for fear of hitting their own ships. We *will* launch missiles and then reinsert before they can maneuver out of their own way. It seems a simple and effective plan. Not that I could've created it, but on looking at it now. What am I missing?"

"*Mistress, they'll be using their plasma cannon, we're so close,*" Cory said. "*The big ships, maybe even the destroyers, chances are they'll make out all right. But the Sissie—we don't have the hull to take the hammering they'll give us. It's nobody's fault, I don't blame the admiral or anything. But it's . . . well, I've been honored to serve with you and with Mister Leary, mistress.*"

"Ah," said Adele. Beads on a holographic display looked the same no matter what the scale was; she hadn't considered that this time the actual range was short enough to make plasma bolts a real danger. "I take your point, Cory."

The outer airlock rang; the second rigging watch was coming in. Adele understood why Daniel wouldn't want personnel on the hull during the coming sleet of ions, though as Cory said—it probably didn't make any difference.

"*And as for them not being able to use missiles themselves, mistress?*" Cory went on. "*That's saying they shouldn't use missiles, but I'd be surprised if one of them didn't. There'll be some missileer who's eager or scared or who just doesn't think about there being friendlies on the other side of us. They'll launch, I'd bet you.*"

"Thank you, Cory," Adele said. "I agree that one can usually predict that people won't think through the results of their actions. Or anything else."

She was more than usually disgusted with herself to be educated by Cory on two separate points in a short conversation. The second matter involved the behavior of normal human beings, though, and that was a subject about which Adele had never imagined herself to be a competent judge.

Hatches clinged again; the aft airlock provided a

faint distant echo to the one just outside the bridge. The riggers didn't have electronic links in their suits, so Woetjans keyed the flat-plate communicator beside the lock to report, "*Six, this is Rig. Both watches are shipside, sir.*"

"*Roger, Bosun,*" Daniel said. "*Break. Vesey, are you forward or aft, over?*"

There was no response. Adele folded two of the corvette's three microwave horns into their traveling position against the hull. From what Cory suggested, they wouldn't survive in the extended position. If the hull was breached—again as Cory suggested—it didn't matter a great deal whether or not the transceivers were functional, but it was a matter of pride to Adele that she took care of her equipment.

"*Sissie Five, report at once!*" Daniel barked. The demand echoed itself through the PA system.

"*Ship, extracting in thirty-five seconds,*" called Blantyre from the BDC. After a pause, "*Extracting in thirty seconds.*"

There was no response from Vesey. Woetjans called, "*Six, this is Rig. Polatti was last through the aft hatch. He says the lieutenant told him she was going forward. Sir, I swear I didn't see any sign of her when I closed the lock and brought in the port watch. I'm going out to get her. Rig out.*"

"*Negative, Woetjans!*" Daniel said. "*Do not—*"

"*Extracting!*" called Blantyre.

"*—exit the ship! Do not leave the ship!*"

The inner airlock clinged open. Then Adele saw flashes of heat and her nose smelled purple as the *Princess Cecile* returned to normal space, in the jaws of an Alliance squadron.

CHAPTER 28

Jewel System

Daniel framed his display with the six attack boards and gave pride of place in the center to the Plot-Position Indicator, even though at the present instant it was a pearly blankness. The universe now bathing the *Princess Cecile*'s sensors had different physical constants from those of the universe of men. The very concepts of matter and energy as the PPI understood them would be meaningless until extraction was complete.

Extraction. . . .

For an instant, Daniel felt that his hair had turned inward to grow through his body, licking every nerve with a tongue of fire. Then the *Sissie* was back in sidereal space and rushing straight down the throat of a dragon.

The *Express* and *Escapade* had extracted early again. Both wings of the Alliance squadron were swinging their plasma cannon onto those first targets blurring out of the Matrix. If the destroyers' captains survived, they'd have to expect Admiral James calling them on the carpet.

441

The precursor effects to an extraction didn't hint at the size of the vessel which was disturbing space-time; the Alliance ships were reacting as though the new arrivals were RCN dreadnoughts. It didn't surprise Daniel as he refined the *Sissie*'s attack on the *Pleasaunce* to see that the *Rip Waechter* was launching a spread of eight missiles. The captain of the Alliance light cruiser must've ordered the attack the instant he saw that the enemy was appearing so close by; he'd lacked the time or inclination to countermand those orders when instead a pair of destroyers materialized.

"*Six, I have a solution!*" Borries said. "*I have a solution, over!*"

Daniel had a solution also, but as his finger reached for the EXECUTE button his eye followed the projected tracks of the *Waechter*'s missiles overlaid on his attack board. The heavy cruiser *Vineta* and the flagship *Pleasaunce* herself were already engaging the destroyers with their cannon. Quite apart from the damage plasma bolts would do, the bath of ions would prevent the targets from inserting before the missiles crossed their tracks.

"Negative!" Daniel cried as his fingers relegated the preset *Pleasaunce* attack in favor of another of those waiting at the sides of his display. "Negative! Hold for new solution, over!"

A 20-cm plasma bolt from the *Formentera* hit the *Sissie*'s starboard B-ring antenna, vaporizing it and the yards, rigging, top and topgallant sails. The corvette both jumped and slewed, slammed by the expanding fireball as well as twisting in the side-thrust transmitted through the antenna in the instant before it vanished.

Seams started, but the plasma had vented its energy

in the rigging. Daniel knew from experience that by dressing the *Sissie* in a full suit of sails, he could prevent the first bolt, even from a battleship's 8-inch weapon, from reaching the hull.

That was the first bolt only.

The *Princess Cecile* wasn't a proper target for the battleships' guns, but she was the nearest target. Daniel supposed that as a Cinnabar patriot he should be pleased that the enemy was wasting shots which should've been fired at the *Alcubiere*. However—he grinned—he wasn't *that* good a patriot.

"*Six, we've got to launch!*" Borries said, but Daniel'd locked the *Sissie's* missile tubes to the command console. He'd launch when he was certain of his target. The *Waechter's* Chief Missileer hadn't taken time to properly plan his solution, which was going to be a costly mistake.

Admiral James had ordered the Foxhunt element to launch at the *Pleasaunce* before fleeing back into the Matrix, but Daniel had also set up attacks on the four heavy cruisers in the right wing and on the *Formentera*, the left-wing battleship. He dumped the *Pleasaunce* attack and brought up the solution for the cruiser directly ahead of her in line, the *Direktor Heinrich*. He modified the preset slightly, then reached for EXECUTE again.

The *Express* launched two missiles. Daniel wasn't sure how her crew managed to do it, because the destroyer had been hammered by plasma bolts from the moment the *Princess Cecile* extracted. Even if her hull hadn't been penetrated, it'd be remarkable if any sensors had survived to provide targeting information.

"Launching two!" Daniel said.

"Six, dear Gods no, you'll miss ahead!" Borries said.

The corvette clanged as steam blasted a missile clear of its tube, clanged again as the second missile banged out ten seconds after the first, and then rang with three blows in quick succession. The heavy cruisers *Hertha* and *Direktor Heinrich* had caught her with 15-cm plasma bolts which stripped away most of the rigging on the port side. Under normal circumstances being hit by a 15-cm plasma bolt would've seemed like walking into the mouth of Hell, but to those aboard a ship that'd just taken a 20-cm round, the cruiser weapons seemed anemic.

"Prepare for insertion!" Daniel said, his hair standing on end. The lights had flickered off and on again, but during the interim the interior metal surfaces had trembled with pale green corposants. He didn't know how long it'd be before he could cancel the hull charges; perhaps there wasn't enough time in the world. . . .

The jolt of induced current had shifted Daniel's display from the attack board back to the PPI which'd been up previously. On it one of the *Waechter*'s missiles intersected the bead slugged ESC for *Escapade.* The cruiser's missiles'd been aimed as much by luck as skill, but any spacer could tell you there was nothing better than luck—or worse.

Under ideal conditions the *Sissie* would by now have gotten the greasy feel that indicated her substance was severing its material connection with the sidereal universe. She wasn't there yet: too much energy from the ion bolts popped and sizzled in hotspots throughout her hull and rigging.

There was nothing to do but wait. Though—reloads were rumbling toward the missile tubes. Even though launching a second salvo might draw further Alliance attention, the *Princess Cecile* had come here to fight.

The steep acceleration curve indicated the Alliance weapons were dual-converter units, as was to be expected from Fleet warships. The range from the *Waechter* to the *Escapade* was just long enough that the missile would've expended the water it carried for fuel, but the projectile would barely have begun to separate into three pieces. Such a hit would've wrecked a battleship. It turned the *Escapade* into two relatively large assemblies, the far bow and the right outrigger, and sent them spinning away in a fan of scrap and gas. Eighty percent of the destroyer's mass was in that expanding spray.

The *Alcubiere* had launched ten of the twelve missiles that'd have been a complete salvo. The *Pleasaunce* had hit her repeatedly with 20-cm bolts as she extracted in company with the *Princess Cecile*, and not even a heavy cruiser could accept that punishment without noticing it. It was scarcely a surprise that two of the *Alcubiere*'s tubes would've been damaged, either by having their caps welded shut or simply warping when the hull twisted.

The *Pleasaunce* was now using her cannon to fend away the missiles sent toward her by most ships of the Foxhunt element. Not all were well-aimed—the *Antigone*'s eight weren't even in the right plane; heavy gunfire had smashed the light cruiser as she extracted. Her Chief Missileer must've launched blindly as overloaded consoles sizzled on the verge of meltdown.

But some some RCN missiles were on track, serious threats even to a battleship. Jolts of plasma turned a missile's own mass into vapor which streamed away at high velocity and thrust the remainder of the projectile into a vector which would miss the intended target. None of Foxhunt's missiles would touch the *Pleasaunce*.

And as Borries had said, by braking hard the *Direktor Heinrich* ensured that the *Sissie*'s two rounds would miss ahead of her. Both 15-cm turrets in the cruiser's bow were blasting great balls of gas from the projectiles, but that was in what a layman would've called an excess of caution. Spacers didn't believe you could be too cautious, though they'd admit that often enough you couldn't be cautious at all.

The outer hull of the *Princess Cecile* shivered into balance. The *Formentera* continued to pound the *Alcubiere*, and the Alliance light cruisers were working over the five destroyers which'd extracted late. Nobody seemed concerned about the *Antigone*, a drifting hulk, nor the corvette draped in the pitiable remains of her rig.

We're going to get out of this after all!

"Ship, we're inserting!" Daniel said as reality flickered.

As the PPI faded to lustrous emptiness, Daniel saw the two things he'd been hoping for. First, the *Zeno* and *Lao-tze* had extracted simultaneously, three light-seconds out-system of the *Pleasaunce*—which was driving directly toward them at one and a half gravities' acceleration.

And second, the *Direktor Heinrich* was rupturing like a melon hit by a heavy bullet. In dodging the

Sissie's pair of missiles, her captain had braked her into the path of the *Rip Waechter's* initial salvo. Over a tonne of steel had just struck the heavy cruiser amidships, exiting in a fireball of the hull's contents; including her crew.

Adele kept a miniature of Daniel's face at the top of her screen. As a result of the first walloping discharge, it began propagating through her display's holographic volume, displacing—she hoped it wasn't corrupting—the data that was supposed to be there.

She wasn't sure if she was dizzy because of the ion-spawned surge that'd overloaded the lighting circuits or if the thought of her equipment being destroyed was making her sick. Grimacing, she shut off the console, then brought it up again with five quick strokes of her wands.

She'd hope for the best. If the unit was hopelessly compromised, she'd—well, she'd make do. Adele Mundy had experience in making do following a disaster.

"Riggers to the hull!" Daniel ordered. *"We'll be extracting again as soon as we can, people. This insertion's just to get us out of the immediate killing zone, though it may not be as quick as I'd like because of the state of the rig. Woetjans, don't hesitate to dump anything if that'll save time. Time's more important than spars that might be repairable. Six out."*

Adele's display glowed like an oyster shell gaping in the sunlight; then all the directories she'd had open shimmered into place. Even the image of Daniel's face, now frowning with concentration, was in its accustomed location until she closed it with an angry twist of her wands.

"*Signals, this is Cory,*" the midshipman called from the BDC. "*Mistress, me and Blantyre are going out with the riggers. Is that all right, over?*"

Adele frowned. Was she to take the call as a statement of fact or a request for permission? And anyway, who was she to give permission?

"Yes, of course, Cory," she said. "But why, if you please?"

"*Mistress, we've got suits and we're trained as riggers,*" Cory said. "*We figure we'll do more good cutting loose rigging than we could to back up you and Six, over.*"

"Go, then!" Adele said and resumed her inspection of her console.

Borries was planning missile attacks. Sun was making keystrokes on his console with increasing violence, but the display wasn't changing; he'd begun to shout curses at it. If the gunnery station had been damaged seriously, what of hers adjacent to it?

She wondered if she'd lost data. The equipment was designed to oscillate storage between two separate backup units. That way if the main unit failed, the storage cell which'd been off-line at the moment of disaster should be complete up to that last split second.

The problem this time was that there'd been several separate jolts. Only the first had done obvious damage, but Adele was well aware that electronic data could've been affected by something she hadn't noticed. She set the unit to self-test, knowing that it would be an indefinite time before it completed the task; knowing also that until it completed the task, she couldn't trust any operation the console conducted.

A sequence of clangs echoed through the ship. The sound wasn't quite regular enough to be mechanical.

Adele looked around in frowning puzzlement. Sun slammed the heel of his land against his console and shouted, "Bloody *fucking* hell, it's welded and there's not a *bloody* thing I can do about it from in here!"

"What's the matter, Sun?" Adele said. Normally she'd have needed the intercom. With the *Princess Cecile* drifting in the Matrix and only a faint humming from her console, ordinary speech was enough. "And what's the ringing sound, if you know?"

"Ma'am, that's Woetjans cracking the weld holding her hatch shut," said Sun. "Anyway, trying to crack it. From the plasma, you see, same as froze my dorsal turret."

"Oh," said Adele. The explanation was simple and obvious—once she'd been told. So many things were like that—once you've been told.

"If Woetjans can't open it from inside, the crew coming out through the aft ventral hatch'll clear it for them," the gunner continued. He gestured toward his console. "And they'll have to break loose my turret, too; it won't budge whatever I do with the controls."

He grimaced. "I could go out myself once they get the hatch open," he said, "but—well, you know, as soon as we extract there's a chance we'll need the guns; and the ventral turret's fine, no problems."

"I see," said Adele. The crew of the *Princess Cecile* was largely composed of people who liked doing their jobs. Neither Sun nor Borries thought of themselves as bringing death and destruction to other human beings—they were just proud of their skill with guns and missiles respectively.

Adele's smile was cold. Sun and Borries were luckier than she was: their targets were beads on a holographic screen. That made it possible for them to divorce themselves from the reality she woke to so often.

She heard the outer hatch cycle open. Reminded by the sound, she rotated out the communications heads she'd locked into their landing position. The aft unit opened normally but the head amidships didn't budge.

That didn't mean it'd been destroyed, of course; Adele had been out on warships after a battle and knew that plasma or vaporized metal could paste a tangle of rigging to the hulls. The midships head might be perfectly all right once the swath of sailcloth had been removed from it.

The bow head, the one she'd left up, had vanished. The readout on her display indicated a gap in the circuit feeding the unit.

"I bet I could shoot 'em free," Sun said. "Just one round, not even both tubes, and the recoil'd crack the weld."

He looked over hopefully to see if Adele was agreeing with him. She gave him a stony glare.

"Right," he muttered. "I dunno what's in front of the guns now, and anyhow the riggers're on the hull. Well, they'll clear me, they know how bad we need the guns."

"*Ship*," announced Daniel, "*we'll be extracting in sixty, that's six-zero, seconds, out.*"

Adele looked at her console. Everything was reading normally. She'd been lucky; which made her think—

"Sun," she said, "what happened to Vesey? If she was outside when we were hit?"

"Well, it could be she's fine," Sun said, but he twisted his head away and spoke so softly that Adele could barely make out the words. "Why she's out there to begin with, though, it's not my place to say."

"What!" snapped Mundy of Chatsworth, straightening at her console. *Does this little oik think he can conceal information from* me?

"What he means, ma'am," said Hogg unexpectedly from the back of the command console, "is that the Cazelet boy's too busy mooning after you to give Vesey so much as a look. She hasn't been too tightly wrapped ever since Dorst bought it, so maybe she just decided not to come in."

Adele stared at him. Hogg looked back; not challenging her, just a dumpy countryman the wrong side of fifty perched like a sack of potatoes on a jumpseat. But not afraid, either; or anyway, not about to shirk his duty to the Leary family because a member of it might shoot him for answering the question she'd asked.

For in Hogg's mind, Adele was a member of the Leary family. In Daniel's mind, and in her own too, she supposed.

Adele collapsed her display. "Tovera," she said, "is this true?"

"Yes, mistress," Tovera said. "I think Blantyre tried to talk to Vesey, but it didn't go well."

"And I had a chat with the kid while we were on Pelosi," Hogg said evenly. He crossed his hands over his paunch, but he was as tense as Adele'd ever seen him. "It seemed to me that being a gentleman didn't mean looking right through a nice girl like she was a piece of glass, you know? I think he'd've taken a swing at me if he hadn't decided it was beneath him."

Tovera giggled. Hogg looked at her and said, "Say, it wouldn't be the first time I've give a young gentleman a spanking when he acted up. I haven't forgot how t' do it."

"Thank you, Tovera," Adele said. Her lips were dry. She brought up her display. It appeared to be operating normally, though she wouldn't know for certain until they returned to sidereal space and received sensor inputs. "And thank you, Hogg."

I should stick to machines, she thought. *But even when I do, I create disasters. I don't belong in a world of human beings!*

"*Extracting!*" Daniel announced.

The shiver of universes forming within one another was a relief from the leaden misery in Adele's heart.

Daniel stabbed the EXECUTE button and shivered at the start of the process of extraction. He felt as though he'd swallowed a tortoise whole and was now trying to vomit it out with its shell carving away whatever remained of his esophagus.

It'd taken two minutes in the Matrix instead of the one Daniel'd expected before the *Princess Cecile* was far enough from the kill zone for him to extract into normal space again. The corvette was small and flimsy; worse, more than half her personnel were on the hull with no protection. The fireball from a single plasma bolt would cook them all.

Pushing the button wasn't usually Daniel's job anymore. It was the sort of mechanical ash and trash duty which he left to whoever was senior in the BDC while he focused on the course or the attack or the latest tidbit which Adele'd dredged up from the Gods knew where.

If Vesey'd been aboard, he'd have handed the command over to her and gone out to help Woetjans. The bosun had an eye for how to proceed on what looked to most people—certainly looked to Captain Leary—like an impossible tangle. Woetjans would be sorting the debris like a professional gambler shuffling with never a miscue.

Daniel would only've been muscle under Woetjans' direction, but despite spending too bloody much time on his butt he still had a good set of muscles. It'd be nice to walk through the woods of Bantry again with Hogg, carrying shotguns but mostly just reconnecting with the living creatures of his childhood.

A lot of people had died today. He was sorry for every one of them and especially sorry about Vesey; but he was RCN and the battle wasn't over yet.

The corvette's return to sidereal space was as shockingly sudden as being dropped in ice water. The PPI came live. The *Sissie*'d crawled to get here, but she'd extracted where he'd wanted her: thirty light-seconds from the kill zone between the Alliance wings. They were well above the plane of the Jewel System's ecliptic.

Images of the corvette's outer hull formed a montage on the bottom half of the command display. They showed sixteen angles at a time, shifting as different shutters opened. Daniel ignored that for the moment while he checked how the battle'd developed while he was directing the *Princess Cecile* to safety.

The battle had developed very well—for Cinnabar.

Both RCN battleships had launched a maximum-effort salvo at the *Pleasaunce*. That meant forty-seven missiles from the *Zeno*, a very good percentage of the forty-eight tubes she mounted, and a perfect thirty-six missiles from the *Lao-tze*.

A battleship's hull torqued more than that of a corvette. Stresses concentrated at weak points on the exterior, frequently jamming shutters or even crumpling a missile tube within the fabric of the hull. For an old ship like the *Lao-tze* to manage a full launch implied both remarkable preparation and luck.

The paired salvos were overwhelming. The *Pleasaunce* was at zero deflection to the oncoming missiles, so she hadn't a prayer of maneuvering out of the swept zone. Because her hull was skewed to her line of travel, she was able to swing eight 20-cm turrets onto defense. Half a dozen projectiles showed on the PPI as expanding balls of gas, but not even a battleship could fend off an attack of that magnitude.

A missile struck portside on the *Pleasaunce*'s axis, just behind the bridge. Because of the quartering angle it traveled through much of the hull before exiting to starboard as a fireball a hundred feet forward of the stern. That by itself turned the battleship to blazing junk, but three more projectiles hit the wreck within a matter of seconds.

One of the missiles had been vaporized without being nudged from its programmed course. As a final insult, it swept as a cloud of glowing steel into the remains of the stricken dreadnought which was by now a larger cloud. Daniel expanded the scene momentarily; it looked like an astronomical image of galaxies colliding.

Daniel wiped the display again, his lips pursing on the sour image. *May their souls find peace.* He didn't in the least regret the destruction of one of the Alliance's newest and most powerful battleships, but he'd have preferred it to happen when the ship was in harbor with only an anchor watch aboard.

Mind, if he'd been captain of the *Zeno*, he'd have felt a thrill when he pushed EXECUTE; there was no way he'd have left that duty for his Missile Officer. This was a war, and the best way to end it quickly was to drive the Alliance Fleet from the cosmos. Destroying a planetary-class battleship was a good start, and forcing a heavy cruiser into similar ruin was a *bloody* nice piece of work for a corvette!

The Barnyard element was launching a second salvo, but for now Daniel gave his attention to the *Princess Cecile*'s damage. There should've been sixteen images at a time cycling on his display, but at the moment seven were either black, indicating the lenses were covered, or iridescent because there was no signal to feed them. One of the black squares suddenly cleared as a pair of riggers lifted a ten-foot length of spar and the blobs of sail melted to it. They shoved the tangle out into space.

The *Princess Cecile* was Kostroman-built. She'd been a reasonably well-found vessel when Lieutenant Leary captured her, but when the prize money started flowing in he'd brought her equipment up to RCN standard.

Among other things, he'd replaced the original hull cameras with triple units so that he could twice rotate new lenses into place in event of damage to the one which'd been in use. He did that now to those connected to pearly images, though one of the four simply went black when the head was replaced.

The Navy Board expected its warships to be damaged in service. Not all of them were, but no ship under Daniel Leary's command had been that sort of exception.

That was certainly the case with the *Sissie* on her present deployment. The injury to the rigging was much worse than Daniel had expected: he'd known the three 15-cm bolts from cruisers had stripped all but the A-ring antenna from the port side, but some of the yards had become secondary projectiles. Because of the angle they'd sheared four ventral antennas off just above the mainsail yards.

No wonder the *Sissie*'d handled like a pig in the Matrix! They could jury-rig her using spars, but Daniel'd have to pick his courses very carefully if he were going to bring her home before they all had long white beards. That was all right if they were going home, but heaven help them if the corvette had to go into action again without a lengthy spell in a shipyard first.

They'd be short of sail fabric as well as replacement spars. Well, perhaps the magazines in Port Delacroix could help—though the *Princess Cecile* was scarcely the only member of the Diamondia Squadron needing repair.

If necessary, Admiral James could commandeer the rigging from the freighters in the Outer Harbor and pay the owners in treasury warrants. The civilians wouldn't be happy about it, but spacers who'd just saved them from the Alliance wouldn't be in a mood to listen to moaning. Certainly Daniel wouldn't.

The images flipped one after the other like tumbling dominoes as the pickups rotated around the four angles each covered. Another wall of debris lifted and sailed off in its own separate orbit. Past the legs of the spacers who'd thrown the tangle—the team was Blantyre and Cory, each with a short come-along—Daniel saw the port outrigger. A plasma bolt had seared away the end, including one of the High Drive motors.

Are the remaining internal partitions tight? We'd better learn before we make a water landing.

There must be fifty people out on the hull. Both rigging watches were there as a matter of course, but in addition to the midshipmen every Power Room tech with a hard suit was helping to cut away the wreckage. The *Sissie*'d escaped without hull damage, but every spacer knew that a dreadnought battle was no place for a corvette which had to move at a waddle.

Though—when Daniel glanced again at the PPI, it seemed to him that the battle was over. The cruiser *Vineta* was maneuvering to pick up survivors of the *Pleasaunce*. There wouldn't be many even if the crew'd donned suits before the action, but perhaps a hundred of the thousand or more might survive if they could be gathered aboard another ship while their air supply lasted.

The Alliance left wing, the *Formentera* with the light cruisers *Durston* and *Waechter*, were headed toward open space, shaking out their rigs in preparation for inserting into the Matrix. They didn't launch missiles because the remains of the right wing screened the RCN battleships.

It crossed Daniel's mind that the *Formentera* and her escorts might reappear and turn the battle around by attacking from an unsuspected angle . . . but that was how *he* thought. It was unlikely that an Alliance captain who'd just watched his sister ship being blown to vapor along with the admiral commanding would be planning attacks on an enemy of twice his force.

The *Zeno* and *Lao-tze* had launched a second

salvo, this time targeting the heavy cruisers *Hertha* and *Viceroy Adelbert*. Daniel was relieved to see that the older battleship got off only twenty-nine missiles this time. He had as high an opinion of the RCN's professionalism as any man alive, but if the *Lao-tze's* launch had been perfect again, he'd have to believe that Captain Stickel was in league with the Devil.

The two cruisers were accelerating in their original directions of travel. Because both had been going away from the Barnyard element—they'd come out of the Matrix on reciprocal courses to that of the flagship—they'd be able to reinsert before the missiles reached them.

The *Vineta* was preparing to insert also. Her captain's instinct to help a fallen comrade had put the expanding cloud of the *Pleasaunce* between her and the RCN battleships, so the incoming salvos weren't directed at her. A heavy cruiser shouldn't have been worrying about rescue in the middle of a battle, but in this case mistaken compassion had saved the lives of her whole crew.

The *Zeno* began firing the cannon in her four forward turrets at the *Hertha* and *Viceroy Adelbert*. The surviving Alliance vessels hadn't launched missiles before turning to flight, so the battleship's weapons weren't needed for self-defense.

The distance was too great for bolts to do damage, but they'd make it difficult for the cruisers to insert. Even if the targets were outside the core of the flux, the sprays of ions unbalanced the ships' surface charge. The *Lao-tze* added her gunfire to the *Zeno's*, either responding to command or simply picking up on her consort's good idea.

The destroyers which'd been picketing Diamondia chose this moment to extract. Presumably they'd intended to join the left wing, but in the event only the *T72* was where it should have been. The *T65* appeared closer to the *Alcubiere* than to the position of the left wing before the Alliance vessels began running.

Daniel thought the *Alcubiere* was derelict. To his amazement and delight, she slammed a pair of 6-inch plasma bolts into the *T65*'s belly, blasting both out-riggers and the High Drive motors. The destroyer immediately began blatting her surrender on the 20-meter and microwave bands. Her fellow slipped into the Matrix with the remainder of the left wing and the *Vineta*.

The *Hertha* and *Viceroy Adelbert* disintegrated under more hits than Daniel could count even when he slowed down the action. It was like watching ships of sand when the tide swept in.

Daniel took a deep breath and let it out. He felt his muscles begin to relax for the first time since Admiral James had transmitted course data to the Foxhunt element.

"Ship," he said, though more than half the crew was on the hull at the moment where they couldn't hear him. "This is Six. Well done, fellow Sissies. Bloody well done! Six out."

On the hull montage, Daniel saw two riggers twist a length of spar out of the sail it was holding stretched against the hull. To his surprise they dropped the tubing to the side instead of cutting it free and launching it into space.

The imaging head rotated to a different lens; Daniel

switched it back manually to watch the riggers kneel. When they rose, they were lifting a figure in a hard suit. The silver-painted right arm meant it was Vesey. They started for the forward airlock, one of them gesturing in sign language to alert their watch commander.

Daniel licked his dry lips and brought up a navigation display. Shortly he'd plot a course to the wreck of the *Direktor Heinrich*. The *Princess Cecile* sailed like a barge just now, but it wasn't far to go. They'd save who they could from the crew of the cruiser they'd destroyed.

First, though, they'd pick up Matthews and Cazelet. That pair had gone a long way toward winning the battle. . . .

EPILOGUE

A cross made from two huge stones topped the crag on which Adele stood with Lieutenant Vesey; each slab must weigh more than twenty tons. The structure was artificial, but it surely predated the human colonization two hundred years earlier. Scaly vegetation grew like orange-brown-cream paint on its south face.

Adele reached for her personal data unit but then quickly snatched her hand away. The megaliths of Diamondia weren't the reason she'd had Tovera set her and Vesey down here. The aircar waited for them on a plateau half a mile away—in sight, but well out of hearing.

Vesey hadn't spoken during the flight from the emergency hospital, a high school into which Medicomps and trained personnel from the larger warships had been moved. She remained silent as she looked down on Port Delacroix and beyond. The water in the Inner Harbor was pale green. In the Outer Harbor it was dark blue, and the open sea was sullen gray.

Adele followed the lieutenant's eyes, then frowned. Rather—again—than taking out her data unit, she seated herself on a slab of basalt and said, "Where are the *Alcubiere* and *Antigone*? I didn't think they'd been destroyed in the fighting."

Vesey glanced at her and managed a faint smile. Before answering, she sat a little more than arm's length away. Though she moved very carefully, the burns to her right arm and the bone bruises to both femurs were healing. Adele'd checked Vesey's medical records—of course—but she knew from personal experience that someone who a computer said was completely recovered might feel pain stab where the bullet'd struck six months previously.

"The *Antigone* may well be a constructive loss like the *Express*," Vesey said. "She's in orbit now, but it may make better economic sense to salvage her fittings and scrap her here on Diamondia."

Her voice was soft but without any music. Like Vesey's hair and her figure, it was plain. She had a fine mind, though, a mind that both Adele and Daniel could respect.

"The *Alcubiere*'s going to be repaired," Vesey continued. "On Cinnabar, of course. But she's lost half her plasma thrusters so it'd have been too dangerous to land her now. She's being jury-rigged in orbit, and Admiral James sent up thrusters for the crew to install during the voyage home."

A plasma bolt had blown a starboard topsail yard across the back of the *Princess Cecile*, trailing a shroud which'd struck Vesey at mid-thigh and slammed her to the hull. That'd saved her life, because except for her right arm she'd been under the topsail when the next three bolts hit.

Adele thought of returning to Cinnabar a year

before in the captured *Scheer*, renamed the *Milton*.
Very deliberately she said, "I don't suppose Captain
Bussom would appreciate Daniel giving him pointers
in how to sail long distances in a jury-rigged heavy
cruiser, would he?"

Vesey stared at her wide-eyed, then realized Adele
was making a joke. She snorted a tiny laugh, probably
as much at Adele's perfect deadpan as from thinking
about Captain Bussom's reaction to getting shiphandling
advice from a junior commander.

"No, mistress," she said. "I don't think I'd recommend that Six do that."

They both looked down at Port Delacroix for a
moment. The buildings were largely built from blocks
of porous volcanic tuff. The gray stone had been
whitewashed. It'd be dazzling later in the day, but
now in the early morning the half-bowl of hills into
which the town and harbors nestled blocked the direct
sun. The roofs were brown tile, golden when lighted
but at present drab.

Besides the losses and the missing cruisers, two
destroyers were in orbit on picket duty. Even so the
Inner Harbor was full of ships, prizes which'd surrendered rather than be destroyed along with the base
on Z3 after the battle. Only one of the seventeen was
of any size, a 3,000-tonne freighter which'd arrived
the day before with resupply. The rest were light
craft which'd been sent to the Jewel System to grind
through the planetary defense array.

None of the vessels was of remarkable value by
itself, but altogether they'd eventually constitute a
pretty trissie in prize money. The amount would
be divided among the crews of two battleships and

assorted lesser craft, with the Admiral Commanding getting an eighth; nonetheless it'd take even common spacers several days to drink up their portions.

"I don't think anyone objects to Admiral James' share," Adele said, voicing her thoughts. "His plan was very effective, though it was hard on Foxhunt."

"That's how it worked out this time," Vesey agreed. She didn't turn to face Adele. "But somebody had to hold the Alliance's attention while the admiral got his battleships into position."

She shook her head very slightly. "We're RCN, after all. We all understood that when we took the oath."

"Yes," said Adele. Using the same precision as she'd employ when aligning her sights, she said, "And do you also understand that Daniel needs you, Lieutenant?"

Vesey'd been leaning forward slightly. She jerked upright and almost slid off the slab of rock. It sloped enough that the seat of her utilities didn't grip well enough to withstand violent motion. She looked at Adele with a mixture of anger and hurt, but she didn't reply.

"Well, *do* you understand?" Adele said.

"Nobody needs me!" Vesey said. "Do you think that isn't obvious? I didn't expect you to bring me up here to lie to me, mistress!"

Adele nodded, pleased to have gotten a reaction. What she'd been really afraid of was that Vesey had shut down completely, because then there wouldn't have been any hope.

"You're right," she said calmly, "I misstated the matter. What I should have said was that Daniel needs *someone* whom he can trust for astrogation and shiphandling. He doesn't need someone to fight the ship, of course; he'll do that himself until the day he dies, and I shouldn't wonder if he managed to stay alive regardless till he's seen off whatever enemy he's facing. Can you agree with that statement of facts, Lieutenant?"

Vesey licked her lips. She sat on the rock again, bracing herself with her hands, to give herself time to frame a response. "Yes, mistress," she said warily.

"He says you're the best astrogator he knows besides himself," Adele continued. "Further, that your shiphandling's good and getting better. Again, do you accept that I'm telling the truth? About Daniel's opinion, that is; you don't have to accept that as correct."

Vesey nodded but lowered her eyes. "I'm honored by Mister Leary's good opinion," she said. "I . . . my shiphandling needs a great deal of work."

"Perhaps," said Adele with a dismissive sniff. "Regardless, it's clear to me that Daniel considers you the ideal First Lieutenant for him. I grant that you might not be as well suited to a captain who'd find your skill intimidating."

"*Me* intimidating?" Vesey murmured, but her smile was an honest one. It faded and she said in the direction of the port, "Mistress Mundy, I really appreciate what you're doing, but it seems so *pointless*."

"Unlike Daniel, I don't need anyone at all," Adele said as though she were ignoring the comment. "Not Daniel, not Tovera."

She turned a hard smile toward Vesey. The lieutenant watched her sidelong.

"I certainly don't need you, Vesey," Adele said. "If all the people I've ever met suddenly vanished, I could go back to the Library of Celsus and spend the rest of my life doing research. I could make myself a little nest there, like a rat in the insulation between the hulls. The only catch is—"

She smiled again. She knew from having seen herself in mirrored surfaces in the past that you could sharpen a knife on her expression.

"—that'd I'd be dead. Dead as a human being, that is. And having spent much of my life dead in just that fashion—"

She paused, furrowing her brow with a real question. "In fact," she said, "I think that I was dead for all my life until I met Lieutenant Leary on Kostroma. Having done that, as I say, I've decided that it's better to be alive until it's time to be buried."

Vesey started to smile. Her expression hardened and she turned her head toward Adele again. "Mistress," she said harshly. "You don't care at all about Rene, do you? Master Cazelet, if you prefer."

"I most certainly *do* care for Rene," Adele said. "I'm responsible for him to Mistress Boileau, to whom I owe—"

She shrugged. "Whatever you please. My life, which doesn't matter. My education, my honor, my self-respect—everything that's important to me as a Mundy and a scholar and a human being."

She allowed the humor of the situation to show in her expression. "Now," she said, "if you mean that I don't have the least romantic passion for Rene, of course I don't. I don't have the least romantic passion about *anybody*. In particular—"

Adele stopped. "Look at me, if you please, Lieutenant," she said sharply.

Vesey jerked her head up and reflexively stiffened as though coming to attention. Pain drove out a gasp, quickly silenced. "Mistress," she said obediently.

"In particular," Adele continued as though nothing had happened, "I don't feel any romantic passion for Daniel. But if the word 'love' has any meaning in human affairs, I love him."

"I thought . . ." Vesey said. She turned her head away, clearly unaware of what she was doing. "Rene's smart and *quick*, and he knows so much already. Oh, not astrogation the way I do; but more about life, mistress, more than I ever will. And I thought . . ."

She put her face in her hands. "But I couldn't be you, and no one else matters to Rene!" she said through sudden tears.

Adele wondered if Daniel would've known better what to do. He must've had a great deal of experience with crying women, though Adele suspected he was the sort to bolt for the nearest door.

Whereas the late Timothy Dorst would've put his arms around Vesey and told her he loved her; which he doubtless had in a dim but very manly fashion. Well, that wasn't helpful in the present circumstances either.

Presumably Vesey would regain control of herself. Letting her cry until she did so seemed as good a plan as any. Adele turned her eyes toward the activity in the harbor.

She smiled faintly. The visor of her commo helmet would've allowed her to magnify the scene, but she hadn't considered using it. What she *had* started to do was use her personal data unit to enter the command console of one of the starships below—the *Princess Cecile* was the obvious choice, but she could pick the flagship—and view the harbor through the ship's external optics.

Surface craft shuttled back and forth across the Inner Harbor. One was a repair boat and there were two government barges, but most of them were bumboats which Admiral James had pressed into service to haul spars, sails, thrusters, and High Drive motors from Alliance prizes to RCN vessels which needed repair.

As Adele watched, a quartet of houseboats which usually sold oranges, pork sausage, and sex to spacers on board their ships crawled toward the destroyer *Exmouth*. Barely awash between them was what must've been a main antenna from the captured freighter. The destroyers on picket duty changed every six hours. When they did, the relief vessels lashed stores for the *Alcubiere* to their outriggers.

The *Princess Cecile* was, according to Daniel, ready to lift as soon as Admiral James gave clearance. Under Pasternak's direction the crew'd put a temporary patch of structural plastic on her port outrigger instead replacing the whole unit here on Diamondia. She now wore spars and sails stripped from an Alliance minesweeper and had taken a High Drive motor as well.

Vesey fumbled in her hip pocket for a handkerchief. Sniffles had replaced her sobs.

Adele waited for her to blow her nose; then, still looking down into the harbor, she resumed, "Vesey, I've learned that there's no end of new and different ways for me to fail. I shouldn't wonder if the last thing I do in life is make another mistake. Given the kind of work you and I do—"

She turned to Vesey and smiled as broadly as she ever did. That wasn't, of course, very broadly.

"—it's not unlikely that we'll be dying *because* we made a mistake. Still, we're both very good at our jobs. The RCN will regret losing us."

A bell somewhere in the town began ringing. *Is it religious, or does it have something to do with today's festival?*

Adele had gotten the data unit halfway out of its special thigh pocket this time because she'd been concentrating on this stressful business with Vesey. Sometimes her reflexes got in the way.

Still, she hadn't drawn her pistol.

Adele would much rather have been in a gunfight than holding this conversation, but it was part of the job she did for Daniel and the RCN. Nobody had told her so, but she was Mundy of Chatsworth: nobody needs to tell a Mundy her duty.

"Mistress . . ." Vesey said. She stopped, apparently because she didn't know how to go on. That saved Adele from having to interrupt her.

"Something that the RCN didn't have to teach me, Lieutenant," Adele said, "is that you don't quit. Quitting would dishonor your family. My present family is the *Princess Cecile* and beyond it the RCN. Not long ago I came closer than I care to remember to quitting."

"You, mistress?" Vesey said in amazement. Her back straightened again.

"In a manner of speaking," Adele said with a cold smile. "I made an effort to let the Pellegrinians kill me. Fortunately, they were bad shots and I'm a very good one. I'm glad of that now, because my honor really does matter to me. Odd though that probably sounds from someone who has no faint vestige of a religious impulse or interest in philosophy."

Vesey swallowed. "I don't think it sounds odd, mistress," she said quietly. "Nobody who knows you could doubt that."

"Be that as it may," said Adele with a sniff. "The important fact is that we both have been granted opportunities to recover from our mistakes."

She looked stone-faced at Vesey and went on, "When will you be reporting aboard the *Sissie*? I believe you were discharged from the hospital this morning, were you not?"

Vesey's face scrunched, but she didn't resume crying. She cleared her throat and said, "Mistress, will Captain Leary let me come back?"

"Yes," said Adele. She didn't amplify the statement. She was almost certain that Daniel would be glad to have Vesey return as his First Lieutenant. If necessary, however, she'd ask him to do so as a favor to her.

Adele smiled faintly. Daniel owed her a great deal. Nothing like as much as she owed him, of course, but that was the way friendship worked.

"Mistress," Vesey whispered. "If he'll have me, I'll . . . I *want* to come back. More than anything in life, I want to come back to the *Princess Cecile*."

"Very good," Adele said. She stood and waved to Tovera. Dust immediately puffed from beneath the aircar; a few seconds later the sound of the fans running up reached her ears. "Then let's go to the *Sissie* and get ready for the Governor's reception. I haven't looked at my dress suit since we lifted from Cinnabar."

She added with a dry smile, "I'm going as Lady Mundy, since a junior warrant officer wouldn't be allowed into the Residence."

Vesey felt alone, and because she felt that way she *was* alone. It wasn't true in any objective sense, but people don't live objectively.

Not even Adele Mundy was truly objective, not in the cold dark hours before dawn.

Daniel turned a little more quickly than he should've done and felt a touch of vertigo. "Whoops!" he said, touching the terrace railing with his left hand. "The punch has more of a kick than I'd imagined."

The girls giggled, which is what they'd probably have done if he'd slit his throat here on the terrace in front of them. Suzette was a sultry brunette, Tatiana a blonde as pale as a cirrus cloud, and Kitty paired red hair with green eyes. They were all young, all stunningly beautiful, and all very obviously interested in the dashing Commander Leary.

A year ago Daniel would've said he'd died and gone to heaven, and the fact that the trio's combined IQ appeared to be comparable to that of Miranda Dorst alone should've been the icing on the cake. Well, maybe he hadn't drunk enough after all.

He turned and looked out over the harbor. The raised dorsal antennas of the warships were strung with lanterns of pastel paper which illuminated only themselves. When they trembled in the mild breeze, they seemed to be floating.

To most eyes a mere corvette made a poor show compared with the huge battleships, but the rush of affection Daniel felt when his eyes fell on the *Princess Cecile* staggered him anew. He remembered the first time he'd stood at her masthead and looked up at the blaze of the Matrix. In that instant he'd realized that he was captain of a starship and that the whole cosmos was his. . . .

The *Zeno*'s band was playing a waltz nearby on the upper terrace; they'd trade off with their counterparts from the *Lao-tze* in another hour, so that all the bandsmen had a chance to celebrate too. Given that the *Lao-tze*'s personnel were having their party now, the quality of the music was likely to deteriorate after the handover. The guests generally were lapping down the punch as fast as Daniel was, however, so nobody was likely to complain.

"Oh, Commander," said Suzette, rubbing Daniel's heavily embroidered scarlet sash with her fingertips. "Does this mean something?"

"It does, doesn't it, Danny?" Kitty said, fondling his chest from the other side. Tatiana simply giggled.

An inside-illuminated dragon floated across the harbor. Daniel wasn't sure whether it and the several similar displays—a whale, a swan, and some sort of spiky, rounded creature—were balloons being guided by small boats or if they were made from paper over frames which the boats supported on poles. They were civilian efforts, part of a local tradition.

"This means I'm a Royal Companion of Novy Sverdlovsk, my dear," Daniel said. He held his smile even though the silk and cloth-of-gold lay on top of ranks of additional medals which Suzette's forceful caresses were driving into his chest. He didn't imagine the sensation could be very erotic for her either. "I'm told it gives me the right to drink from the king's own cup at banquets if I'm ever on Novy Sverdlovsk—which heaven forbid."

The girls giggled harmoniously. He wondered if they'd taken a course in Synchronized Laughing.

Admiral James had ordered that his officers attend the Governor's fete wearing full Cinnabar and foreign decorations. In a naval gathering that would be bad taste—particularly for a junior commander—but the intention here was to overawe the civilians. Because much of Daniel's service had been on distant planets with a gaudy sense of showmanship, he made a better display than some of the RCN captains present.

Having said that, Daniel wore the Cinnabar Star at the head of his top row of medals. RCN officers would ignore the Strymonian aigrette and the sash from Novy Sverdlovsk, but they'd respect the Star.

"Commander, come and dance," Suzette wheedled, tugging on the sash as though it were a leash. "Won't you dance with me, pretty please?"

There was dancing on the upper terrace. When Daniel looked up, he saw Adele sweep by in a gigue with Captain Bussom. She was in her occasional disguise as Lady Mundy, wearing a light gray suit slashed with violet. Formal dancing was an aristocratic skill which Evadne Rolfe Mundy had therefore seen to it that her bookish daughter Adele learned.

Pastel lanterns like those on the ships lit the grounds of the Governor's Residence. They cast a comfortable dimness over the faces of people who'd drunk too much tonight or eaten too much over the previous decades.

"My dear—" Daniel began. His tongue stopped and he looked up to the higher terrace again to be sure of what he thought he'd seen in the corner of his eyes.

He really had: Vesey was dancing with Adele's young ward, Rene Cazelet. The boy wore an attentive smile, while Vesey looked flushed. That might simply be strain from dancing despite having been so badly bruised during the battle. Still, she seemed to be having a good time.

"Dancing makes me feel all funny," said Tatiana, stroking Daniel's cheek with her fingertips. "Dreamy, sort of, if you know what I mean, Danny."

She didn't look any more dreamy than a cobra tensing to strike, though Daniel was confident that her intentions weren't in the least hostile. So long as she got her way, at least.

"My dears," Daniel resumed in time to forestall Kitty's no-doubt similar suggestion, "I really don't think I'm in the mood for dancing just now. As a matter of fact, I seem to have finished my punch and—"

He broke off again, gesturing with an index finger to call the girls' attention to the fact they were about to have visitors. A big man in uniform with a tall, slim woman at his side was striding toward them.

"Good evening, Captain Stickel," Daniel said brightly, standing straight instead of letting the stone railing carry some of his weight. Michael Stickel was captain of the *Lao-tze*. Daniel had seen him in passing when the Residence was the Diamondia Squadron Headquarters, but they hadn't met formally.

"I've been looking for you all night, Leary," Stickel said. "I should've guessed you'd be a proper RCN officer and keep close guard on the punch bowl."

From some lips that would've been an insult, but it sounded friendly this time. Daniel said, "May I introduce my charming companions, Captain?"

Bloody hell, he didn't know any of their last names. Nothing unusual in that, of course, but under the circumstances it was going to be awkward. He was pretty sure that one of them was Governor Niven's daughter, but even that wasn't a help: the Governor was as bald as a cue ball.

"No, you bloody may not," Stickel said. "Ollie my dear—" It came out as one word, *olliemadur*. "—why don't you go powder your charming nose."

It wasn't a question the way he said it.

"And take Leary's little friends along with you," he added, "so that he and I can have a man talk, the two of us."

Daniel didn't mind Stickel shooing away the girls, but he wondered whether the senior captain would've been so brusque with Adele. He smiled faintly. Perhaps he would have been—the first time. He wouldn't repeat the insult after he'd met Lady Mundy, however.

"I was just up there talking with Kithran," Stickel said, nodding toward the Residence, beyond the railing of the upper terrace. The windows were brightly lighted, save for those of the ground-floor room which Admiral James had taken for his private office. "He's still working on the bloody report to the Senate which he says—"

Stickel glared at Daniel. His hair was iron gray and cropped short. Between that and his craggy face, he looked more like an aging bruiser than a respected senior captain in the RCN.

"—you're taking to Cinnabar tomorrow morning. It seems to me that it could wait another day or two, given that blockade runners carried the news back before we'd finished putting crews in all the prizes."

"I assure you, Captain," Daniel said calmly, "the decision on timing was His Lordship's alone. This won't be the first time I've felt what a hangover does to the process of inserting into the Matrix, but it isn't an experiment I wanted to repeat."

Stickel roared with laughter. "Well," he said, "Kithran was a pigheaded bastard when we were at day school together, so I didn't imagine a corvette commander had started leading him around by the nose. Still, I think even an admiral can take a night off for a party, don't you, Leary?"

"Yes sir, I certainly do," Daniel said. He grinned broadly. "But I didn't think it was the place of a corvette commander to tell His Lordship that."

Stickel laughed again. "Well, I *did* tell him," he said, "and it made bugger-all difference. There was nothing for it but that he should hash over my report again before he does his own final. You gave him your report too, eh, Leary?"

"Yes sir," Daniel said. "I believe His Lordship compiled the reports of all captains in the squadron. Or senior surviving officers in the case of the *Express* and *Escapade*, I suppose."

Fireworks streamed skyward from both sides of the narrow passage through the mole separating the Inner and Outer Harbors. The *boomp!* of mortars reached the terraces only seconds before the shells burst into stars. Those in turn burst into lesser stars, rattling like the wind through bamboo blinds.

Stickel watched for a moment. "Pretty toys for children," he said with a harshness Daniel hadn't expected. "Children and civilians. We could tell them about real fireworks, couldn't we, Leary?"

"Yes sir," Daniel said. He thought about the *Sissie*'s bridge going dark except for the yellow-green deathlight which sizzled from all metal surfaces. He licked his lips and wished he hadn't finished his drink.

"But they wouldn't understand," he said. He seemed to be hoarse. "And sir? You and I are out there so that they don't have to learn, aren't we? So that the civilians here and the ones back on Cinnabar never learn."

"Well said, boy!" Stickel said. "Bloody well said."

His voice got rougher and he said, "Your father's Speaker Leary, I hear?"

"Yes sir," said Daniel. He was asked the question frequently. There was nothing to do but return a flat answer and hope that was an end to it. "We're not close."

"Bloody dangerous man to be close to," Stickel said. "But nobody ever said he was stupid, and I see his son isn't either."

More fireworks thumped, popped, and rattled. Blue and golden streamers trailed down toward the water. Daniel would very much have liked another mug of punch. Or a mug of raw alcohol from the Power Room with just enough water to keep it from lethally drying his mouth and throat.

"Well, that's neither here nor there," Stickel said. "We're not politicians."

His face hardened and he said, "You're *not* a politician, are you, Leary?"

"No sir," Daniel said, "I most certainly am not. Sir!"

He was reacting like a cadet at the Academy being grilled by a member of the cadre. He hadn't expected this tonight, though Stickel didn't seem hostile—only forceful. *Very* forceful.

"Kithran tells me that you launched your missiles to nudge the *Direktor Heinrich* into one of their own that they wouldn't notice because they were concentrating on you," Stickel said. "Is that true, Leary? That you planned it that way?"

"Captain," said Daniel, feeling an icy mixture of anger and fear, "I didn't put anything of the sort in my report."

"I know what you put in your report, boy!" Stickel said. "I've read the bloody thing, haven't I? I'm asking you if that's what you *did*, because Kithran says it is."

Daniel licked his lips again. "What His Lordship says is correct," he said, "but I did not say that to His Lordship or to anyone else. Until just now, sir."

Stickel laughed explosively again. "Well, I owe Kithran a case of brandy, then," he said. "I swore nobody was that good. I thought you'd gotten lucky—or anyway, *we'd* gotten lucky, since you weren't claiming the hit yourself."

"Well sir . . ." Daniel said, feeling himself relax. He'd thought he was being accused of lying or—possibly worse—bragging. "I must say that *I* didn't believe the *Lao-tze* launched thirty-six missiles in her initial salvo. I'd have bet much more than a case of brandy against that happening. I'm *very* glad that I'd have been wrong."

Captain Stickel beamed. "You noticed that, did you?" he said. "That was nice work, but I can't take much credit for it. I will say that my *Lao-tze*'s got the best bloody crew in the RCN, bar none!"

"I won't argue with an officer of your rank and merit, Captain," Daniel said, hoping his smile was broad enough to blunt the very real edge to his words, "but if we were civilians I'd ask you aboard the *Sissie* and we'd see what we saw."

"By the *Gods*, Leary," Stickel said, but he was laughing again. "I heard you have ginger! I guess otherwise you wouldn't have the record you do. Say—when we're both back in Xenos, which I hope won't be any longer than it has to be, you look me up. We'll have dinner at my club and we'll talk, you and me."

"Thank you, sir," Daniel said. Bloody hell, this could've gone *badly* wrong; but it hadn't. "I'll be honored to accept your invitation."

"Excuse me, Captain?" said a cool, perfectly modulated voice.

Daniel looked up. Cassandra McDonough, Admiral James' flag lieutenant, looked expectantly over the railing of the upper terrace. She looked very good in Dress Whites, but Daniel could as easily imagine making love to a porcelain figurine.

"His Lordship would appreciate a few words with Commander Leary," McDonough said when she had their attention, "before he seals the courier pouch."

Stickel snorted. "What did I tell you, Leary?" he said. "The man *will* have everything just so before it goes off to Navy House. Go cross his tees for him, boy—but remember what I said about dinner."

"Yes sir!" said Daniel as he strode for the steps to the upper terrace. "I most certainly will."

McDonough waited for Daniel to get up the flight of broad stone stairs before turning to precede him around the fringes of the dancing. The band had resumed with a hornpipe which bounced over the happy murmur of voices. Couples swung into the quick rhythm or drifted off the chalk-bounded dance floor to wait for a less strenuous measure.

Daniel and his guide entered through a lounge with

a coffered ceiling. Its cells were skylights; another volley of fireworks trailed sparkles in the sky above them. Half a dozen members of the Governor's staff sat smoking on the black leather chairs; a servant with a tray of drinks bent to serve them.

The civilians followed the two officers with their eyes. Daniel nodded pleasantly in acknowledgment, but Lieutenant McDonough paid them no more heed than she would've done for balls of mud on the area rugs.

There usually wasn't any love lost between the civil and military staffs of a protectorate. Here on Diamondia the naval personnel treated the civilians as cowards who'd fled rather than take the risk that an Alliance raider would sneak through the minefield and target the Residence; the civilians had considered RCN officers pushy from the moment they arrived and had found them next to unbearable since their victory. Daniel supposed both sides had the right of it.

McDonough tapped on the elegantly carved north door. "Your Lordship, Commander Leary is here," she said in a quiet, penetrating voice.

"Enter!" said James. McDonough opened the door, nodded Daniel through, and closed it firmly behind him.

The office had started out as a sitting room, but James had installed a standard RCN console in place of what'd probably been a glass-topped table. The result was serviceable though a little odd; the maroon banquette on which James was sitting in one corner made a particular contrast. Mirrors etched with hunting scenes covered two walls.

The admiral had a courier pouch in his lap. He was in his sleeveless undershirt; the tunic of his Whites, stiff with medals and braid, hung over the back of the console. He gestured Daniel to the other arm of the banquette.

"Sit down, Leary," he said. "I want to talk with you privately before I seal this."

He tapped the pouch and continued, "And I *mean* private. There's no rank in this room until I tell McDonough to open the door again."

James sounded tired, but this time in a good way. The exhaustion he'd displayed when Daniel first met him on the terrace of the Residence had been as much depression as overwork.

Daniel settled onto the maroon leather in a gingerly fashion. He wasn't going to argue with an admiral, but he knew how bloody dangerous these "all pals together" situations were for a junior party who was fool enough to take his senior at his word.

A mirror-backed wall sconce above the banquette lighted Daniel very well. James hadn't seen him in full dress before. He guffawed and said, "Well, you're a sight for sore eyes, aren't you, Leary?"

"Sir, I feel like a clown," Daniel said sincerely. "But you said 'Cinnabar and foreign medals.'"

James chuckled. "So I did, and you're certainly one up on Niven and his pretty boys in their frock coats," he said.

In a slightly softer tone he added, "A bloody impressive clown, Leary. I've read your record. Fruit salad's easier to come by than a record like yours."

Daniel cleared his throat. "Ah, thank you, sir," he muttered.

James tapped the courier pouch. Sealing it would arm a layer of thermite in the lining of the case. Opening the pouch by force would incinerate the contents, along with the person applying the force and probably the room in which it happened.

"I suppose you hope that my report recommends you for promotion because you tricked Guphill into sending away half his squadron," James said bluntly. "Don't you?"

"Sir, I'd never suggest what ought to go into my commanding officer's after-action report," Daniel said. *"Never."*

"I didn't ask what you'd suggest, Commander," the admiral snapped. He'd been under strain for a very long time, and victory brought its own different stresses. "I said that's what you hoped. Isn't it?"

"No sir," said Corder Leary's son, not a politician but a man who knew politics from the inside out. "I very much hope you would *not* put that in your report to Navy House, because it involves matters beyond the remit of the Admiral Commanding the Diamondia Squadron. At the very best, the Navy Board would regard the recommendation as an impertinence and ignore it. More probably, particularly given my history with Admiral Vocaine, the Board would assume I'd somehow nobbled you—"

James snorted.

Daniel flashed him a hard smile. "Yessir," he continued, "but they would. And they'd post me to the job of latrine inspection on West Bumfuck in response."

James chuckled. The sound was rusty as though he hadn't laughed in a while.

"I don't know that it'd be anything quite so dire, Leary," he said, "but it wouldn't have a good result, no. So I haven't done it. I do note that the intelligence of enemy movements which the *Princess Cecile* brought was of inestimable value, and that Captain Leary handled his corvette with the skill and courage to be expected of an RCN officer."

"Thank you, sir," Daniel said. He was just as sincere as he'd been when he said he looked like a clown.

"If you'd managed to get yourself killed the way Powell and Meltzer"—the captains of the *Express* and *Escapade*—"did," James continued, "I'd put you in for a Cinnabar Star. In your case, a wreath to the Star. But you don't get even that."

"That's all right, sir," said Daniel, smiling. "Perhaps I'll have better luck next time, eh?"

James laughed again. "Perhaps you will at that, Leary," he said. "Well, it's happened to plenty of others who swore the oath, hasn't it?"

His right index finger ran along the seam of the courier pouch. "I dare say it'd have happened to most of us in the Diamondia Squadron if we'd had those two battle cruisers to deal with also," he said.

Daniel didn't speak. His eyes were on the painted screen on the wall behind the admiral. It showed a scene on the deserts of Ryndam, a voorloper stalking a casiline bird whose vestigial wings ended in defensive spikes. Did Governor Niven come from Ryndam, or had some interior decorator liked the contrast the screen made with the harbor outside?

An open plastic writing sheet lay on the small table at James' end of the banquette. He picked it up, glanced at it again, and handed it to Daniel.

"I'm sending a personal note to my cousin in the pouch, Leary," James said. "Go on, read it."

Daniel took the document but didn't let his eyes fall onto the writing yet. "Ah, your cousin, sir?" he said.

"What?" said James, a trifle sharply. "Yes, my cousin. You didn't know that Eldridge Vocaine's my wife's aunt's son?"

"Oh," Daniel said. "I didn't know that, sir."

Pursing his lips, he looked down at the letter. The richly grained plastic had a high gloss; he found he had to adjust the angle slightly so that the admiral's firm, black writing wasn't lost in the reflection of the light sconce.

> *The Residence, Diamondia*
> *7 Three 18*
>
> *My dear Bucko—*
>
> *I hope this finds you well. It leaves me a bloody sight better than I expected would be the case a week ago.*
>
> *In my formal report, I recommend a number of my officers for awards and promotion. I'd appreciate it if you'd see all this business through what seems to an outsider like me to be an impenetrable bureaucracy. I'd regret being forced to make a public protest simply because some faceless, bone-idle twit in Navy House was sitting on his hands instead of processing my request.*
>
> *There's a matter which I've not put in my report because it's not my place to do so. You succeeded beyond anyone's dreams with your plan to destabilize the Bagarian Cluster so that the Alliance couldn't reinforce the Jewel System. In fact, you managed to draw off half Admiral Guphill's squadron, enabling me to deal with the remainder in a thorough fashion.*

If (as I expect) I'm asked to address the Senate on my return to Xenos, rest assured that I will give full credit to you, coz, for your plan; and to your agent, Captain—as I expect his rank will be by then—Leary, who so brilliantly executed it.

Hug Maisie for me, and tell Aunt Madge that I'll be bringing her a jar of Ceralian honey on my return.

Yours in haste—
Gams

Daniel handed back the thick sheet. "Thank you, sir," he said very quietly.

James folded the four corners in, then folded both outer quarters of the new rectangle inward. He held his signet to the seam; after thirty seconds, the gold catalyzed the plastic with a hiss, sealing the letter around a stylized K.

The admiral flipped the letter over and on the face wrote *Vocaine, Navy House/Eyes Only*. That done, he added the letter to the pouch, which he sealed. Then he rose from the couch.

"I'll have McDonough bring it to the *Sissie* in the morning, Leary," James said. He walked to the console and began to put his tunic back on. "No sense you having to worry about it tonight. Now, go out and have some fun. You've earned it."

"Thank you, sir!" Daniel said. "I—well, thank you, sir!"

Lieutenant McDonough opened the office door; there must've been a signal Daniel hadn't seen. He floated by her.

I've got to find Adele, he thought.

As Daniel stepped out the door onto the terrace, a volley of fireworks burst over the harbor, red and gold and splendid.

The following is an excerpt from:

IN THE STORMY RED SKY

DAVID DRAKE

Available from Baen Books
May 2009
hardcover

CHAPTER 1

Bergen and Associates Shipyard, near Xenos on Cinnabar

"Heart of Steel are our ships!" played the band on the quay. The Bergen and Associates shipyard was decked with bunting and packed with temporary bleachers for this unique occasion. *"Heart of Steel are our crews!"*

Like Adele Mundy, the twenty-four bandsmen wore the white first-class uniforms of the Republic of Cinnabar Navy. Unlike Adele, they were used to Dress Whites. She almost never wore them.

"We always are ready!" played the band.

Ordinarily Adele had nothing against great public gatherings in which everybody put on their best clothes and stood around wasting time. She simply found an out-of-the-way corner and amused herself by using her personal data unit to hack into whatever nearby database seemed the most interesting.

She couldn't do that here, because the ceremony was in honor of her friend Daniel Leary; soon to be Captain Daniel Leary.

"Steady crew, steady!"

The band had been playing marches for twenty minutes, filling time while frantic officials took care of the final details of the ceremony. Adele didn't pretend to be knowledgeable about music, but she could tell when everybody kept the same time and the notes followed one another in a proper pattern. Both were true here. She frowned, wondering where the musicians came from.

"We'll fight and we'll conquer for we never lose!"

Adele carried her PDU in a thigh pocket which she'd insisted on in complete disregard for the uniform regulations. Her fingers twitched toward it, but she restrained them with conscious effort.

Though Daniel wouldn't mind, others would think that Lady Mundy didn't respect him. She'd rather die than allow that false notion to spread.

"That's the *Lao-tze*'s band, mistress," said Sun, her long-time shipmate and Daniel's as well. He was now a senior warrant officer, gunner of a heavy cruiser, as a reward for his loyal service—and because he'd survived. "They was with us in the Jewel System, you remember."

"Yes, Sun, I do," Adele said dryly. She wondered how the crew of the battleship *Lao-tze* would react to the implication that they had accompanied the corvette *Princess Cecile* during the Battle of the Jewel System.

Though in truth, the *Sissie*—or at least her captain, Daniel Leary—probably did have more to do with that RCN victory than any other ship present.

A private shipyard like Bergen and Associates ordinarily worked on ships of 1500 tons or less. RCS *Milton*, a heavy cruiser of 13,000 tons, filled the pool and dwarfed the yard's equipment. She'd been repaired here not only because of the demands put on RCN facilities by all-out war with the Alliance but also because the 'Associates' in the yard's name was Corder Leary, no longer Speaker but still one of the most powerful members of the Cinnabar Senate.

"*We ne'er see our foes but we wish them to stay,*" boasted the *Lao-tze*'s band musically. "*They never see us but they wish us away!*"

The *Milton* would lift with a crew of nearly five hundred, a hundred short of establishment but remarkably good when the RCN needed crews worse than it did ships. The spacers were here, packed into corners and angles; standing on the gantries and lining the cruiser's extended antennas.

"There's never been anything like this before!" said Woetjans, the *Milton*'s bosun. She was six and a half feet tall and would've been abnormally strong even for a man of her size. Like Sun, she'd risen by following Daniel Leary, but it'd been at Adele's side that she'd taken three slugs through the chest. Woetjans claimed to have made a complete recovery, but her face, always craggy, now was cadaverous. Sometimes a gray flash seemed to cross her eyes.

"*If they run, why we follow them,*" played the band, "*down to their bases.*"

Woetjans was looking at the shipyard offices above the shops. There, sheltered from direct sunlight though the sashes were swung up from the windows, Daniel's elder sister Deirdre sat with four Senators who were allied with her father. "And nobody bloody deserved it like Six does, neither!"

"*For we can't do more if the cowards won't face us!*" played the band, climaxing the stanza with a flourish before swinging into the chorus again.

Adele's lips quirked in a tiny, bitter smile. Perhaps she was only projecting her own heart when she thought she saw bleakness in the bosun's. Adele's ribs occasionally twinged from a wound in the further past, but if physical injuries had been the worst damage she'd taken in RCN service, she'd have slept better.

"I never dreamed of this," said Borries, the Chief Missileer. He was a Pellegrinian by birth, but he'd decided not to return to his home world after he survived a battle which took the life of the eldest son of Pellegrino's dictator. "We're great men because we're with Captain Leary. *Great* men."

"Woetjans and I might disagree with you," Adele said with a straight face. The society of outworlds like Pellegrino was more sexist than the norm of the civilized regions ruled by Cinnabar and the Alliance. "About being men, that is."

"Sorry, ma'am," Borries muttered, flushing. "I didn't mean that, truly."

RCN signals personnel were quite junior. According to the Table of Organization, Adele should have been out on the fringes of the crowd with the common spacers instead of standing beside the dais with the senior warrants.

The crew, however, had insisted she take a higher place than her rank justified. She was Mistress Mundy, Captain Leary's friend and a real lady. Adele knew that it wasn't her title, Mundy of Chatsworth, that impressed the spacers but rather herself—or at any rate, her legend.

To hear the crewmen's stories, Mistress Mundy could learn all a databank's secrets by looking sideways at it and she could shoot her way through a regiment of Alliance soldiers. Those were gross exaggerations—but there was a core of truth to both statements.

The band swung into a cheerful ditty called *The Rocketeers Have Hairy Ears*. Spacers in the *Milton*'s rigging cheered wildly, and both Daniel and Admiral Anston on the low dais grinned.

It struck Adele that Captain Stickel of the *Lao-tze*

had a robust sense of humor. She'd found a number of different versions of the piece involving Engineers, Cannoneers, and Mountaineers. The various lyrics ranged from obscene to absurdly obscene.

Adele looked toward the dignitaries in the office. Daniel's father wasn't present. Corder Leary and his teen-aged son had broken violently on the day Daniel joined the RCN. The elder Leary had made a great number of enemies in a career focused on gaining wealth and power. In particular, he'd crushed the Three Circles Conspiracy in a series of proscriptions that took the lives of many of Cinnabar's political elite, their families, and their associates.

No one—no survivor—was willing to deny that the bloody response to treason had been necessary, but afterward even Corder Leary's closest associates—he had no friends—looked at him askance. He'd had to give up the speakership, though most people still referred to him by the title as a mark of honor and of fear.

Adele had escaped the Proscriptions by the chance of having just left Cinnabar to study in the Academic Collections on Blythe, the intellectual heart of the Alliance of Free Stars. Her parents and ten-year-old sister Agatha had provided three of the heads nailed to Speaker's Rock in the center of Xenos, however.

Adele's left hand twitched. The tunic of RCN Whites didn't have pockets, and she hadn't added a concealed one for the small pistol she normally carried. Senator Mundy had seen to it that his children became dead shots to prevent the sort of challenges which his political radicalism might otherwise have drawn. The ability to shoot accurately with either hand had benefited Adele in the slums she'd frequented when the Mundy fortune was expropriated during the Proscriptions.

Since she'd met Daniel her pistol had helped him, the RCN, and the Republic of Cinnabar. It had kept

Adele alive in difficult circumstances; but when the faces of the dead visited her in the hours before dawn, she wasn't sure that survival had been a benefit.

She wasn't wearing the pistol today; and besides, Corder Leary wasn't present at the ceremony.

She forced herself to relax, smiling faintly. Many people thought that Adele Mundy was emotionless. She worked to conceal her emotions and she certainly didn't let them rule her actions, but they existed. Until she'd met Daniel and become a part of the RCN family, the main emotion she'd felt was red fury. Courtesy alone would've made her conceal that to the degree she could.

Daniel caught Adele's eye and grinned more widely. She thought it was the first time she'd seen him looking comfortable in the closely tailored Dress Whites. Daniel was fit, but he tended to put on a few pounds if he didn't watch himself. The rounds of dinners and parties which Xenos offered to a naval hero on leave would've made temperance difficult for even someone less sociable than the dashing young Commander Leary.

His first-class uniform fit now because Miranda Dorst, standing with her mother in the front of the crowd facing the dais, was an accomplished seamstress among her other talents. Daniel had never lacked for female company, though he'd had high standards: his companions had to be very young, very pretty, and very intellectually challenged. They'd generally lasted a day—more often a night—and Daniel never even pretended he was going to remember their names.

Miranda was young enough. Her brother Timothy had been one of Daniel's midshipmen before his duties put him in the way of a 20-cm plasma bolt from the cruiser *Scheer*, before its capture and commissioning into the RCN. It was now the *Milton*, towering above the ceremony.

Miranda wasn't strikingly attractive, though Adele had noticed that she became oddly beautiful when she was in Daniel's company. It was as if she were a silvered reflector behind Daniel's brilliant flame.

And unlike the bimbos who'd preceded her, Miranda Dorst appeared to be very clever indeed. Her brother had been a fine officer: brave, well-liked, and equipped with an instinct that took him to the throat of an enemy. He'd have risen high in the RCN, had he survived.

Intellectually, though . . . Well, the best that could be said was that Midshipman Dorst studied very hard and that his personality encouraged others to give him all the help they could. It was unscientific, but anyone who'd met both siblings had to wonder if the sister had gotten a double share of intelligence.

Adele let her eyes return to the crowd facing the dais, though her mind was still on her friend Daniel. She was smiling as widely as she ever did. He was a reasonably good-looking fellow of average height. He was young for a full commander, and soon he'd be the youngest captain on the Navy House list. You'd see nothing special in an image of him, not even a three dimensional hologram.

In person, Daniel gave the impression of being twice his real size. His engaging smile lighted a room, and if he'd chosen to make women a business rather than a hobby, he'd have lived very well.

Adele had always been alone before she'd met Daniel Leary. Since then she had gained Daniel as a friend, and through him the companionship of not only the ship's company he commanded but also the whole RCN. She had a *real* family, in a fashion that the politically focused Mundys had never been to a studious girl like Adele.

The *Lao-tze*'s band was trooping off the quay, playing *What Do You Do With a Drunken Spacer*. Replacing them were young men and women, ten of each in parallel files, wearing white shirts and black trousers. They wore shoes as well, but from their awkwardness Adele suspected that for some it was the first time they'd put on any footgear but shapeless farm boots.

It was a cool day, but the newcomers were sweating profusely. Adele smiled in rare sympathy. She'd felt lost and out of place many times in her life, so she could easily identify with these poor folk.

She wasn't lost any more: she was a member of the RCN.

Adele looked up at the yard offices where Corder Leary would have been had he attended the ceremony. If that cold, brutal man hadn't had her parents and sister murdered, Adele Mundy would never have found the RCN and the place in the universe where she fit.

She didn't believe in Gods or fate or even purpose in any real sense. But sometimes it puzzled Adele to see how very unpredictable the consequences of an event could be.

Daniel Leary had spent much of his youth in this shipyard, listening to Stacy Bergen and other old spacers tell stories. Uncle Stacy was a legendary explorer who'd opened more routes through the Matrix than any other officer in the RCN. He'd showed his young nephew how to conn a ship from the masthead, *feeling* a path through the infinite bubble universes instead of simply calculating one. More important, Daniel had learned to love the romance of star travel because Uncle Stacy and his friends did.

Though now Daniel owned Stacy's half of the shipyard, he was still a boy full of wonder and delight every time he walked through its gates. Like the swirling majesty of the Matrix, Bergen and Associates was a magical thing which hinted at infinite secrets.

Daniel instinctively glanced at the sky, though he knew better than most that if there really was a heaven, it wouldn't be found by going upward. "Thank you, Uncle Stacy," he whispered, his lips barely moving. "This wouldn't be happening except for you."

He stood in the middle of the dais. To his right were the *Milton*'s three lieutenants, while to the left stood six retired officers who'd served under Stacy Bergen at some point in their distinguished careers. They were honoring Commander Bergen by attending the promotion of the nephew who'd been like a son to him.

When young Daniel hadn't been spending time in the shipyard, he'd been on the family's Bantry estate learning to hunt, fish, and generally appreciate the natural world. His teacher had been a retainer named Hogg who looked—then as now, standing behind Miranda and her mother—like a simple-minded rustic who'd dressed in a random collection of old clothes.

Hogg was rustic, all right, but a variety of concealed pockets were sewn into his baggy garments. On Bantry the pockets were for poached game; now they hid a variety of weapons, in case somebody on a distant world thought he'd make trouble for the young master. The man who'd regularly snapped the necks of cute furry animals for his dinner had even less compunction about dealing with wogs who got in the way of a Leary.

And though Hogg was likely to be direct, there was nothing simple about his mind. Sharpers who thought they'd clean the rube out in a poker game learned that very quickly.

Mistress Heather Kolb, the wife of Bantry's overseer, marshalled her paired choruses so that they faced the dais rather than the crowd. She'd told Daniel that the estate's youths and maidens—if they *were* maidens, then things had changed since Daniel was a youth at

Bantry—had begged to appear at the young master's promotion ceremony.

Daniel had been disinherited when he broke with his father. He wasn't any kind of master now, but he was still a Leary, and he knew the tenants of Bantry would've been crushed had he snubbed them. He'd granted their wish, but from the terrified faces they raised to him, they'd have been much happier cleaning offal from the estate's fish processing plant.

Admiral Anston, who'd been Chief of the Navy Board until his heart attack, shuffled toward Daniel from the group of retired officers at the end of the dais. Daniel felt a twinge to see with what difficulty the old man moved.

Everyone in the RCN respected Anston, perhaps the finest chief who'd ever blessed the service. Daniel had met him a few times one-on-one. He didn't claim to know the admiral well, but he'd known him well enough to feel personal as well as professional regret at Anston's ill health.

"Any notion of what's holding up the show, Leary?" Anston said. "I told them I didn't want a bloody chair here on the stage, but I'm half regretting that now."

"Sir, I'll get you a chair at once!" said Daniel in horror.

"You bloody won't," said Anston forcefully. "But I'll put a hand on your shoulder if I may. Old shipmates together, you know."

"Sir, I'm honored," Daniel said. He didn't add flourishes to the words; the truth didn't need embellishment.

The older man let himself sag against Daniel's arm; he was light as a bird. Illness had melted away his flesh and turned his ruddy complexion sallow. Daniel thought of repeating his offer of a chair, then swallowed the unintended insult and said, "I believe they're waiting for two more senators to arrive, sir. Ah, I believe this was some of my sister's doing."

Anston laughed with unexpected good humor. "Bloody

politicians, eh, lad?" he said. "But maybe it'll do us some good in the Navy Appropriation. I know the Learys too well to ignore their judgment when it comes to politics."

He coughed. "No offense meant."

"None taken, sir," said Daniel. "But that isn't me, you know."

"Pull the other one, Leary!" Anston said, glaring at Daniel like a sickly hawk. "Yes, you're a fighting spacer, but you're a bloody politician too or you wouldn't be here. And don't you think *I'm* the one to know a man can be both?"

Daniel found himself grinning. "Well," he said. "Thank you, sir."

Mistress Kolb slashed her baton down and up three times with as much determination as if she were beating a rat to death in her pantry. The last stroke was toward the male chorus, which dutifully responded, *"Mighty Cosmos, all enclosing, filled with worlds and peoples bold . . ."*

Anston bent close to Daniel's ear. "Who're the liberty suits on the gantry? They're not your crew, are they?"

"As You wax and wane eternal, one stands out of all You hold—"

"No sir," said Daniel. "They're the shipyard staff. My Uncle Stacy believed in hiring old spacers where he could, saying that they knew their way around a ship better than any landsman and knew the cost of bad workmanship to the folks who'd have to repair it in the Matrix. We've just followed his lead."

"Cinnabar, the crown of all worlds," sang the youths. *"Cinnabar, Your chosen world."*

"And it's not charity!" Daniel said, with perhaps a touch more vehemence than was helpful to being believed. "An experienced spacer is often more use in a shipyard than a landsman who has all his limbs still."

"I never heard complaints about the work we contracted out to the Bergen yard, boy," said Anston softly.

Liberty suits were RCN utilities decorated with embroidered patches and, along the seams, colored ribbons bearing the names of the various ports the spacer had called on. A senior warrant officer like Woetjans went on liberty in gorgeous motley, an object of admiration to all who saw her.

The *Milton's* crew were in duty uniforms for this ceremony, but the yard personnel could wear what they pleased. If that was liberty suits, then they'd earned the right. The peg legs, pinned-up sleeves, and eye patches were proof of that.

And they *were* bloody good workmen!

Mistress Kolb poised her baton. It was a sturdy thing, suitable for battering an opponent into the floor; Daniel wondered fleetingly just how she'd rehearsed her choristers. She cut it down, toward the girls. They caroled, *"Fate, Thou Who worlds rules, never bending . . ."*

Admiral Anston swayed. Daniel put his hand on the older man's waist, taking more of his weight. Anston muttered a curse, but he got his strength back and straightened.

"I never let the bloody politicians stop me before," he said. "That isn't going to change now."

"Fixed Your course, to triumph tending . . ." sang the girls. The brunette on the left end had a remarkable pair of lungs in a remarkable chest; Daniel remembered her elder sister well.

Daniel smiled. He supposed he and Anston looked odd, gripping one another in the middle of a crowd waiting for something to happen, but the two of them were the only folk here who could do as they pleased without people looking askance. Daniel wore only his Cinnabar decorations, not the gaudy trinkets he'd been given by foreign governments. Even so, Anston alone of the officers present had a more impressive chestful of medals.

"*Cinnabar, the crown of all worlds,*" sang the girls. "*Cinnabar, Your chosen world.*"

Anston turned slightly to look at the spacers lining the *Milton*'s hull and yards. "You've got a full crew, or the next thing to it," he said approvingly. "Volunteers, I shouldn't wonder."

The joined choruses were praying that Fate and the Cosmos would continue to bless the youth of Cinnabar with purity and their elders with wisdom and peace. It was all silly if you thought about it. Daniel had been a youth recently and a senator's son all his life; he had no high expectations of purity, of wisdom, or certainly—he was also an RCN officer, after all—of peace.

But the *Festival Hymn* struck him much the way each fresh sight of the Matrix did: it rang a chord echoing deep in his heart. Call it childish superstition or patriotism or just the urgent wonder of the not-yet-known—it was there, and Daniel was glad for its presence.

"Yes sir, volunteers," Daniel said, grinning with rightful pride. Spacers *wanted* to serve with Captain Leary. "The change in regulations permitting spacers to follow the officer of their choice had a good effect on the *Milton*'s recruitment."

Anston shuddered in what after a bad moment Daniel realized was laughter, not a coughing fit. "Vocaine didn't have much choice," Anston said, swallowing the last of a chuckle. "Every successful officer in the RCN was on him to stop locking their crews up between commissions and parceling them out to whichever ship was short; which all ships are, we don't have enough spacers. He may dislike you, Leary, but not even the Chief of the Navy Board can ignore what school chums like James of Kithran are telling him."

"It worked out well for me," Daniel said mildly. He wouldn't brag to Anston, and anyway he didn't have to.

He cleared his throat and added, "I was a little surprised, because, well, we both know that the *Milton*'s an oddball ship. We know it and every spacer on Cinnabar knows it. And I couldn't promise them loot, not on this commission. But they still came in to volunteer."

The male chorus boomed out the names of the many worlds frightened by Cinnabar's armed might. The women answered with a similar catalog of worlds which had embraced Cinnabar's mercy and protection and thus were being guided to peace and prosperity.

Daniel had seen a good deal of how Residents from the central bureaucracy in Xenos governed planets which had fallen under Cinnabar's control; the reality was less idyllic than the *Hymn* would have it. Nonetheless, Cinnabar's rule was greatly preferable to the system of organized rapine by which Guarantor Porra's minions administered members of the Alliance of Free Stars. Politics and life are the art of the possible.

"Oddball?" repeated Anston. "A bloody *stupid* design, I'd call it. Four eight-inch guns instead of eight six-inch on the same hull means you don't have either the coverage or the rate of fire to deal with incoming missiles. Sure, an eight-inch packs a wallop when it hits, but three or four six-inch bolts do more good anywhere but at long range. And you shouldn't be burning out your tubes at long range anyway."

"Yes sir, as far as defensive use goes," said Daniel, being very careful not to let his tongue get away with him. *The* Milton*'s my ship, or next thing to it!* He coughed. "But eight-inch bolts are *very* effective against other ships. As I know well, having been on the receiving end of them."

The admiral laughed again. "Sorry, Leary," he said,

"sorry. I guess you'd make a garbage scow look like a useful warship if you took her up against the Alliance. And we have our share of peacetime designs, too. But as for spacers joining you—"

He glanced up at the cruiser's yards, then met Daniel's eyes again.

"I know you didn't promise them loot, but they're certain that Captain Leary knows what he's doing and knows how to take care of his crews. And besides, boy, they know how lucky you are and probably figure you'll find them loot besides. Which is what I think too, by the Gods!"

"Sir . . ." said Daniel. He paused to organize his thoughts. "Sir, I appreciate your confidence, but we'll be shepherding a senator to the Veil as an ambassador. As I'm sure you know. We won't see action, let alone gather up prizes, if we do our job correctly. Which I certainly intend to do."

There was a bustle beyond the raised windows of the shipyard office. Looking into the shadowed darkness from this low angle, Daniel could only guess that the missing senators might at last have arrived.

The workmen on the gantry had a better view of the interior, however. In the center of the trestle stood the man who'd been Lieutenant Mon when he served under Daniel on the *Princess Cecile*. Mon was a skilled and methodical officer, but a run of bad luck had gained him the reputation of being a jinx. That doomed his chance of success as a ship's captain, whether in the RCN or the merchant service, but he'd proven an ideal manager for Bergen and Associates while Daniel pursued his naval career.

Mon's reserve commission gave him the right to the Dress Whites he wore today, though they bulged at every seam; nobody had let out his set with the skill

Miranda had lavished on Daniel's. He'd chosen to wear his uniform for the same reason his workmen were in liberty suits: this was the RCN's day.

Three serving officers came down the outside stairs from the yard offices. The last was Captain Britten, the head of the RCN's Personnel Bureau; Daniel assumed the male lieutenant commander and the female lieutenant preceding him were aides from the bureau. They made their way toward the dais as briskly as the crowd could part before the aides' crisp orders.

Mon raised his arms and snapped, "Ready!" in a carrying tone. Then he dropped his arms and shouted, "Hurrah for Mister Leary!"

"Hurrah for Mister Leary!" the yard staff bellowed in answer. Obviously they'd rehearsed this.

The cheer silenced the crowd like a trumpet call. For a moment the chorus of girls sang piercingly of fruitful lands and fecund seas; then Mistress Kolb chopped her baton down. The assembled flower of Bantry bowed low to Daniel, their faces flushed and beaming. Turning, they bounded off the quay with a cheerful enthusiasm that made a striking contrast with their stiff, terrified approach.

The delegation from Navy House passed between the two choruses. The lieutenant commander handed a ribbon-tied scroll to Britten; then both aides halted, leaving the captain to take the single step onto the dais alone.

Britten transferred the scroll to his left hand, then came to attention facing Admiral Anston. He threw a much sharper salute than Daniel would ever have been able to do. It was unexpected and completely appropriate.

Anston no longer had an active commission, but he was largely responsible for the RCN's present strength. Britten, who'd spent much of his career as a Navy House bureaucrat, was well aware of his former chief's importance.

"A pleasure to see you again, Admiral," Britten said.

"Ah . . . would you care to say a few words? There's a directional microphone upstairs—"

He gestured with his chin toward the yard office.

"—feeding the loudspeakers. I'll just signal them to aim it at you."

"Well, to tell the truth, Darwin," Anston said. "I talked to my friend Vocaine last night and he's authorized me to deputize for him. I hope you don't feel that I'm stepping on your toes."

"By the Gods, sir!" Britten said, holding out the scroll. "You certainly are not."

Anston untied the document. He was standing unsupported, which made Daniel's eyes narrow with concern. For the moment at least he seemed as solid as a bollard. Taking a broad-nibbed stylus from his sleeve—Dress Whites didn't have pockets—he said, "Give me your back as a table, Darwin."

Britten obediently turned and hunched slightly to provide a slanted writing surface. Anston crossed out the signature of Klemsch, Secretary to the Navy Board, and wrote his own above it.

"All right," he muttered, putting the stylus away as Britten scuttled to the side.

Anston looked at the yards of the *Milton*, solid with spacers, then faced the crowd. Britten pointed toward the office and swung his finger toward Anston before dropping his hand to the side.

"Fellow spacers!" Anston said. The new speakers on both sides of the office boomed back his words, but his unaided voice was stronger and steadier than it'd been when he was talking to Daniel. "Fellow spacers, senators, and citizens of Cinnabar!"

Daniel grinned without intending to. It was typical of Anston that he'd give spacers pride of place over members of the Senate. He probably would've been more politic if he were still in office, but as a private citizen he could make his personal preferences known.

Anston waved the crackling document to the crowd. It was real parchment, impressed with two red wax seals from which fluttered a blue ribbon and a white ribbon.

"This is no longer my duty," Anston said, "but I'm glad to say that I find it a great pleasure."

Spreading the document with both hands and moving it slightly outward to where his eyes could focus comfortably, he read, "By the powers vested in me by the Senate, I hereby appoint Daniel Oliver Leary to the rank and authority of Captain in the Navy of the Republic of Cinnabar—"

Hogg cheered like a boar challenging the world. The Bantry contingent joined with enthusiasm, followed by almost all the other civilians at ground level. Madame Dorst started to cheer also, but Miranda laid her fingertips over her mother's mouth to shush her.

Daniel held himself at attention, blushing with embarrassment for what his friends had done. Anston looked nonplussed for a moment; he'd probably never attended a promotion ceremony at which many of the spectators were civilians who didn't know the drill.

When the noise died down, he resumed, "The rank of captain, as I say, his duties to commence with the reading of this order. This is signed by Darwin Britten, Captain, Chief of the Bureau of Personnel, and countersigned by Admiral Eldridge Vocaine, President of the Navy Board, by George Anston, his deputy for this purpose."

Anston let the parchment roll itself up and handed the scroll to Daniel. "Captain," he said, "allow me to be the first to give you the salute in your new rank."

He shot his right hand to his brow, wincing as his arm rose above shoulder level. Nonetheless, he completed the salute.

Daniel returned it, his eyes blurring with tears. This was all quite improper: admirals don't initiate an exchange of salutes with junior officers. It was the greatest honor anyone had ever paid him.

People were babbling and cheering. Captain Britten helped to support Anston, moving him back from the crush of folk mounting the dais to congratulate Daniel.

Hogg bumped Daniel from the side. "Hold your bloody arms still, young master!" he said. "Else I'm likely to put one of these pins through your wrist while I give you your new stripes. And won't you look silly then, all blood over your white uniform?"

"What?" said Daniel. "Oh, sorry, Hogg."

He held both forearms out from his body while his servant pinned a narrow gold stripe around the right sleeve above the two broad stripes of a commander. The *Milton*'s crew cheered from the yards like a choir of hoarse, profane angels.

Hogg moved around to Daniel's left arm. "And if they look a bit worn . . ." he said. "That's because they're the pair off Admiral James' old captain's uniform that he told me to fetch for you when I got back to Xenos. I guess it's not much of a comedown for them to go on a Leary's sleeve, is it, young master?"

"I'd like to think it wasn't," Daniel said, his eyes glittering again. He was no longer sure that Anston's salute was the greatest honor he'd ever receive.

—end excerpt—

from *In the Stormy Red Sky*
available in hardcover,
May 2009, from Baen Books